ALONE BUT FOR the trees and roses and a few birds settling in, I lifted my flute and found a simple melody. Somewhere in the woods, a bird repeated a few notes. I smiled and played again, and the bird sang back.

Strange, but I couldn't identify the bird. It didn't sound like a shrike or mockingbird. A thrush? No, the voice was too otherworldly.

Peering into the darkness, I played a few measures of my minuet—the one I'd written not long before Templedark—and the bird . . . something . . . sang it back. It wasn't a bird.

"What are you doing?" Sam came outside again, his arms filled with a stand, a book of music, and his flute.

"There's something out there." I couldn't see. The front light stretched and vanished only halfway down the path, and the trees huddled beyond its reach. Rosebushes shivered in a cool breeze, and in the woods, someone moaned long and mournful.

My stomach dropped. I knew that sound.

"Sylph."

BY JODI MEADOWS

ASUNDER

JODI MEADOWS

KATHERINE TEGEN BOOKS
An Imprint of HarperCollins Publishers

Katherine Tegen Books is an imprint of HarperCollins Publishers.

Asunder

Library of Congress Cataloging-in-Publication Data
Meadows, Jodi.
    Asunder / Jodi Meadows. — 1st ed.
        p.   cm.
    Sequel to: Incarnate.
    Summary: After the devastation of Templedark, eighteen-year-old Ana
must stand up for the additional newsouls and figure out the mystery of
their—and her—existence.
    ISBN 978-0-06-206079-2 (pbk.)
    [1.   Fantasy.   2.   Reincarnation—Fiction.   3.   Identity—Fiction.]
I. Title.
PZ7.M5073As   2013   2012009696
[Fic]—dc23   CIP
                                                            AC

Typography by Joel Tippie
13 14 15 16 17   LP/RRDH   10 9 8 7 6 5 4 3 2 1
❖

First paperback edition, 2014

To my dad, for encouraging my love of the fantastic.
I miss you.

ASUNDER

1

MEMORY

MY LIFE WAS a mistake.

As long as I'd been alive, I'd wanted to know why I'd been born. Why, after five thousand years of the same souls being reincarnated, my soul had slipped through the cracks of existence and burdened the people of Heart with such *newness*.

No one could tell me how I happened, not until the night I'd found my way into the temple with no door, trapping myself with the entity called Janan.

"Mistake," he'd said. "You are a mistake of no consequence."

I knew, as I'd always known, that I was a soul asunder.

Outside the temple, the night had spiraled into chaos. Sylph burned, and dragons rained acid from the thunder-torn sky.

The numinous light of the temple had vanished. The father I'd never known appeared and told me the same as Janan: I was an experiment gone wrong.

My life might have begun as a mistake, but I wouldn't let it end as one.

Spring slipped across Range, a verdant blanket stitched with new life. Trees blossomed and young animals peeked from the forest, and the people of Heart cleared a stretch of land north of the city, just beyond the geysers and mud pits that steamed and bubbled as winter eased its grip on the world.

Instead of crops, they planted dozens of black obelisks, each carved with loving words, achievements, and the name of a darksoul: a soul who wouldn't be reincarnated; a soul lost during the battle of Templedark.

Every citizen of Heart took on a task. They gathered physical reminders to place by the obelisks, combed through records to find videos of darksoul friends, or assisted in the construction of the Templedark Memorial.

Sam and Councilor Sine combined their efforts, composing music and writing laments. They created different melodies and lyrics for every darksoul. I wanted to help, though I didn't know most of the darksouls well enough to contribute.

When spring bowed to summer and the memorial was finished, everyone in Heart met on North Avenue and formed two lines.

Two by two, we passed beneath the Northern Arch.

Two by two, we filed out of the white city.

Two by two, we entered the Templedark Memorial.

Our lines split there, and we followed the iron bars of the fence. Wind gusted through, making the whole place smell of roses and tinges of sulfur from a nearby geyser. Steam drifted through the cerulean sky.

The procession took ages. By the time we all arrived, people stood three deep around the field of high monuments. Everything was silent, save rustling leaves and the gasp-heave of weeping. Next to me, my best friend, Sarit, squeezed my hand tight and blinked tears off her dark lashes. Our dresses tugged in the wind while we waited.

A bell tolled in the center of the memorial, one peal for each soul lost.

What happened after death? Where did you go? What did you do? The scariest possibility was that we might. just. stop.

After another moment of aching hush, Sine pulled away from the perimeter and took a microphone. "Today, we gather to remember those who fell during Templedark. We come to honor their lives and deaths, and begin the long process of healing not only our bodies and city, but also our souls. . . ."

Most people kept their heads down, the weight of grief so evident in their slumped postures I feared they might collapse. Others stood stoic, blank, as though their minds were somewhere very far away.

But here and there I caught eyes seeking mine; I exchanged sad smiles with almost-friends. Most were people I'd warned about dying during Templedark. There wasn't much to say about it, but they were nice to me, and our encounters were always cautiously hopeful.

Sine finished her speech.

One at a time, someone stood for each darksoul to recount lifetimes and memories. Sam and Sine performed the music they'd written. Small screens went into the base of each obelisk, set to play a video of the darksoul, or play a recorded copy of the music written for them.

Then we turned our attention to the next darksoul.

At the end of the day, we filed out of the memorial, same as we'd come in. Friends stayed at Sam's house with us, but everyone was so raw with sadness there was no joy in the companionship, and the next morning, we walked back to Templedark Memorial.

It took four days to remember the lives of almost eighty souls, and as we left the field of black obelisks for the final time, people kept glancing at the empty places in the back: room for more darksouls, because we couldn't be sure about when a few people had died. Some might still come back.

Over the next weeks, some people went on like it never happened, but there were rumors of people sleeping in the market field or destroying everything in their homes. Others supposedly didn't leave their houses for weeks at a time.

I went back to my lessons—what lessons were still being offered—and tried to find happiness with my friends and music, but the strangeness of the community's behavior smothered me. No one seemed to heal.

As summer hurtled toward autumn, the mood sagged from melancholy to disconsolate, and the pulse in the walls grew unbearable. The city wall. The Councilhouse walls. Even the exterior walls of everyone's homes. The slow throb of life inside stone made my skin try to crawl off.

I couldn't take it anymore.

"I have to get out," I told Sam. "I need to get away. Will you go with me?"

"Anywhere," he said, and kissed me.

We left Heart just before summer faded into memory.

"You've been quiet," Sam said as we left behind the geysers and mud pits, the fumaroles and rime-whitened trees.

"Nothing's wrong." Oops. We hadn't gotten to that part of his questioning yet.

He snorted. "Okay. What's on your mind?"

I lengthened my strides to keep up with Sam and Not as Shaggy as His Father, the pony that bore most of our bags. We called him Shaggy for short. My backpack straps dug into my shoulders, but I carried only a few essentials—in case we somehow got separated—plus the temple door device, and my notebook. Sam had taken to calling it my diary, but I didn't keep track of my days in there.

"Nothing in particular, I guess." I glanced back at Heart, from here just a seemingly endless expanse of white ripples and curves over the plateau. The immense central tower stood partially obscured by late-summer foliage. The city looked peaceful from far away. "I feel better getting out of there."

"The walls?" He said it like he understood, but the walls didn't feel bad to anyone but me.

"Yeah." I slipped my thumbs beneath my backpack straps, relieving some of the pressure on my shoulders. "Did you see Corin when we went through the guard station?"

"Corin?" Sam raised an eyebrow. "He didn't do anything."

"No, he didn't." I kicked a fallen branch off the road. Pine needles scraped the cobblestone. "He just sat there at his desk. He didn't say anything. He didn't acknowledge us. He barely moved."

"He's grieving," Sam said gently. "He lost souls very close to him."

"Then why does he go to the guard station every day?"

"What else should he be doing?"

"I don't know. Staying home? Staying with a friend?"

Sam's eyes were dark as dusk, and his voice deep with a hundred lifetimes. "It doesn't always make sense, the way others grieve. I can't imagine what I'd be like if I'd lost you, but it would probably seem very strange to others."

8

Because I was the newsoul, and why would anyone grieve that much over me?

Then again, I knew how I'd behaved during Templedark. Fearing for Sam's life, I'd hurtled through fields of dragon acid, dodging sylph and laser fire. I'd felt like someone other than myself, like I might do something crazy if I didn't find Sam, because how could my world be right without him?

"I don't like the way grief feels," I said at last. "And I don't like the way it feels when other people grieve." Which sounded like I thought they should avoid the emotion because it made me uncomfortable. No, what did I really mean? "After the dragons attacked the market, I wanted you to feel better. I wanted to do anything I could to help, to make you stop hurting, but I didn't know how. I tried and . . ."

Sam nodded. "It makes you feel helpless."

"I don't like that."

"Me neither." He pushed a strand of black hair from his eyes. "I've felt like that about you, helpless to make you feel better."

"Really?"

He flashed a strained smile. "When we first met. You trapped the sylph in an egg, letting your hands get burned so you could rescue me."

Sylph. Just the word made me shudder and check the woods for unnatural shadows. Too easily, I could remember the inferno racing through my hands, up my forearms, and

9

the red-and-black skin all bubbling with blisters.

"You tried to be so strong after that," Sam said. "And you *were* strong, but I knew how much it must have hurt. I wanted to take the pain from you, but I couldn't. I felt helpless."

"Even though we'd just met?"

Sam only smiled and touched my hand, and we shifted to the safer topics of music he wanted me to learn, and debating whether or not Sarit would actually make good on her threat to come after us if we didn't return to Heart before winter.

Late summer bathed Range in shades of green. Clouds drifted across the sky, catching and tangling on mountains like gauze. A hawk careened in from above, calling his territory, and a family of weasels startled at the sound. They tumbled to hide in the brush, even though the hawk was far away.

When night fell, we set up a tent and sleeping bags and discussed music over dinner, then went outside to take turns on the flute he'd packed. I liked waking up across the tent from him; seeing his messy hair and sleepy smile first thing chased away my lingering fears and sadness.

We made good progress across Range, and finally we reached our destination: Purple Rose Cottage.

The last time I'd seen Purple Rose Cottage, the roof bore daggers of ice, and the path uphill had been slippery with snow. Li had stood in the doorway, tall and beautiful and fierce, and she'd given me a broken compass so I'd lose my way and fall prey to sylph.

Now Sam and I stepped out of the forest shade and trudged up the hill. Sunlight warmed my face and arms and made the cottage glow brown and almost unfamiliar with how welcoming it looked. Rosebushes huddled around the wall, indigo blooms just fading as summer came to a close. Vegetables lay half-eaten and rotted in the garden; no one had been here to harvest and put them away for winter.

We spent a couple of days getting the cottage cleaned up, arranging our things in the bedrooms and kitchen, and not discussing anything more difficult than who was in charge of coffee each morning. It was nice living with Sam without the heartbeat-filled walls boxing us in.

Our third evening in Purple Rose Cottage, Sam asked me to wait for him outside.

The cool air gave me goose bumps, but I waited on the grass by a bush of indigo roses. Low sunlight shot around the cottage, casting the forest in shadow and gold-green and hints of russet. The door shut, and Sam walked over carrying a large basket.

"Help me with this?" he asked. Together, we spread a blanket on the grass to sit, and his eyes shone in the dimness. "I want to give you something." From the basket, he removed a long wooden box. Faint light from the window made the polish glisten. When had he packed that? "This is for you."

"You didn't have to get anything for me. I have everything I need."

He smiled and regarded the box, his hands covering the gilt latches. "It's a gift, like friends gave Tera and Ash for their rededication ceremony."

That had been a special occasion, celebrating their eternal love. Today was nothing, as far as I could remember. Still, the idea of a gift delighted me, and I tried to squeeze my fingers between his to look. There were patterns carved into the wood, but I couldn't see them. "What is it?"

His hands trembled as he pulled up the latches, and the box was soundless as he turned up the lid.

Light glimmered across two lengths of silver, catching on a row of keys and delicate swirls engraved into the metal.

It was a flute, one I'd never seen before.

A rush of wind stirred the trees and stole my quiet "Oh" as Sam pulled the flute from its case and pieced it together. His eyes were dark, wide with anticipation and something else as he offered the instrument with both hands. "It's beautiful," I whispered.

"I hoped you would like it." The flute nearly vanished in his hands, though it seemed normal-sized when I rested my fingertips on the cool metal. "Take it," he urged. "It's yours."

"Why?" My question didn't stop my fingers from wrapping around the flute, from pulling it to my lips. My breath hissed over the mouthpiece as my fingers found their places on the keys.

The heat of his body warmed me as he leaned closer.

"Here." He nudged my right thumb farther down the tube. "And your chin." He tilted my face up slightly, his fingers lingering over my skin.

Our eyes met, both of us suddenly aware of his other hand flat on my ribs, unconsciously adjusting my posture. "Better?" I breathed.

He watched my mouth and nodded. "Play for me."

Play what? He hadn't brought out music. But as sunlight began to fade, making the indigo roses turn ink-dark and early snow glow on the mountaintops, I played a long, low note that filled the cottage clearing with a haunting reverberation.

The note created a bubble of warmth around us. It tangled around vines, caught in rosebushes, and pushed out toward the mountains that rose like distant walls. I found a breath, and my fingers climbed a half step up.

The flute stretched its sound. It fit me as precisely as though it had once been part of my body and now we were reunited. My hands and mouth and lungs knew this flute, and I knew this flute would do anything I could ask of it, and more.

I climbed notes until a pattern emerged, as sweet and haunting as the flute's sound. The melody took shape and flew on sure, steady wings. Music filled me until it seemed I might burst.

When I lowered the flute, Sam leaned toward me, a

satisfied smile on his lips. "It suits you."

"It's perfect." I caressed the silver, engravings sharp and new beneath my fingertips. They looked like ivy, or something delicate and twisty. "Did you make it?"

"Some. I had a friend do a lot of the work. How was I going to hide it from you otherwise?"

The metal was warm from my playing, and I couldn't stop staring at the way it looked in my hands. It was *perfect*. "I want to play it all the time."

"Good." Sam grinned widely. "Because you will." His tone turned conspiring. "I wrote some duets for us."

My heart stumbled over itself. "Really?"

"I want to keep this moment forever, the way you're smiling right now."

"You may." I placed the flute in my lap and brushed my hands over my mouth, pretending to grab my smile as though it were bits of wool or clouds. "Here." I pressed my imaginary smile into his hands. "This is for you."

He held his fists against his heart and laughed. "It's just what I always wanted."

"I have more whenever you want them."

"All I have to do is give you new instruments?"

I shrugged. "We might be able to find other things worthy of smiles."

He cupped my cheek and kissed me. "Ana, I . . ." The way his voice had softened, deepening with emotion, made me shiver. He pulled back. "I'll get you a jacket."

Whatever he'd been ready to say before faded into the cool night. "No, you know what would help me warm up? If you got the other flute and music."

"You're ready to start now?" He lifted an eyebrow.

"You can't give me a pretty new flute and expect me just to put it away." I clutched the instrument to my chest.

"Then I'll be right back." He kissed me again, then got up and vanished into the cottage, turning on the front light as the door shut behind him. Good idea, if we were to read music.

Alone but for the trees and roses and a few birds settling in, I lifted my flute and found a simple melody. Somewhere in the woods, a bird repeated a few notes. I smiled and played again, and the bird sang back.

Strange, but I couldn't identify the bird. It didn't sound like a shrike or mockingbird. A thrush? No, the voice was too otherworldly.

Peering into the darkness, I played a few measures of my minuet—the one I'd written not long before Templedark—and the bird . . . something . . . sang it back. It wasn't a bird.

"What are you doing?" Sam came outside again, his arms filled with a stand, a book of music, and his flute.

"There's something out there." I couldn't see. The front light stretched and vanished only halfway down the path, and the trees huddled beyond its reach. Rosebushes shivered in a cool breeze, and in the woods, someone moaned long and mournful.

My stomach dropped. I knew that sound.

"Sylph." The light made harsh shadows across Sam's face. "Is that a sylph? Here?"

"It didn't sound like a sylph before. I thought it was a bird. It was mimicking my playing."

Shock flickered in Sam's expression as he squinted into the dark. "Surely they wouldn't be this far into Range. Or— mimic you."

I licked my lips and played four notes, and the repeat came from closer. Just beyond the light, a shadow writhed. Then another, to the left, and a third still in the forest. There were so many, maybe as many as there'd been the night they chased me off a cliff, into Rangedge Lake.

Sylph burned, reeked of ash and fire, and they were without substance. The lore was complicated and contradictory. Some said they were shadows brought to a terrible half-life, thanks to fumes and heat from the caldera beneath Range. Skeptics maintained sylph were simply another of the planet's dominant species, like dragons or centaurs or trolls; people should be cautious, but not assign them any special history or powers.

Whatever they were, I'd had more than enough experience with them for one lifetime.

"Sam." I hardly recognized my voice, so opposite the storm

of fear building inside me. "Get all the traps you can find."

Several more sylph picked up the notes, singing as though it were a short round of music. The sound grew, pressing closer, and abruptly stopped.

A sense of *waiting* grew heavy in the air. A heartbeat later, a sylph whistled a scale.

Sam touched my elbow. "You need to get inside. The walls are protected."

"Protected. Not sylph-proof." I lifted my flute. "I think—" My breath hissed across the mouthpiece and made all the sylph tense, push closer. I retreated until my skirt caught in a rosebush; thorns pricked through the cloth. "I think my play-ing keeps them distracted. Get the eggs. Set the traps. If the sylph attack, I'll go inside."

And hope I was fast enough to reach the door before they burned me alive.

"I'll hurry." Sam vanished into the cottage.

Heat billowed from all sides as the sylph swarmed closer. Heart pounding, I began to play.

2
SHADOWS

DARK TENDRILS FLICKERED in and out of the light. The moaning grew softer as I played a major scale—and they sang it back.

Every scale I played, every arpeggio and trill, the sylph echoed it and hummed closer. Heat brushed against my skin like breath as the shadows drew ever nearer, but did not attack. The scent of ozone filled the clearing, though, and the front light seemed to grow dimmer.

"Good Janan!" A boy's voice came from the bottom of the path.

Every sylph went rigid and shrieked, and a wave of heat rolled toward the cottage. I gagged on the taste of ash, and sweat prickled over my skin.

"Stop!" The word was out before I could consider the wisdom of shouting, but the sylph froze. Adrenaline surged through me, making my head buzz with terror and my voice too high and pinched. "Stay where you are," I called to the newcomer. "Stay out of their way."

Silence. Either he had run, or he was doing as I said.

I couldn't breathe through the heat. Too easily, I could recall the sensation of a sylph burning my hands. The blaze, the lightning pain, and then nothing.

These hadn't burned me—yet—and if music would keep them from trying, I'd give them music. Sam would be out soon with the sylph eggs. I hoped.

Sweat pooled between my chin and the flute as the heat intensified, but I could *feel* their attention shifting back to me as I drew a breath, struggled to focus, and blew a stream of air across the mouthpiece. Haltingly, I played one of the first sonatas I'd learned. It was a sweet, unassuming thing called "Honey," which Sam had named for Sarit and her apiary five or six lifetimes ago.

My hands and jaw shook, but after a few moments, the sylph heat faded. One or two tried to sing along, and more caught on as I kept playing.

The sylph danced, black knotting with black. Ropes of darkness reached toward the stars, twisting with one another until they melted into one writhing shape.

They seemed to . . . enjoy the music. A little more confident,

I stepped closer and they moved back—as though I were a light they couldn't stand to be near. But they kept singing, kept twisting. They kept *dancing*, even as we moved away from the cottage.

Sylph had always been terrifying shadow predators, but these were behaving unlike any sylph I'd ever met. Not like the ones that had chased me on my eighteenth birthday, or the one that had burned my hands the day after. They weren't even like the ones that had been at Templedark, though those had behaved strangely as well, fleeing from my father.

But this. Dancing. This was not sylphlike behavior at all.

The sonata came to an end. I smothered a moment of panic—would they be angry?—but the sylph hmmed and murmured the melody here and there, like echoes or making sure they hit the right notes.

One at a time, sylph drifted down the path, humming as they went.

Brush rustled, and a flashlight beam bounced across the yard as the newcomer hurried out of their path. When they were gone, the boy climbed the hill, sagging under the weight of his enormous backpack. "What did you do?" he asked.

I clutched my flute to my chest, waiting for my heartbeat to slow to a normal speed. I had no idea what I'd done. They heard the music, sang along, and went away. It was very odd behavior.

The boy didn't wait for an answer. He pulled his backpack

off and dropped it to the ground beside him, glancing over his shoulder like he thought the sylph might change their minds. Did they have minds? They were incorporeal shadows, affecting the world only with their heat. My hands prickled with memory of sylph burns and my phoenix feeling from months ago. The pain had been excrutiating, but when it was over, my scars had been burned away.

"Were they after you?" I asked.

He shook his head. "I don't think so. I was walking here and heard your playing. I thought you might be—" He shrugged the words off. "Then I saw the sylph as I approached the path. That's it."

"Hmm." I looked beyond him into the forest, but night-time hid everything, especially sylph.

"I'm sorry," he said, offering his hand. "I've been rude. I don't think we've met in this life. Cris."

"Cris." I glanced at the cottage as Sam's rushed footfalls came toward the front door. "Purple rose Cris."

He made a smile that might have been a grimace. "Yes."

"Sorry, I meant blue." According to everyone, Cris had bet he could grow the perfect blue rose, supposedly a genetic impossibility. Four lifetimes of rose breeding later, everyone said the results were purple, and Cris left his cottage. *This* cottage, which people called Purple Rose Cottage to mock his attempt.

"Don't worry about it." Another smile-grimace. Cris was

tall and narrow, with sharp points at his cheekbones and chin, accented by short hair. Physically, he was maybe only a couple of years older than Sam and me. In reality . . .

They were all much, much older.

The front door flew open, and Sam stood there with an armful of sylph eggs. He scanned the clearing, breath heaving. "Where are they?"

"They flew away." The bar of keys on my flute dug into my ribs where I held it too tightly. "We got Cris in trade."

"Cris." Sam's voice slipped, and there was something while the boys looked at each other—something I couldn't understand.

"Dossam. I heard you were . . ." Cris shifted his gaze to me. "Then you must be Ana."

"Yes."

Awkwardness pulled in all directions: the awkwardness of being me, the newsoul; the sylph that had seemed happy to go away after singing; whatever history Sam and Cris had. Friendship? Hate? Some sort of falling-out? Sam hadn't talked about Cris much, and everything I'd ever read about or by Cris—mostly gardening notes—made him seem like someone who kept to himself.

"Sorry," Sam said, coming back to himself. "The sylph are gone?"

I nodded.

"Then we should get inside before they come back. Cris,

are you staying?" Sam backed into the cottag⟨
the sylph eggs in a basket, making a metallic⟨
hurried to help me with the blanket and mus⟨.

I glanced at Cris, inclining my head toward the ԁʋʋ⟨
another invitation. It was his cottage anyway. I didn't know
if he built it specifically for the roses, or if he'd built it long
before, but it carried their name.

He grabbed his backpack and followed me up, eyeing the
roses as he walked past. "Someone's been taking care of
these." He lifted an eyebrow at me. "You?"

"They didn't deserve to be abandoned just because they
weren't what you expected." The words cut out sharper than
I intended, and both Cris and Sam winced as we filed inside.
"Sorry," I muttered.

"I'll make tea." Sam shut the door. "You still prefer coffee,
Cris?"

"Please." Cris smiled—sort of—and left his backpack by
the basket of sylph eggs. "I wasn't expecting to find anyone
here."

"You'll stay, of course. We'll work out sleeping arrange-
ments." Sam took Cris's jacket and hung it on a peg, while
Cris looked between us as though he were reevaluating
something. Was he surprised that Sam and I didn't share a
room? A bed?

A few minutes later, Cris had washed up and Sam was in
the kitchen, boiling water and preparing mugs. Cris and I

sat in the front room, me on the threadbare sofa and him on the chair across the low table. Neither of us said anything, and my thoughts flashed back to the sylph and their strange actions. What had they been *doing*?

"I thought you'd be bigger," Cris said.

"What?"

He had the decency to blush. "Sorry. I just meant that you're the newsoul. Even being away for four years, I've still managed to hear the fuss everyone makes. I thought you'd be giant or have tentacles, but you're not. You're kind of pretty."

"Oh. Um." I wished I had something to do with my hands. Anything. Besides Sam and Sarit, no one had ever said I was pretty. Sam's friend Stef had called me cute, but that hardly seemed the same thing. "Thanks. I guess."

"So you're studying music with Dossam?"

A thrill raced through me, and I couldn't stop myself from grinning at the flutes and music resting on the table. It had always been my dream to study with Dossam. Sam. I'd wanted music from the first moment I heard it, and Sam gave it to me every day. But Cris didn't need to know that much about me. I just nodded.

"What about the roses? You took care of them, even though you thought no one wanted them."

"People don't want a lot of things, but they get them any-way." Such as newsouls, or roses of indeterminate color. "I liked the roses for what they were."

Cris offered a dazzling smile, like I'd just said something amazing or profound. "I'm glad someone appreciated them."

"Hmph." I wished Sam would hurry with the tea. Then I could pretend to focus on not spilling. "We had things in common, the roses and me. That's all." I wanted to kick myself for being rude, but Sam came into the room with a tray of mugs and rescued me from more humiliation. The way he looked at me said he knew it, too.

"Where have you been traveling, Cris?" Sam sat beside me and offered a mug of tea. I wrapped both my hands around it, grateful for the distraction.

"Lots of places. I went across the continent, cataloguing different species of plants, their rate of growth, looking for more edible plants that we might be able to grow in Heart. . . ."

"You walked the whole way?" I asked. "For four years?"

He nodded. "That's the best way to see plants you might like to eat."

No wonder he was as thin as a wire. But he looked strong and sharp, like he *could* walk across the world. I didn't know much about lands outside Range, but I knew this continent was huge, with mountains, plains, deserts, and marshes. You could walk a thousand leagues from the east to the west and still miss so much. That is, as long as nothing killed you the moment you stepped foot outside of Range.

"Didn't you get lonely?"

"Sometimes, but I had my SED." He patted his breast pocket. "Which is how I heard about something called Templedark. What happened?"

I shuddered, and Sam pressed a strong hand on my spine. "My father made Templedark," I said. Though maybe I shouldn't claim Menehem. I hadn't known him—only through his diaries and the way just his name seemed to make everyone roll their eyes. I'd met him for only a short while the night of Templedark, before he died. "Menehem did something to the temple to stop Janan from being able to reincarnate anyone who died that night. He captured dozens of sylph from outside of Range, then released them in Heart. Dragons came that night, too."

Cris jerked his gaze toward Sam, who'd gone still and pale at the mention of dragons. "And you—" Cris smoothed his perplexed expression. "You made it through. That's good."

"Ana saved me." Sam's hand settled on my hip, pulling us close. "She saved me from dragons twice."

Questions stretched in the air between Cris and us, a piano wire pulled so taut it might snap. "So, Ana," Cris said, "you know about Dossam and dragons?"

I nodded.

Sam was still ashen. "I told her about the way they come after me. She knows."

The thinking line had carved itself between Sam's eyebrows; sometimes it was a worry line, or a stress line. I rested my hand on his knee and drew his gaze, and when our eyes met, the line melted away. "It's okay," I murmured. "I'll protect you from the dragons." It was a joke, mostly, just to make him smile. Because what could I do against dragons? They'd killed him thirty times.

Thirty.

But Sam wove his fingers with mine and smiled. "I know you will." It didn't sound like teasing at all.

"Fascinating." Cris wrapped his hands around his mug, his tone light and amused, but tinged with something sad. He sipped his coffee, as though to hide the emotion. "One new-soul, and Sam's problem with dragons is fixed."

"I wouldn't say that." I glanced toward the window, like sylph or dragons might be peeking in right now. "There've been two dragon attacks since I came."

"They always come in twos." Cris rested his mug on his knee. "You were just unlucky enough to be here for their first visit in quite some time."

"And we were all unlucky enough they chose to come during Templedark." Sam lowered his eyes, the memory of Templedark still fresh and heavy. "The sylph and the dragons proved too much. Everyone panicked. We lost more than we should have before anyone realized what Menehem had done: he made the temple go dark."

When I closed my eyes, I could still see the strange darkness where the iridescent light of the temple should be.

Except it *shouldn't* illuminate. What kind of building glowed in the dark?

One with Janan in it.

"Stopping reincarnation. What a thing to do." Cris shook his head, then leveled his gaze on me. "Did Menehem— before? You?"

Oh, Cris was quick. "By accident. That was why he left eighteen years ago—to find out what he'd done." I shrugged, feigning nonchalance. "Only Menehem knows why he wanted to end so many others. Maybe he'll tell us when he's reborn."

That wasn't quite true, I knew. But not knowing how Cris felt about Janan—some people really cared, while others hadn't believed for millennia—I didn't say any more. Menehem had given me two explanations. The first made it sound as though he were doing me a favor: attempting to let more newsouls be born.

The other reason Menehem had given me seemed most genuine: he'd wanted to prove Janan's existence either true or false. It had been scientific curiosity, nothing more.

Cris glared into his coffee. "I'm sure the Council will be very curious to find out exactly how he created Templedark so they can prevent anyone from ever doing it again."

"I'm sure they will be." Did my voice shake? It seemed like Menehem's research notes were a bright beacon shining from my room. He'd left them for me after he died, and

I hadn't wanted to leave them in Heart. The folders and diaries, the door device, the mysterious books I'd stolen from the temple—it was a wonder everyone didn't know about them just from the guilt on my face.

But I wasn't ready to tell anyone about my visit into the temple or Menehem's research, and Sam had agreed. I didn't know exactly how the Council would react, but it definitely wouldn't be good.

Sam looked at Cris, a strange and awkward hopefulness in his tone. "You're on your way back to Heart now?"

"I think I'd better be," Cris said. "Sine's message indicated they'd need assistance reorganizing the genealogies now that so many won't return."

"I'm sure they'll appreciate your help," Sam said, not explaining to me how a gardener would be useful for genealogies.

They talked until everyone's mug was empty, keeping the conversation to simple things, like the best road to take into Heart, and warnings about bears and wolves in certain parts of the forest. They concluded with a polite argument about who would take the other bedroom, and Sam won, which meant he slept on the sofa.

As the calming herbs in my tea took effect, I wished the boys good night and went into my room, trying desperately not to think of the sylph.

Moaning wind roused me from fiery dreams.

My bedroom looked the same as it always had, dusty wood floors and walls all bathed in darkness, but something was different. Not the shadows, but the sounds. The wind had never made this particular wailing in the eighteen years I'd lived in Purple Rose Cottage.

I went to the window and pushed open the shutters.

Stars blazed far away, trees hugged the earth and sky, and the rosebushes breathed perfume that didn't quite mask the lingering reek of ashes. The night was perfectly still, but the moan persisted.

A shadow moved.

They twisted all along the path up to the cottage, whistling, humming, singing. A melody I'd played earlier lifted and faded in the strange song. A moment later, another familiar tune piped up, and the others built on it with harmony and countermelody. Unearthly music filled the night, subtle enough that it might have been wind on the corner of the cottage. Strange enough that it had pulled me from sleep.

There had to be a dozen sylph outside my bedroom, and though they were eyeless, I could feel them *looking* at me.

A whimper escaped my throat.

A gasp sounded in the front room, and blankets crumpled to the floor. Soft thumps made their way to my bedroom door. Sam. I knew the cadence of his footsteps.

I raced to the door and dragged it open.

In the dimness, Sam glanced me over, as though to make sure I wasn't bleeding—why would I be bleeding?—and then swept me up in a tight hug. "Are you all right? I heard you—"

He stilled as the sylph sang outside, echoes of music he'd composed.

"Oh." His breath rustled my hair as he released me, and together we made our way back to the window. Warm air pushed inward, smelling faintly of ash and ozone.

One by one, the sylph finished their music.

One by one, the sylph drifted down the cottage path, leaving nothing more threatening than a song.

"What does it mean?" Sam whispered. He cocked his head, as though listening for sounds of Cris stirring in the other bedroom, but relaxed. Cris must have been a deep sleeper, or tired from walking everywhere.

"It means I need to stop avoiding Menehem's research. The sylph were terrified of him during Templedark, and it was his research on the sylph that affected Janan's temple. I need to understand why. And why they'd sing outside my window." Though it was unlikely Menehem would be able to answer that question. As far as I could tell, he'd never been concerned with thoughts or feelings or motivations of others; he couldn't grasp them.

Sam dropped back his head in resignation. Our peace was too short-lived. "What do you want to do?"

I stared into the darkness, but nothing moved, and the sylph odor abated. "I wish we could stay outside of Heart, just playing music all the time. But in houses. I don't want to walk around for four years like Cris."

"Pianos are too heavy to carry in a backpack, anyway." He kissed my forehead, stubble scratching my cheek. "You know people there like you."

"Sarit, Stef, Sine—other people whose names begin with *S*."

He chuckled. "Armande, Lidea, Wend, Rin, Orrin, Whit. Lots of others. Templedark was horrible, but it did show people you cared. How many did you save that night?"

I didn't answer because I didn't know. The night had been so frantic, and mostly I'd been looking for Sam.

Warm fingers curved over my cheek, and he drew my gaze upward. "Are you worried they'll change their minds about you?"

How did he always know my real fears? "No one calls me nosoul anymore, but how long will that last when they find out sylph don't chase me anymore? Cris saw them reacting to my playing."

"He won't tell anyone. You can trust Cris."

I wished I had Sam's confidence that people would remember I wasn't out to destroy their existence. Maybe that was why I was reluctant to look into Menehem's research, but I couldn't let fear of others' reactions stop me anymore.

"All right. We go east of Range, where Menehem did his experiments." I closed the shutters, locked them. "I don't want anyone to know we're going there. The Council won't like it."

"No," Sam whispered darkly. "They won't."

"We leave as soon as Cris does." And then, I hoped, I would find out what Menehem had done to the sylph, and their connection to Janan. But mostly, I needed to find out what they wanted from me.

3
SCORCH

CRIS LEFT THE cottage as the sun rose. I lay in my lumpy bed, listening to a stranger move through the next room, through the washroom, through the front room. I was still getting used to other sounds in this house belonging to Sam, not Li, and Cris's sounds were different yet. His steps were longer than Sam's, and not . . . heavier, but more solid somehow.

Just as I realized I should see him off, low voices came from the front room. "Will you tell Ana I said good-bye?"

"She's awake, if you want to tell her yourself." Sam's voice was groggy, but he'd probably awakened as soon as Cris's feet hit the floor.

"I'm sure she'd rather go back to sleep. I'll see you both in

Heart." Cris hesitated. "You mentioned she's taking lessons from people. Perhaps she'll want to try gardening."

"Perhaps." Sofa springs made their someone-sitting-up groan, but it wasn't Li's motion. It would never be Li again. Sam's voice came almost wistfully. "It was good seeing you again, Cris."

"And you." A moment later, the front door squeaked and shut.

It was hard to find time to practice while traveling, but Sam insisted there was more to music than playing an instrument. Theory was just as important, and we listened to as much music as we talked about, our SEDs synced to play the same things.

Sonatas, minuets, arias, symphonies: these things accompanied us through the forest, all golden-green woven with the fire of oncoming autumn as we walked northeast through Range.

"Are you worried sylph will hear the music and come after us?" I asked Sam once.

"No." He paused. "Not *too* worried while we're in Range, at least. And we have sylph eggs. Purple Rose Cottage is at the edge of Range, so there weren't as many traps between them and us. It's unlikely they'd follow us."

Unlikely, but not impossible. Sylph had been doing all sorts of unlikely things lately. A few heat-sensing traps might not make much of a difference. "What about when we get to Menehem's laboratory?" I asked. The map he'd included in his diaries indicated the building was just beyond the border of Range, drifting into troll territory.

"We'll have to be more careful there, but I'm sure the building itself is well protected."

"Hmph."

I shouldn't have been worried, though. When we arrived at the coordinates Menehem had left, we found an ugly iron building the size of a barn. Solar panels covered the roof, while cisterns hugged the sides.

Trees stumps dotted the area, some as big as dinner tables. Here and there, the grass had been scorched black. Not by lightning. Sylph? But how?

I knelt and dragged my fingers through fine, midnight powder. Ash. It trickled away in a gust of wind, leaving my fingers stained with dusk.

Sam stopped beside me. "What do you think happened?"

As if I had any clue.

"Not sure." I pulled out my SED and made a quick video of the entire area. "Eerie," I muttered as I saved it in a private, protected folder Stef had taught me how to make. I doubted she realized exactly what I'd be doing with my privacy, though; she'd probably assumed it was simply because I didn't want to risk any of *them* finding my secrets, since I hadn't yet started a diary for eventual sharing like everyone else.

A message flashed in the corner of my screen. Sarit had sent a photo of a jar of honey with a teal ribbon tied around it, and "For Ana" written in her flowing script.

"What are you smiling about?" Sam nudged me with his elbow.

"Sarit." I showed him the photo. "I think it must be a form of bribery."

"She misses you. I would, too." Sam gazed up at the monstrosity of a building while I sent a message back to Sarit, letting her know her bribe would have more effect if I hadn't remembered to pack a small jar. She would try again when I ran out. "Ready to go in?" Sam asked.

"Ugh. I can just imagine how comfortably we'll be living until we go back to Heart."

He chuckled and motioned toward the cloudy sky. "At least we won't get rained on. Do you want to take the bags in and I'll put Shaggy in the stable?"

I looped bags over my shoulder and blew Sam a kiss as I headed for the front door. Menehem had left me a key and a code, though it could have been easily broken by anyone who cared enough to try. A soul-scanner would have been more secure, but maybe he'd been planning on leading me here; I wasn't in the main database and wouldn't have been able to get in. He couldn't have predicted I'd have Sam with me.

Inside smelled like something had died months ago. Certainly the building was protected from sylph, thanks to all the iron, but it wasn't protected from dust, small animals, or general grossness.

Lights flickered on as I dropped the bags and stepped into the front section, filled with cabinets and rickety furniture for a parlor, bedroom, and kitchen. Another room—a washroom, I hoped—was blocked off in the back.

Beyond the front area, I found a lab with tons of equipment I couldn't identify, huge glass and steel containers, and *stuff.* It looked like Menehem had been collecting lab-type junk for a lifetime.

A stair to the upper story revealed a dark data console and a small library's worth of research. It seemed he'd also stored off-season clothes and supplies here, because I discovered crates of jackets, skis, and other things. The scent of cedar—to ward off bugs—flooded the area.

"Ana?" Sam's voice came from below, and I clomped back down the stairs. "Anything exciting up there?" He was gazing around the lab when I found him, probably looking for a mop or button that would miraculously clean the layers of dust and grime. Menehem hadn't even been gone a year, but it didn't take long for nature to start reclaiming things.

He probably hadn't been the cleanest person to start with.

"Just lots and lots of research and junk." I sighed. "This is going to be like reopening the cottage, but even worse, isn't it?"

"Do you want to sleep in here with everything like this?" He lifted an eyebrow.

"We could sleep outside. I'd risk the sylph."

"How about cleaning the living area today, then we'll worry about the rest?"

"Fine." I dragged out the word, but mostly I was complaining to complain. I didn't mind cleaning up if Sam was nearby. "But my cooperation comes with a price."

"What's that?" His posture relaxed, voice warming like he knew already. And when I smiled and tilted my face upward, he kissed me so sweetly my entire body hummed with adoration and desire. Could anyone else ever make me feel this complete?

No. Only Sam.

It had always been Sam.

Almost a week later, we'd tossed out a decaying raccoon and scrubbed the living quarters and lab until they didn't make us want to run back to Heart and shower. Sam fished twigs, dead bugs, and a snake out of the cisterns—I double-checked that the water purifier had new filters and solution—and finally we were able to get started on the research we'd come to do.

We sat at the splintering kitchen table, diaries and papers spread out around us. I pointed at a notebook. "This journal matches up with what we already know: he'd been trying to find ways to stop sylph. He started with iron and was looking for ways to make sylph power the eggs with their own life force; that way they'd keep sylph trapped long after the batteries ran out. But that didn't work, so he went back to chemicals."

"He was always best with chemicals," Sam agreed.

"During the first Templedark—the night Ciana died—he was doing his experiments in the market field." Then Ciana hadn't been reborn. I'd replaced her.

"Because, of course, that's a logical place to do experiments."

"You know Menehem." My heart pinched for only a moment—if Menehem hadn't been so irresponsible, I wouldn't be here—but Sam touched my hand. His knee bumped mine. His comment had been only about Menehem, and involved zero regret about the way things had turned out, even though the world had lost Ciana. I tried to smile.

Strong fingers tightened over mine, and he lifted his eyebrow, waiting for something. Acceptance. I was getting better at reading Sam, if not many others.

I smiled again, squeezed his hand, and we both relaxed. "So whatever he was doing in the market field," I went on, "there was some kind of minor explosion, and a vapor went up. That's when the temple went dark."

"From the gas," Sam said. "Then he came here to figure out how to reproduce the mistake, because he didn't know what he'd done to get that reaction."

"Right." I flipped a few pages and pointed at a list. "These are the chemicals he used." It was a long list.

"I don't know what those are."

"Hormones, some of them. I recognize a few from Micah's biology lessons." I glanced toward the lab in the back. "There are stores of the chemicals in there. Most of them are labeled, even. *And* he wrote down the final recipe, though I'd like to study his experiments a bit more first."

"First? Before trying it yourself?" Sam frowned. "I don't know if that's a good idea."

I flinched. "You don't think I'd try to make another Templedark, do you?"

"No, *I* know you'd be doing it for research, but what if the Council finds out? We both know what they'd assume."

I slumped and planted my chin on my fist. "You're right."

"Besides, you've told me that sylph were *fleeing* Menehem during Templedark. That makes me think he was hurting them."

"Are you worried about hurting sylph, Dossam?" I flashed a dry smile.

He spoke gently. "I just don't think you'd want to hurt anything, even sylph."

I lowered my eyes. "No, not even sylph." After the weeks it had taken for my hands to recover from sylph burns, I might not have minded. But the night of Templedark, when Meuric had led me into the temple and tried to trap me, I'd stabbed him in the eye with a knife and shoved him beneath

41

an upside-down pit. He'd fallen upward, body still flailing. That had been self-defense, but the guilt still writhed inside me. I should have come up with a better solution to my problem, but it was too late now.

Sam put his arms around me.

"I don't want to hurt them," I said, "but the more I understand about this, the more I understand about Janan. Whatever Menehem did, it stopped Janan for a little while. The rest of you don't feel it, but the white walls feel *horrible* to me. And the temple makes me feel—" I blinked away tears. "He's not good, Sam. Whatever Janan is, it's bad. It's evil."

"All right." Sam pressed himself against me, as though he could shield me from something like Janan. As though he could even comprehend my fear of Janan when he didn't fear Janan at all. I probably sounded crazy to him, thinking the heat and pulse of the walls were wrong. My seemingly irrational dislike of sleeping close to the exterior walls of buildings was unique, but I couldn't even lean against the wall. It made my stomach twist with unease.

I was right, though. There was something *off* about Janan. Inside the temple, he'd called me a mistake, which implied that he had a plan. He'd also said I was "of no consequence," which implied that he didn't view me as a threat.

I aimed to be a threat.

Sam combed his fingers through my hair, down the back

of my neck. "I wish I understood what it feels like for you. I wish I could make it right."

He didn't want to make *me* right. He wanted to make things with Janan right.

I liked that he didn't think I was wrong. I liked that he believed me. That he trusted me, in spite of how I must have looked.

The building creaked in the wind as night settled, and my hair muffled Sam's words. "I'm just worried that if we go too far into Menehem's research, regardless of our intentions, someone will think we're creating another Templedark."

"Even our possessing his research will be too much for some people," I whispered. "Maybe I have more friends now, but Meuric wasn't alone in his feelings about newsouls. Not nearly." Right off, I could think of five people who'd made their dislike clear, and lots more who just didn't bother acknowledging me.

Sam nodded, his expression etched with frustration.

"I don't want anyone to think I want another Templedark, but Menehem's poison is the only thing I know that affects Janan. I just— I want a weapon, Sam. You gave me a knife when I told you someone followed me home one night. A knife won't work against Janan. We only know one thing that affects him, and this is it. I want to understand how. I want to discover if maybe there's another way I can protect myself."

I wanted to feel safe, but that would never happen in Heart, and I wouldn't ask Sam to spend this lifetime in a dusty cabin just for me.

"Let's go through the rest of Menehem's research," Sam said. "I'm sure he recorded videos and every possible variation in his results. Will that help?"

"It's a start."

4
WATCHERS

SAM WAS ALREADY sleeping on the sofa when the noise came, a soft shriek of wind that sent splinters of fear through my chest. I scrambled for the window.

Dusk had fallen, and the view from the window nearest my bed revealed only twin mountains against starlight, and lots of trees in between. Brittle leaves rushed in the wind, and I relaxed. Real wind. Real wind in a strange place. I didn't know the sounds of this building like I knew those of Purple Rose Cottage. I wasn't familiar with the particular way wind cut across the iron corner in the northeast, or which trees groaned. I didn't know their voices.

The sound remained, but the branches, half-dressed with autumn, became motionless.

A square of light fell from my window onto the grass when Sam clicked on the nearest lamp. "What is it?" He stopped at the foot of the bed, yawning.

"They're watching." I grabbed my flashlight from the nightstand, gave the tube a few sharp twists, and shone the light toward the woods.

Shadows skittered away, yelping and whining, but they didn't come closer. When I pulled the beam toward the lab again, the shadows relaxed and resumed their places at the tree line.

"Watching?" Sam touched my shoulder and peered out from behind me. "How many are there?"

"A lot." I closed the window and pulled the shade. We were probably safe inside the iron building. Probably. "Do you think any of these are the same sylph that attacked me on my birthday?"

"I don't know." Sam clicked off the light. "If they are, why behave differently now?"

Mysteries and more mysteries.

The sylph didn't leave that night, or the next, or the next. They never moved closer, never threatened or attacked, but they were always there. Watching.

Over the next few weeks, I learned why it had taken Menehem eighteen years to re-create and perfect the results of the first Templedark.

The process of creating and dispersing the poison was a complicated one. Sam and I watched video after video of Menehem explaining different theories and tests to the camera. The hundreds of combinations ran together until one finally gave the response Menehem had been looking for.

Sam and I sat curled on the sofa together, his arm around my shoulders. I had a notebook balanced on my knees so I could write down stray thoughts. The screen, which Menehem had hidden in a wall, showed a summer day with my father bustling about the yard with cans of aerosol poison, which he'd created using a machine in the back of the lab.

"Aerosol," he explained to the camera for the hundredth time, "has proven to be the most effective delivery system. It allows the hormones to be both solid and suspended midair. For sylph, both corporeal and incorporeal, almost a paradox themselves, fighting them with a substance that behaves the same way seems the most logical.

"The problem has been finding just the right amount of each hormone and timing the exposure, but I believe that I've finally found a combination that will work. I started with . . ."

He droned on for a while, repeating many of the same things he'd said before. Then he ambled toward a large speaker by the building and flipped a switch. Music crackled and settled, and a haunting piano sonata flowed across the small field and toward the nearby creek. Music streamed toward the mountains, filling the entire area with melody.

As they'd done in nearly every other video, sylph appeared in the distance.

Shadows glided toward the speaker, writhing like flames. Tendrils of darkness shot out of them, like hands reaching for the sky. Under the familiar sounds of Sam's piano playing, the sylph voices rose up to sing along.

I glanced at Sam. "Is that weird? That they like music so much?" As I had, Menehem seemed to have discovered their response to music by accident. Then he'd begun using it as a lure.

"Maybe. Who can tell with sylph?"

Perhaps they thought Menehem had captured one of their own. Would they have cared if Menehem had trapped another sylph?

On the screen, sylph drifted around the yard, ignoring the small canisters placed about. When there were nearly a dozen sylph singing along to the sonata, Menehem pressed another button.

The canisters spewed aerosol, hissing loudly. The sylph ignored it; if these were the same sylph as had been in previous videos, they were used to this part, too. The gas had never done anything to them.

This time, the sylph dropped.

Two or three at first. They twitched and seemed to glance around—how could they *glance* if they had no eyes?—and then sank into puddles of darkness.

Another sylph shimmered and fell. And another.

Soon, Menehem flicked off the speaker and the field was silent.

"I did it," he said. "Finally, I did it!" Menehem jumped and whooped, giving me an odd sense of embarrassment for him.

Sam shifted uncomfortably, and I doodled roses in the margins of my notebook while we waited for Menehem to compose himself on the screen.

"It looks like they just fall asleep," Sam said.

"The music draws them in, and the gas puts them to sleep." I nodded and leaned forward as Menehem approached one of the sylph puddles. I almost felt bad for them, being experimented on. Sam was right. I didn't want to hurt them—though these didn't look like they were *hurt*, exactly.

Menehem knelt by the nearest sylph and pulled a device from his pocket. "Temperature is abnormally low for a sylph." He stuck his hand into the sleeping sylph. "It's warm, but not uncomfortable."

My heart jumped and sped. "Sam." Why would anyone *put their hand* inside a sylph?

"I see it." He touched my hands, squeezed them. "They're fine now. Healed completely, remember?"

I nodded, but the sensation of burning wasn't something I'd ever be able to forget.

As we watched, a couple of sylph twitched and shifted in their sleep. Could sylph dream?

Suddenly, the one Menehem had touched shot into the air, towering over the chemist. Grass sizzled, and the sylph shrieked so loud and high that Sam and I both covered our ears.

Other sylph awoke, equally enraged. Smoke billowed where they burned the grass. They converged on Menehem and—

And they *seemed to think about it*. Something passed among the sylph. Communication? I couldn't tell. It was so fast, and they were still keening. . . .

At once, all dozen sylph fled the area, leaving patches of scorched earth behind. Menehem slumped to the ground, an unused sylph egg rolling from his hand. He'd almost been killed.

He'd almost been burned alive, but the sylph decided not to do it.

"What . . ." I stared at the screen until Menehem soberly got up to declare this portion of the experiment finished. The video stopped. "Did he even realize the sylph chose not to kill him?"

"Hard to say with Menehem." Sam switched to the next video but didn't play it yet. "It didn't last very long, what he did to the sylph. A few minutes at best."

I checked one of Menehem's diaries. "This says the initial dose was small. He eventually increased the doses, but they grew resistant."

Sam nodded. "And the dose he gave to Janan?"

Oh. If it affected both sylph and Janan the same way, then it was logical to assume Janan would develop a tolerance, too. I checked Menehem's notes, flipping several pages toward the end. "It was a massive dose. At least a hundred times larger than the biggest dose ever given to the sylph."

"So what he did during Templedark won't work again."

I shook my head. "No, looking at the logs, the tolerance grew quickly and exponentially in sylph. If anything were to affect Janan again, it would have to be—I can't even comprehend. There'd have to be a lot of it, and it would take months to make, even with that machine in the back doing all the work. The delivery would have to be unbelievably enormous."

"Yeah." Sam considered for a moment, then touched my wrist. "At least there's something good in this."

Was it bad? I wasn't sure how I felt about it, let alone whether it was good or bad.

"Should anyone accuse you of wanting to attempt another Templedark, we have proof it isn't possible."

Newsouls were supposed to be impossible, yet I'd been born.

Getting into the temple should have been impossible, yet I'd been inside.

Poisoning Janan again wasn't *impossible*. With a bigger dose and a bigger delivery system, it could be done. I just didn't know how. Or whether I should.

Inside the temple, Meuric had hinted about something horrible happening on Soul Night: the spring equinox of the Year of Souls. That threat nipped at my thoughts.

"We still can't tell anyone about the poison," I said. "I don't want the Council—or anyone—to know we came here and looked. They'll assume the wrong thing. They'll assume I'm like Menehem, and I'm not."

"I know." Sam lurched up from the couch and paced the room, shoulders and back stiff.

After a while of watching him walk ditches in the floor, I asked, "Are you okay?"

"Yes." He stopped and sighed. "No. Sorry."

Sorry for saying yes when he didn't mean it? Or sorry that he wasn't okay? I waited for him to go on.

"I've never gotten involved in disputes. I don't like them. Even in the beginning, I stayed away from conflict." Emotions shifted over his face, and he looked at me. "I'm on your side, Ana. Every time. Before, it was easy to stay out because I didn't care. I just made music, and no one expected anything more from me. But with you, I do care."

And by being with me, the controversial newsoul, his life had changed. What he'd been before—notable for only his music—was gone. Now he was notable for living with, and frequently kissing, the newsoul, and that forced him to take a side. Mine.

"I'm on your side," he said again. "But I have to admit the

idea of being *in* something is frightening."

I pushed my notebooks to the sofa and crossed the floor to Sam. His cheeks were warm beneath my palms, and stubble scraped my skin. I wanted to—*something*. Thank him. Reassure him. Make him know how much I appreciated him and cared about him. Express everything I felt, but nothing that found its way to my tongue felt big enough. So I brushed a kiss over his mouth and stayed silent. His hands tightened on my hips.

Moments spiraled between us, ripe with words unsaid, until finally I pulled away and gathered up my notebooks to work at the table. He'd relaxed a little; that was what I'd wanted.

"What *are* the sylph?" A book slid from my pile and hit the floor with a loud slap.

"Shadows?" Sam bent and retrieved the book smoothly, and sat across the table from me. "Fire? I'm not sure what you're asking. They're just sylph."

"But they're—" I dropped to the chair. "Are they like people? Do they think? Have emotions? Societies?" They seemed like creatures with reason in the videos we'd just watched. They'd made choices.

Choices I didn't understand.

"I don't know." Sam eyed me askance. "What are you thinking?"

"I'm not sure. I mean, we know centaurs live in

communities, right? They have language, traditions, and hierarchy. They go on hunts together."

He nodded.

"And trolls? They're the same?"

"Different, but yes. They live in communities, too."

"What about dragons?" I didn't want to ask him about dragons, all things considered, but I was chasing a point. An idea. A question.

"From what we've been able to tell, yes. And rocs nest with a mate and care for their chicks until they're old enough, like eagles do. Unicorns live in herds. They're not human, none of them, but they do seem to be *more*." He studied me with those dark eyes. "You're trying to figure out sylph."

"Aren't you?" I glanced out the window, where ranks of sylph still guarded the building. "We know so much about everything else surrounding Range, but not sylph. We see them in swarms sometimes, or off by themselves, but we don't know if they stay with the same group or just join up with any other sylph they meet. We don't know if they eat, how they think, whether they reproduce. Are there a limited number? We haven't been able to kill them, but what about other creatures? Centaurs are intelligent. Can they kill sylph?"

Sam just stared at me like I'd grown a second head. "I don't know. Sylph are all over the world, rather than generally keeping to one region, like we do, or dragons or centaurs or trolls."

"There are bears and flies all over the world, too, but sylph aren't like bears or flies."

"No," he agreed. "They're much different."

"But *how*? Please tell me you at least understand the questions I'm asking, even if you don't know the answers."

"Of course." Sam frowned, eyebrows drawing together to carve the thinking line. "Why wouldn't I understand your questions?"

Lightning struck inside my chest. He couldn't even remember that sometimes he didn't. It was okay, though. Most people couldn't remember things about the temple, or Janan, or understand why I asked so many questions. I said gently, "What's inside the temple, Sam?"

"Nothing. It's empty."

"How do you know that? Have you been inside?"

He shook his head, looking confused. "There's no door."

My fingers skimmed the silver box I'd taken from Meuric during my trip into the temple. The door device was too dangerous to leave behind. Doors could be created, and the temple wasn't empty—not completely. I'd stabbed Meuric and left him there, and I'd taken a stack of books from inside the temple; there were still more there.

Sam followed the motion of my hand. "What is that?"

"A key, I think." I waved his next question away. We'd had this conversation a few times already. He just couldn't remember. "And in your life before this one, you went north?"

"Yes. There were dragons." A shudder passed through him.

I wished I hadn't brought it up.

"But before the dragons, you said you came upon a huge white wall."

Slowly, he nodded. "There was snow everywhere. The wall was pitted with weather. It seemed familiar, but strange, too." The haze vanished from his eyes. "We were talking about sylph."

No, we were talking about why he might not understand my questions.

And knowing what I did about reincarnation, what entity was responsible for it, I could make a pretty good guess as to why Sam—and everyone else—struggled with certain subjects.

Janan didn't want them to know.

Janan didn't want them to question.

Janan kept a huge secret in that temple, in those books, and somehow the sylph were connected to it.

I just had to find out what it was—and use it against him.

5
WORDS

AFTER MORE RESEARCH and note consolidation than I could stand, I slumped on the rickety bed to check my SED. It had been chirping with messages all morning; they were from Sarit, asking me to call.

I shifted to the communicator function.

"Ana!" Sarit's voice squeaked with joy. "What have you been doing all day? I've been waiting and waiting."

I giggled. Sarit was amazing. No other oldsoul would complain about waiting. Everyone else, Sam included, was ridiculously patient. "You know Sam. There's always more work with him."

Sam glanced up from the sofa where he was writing in his diary. He looked adorably baffled about why he was getting blamed for something, and I winked.

"Oooh." Sarit drew out the sound. "Work. I'm sure that's all you've been doing."

"Well." I giggled again, remembering earlier when we'd taken a break to cook lunch, and later had to eat burned rice and vegetables because we'd been too busy kissing to remember to stir.

"That's what I thought." Sarit laughed. "I can't wait for you to come home. I want to see the flute and hear the duets. Just the idea is making me wilt."

"That's why you're one of my favorite people." I leaned back on my pillow. "But tell me about the fifty thousand messages you left. What's so important?"

"Okay, there are two things. First, did you feel the earthquake?"

"Earthquake? No." I glanced at Sam, my eyebrow raised. "Did you feel an earthquake?"

He shook his head.

"Neither of us did," I said to Sarit. "Was it big? Is everyone okay?"

"Oh, yeah." She sounded breezy. "Everyone's fine. It was small, really. There are always earthquakes in Range, though most are too tiny to feel. But you know how everyone gets. They're all wishing Rahel were still here; she looked after the geological and geothermal aspects of Range. It just makes people feel safer to have someone like her saying there's no danger."

"Ah." I shifted, hating when anyone mentioned a darksoul. It wasn't that I wanted people to pretend they'd never been here, but friends' pain was too sharp. "What was the second thing?"

Her tone lightened. "Well, you remember how you were asking about what happens during a rebirth?"

"Yeah . . ."

"But no one invited you and you said you felt awkward just showing up?"

"Yes?" After Templedark, several pairings had been approved by the Council; they needed to start getting souls back, and not *everyone* who'd died that night became a darksoul. Lots would return, like Menehem.

"Lidea was asking about you last night. She wanted to know when you and Sam would be back, because she was hoping you'd be there when she gives birth."

"Really?" I bounced. "You're not tricking me so I'll come back to Heart early, are you?"

"No!" Sarit lowered her voice, as though telling me a secret. "She said she wouldn't be alive now if it weren't for you. And she was asking about *you*, really. Not even Sam, but he's probably expected if you're going."

"Wow. Okay. When is it?"

"They're thinking it will be just a couple of weeks"—her tone turned sly—"so you should probably come home now."

I snorted. "I knew there was a catch."

"And a bribe. Come home and I'll give you another jar of honey. A bigger jar. I'm sure you've run out of the little one by now."

It was true. "You do know the way to my heart. I'll tell Sam I can't pass up an offer like that."

"Good! Okay, go tell him. See you soon, my little moth!"

"Ew. Really?"

"I have a whole list of bugs for you. Bye!" She hung up.

"What did she call you this time?" Sam put down his diary and stretched.

"A moth." I checked for other messages, but Sarit's were the only ones. "I think she's trying to wear me down about the butterfly thing."

"Is it working?" He stood and glanced out the window. His expression didn't change, though, which meant the sylph must still be out there.

"Nope. She can call me whatever bug she wants. I'm not a butterfly."

"No." Sam gave a quiet half smile. "You aren't."

Shortly after we'd met, Sam had compared my life to a butterfly's, saying that to others I was fleeting, inconsequential. I'd long ago forgiven the insult, but I'd made the mistake of wearing a butterfly costume to a rededication masquerade earlier this year. The nickname had stuck, mostly as an endearment, though knowing my distaste for it, Sarit searched tirelessly for alternatives.

"It sounds like we're going back to Heart sooner than scheduled?" Sam hesitated, then sat on the corner of the bed. He'd been sleeping on the sofa only a few strides away, and he claimed he wasn't uncomfortable there, but I kept wondering if we might both be more comfortable if he were here. With me. I didn't say anything, though.

"Yep." I stretched to put my SED on the small nightstand, next to my private notebook. "We've been invited to a rebirth, and I really want to go. I think we're done here, anyway."

Sam tracked my motions, something deep and undefinable in his eyes when I settled against the pillow again. "You know I'd go anywhere with you, Ana."

I smiled. "Keep saying that and I might start believing you."

"It's true." He scooted closer, now by my hips. "Where do you want to go?"

"To the moon?"

He grinned. "I like that you think big."

"What about to the bottom of the ocean?" I'd never even seen the top of the ocean, but why stop there? "We could go to the very bottom and explore. Can you imagine what kind of creatures must live under all that water?"

"I think *you* can, and that's what I—" He dragged in a

breath. "I want to tell you something."

"What is it?" I pushed myself up straight, and suddenly we were very close together and the mattress sagged awkwardly under our combined weight. He hooked his arm around my waist to keep me from falling over as I let my hands slide downward so my fingers curved over his arms.

"Ana—" He kissed me, gentle and sweet, but filled with an intoxicating urgency. His arm tightened around me, drawing me nearer. He kissed a trail down my neck, as far as he could go before my shirt collar stopped him, and then he stayed there. Breathing hard.

I almost asked again what he wanted to tell me, but maybe I didn't want to know. Maybe it was something bad and that was why he'd kissed me like that. Maybe he thought it would be so horrible I'd never speak to him again, but surely he knew he meant everything to me.

"Sam?" I combed my fingers through his hair, soft and thick and dark. I liked the way he kept it, a barely contained disaster. "What is it?" I whispered.

He drew himself up, kissed me again, and spoke the words against my lips. "I love you, Ana."

My breath caught in my chest.

The words. They made my heart beat faster. I wanted to be able to tell him how I felt, and what he must have been waiting to hear, but even thinking the words made me sweat. Nosouls couldn't love. That was what my mother had told me for eighteen years, and she'd slapped me if I even said the word.

But I *wasn't* a nosoul. Newsoul, yes. Still, was I truly capable and deserving of love?

"It's okay," he whispered, and his worry turned into understanding. Of course he understood; he always did. "It's okay if you can't tell me. Or if you don't feel the same way about me. I just wanted to make sure that you knew I do love you."

The words sent chills across my skin. "Thank you." I tried to smile to reassure him, but nothing would come.

"I love you." He said it as though repeating himself would convince me.

The tightness spread up to my throat, making tears blur my vision.

"Ana." He turned my face up, brushing his thumbs across my damp cheeks. "Why are you crying?"

"I don't know." A sob erupted with an ugly heave. I couldn't breathe anymore.

Sam wrapped his arms around me, holding me tight against his chest. My tears soaked his shirt, and when my nose ran, he pressed a clean handkerchief into my hand. I clutched the square of white cloth. Clutched Sam. Part of me wanted him to go away so I could cry in peace, but I didn't want him to leave.

He rocked me until my sobs waned to sniffles, not asking *why* again. And he didn't take back the words. *That* word. I didn't want him to take it back. I wanted him to feel that way about me.

I wanted it. I couldn't bear if he took it away.

"Lie down," he whispered.

I did, wiping a dry corner of the handkerchief over my face as he pulled a blanket over me.

"Do you want a cup of tea?"

"No." Weeping had shredded my voice. "I want you."

"Okay." He bent to untie his shoes, then kicked them off and stretched out on the narrow bed beside me. Achingly close. Too close, because our knees and elbows got in each other's way, even through the blanket. Not close enough.

I shut my eyes so I didn't have to see his concerned expression, his confusion, or the hurt. If I could have explained somehow, I would have, but there was nothing where an explanation should be.

He brushed hair off my face, strands stuck to damp skin, and finally I drifted in and out of restless sleep. But he was there every time I opened my eyes, stirring awake when I moved.

Darkness blanketed the world as I crept up to wash my face and throw the handkerchief in the laundry pile. Night had fallen. Outside, sylph crooned half-familiar songs, making me pause.

"Ana." Sam rolled over to face me, and I darted back into bed before he decided to go to the sofa.

The blanket was still warm from his body, even though he lay on top of the covers. "Thank you," I whispered.

"For what?" He leaned on his elbow, face just above mine in the darkness. Kisses breezed over my forehead, my cheeks.

For not running away when I started crying. For not taking the words back. For saying the words in the first place.

"I don't know. For everything."

Dawn slanted through the east-facing windows in gold banners. Sam was in the kitchen area, preparing coffee, and all our bags were waiting by the front door.

He scraped the sides of the empty honey jar before stirring my coffee, then smiled over. "Hey."

"Are the sylph still out there?" I rubbed sleep from my eyes and scooted off the bed. The rest of the covers were cold; he must have been up a long time, getting ready for us to leave. "Do you think they'll let us by without trouble?"

"They haven't bothered us yet." He took our mugs and came to sit beside me, handing me my coffee.

It was true. We'd gone outside to clean, to get fresh air, to take care of Shaggy, and the sylph hadn't done anything more sinister than study us.

Ceramic warmed my hands as I breathed in bitter and sweet steam. "Sam, about last night . . ."

He inclined his head toward me, black hair falling across his eyes.

In all the months I'd known him, he'd never said my feelings were stupid. He never made me feel *wrong* or dumb. He'd always taken me seriously. I could trust him.

"I don't know why I reacted like that, after you said—" I stared into my coffee. "I didn't want to start crying. It's embarrassing. I'm sorry."

He caressed my cheek, my neck. "There's no reason to be embarrassed or sorry. It's fine. I think . . . I think I understand."

"Can you explain it to me?" I choked a laugh. "Because I don't understand at all."

"No, because if I'm wrong, *I'll* be really embarrassed."

"Thank you." I leaned on his shoulder.

He kissed the top of my head, and we stayed quiet as sunlight moved across the floor. "After someone followed you home, I gave you a knife."

"Yes." I shivered closer to him.

"Did it make you feel safer?"

I considered. At first, I'd tried to squirm away from the weapon, but it was beautiful and had later saved me from Meuric. I carried it everywhere now, though I tended to use it for holding down paper more than stabbing.

"Yes," I said at last.

"All right." His voice grew distant, disturbed.

"What is it?"

"Nothing you need to worry about." Sam was a rule

follower. He didn't do things that might get him in trouble. He plain didn't think about trouble at all.

But whatever he had in mind now, it was as un-Sam-like as the sylph outside.

6
GRATITUDE

A COUPLE OF hours later, the sylph watched us go. They stayed by their trees, moaning pitifully and huddling together when a chill wind snapped through, but they made no motion to follow us. I had pockets full of sylph eggs, just in case.

As Sam and I headed west into the woods, the pony on a lead behind us, the sylph wailed and sang part of a symphony we'd been listening to the other night.

I shivered deeper into my coat. What did they want? Nothing in the lab had offered an explanation. Aside from the poison, I was just as confused as before.

"Come on," Sam said, gentle as ever when pulling me from fearful contemplation. "We need to decide something very important."

"What's that?" I tugged my hat over my ears and adjusted my fingerless mittens, trapping in as much heat as possible.

"Which duet we'll play for Sarit first. Do you have a preference?"

I grinned and let him distract me with talk of music for the next several hours, though both of us kept checking over our shoulders for shadows that didn't belong.

During our hike from Purple Rose Cottage to Menehem's lab, autumn had only been creeping into the leaves, weaving red and gold and russet with the green. Now, as we pushed toward Heart, an autumn carpet crunched beneath our boots.

A deep roar sounded, long and rumbling. I stiffened and reached for my knife—as if it would do any good if we were about to encounter a bear—but Sam just took my forearm and drew me off the road.

"Stand back here." As the roar grew louder and higher, Sam slipped one hand around mine and held tight to Shaggy's harness with the other.

It wasn't a bear growl; the sound was too long and even and mechanical. A low-flying air drone approached in a torrent of leaves. Metal glinted in dappled sunlight, the only thing I could see through the leaf storm, and the noise grew so shrill I covered my ears.

Then the drone was gone, its sound falling lower as it vanished down the road. Leaves rained down on the sides of the road, showers of gold and red and russet, leaving the cobblestones mostly clear.

"It's safe now." Sam drew Shaggy and me back onto the road.

"A drone to clear the roads?" I gazed after the thing, but it was long gone. Only flurries of autumn leaves gave evidence to its passing. "How does it know where to go? And why is it so loud?" Labor drones were typically quiet.

"There are sensors under the roads, which tell if there's anything covering it for long periods of time. Rain doesn't matter, and moving traffic doesn't set it off, but snow and lots of leaves do. Even dead animals. It can tell what kind of material is covering the stone, and appropriate drones get sent out."

"Stef's idea?" It sounded like something she would insist on, keeping the roads clear even when traffic outside of Heart was uncommon.

"And the noise they make." Sam tugged Shaggy's lead and the pony snorted, ears twisting to listen to the retreating drone. "We found out quickly that with the quieter models, animals didn't know what to do. With the noise, they tend to run."

"Instead of waiting to get hit on the head?"

"Exactly. Now," he said, "we need to talk about your posture when you play your flute. You keep letting the end drop. Is it too heavy?" His tone was teasing.

"No," I mumbled, because he was right. It was just laziness.

"You'll get a better sound if you hold your flute straight."

"I know, I know. Do you keep yourself up at night coming up with new things to correct me on?"

He chuckled. "Do you keep yourself up at night coming up with new ways to see if I'm paying attention?"

"That's exactly what I do." Sighing happily, I lifted my face to the perfume of autumn. The scents of turning leaves and decaying grass tickled through me, and as we left the sylph and lab behind, a knot inside my chest began to loosen.

A new tangle formed as we drew closer to Heart, and two days later we woke to clouds falling across the sky in great splashes. The air, so recently crisp and exciting, now felt heavy and close with waiting. As we finished packing our belongings, I hunched deep into my raincoat, wishing it would just rain already.

The sky rumbled and the ground shook. Water poured from the clouds, soaking the remainder of the journey to Heart with misery.

The rain pounded on us at all hours, dripping through the autumn foliage and revealing thin spots in our tent that night. The temperature dipped, and by the time we approached Heart the next day, my wool clothes were sodden and smelly, chafing my skin. I entertained vivid fantasies of a hot shower.

At last, the city wall shone white atop the plateau, and beside me, Sam muttered something in relief. Beneath his hood, his expression melted into what mine must have looked like when we'd *left* Heart.

But seeing the pristine white tower that soared into the clouds, muscles in my neck and shoulders crawled with tension, and all I could think about were Janan's words to me: *mistake. You are a mistake of no consequence.*

I jerked my gaze downward, pulled in a breath, and twisted my hands around in my mitts to distract myself. Even with the sylph, our weeks away had erased the stress I'd barely realized I'd been living with in Heart. And it took only one look to bring it back.

"Are you all right?" Sam's voice came just over the pounding rain. "Ana?"

I nodded. "Let's get it over with."

Geysers steamed fiercely in the cold, making the whole plateau misty and difficult to navigate.

"Stay on the road," Sam reminded me, though it wasn't necessary. Some of the ground here was very thin; beneath us, an immense chamber of magma pulsed and boiled, releasing its energy in bursts of steaming water and bubbling mud. Nevertheless, I let him guide me to the Eastern Arch, and waited while he pressed his hand against the soul-scanner. A moment later, it allowed our entrance.

Inside the guard station, we dried ourselves and Shaggy, and sent the pony with the guard on duty so he could be fed. The guard smiled at me. I sort of recognized him from

Templedark. Had I warned him against dying? The whole night had been too chaotic for clear memories, and he took Shaggy and left before I could ask.

"Do you want to wait here until it stops raining?" Sam asked when we were alone.

"No, we might as well walk to the other side of the city now. Who knows how long it will be before the storm passes?" I pulled out my SED and sent a message to Sarit to meet us at Sam's. "But we *are* going to have a big jar of honey waiting for us. Sarit likes rain, right?"

Sam grinned and hefted four of our bags onto his shoulders, leaving two for me. Just those were more than heavy enough.

We headed outside, into Heart, trudging under the weight of our belongings. East Avenue was dark and quiet, except for the driving rain, so we hurried down the road without interruption. Mills and warehouses of the industrial quarter watched us from the south; evergreen trees blocked the northeastern residential quarter, leaving only the occasional street as proof that people lived there.

As we entered the market field—the wide expanse of cobblestone surrounding the temple and Councilhouse—Sam moved to walk between the temple and me. He didn't say anything about it, and he knew I didn't like the temple, but I wasn't sure it was an entirely conscious move, either.

We turned onto South Avenue. A side road here and there,

and finally we came to his walkway, covered with wet leaves and broken twigs. The fruit trees were bare, and at one side of the house, chickens and cavies' buildings were nearly invisible in the rain.

"Ready to get out of the weather?" Sam asked, hitching his load of bags again.

Yes, definitely, but I wasn't eager to box myself into one of the identical houses of white stone. Walls shouldn't have heartbeats. They *shouldn't*. And as welcoming as Sam's house was otherwise—pine-green shutters and doors, rosebushes below the windows, and a generous garden—it was still made from that stone. It had windows and doors in the same places as every other house in Heart. It wasn't natural.

Still, I didn't want to stand out in the rain staring. I followed Sam indoors and dropped my bags on the mud rug. Water soaked the wool threads immediately, turning the gray a shade darker.

Sam stripped off his outer clothes and boots, leaving them behind as he moved between all the instruments in the parlor. The sheets covering the piano, harpsichord, cello—all the large instruments on the floor—had been moved away already, probably courtesy of Stef or Sarit.

I unloaded all my wet belongings and clothes, muscles creaking with relief, then hurried up the spiral staircase and into my washroom for a shower.

When I was warmed through, dry, and clothed in a

dove-gray sweater and thick black pants, I skipped down-stairs to find Sarit and Stef making tea in the kitchen.

"Ana!" Sarit abandoned the kettle and wrapped me in a hug. "You're back! And just in time. I got a message earlier saying that Lidea went to the rebirthing center this after-noon, and Wend will send a message when we should come. They'd have been so sad if you couldn't make it."

"Ugh, the rain, though." I pulled my damp hair into a quick bun. "Our tent had a leak. I've had quite enough of the rain."

"But you're going, right?" Sarit narrowed her dark eyes at me. "Because I will put you in one of my tiny bags and carry you if I have to."

"I'll go! Anything but the tiny bag." With Sarit appeased, I shifted and hugged Stef before accepting the hot mug of tea she offered. "Missed you."

She shook back a length of blond hair and kissed my fore-head. "You too."

We headed into the parlor, where Stef and I sat on the sofa, and Sarit perched on the piano bench. "Think he'll notice?" She glanced toward the stairs; Sam was somewhere up there, fin-ishing washing or unpacking. I didn't even want to think about unpacking, but my bag stared at me from the door, waiting.

"Oh, he'll notice," Stef said. "But he won't mind."

Sarit grinned and caressed the row of ebony and ivory piano keys. "I call this one 'Bumble, Bumblebee.' It's for you, Ana."

I laughed and leaned back to listen while she played a silly tune that seemed to involve more picking notes at random than anything. Eventually Sam came down and sat on the arm of the sofa next to me, and everyone caught up with one another.

In all my years of living in Purple Rose Cottage with Li, I'd never imagined this: sitting in Dossam's elegant parlor, surrounded by glorious instruments I'd only dreamt of seeing, and listening to *my friends* discuss their days.

I had friends.

It was more than I could have hoped.

Stef was fierce and intimidating, possessing this grace so practiced it was unconscious after all these generations. Sitting next to her always made me feel skinny and awkward. And while Stef looked like sunshine, Sarit looked like nighttime, with dramatic dark hair and eyes. They were both so beautiful it hurt.

But they were my friends. *My* friends. They liked me for some reason. And Sam—Sam had said he loved me.

I leaned back, scribbling happiness into my notebook and listening to the melody of my friends' voices.

Sam glanced over and lifted an eyebrow. "Diary?"

With a shrug and a smile, I closed my notebook. I'd show him what was inside when I was ready.

After a half hour of talking and drinking tea, the patter of rain let up, and Sarit checked her SED. "Looks like Lidea is ready for us. We should go while it's safe to walk outside without gills."

We put on coats and grabbed umbrellas, and the four of us went out, Sam and Stef walking together, and Sarit with me. The world smelled of damp grass and leaves, fresh, in spite of the way everything was dying at winter's approach.

"Long trip away," she muttered. "Just you and Sam. A romantic gift of a flute. So have you"—she lifted an eyebrow suggestively—"you know?"

Had I what? Had Sam and I done something together? Something that warranted a suggestive eyebrow? She must have thought I'd be embarrassed to talk about it—which meant whatever it was, I hadn't done it. "No." I bit my lip.

"Really? The way you two were at the rededication, I'd have thought months ago."

Heat rose to my throat and cheeks when I thought about the masquerade, Sam as the shrike and the way he danced with me. My face really burned when I remembered what happened after the masquerade, the way he'd touched me and made me long for something I couldn't name.

But then Meuric and Li had taken Sam prisoner, and forced me to live with Li until Templedark, when I'd escaped. After that . . . "We slowed down," I said. "Really slowed. Nothing has been the same since the rededication. That night was unique."

In both wonderful and horrible ways.

She nodded. "But you're happy with him? Slow, but good?"

"Yes, very." Nervousness fluttered inside of me. "He said he lo—" The word stuck on my tongue, and Sarit waited for me to finish, her dark gaze patient. I gathered the syllables in my mouth again. "He said he loves me."

A dozen reactions flickered across Sarit's face—I caught shock and joy and confusion—before her expression softened into understanding. "And you think . . . what?"

I shrugged.

"I want to know." She bumped my shoulder with hers and lowered her voice, though Sam and Stef were far ahead of us now. "Did you say it back?"

She wouldn't think badly of me. I could be honest. "I didn't."

"Did you want to?"

I pulled my flashlight from my coat and swept the beam across the wet cobblestones. It wasn't quite dark enough to need it, but they'd all keep going long after it was too dark to see. They could navigate Heart with their eyes closed. Sam had done it once when I'd bet him he couldn't.

Sarit touched my wrist as we turned the corner onto South Avenue. "It's okay if you didn't want to say it. Or you just couldn't." She was an echo, just as sweet and understanding as he'd been. Both of them made my heart feel like it might burst with wonder.

"I don't know yet," I said at last. I couldn't even explain to myself why I'd started crying when he told me, and I didn't want to bother Sarit with it. Not now. This would be a happy night. "But he told me again the next day. And the days after."

"Good." She was quiet as we headed toward the Council-house, where the hospital waited. "Don't worry about that other thing."

Ah, the thing that might be embarrassing to talk about. I bit my lip, half wishing she'd been more clear about it, half relieved she hadn't. "Okay."

"It'll happen when you're ready. Just . . . He loves you, Ana. If he said it, he means it. And I love you too. I'm still really glad you're here."

"Why?" I whispered, hardly able to believe she'd said it, too. How easy she made it sound, just freely giving love.

Sarit stopped and regarded me with a wry smile. "Just accept it, Ana. You can't stop your friends from loving you. You can't stop Sam from feeling the way he does. You know I admire that you question things, but this—this doesn't have to be one of them."

Gratitude kindled inside of me, almost choking my words. "Thank you," I said, and we hurried after Sam and Stef.

7
REBIRTH

THE COUNCILHOUSE WAS an immense building with a wide half-moon staircase spreading out from the front. A huge landing waited at the top, just ahead of a series of double doors; sometimes the landing was used as a stage for outdoor concerts and dances, or just announcements. Though since Templedark, there hadn't been much call for celebration.

We climbed the stairs—two at a time for those with longer legs—and stepped around columns and crumbling statues. The human-made parts of the Councilhouse were old and falling apart, worse after Templedark. Nothing had been the same since Templedark.

Sam held the door open for us, and we headed toward the hospital wing. Now that we were almost there, it took all my effort not to skip. "I'm excited to see a rebirth. Do you think she'll let me touch the baby?"

"Probably." Sam fell into step with Stef, behind Sarit and me.

"Good," I said. "That was your last chance to tell me if asking would be rude."

Stef lowered her voice, intentionally just loud enough for me to hear. "Next she'll be wanting one of her own."

One of my own?

A baby?

"Right." I glanced over my shoulder to find Sam looking fascinated by the wall, and Stef wearing a smirk. "Because what I really need is to be responsible for someone. Because I'd be really good at giving a baby everything it needs, thanks to the great example I got from Li." I choked out the last words. I had no idea if I ever wanted to have a baby, but it certainly wasn't *next* on my list of things to do.

Darkness flashed through Sam's eyes, but he didn't say anything.

"The Council is approving a lot of couples right now. I bet you'd be approved, too." Stef acted oblivious to my response, or Sam's discomfort. "We can check the genealogies later to make sure they'd say yes. It's embarrassing when they say no."

The Council had to be careful of accidental inbreeding and unfavorable genes being passed along, and no one wanted to be responsible for future generations suffering poor eyesight or genetic disorders. The practice made me uncomfortable, but to everyone else, it was a way of taking care of their bodies.

She went on. "I think—"

Sam interrupted her, voice deep and dark. "Let it go, Stef."

"Fine. I was just being interested in your lives."

Sam gave a long sigh; that was what the end of his patience sounded like, which I knew from experience. "Passive aggression doesn't suit you," he said. "If you want to talk about this, then we should. But later."

"Later," Stef whispered, tone all pity, and I could almost feel her glare on the back of my head. "I guess I do have that in my favor."

I probably hadn't been meant to hear the last part. My face burned with shame and grief at my own inevitable demise. We didn't know *for sure*, of course, whether I'd be reincarnated after this life, but it didn't seem likely.

Next to me, Sarit's expression was twisted with discomfort.

"Here we are." I spoke mostly to pretend like I hadn't heard Stef's comment, though everyone probably knew better.

The birthing center was a warm, open section of the hospital wing, with silk walls pinned in place by metal shelves. We hurried past the lit Soul Tellers' office, toward the rebirth room with its cheery decorations and array of medical equipment—just in case. They'd stopped using most of it a century ago.

As we entered the crowded room, buzzing conversation paused and people glanced up to see who'd arrived. Lidea was propped up on the bed with her eyes closed, surrounded by a team of birthing assistants.

"Shouldn't be long now," Stef said, folding her coat. "You can put your belongings on a shelf, Ana. Looks like we'll have to stand, though. All the chairs are taken."

"Why are there so many people here?" I placed my coat and umbrella next to her things. "There's got to be at least four dozen. Are they all going to watch her have a baby?"

"Yep." Stef flashed a smile, almost like an apology for her insensitivity earlier.

I'd have to remember this kind of thing attracted crowds, because in the unlikely event I *did* ever have a baby, someone would be in charge of shutting the door.

Sam took my hand and guided Sarit, Stef, and me through the crowd of people chatting, speculating on who'd come back.

"Look," someone muttered, "the nosoul is here."

Shock spiraled though me, shame not far behind. I wasn't a nosoul. I *wasn't*.

Few people used the word "nosoul" anymore, so what had changed? Perhaps it was this birth: Lidea had gotten pregnant *after* Templedark, and everyone was nervous.

Still, I kept my face down as I walked, as though I could hide from the words.

"She'll curse Lidea," and "She's already cursed everyone. Her and Menehem. They planned Templedark," and "Dossam with her. He's no better."

Sam's hand tightened painfully around mine, but neither of us acknowledged the speakers. As much as I wanted to defend myself, this wasn't the time. Maybe I shouldn't have come. The last thing Lidea needed was for my presence to start a fight.

"Often," Sam said, as though we hadn't heard a bunch of people talking about me, "we can predict who'll be born, since there aren't a lot of possibilities. Maybe two or three. Their best friends usually attend the birthing to welcome them back."

We found a spot by the back wall, and I said, "A lot of people lost their friends."

Sam kept his voice soft as he turned his attention to the bed and birthing assistants gathered around. "Yeah."

Wend, Lidea's partner, stood beside her, petting her hair and whispering encouragement. Nearby, someone said she was pushing now, so it wouldn't be much longer.

I stood on my toes, but from our corner, I couldn't see more than Wend's head. There were too many people in front of us, half of them standing. I tugged Sam's sleeve. "I can't see."

Sam eyed the rows of people, and my nice view of their shoulders. "Go to the front." He nudged me. "I'll wait here."

I hesitated—some of these people hated me—but I refused to let them stop me from seeing my friend. I squeezed Sam's hand, then maneuvered through the crowd before I missed anything else. Right in time to see Micah, one of the birthing assistants, adjust the sheet over Lidea's legs and— Ew. It was really going to come out of her.

Sarit sidled up next to me. "Thought you could use some company." Protection, she meant, but I wasn't going to complain.

"Wow." I tried not to gape as Lidea groaned at another contraction. "That can't feel good."

Someone glared at me, and Sarit giggled.

Lidea grunted and—around a white-smocked birth assistant—I saw her face, lined with concentration. Her eyes were closed as if there was nothing else in the world. Just her and the baby.

True, most people weren't *watching*, but she made a lot of weird noises I'd have been embarrassed about. No one seemed to care, though.

It wasn't long before a last push brought the baby and its cry. Everyone cheered and called out, "Welcome back!" while Micah gave the baby to Lidea, who was flushed and sweaty, but grinned happily. Wend unbundled a small blanket and laid it across both of them.

"He's healthy!" Micah's shout made everyone cheer again. She put a dark green cap, embroidered with tiny ospreys and elk, on his head.

Sarit leaned toward me and muttered, "It's a running joke that there are only five or six newborn caps in existence. Everyone just passes them back and forth."

I giggled. "It does look suspiciously familiar."

After a few minutes, the cheering quieted and a pair of Soul Tellers stepped forward. Sarit and I ducked away, back to Sam and Stef.

"That was *amazing*," I whispered, pressing my spine against Sam's chest, relaxing when his arms circled my waist. "And kind of gross. It must have hurt."

"I'm sure she'd be happy to share, if you asked her."

I couldn't decide whether he was making a joke or not. Why would anyone want to talk about childbirth?

Maybe I'd see if the library had a book on it, instead.

Aside from Lidea's cooing to the baby until he calmed, the room grew silent as Emil, one of the Soul Tellers, approached the bed with a small device. It was a soul-scanner, like those used around the city to restrict access to armories and other secret places.

"Baby soul-scanners?" I asked.

Stef nodded. "They're new for the Soul Tellers, only fifty or so years old. Before that, Soul Tellers did blood tests, which were less reliable. They measured chemicals they believed the soul produced."

I hmmed. Sam had once mentioned that certain tests hadn't been reliable, and people would be called the wrong name until they were old enough to complain about it.

"Soul-scanners have been around much longer, of course," Stef went on, "but they work by measuring vibrations of the soul inside the body. Newborns tend to have erratic and excited souls. It took a lot of work to get around that."

"Huh." Maybe they'd thought the scanner was broken when I was born, if the technology was that new. Maybe they'd tried three or four times, and with different scanners, just to make sure.

"Hold his hand still," said Emil. "We should know in just a few minutes." They pressed the baby's palm against the scanner face and then tucked the blanket tighter. Being born must have been terribly shocking, and cold, but he stayed quiet, tucked against Lidea's chest.

Everyone in the room stared at Emil, all anticipation and hope that this baby was *their* best friend who'd been lost the night of Templedark. The number of possibilities was staggering, but worse, underneath rode a current of fear: glances at me, muttered prayers to Janan, and objects clutched to their chest.

The last must have been things belonging to whomever they hoped would return. A box, a key, a silk fan.

Emil lowered the device and gazed around, eyes settling

briefly on me. I tensed as another wave of anxiety passed through the silent room. "Is something wrong with him?" The words barely formed in my mouth, and Sam squeezed me, as if to caution.

"Who is he?"

Lidea's expression twisted with worry. "Please just tell me."

Emil faced her, his tone sober. "He's a newsoul."

8
NEWSOUL

I WASN'T ALONE.

I wasn't the only one.

I wanted to be sick.

All eyes fell on me, and the first ones I saw were angry and accusing. Sam's arms grew tight around me, ready to protect me from the inevitable storm. "Ana . . ."

Sam followed my gaze to the large man on the other side of the room, slowly standing, his glare locked on me. The man was enormous, with shoulders so wide he made Sam look small. Close-cropped brown hair made him look bald, and a few days' worth of stubble darkened his face. His name was Merton; I'd seen him leading anti-newsoul speeches and complaints to the Council.

Anti-Ana speeches, because there was only me.

Until now.

"This is your fault." He seemed bigger for all the rage building up beneath his words. As though anger were contagious, the room began to boil with it. "Meuric was right. Li was right. This one was only the beginning of replacements. Now Lidea has borne another."

On the bed, Lidea stared at the infant in her arms, like she wasn't sure what to do now. Tears trickled down her sweat-streaked face.

"Nosouls will replace everyone," someone in the back shouted. Panic pitched his voice high, and then it was lost under the wave of suspicion-filled mutters.

"We're being invaded!" Merton shouted.

A small cry of agreement went up, hesitant at first, gaining voices swiftly.

"When sylph infest the city," Merton roared, "what do we do? Capture them and send them beyond Range."

People nodded emphatically. A few cheered.

"When centaurs hunt in our forests," Merton went on, "we drive them out with gas that erodes the bonds holding together their two aspects."

My stomach dropped, but Merton held everyone's rapt attention. He looked just as eager to say what they were all waiting to hear.

"Now we need to learn to defend ourselves against this new threat."

He thought of us as monsters. This baby who'd barely drawn breath, and me. Several people thundered agreement. With Merton as the conductor, the shouts and rage crescendoed.

The baby wailed, and Lidea held him close, but she wept too. My friends yelled in my defense, and the birthing assistants ordered people to leave the room. No one obeyed. People kept shouting and pointing, pressing closer to me as the scowls and glares deepened. They practically burned.

Their heat filled me, leaving no room for disbelief or shock. How could I be shocked when some of these people had treated me with nothing but hatred?

But as the shouting grew and the baby screamed, my own anger replaced my fear. Like a geyser, pressure built inside of me, boiling with the heat of the cacophony all around—like the power of the Range caldera. I was ready to erupt.

"Stop!" I wrested myself from Sam's grip and climbed onto a chair. "Enough!"

They all stared—birthing assistants, observers, and Soul Tellers—and I imagined geyser steam wafting through the room, stunning them into silence. Only the baby cried, and then Lidea put him on her breast.

Silence.

Oops. Everyone was looking at me.

On the bed, Lidea cradled the baby to her. Sweat dripped down her temples, and her skin flushed bronze. The room smelled of salt and copper and other things I couldn't identify.

I focused on the geyser feeling, how furious I'd been about everyone scaring the baby, threatening to kill him as if he were some kind of monster.

They would *not* hurt him. I wouldn't let them.

"I was led to believe that you were all rational people who knew how to behave around an infant." My voice shook. So much for being strong like a geyser. "If you want to yell, do it outside. This isn't the place."

No one moved; I wasn't sure this was better than the yelling.

"If not for the baby, please show a little consideration for Lidea. Or don't you care about her anymore?"

That shamed a few people into slinking out of the room. I stayed on my chair as they passed.

"Anyone else?" I mimicked an angry expression Li had always used to force me to confess when I'd been listening to music. It seemed to work, though I felt more like a chipmunk addressing a room full of wolves. "We're here to celebrate a birth. If you can't do that simply because he's a newsoul, you're welcome to leave."

More people left. More than before. A few had the decency

to look ashamed. I didn't bother hiding my disgust for any of them.

Across the room, Merton stood there with his arms crossed, his face crimson and contorted with rage. He stalked toward me.

Everyone watched, and Sam eased toward my chair, but when Merton reached me, he just glowered and walked around me—to the door.

I tried not to let my relief show. If he'd attacked me, there'd have been little my friends could have done. Merton was huge. And strong.

But he was gone for now. I focused on breathing, and trying not to crumple under the stares of birthing assistants, observers, and friends. Most of the hostile people had gone ahead of Merton, so why did my heart speed up *now*? Surely I should have been able to say something coherent in front of people who didn't completely hate me.

"I believe the tradition is to welcome newborns." Welcome them back, anyway. But this one hadn't been here before. He was like me. Newsoul. "I'll go first." I ached for him, this unnamed child facing an existence like mine. At least he wouldn't be the only one.

Sam offered a hand to help me off the chair, and I accepted. The last thing I needed was to fall on my face.

As I approached Lidea's bed, I imagined what the scene must have been like when Li gave birth to me, and the Soul

Tellers announced I wasn't anyone. There'd probably been fewer people in the room. And all of Ciana's friends would have been there.

Ciana, whom I'd replaced.

I doubted anyone had welcomed me to the world.

I stopped by Lidea's bed. Someone had pulled sheets all around her and wiped sweat off her face, though her skin remained flushed with heat and anger and the labor of birth. Black hair hung in tendrils over her shoulders; the baby's hand reached upward at nothing, losing his fingers in the tangles.

Sam stood next to me, and everyone else queued behind him. Except Wend, Lidea's partner; he didn't leave her side.

I searched for the right words, but what did you say to someone who'd had a newsoul? Apologizing seemed wrong, because this wasn't bad, and I'd had nothing to do with it. The only thing that made me sorry was knowing how much everyone already hated him.

"Thank you." Lidea's smile was strained. "For making them stop. For making them leave."

"I couldn't let them continue." What if they'd hurt him? He was tiny, all splotchy red and brown skin, and his face scrunched up with the stress of being born.

She lowered her eyes. "The idea of having a newsoul—it was terrifying. And"—her voice caught with the confession—"humiliating. But holding him now, I'm glad he's here. I love him completely."

My throat tightened from choking back tears. "He's lucky to have you."

"I'm going to do everything in my power to make sure he's happy. I'll keep him safe."

So would I. "I'd like to welcome him. Will you name him?"

"I thought about naming him after you, in honor of your standing up for him." Her eyes were only for the baby. She didn't see the way my mouth fell open. "But that would be confusing, and I don't want to start a trend of all newsouls being Ana."

I hoped not. Li had told me they'd chosen my name because it was part of Ciana's name, symbolizing the life I'd taken from her. The name also meant "alone" and "empty."

"It was a generous thought, but not necessary." And I didn't deserve that kind of honor.

Lidea caressed his round cheeks, small nose. "It did give me another idea." Sweeter anticipation filled the room. "Anid is close."

My heart felt swollen as I reached, glanced at Lidea for permission, and then touched Anid's tiny hand. He didn't seem to notice. "Hi, Anid. Welcome to the world." My voice trembled as I whispered, "I'm really glad you're here."

We were in this together now. Neither of us were alone. Asunder.

He looked toward me with wide, dark blue eyes. He was beautiful, and I wasn't ready to move on, but people waited behind me, so I touched Lidea's hand, then Wend's, and gave Sam a turn. As the line moved, I watched how everyone else was with the baby, trying to memorize the faces of those who'd stayed. Were they friendly, or just polite?

After everyone but the birthing assistants had left, I offered Anid my finger again. His fist closed around it immediately.

"Don't let anyone call you a nosoul again," I whispered to him. "If they do, tell me and I'll take care of it for you."

Lidea looked amused. "Are you corrupting him already?"

"Just a little." I smiled so she'd know I wasn't serious.

"I'm worried," Lidea confessed. "After earlier, all that yelling." She squeezed her eyes shut, and tears shimmered across her lashes. "What if they really try to hurt him?"

Wend appeared by her side, hand on her shoulder. "Nothing will happen to him." When Lidea twisted toward him, he leaned over to hug her.

Sam touched my elbow and murmured, "Ready to go?" I nodded, and we said our good-byes, fetched our belongings, and headed for the exit.

It was raining again when we went outside, and fully dark now. Only the temple glowed, shedding watery light across the market field. Without conversation, we headed back to the southwest quarter of the city where all our homes were located. Sarit and Stef broke off onto their streets, close to ours.

Inside and dried off, I said, "Sam," before realizing I'd spoken.

He paused on his way to the piano, one hand drifting over my hip as he faced me. With his face in shadow, Sam's eyes were even darker, more mysterious, and heavier with the weight of centuries. Millennia.

"Once, you called me a butterfly, because my existence seems so fleeting to everyone else in Heart."

A line formed between his eyes. "Ana—"

"I know you didn't mean it to hurt me, and I know you've apologized a thousand times." I swallowed nerves caught in my throat. "That doesn't make my existence less potentially ephemeral. I could die and never be reincarnated."

"Please don't say that," he whispered.

"You, Stef, Sarit, others—you've made the Year of Hunger bearable. I didn't think I could have friends until you proved me wrong." I reached up for his shoulders, let my hands slide along the backs of his arms. "But the beginning of my life was terrible, and half the people still treat me like I'm responsible for Templedark and every other horrible thing that's ever happened."

He looked downward, like I blamed him for others' actions. "I'm sorry."

"Don't be. None of it's your fault. I just meant to say, I don't want Anid to grow up like I did."

"Lidea and Wend will care for him. So will we."

I nodded. "But it's not enough. You saw what happened in there. People were anxious to welcome back a friend, and then it was *terrible*. Within minutes, people were talking about killing him. If that's any indication of the rest of the city's reaction to his birth, when other newsouls start coming, there won't be anywhere safe. Not in the city. I need to make it safe. Somehow."

"Ana." Sam stepped so close I had to drop my head back to meet his eyes, and the way he said my name—it was same reverence people used in their prayers to Janan. My insides knotted up as he touched my jaw and kissed me. Softly, gently, aching with restraint. "Anything you need from me, just ask. I promise, we'll give these newsouls the chance you never had."

Hearing it in those words made everything so clear. Sam understood me better than I understood myself, and he'd known what I needed all along.

9
LAKE

I'D BEEN RIGHT about the shift in Heart over the next couple of weeks.

Twice, when I went out on my own, someone threw rocks at me. People jeered and called me names. At the market, people refused to sell things to me without one of my friends there. Strange calls came on my SED, just loud breathing. Stef traced them for me and blocked them from calling again. Then Sam started getting calls.

I tried to ignore it. The rock throwing and SED calling were new, but all in all it wasn't much different from when I'd first arrived in Heart. The fear and anger were the same.

Every morning, Sam and I had music lessons and practice. I took Council-required lessons in the afternoon—they'd kick me out of the city if I didn't—and my monthly progress report was coming up. After my long trip to Purple Rose with Sam, I should have been trying to squeeze in more study to make up for time lost, but Lidea called and asked if Sam and I wanted to go to the lake with some friends.

Absolutely.

"What about your paper on the history of geothermal energy?" Sam asked, not quite hiding his smirk as we walked to Lidea's house.

"I'm sure you can see how devastated I am about going to the lake on the last warm day of the year. Spending time with you, with friends— Ugh. I don't know how I'll make it through the afternoon." I grinned and slipped my hand into his.

With Lidea, Wend, Anid, and a handful of other friends in tow, we headed out the Southern Arch, toward Midrange Lake. It was the biggest lake in Range, and mostly used for the city's fish and water supply, but there were a few beaches set aside for enjoyment. Sam and I had gone a couple of times over the summer.

Geyser steam wafted across the barren land between the city wall and the forest, reeking of sulfur. I wrinkled my nose until the wind shifted to blow the stink away from the path.

I held on to Sam's hand, listening while Stef and Orrin inquired about the baby's health, and Whit and Armande discussed the effort to rebuild sections of Heart that had been destroyed during Templedark.

"The Council isn't even trying," Armande complained. "Have you noticed the statues by the Councilhouse? And the relief over the front? Not to mention the stairs."

"Those things are hardly as important as rebuilding the mills and agricultural areas." Whit shook his head. "Lots of private gardens and livestock were destroyed, if not by sylph or dragon acid, then by drone fire and neutralizing chemicals. Even with sharing and appropriating supplies from"—his voice caught—"the darksouls, it's going to be a hard winter."

"Because the Council stored food in buildings that won't stand up to dragon acid."

"Armande," Whit said gently, "even if they'd put everything in the Councilhouse, it could have been destroyed just as easily. Templedark, remember? The walls were useless."

The white stone had repaired itself when Janan awakened, so some people preferred to believe the cracked temple had been only a nightmare.

"Anyway," Whit continued, "you've completely changed the subject. You're upset about the statues and stairs, but don't you think that's a little shallow, considering all the things that *need* to be repaired?"

Armande snorted. "Maybe so, but I'm the one who has to look at them every day."

"You don't *have* to set up your stall. Let people make their own pastries if it's so difficult to look at pockmarked statues."

Armande pressed his palm to his chest. "You're condemning even more people to starvation. Or, at the very least, bad breakfast. Besides, our art is a testament to our society. It's a symbol of our achievements, like your library and Sam's music. It's something to be proud of, and we should take care of it."

I thought about that as we stepped into the shade of fir trees and headed down a smooth path that thumped solidly beneath my boots. We were off the thinnest part of the caldera.

Sam held aside a low-hanging branch for me, then ducked under after.

"Thanks." I glanced back; the branch was as big as my arm. "If you'd left it, we could have had matching bruises on our foreheads."

He laughed. "That's not as romantic as matching hats or belts."

"And that's not romantic at all. Did anyone really do that?"

"Some did. About a thousand years ago." He rolled his eyes, but his grin widened. "I don't think I was ever so happy to see a fashion pass. The hats got worse every year. Taller, bigger feathers, ridiculous shapes. It was terrible."

"Did *you* ever wear matching"—I couldn't believe it was a real thing—"hats or belts?"

He shot a look that said I'd wasted my breath asking. Of course he hadn't. He didn't even like attending the rededication of souls.

My tone slipped toward mocking. "I should have known not to question your sense of fashion."

Sam squeezed my hand, his smile full of mischief. "If you asked, I'd probably find us matching hats."

"You're such a tease."

Another ten minutes and we arrived at the beach, all sand and frothy gray water, veiled by evergreen trees on three sides. Immense snow-blanketed mountains stood on the horizon like walls, shaded blue and gray in this weather. These walls, unlike the one around the city, made me feel safe. Protected.

"The beach looks bigger today," Sam said, as we came off the narrow path, the only access to the beach.

Orrin glanced southward and scowled. "It is. The water line is lower."

"What does that mean?" I asked.

"Nothing, probably." Orrin and Whit exchanged looks, and Orrin shrugged. "We've had a lot of small earthquakes. Nothing you would have felt, and earthquake swarms don't necessarily mean anything. They're just part of living on the caldera."

I knew that. "But would a tiny earthquake change the level of the lake?"

"Maybe." He gazed toward the water, probably wishing Rahel—the soul who'd been responsible for monitoring these things—were still alive. "A crack might have opened in the bottom of the lake. We're on such a thin crust of land here. But I'm sure it's nothing to worry about."

"If you say so." People used the lake for water and fish, so if the level dropped, surely that would have an impact on life in Heart. But I didn't want to get into an argument on such a nice day. When the group stopped in the middle of the beach, I helped Sam spread out a blanket and then squatted by the basket of snacks. Surely Armande had packed honey-glazed buns.

"Don't worry about the caldera," Orrin said, crouching next to me. "Whit and I are taking up some of Rahel's work. If you're interested, you're welcome to join us when you have time."

"Thanks. I might."

He smiled and peered into the basket. "Have you seen muffins?"

Soon everyone was chatting, laughing, listening to waves brush sand. A few cranes and herons braved the day, but most waterfowl had already migrated south. The baby cried, but Lidea held him close, wrapped up in soft wool blankets, threaded with cinnamon-colored buffalo yarn for extra warmth.

Wend flirted with Lidea, while the others talked about their projects or music they were hoping to play together. After admiring Anid's tiny fingers and nose and ears—all pointed out by Lidea, as if I couldn't figure it out myself—I mostly lay on the blanket for hours, writing in my secret notebook and taking in the afternoon's thin near-winter sunlight and the happy sound of friends' voices.

The voices stopped.

Suddenly conscious of the change, I looked over my shoulder to follow everyone's stares.

By the forest, shadows twisted *toward* sunlight. Five sylph. Ten. They emerged from the forest, silent across the sand.

Dread rushed through me, chased by fear. How had they gotten here? What did they want?

"Do we have sylph eggs?" Stef whispered, reaching for the nearest bag.

"No." I didn't have to look. Why would we have sylph eggs when we were so close to Heart? Midrange Lake should have been safe. There had to be a hundred sylph traps all through the forest between here and Menehem's laboratory.

No sylph eggs. What *did* we have?

"Protect Anid," I said, standing. "When you can get him out of here, do it." The sylph on the edges of Range hadn't done anything more threatening than sing at us, but here, with more people? With *Anid*?

I couldn't take the chance of them hurting him.

"What are you doing?" Armande asked, even as everyone stood and made a protective circle around Lidea and Anid. As if that would stop sylph.

No sylph eggs. My jacket pocket held my knife, the temple key, and my SED.

Unearthly cries shivered across the beach as I drew the SED from my pocket and sent a quick message to Councilor Sine, asking for guards and sylph eggs at the lake. Then I shifted to the music player.

"Get behind me." My voice quivered, and my heart beat too fast, but toward the forest the sylph had stopped, and they were *looking* at me. "When they're distracted, head toward the path. Don't run or they'll chase. They're predators. They can't help but chase." No one knew whether sylph somehow ate what they burned, but they *would* chase.

"Don't be stupid," Stef said. "No one's leaving you."

"Please." I shot her a desperate look. "Please just trust me." Maybe these were the same sylph. Maybe they weren't. I had to try.

"I'm staying with you." Sam touched my shoulder, looking uncertain about my plan but determined to remain at my side.

Grateful for his presence, I set my SED volume on high, and strains of a nocturne floated on the air.

The sylph, which had all been curious before, snapped to alertness. All ten focused on me as I stepped to the right, away from the path. Away from my friends.

The breeze picked at the melody, sweeping it across the beach and toward the sylph. They followed the sound bit by bit, edging closer to me like they were afraid I'd take the music away.

The SED had good speakers for its size—Stef had designed everything, consulting Sam for sound quality—so the music was loud and clear as I lured the sylph away from the group. The line of shadows followed me, entranced by the long chords and arpeggios.

"Go." I tried to keep my voice level, hoping Stef, Lidea, and the others would hear me. "While they're distracted."

Orrin and Armande motioned for Lidea and the baby to go first, toward the path off the beach. Pine boughs rustled, but the sylph didn't turn. They watched me, slipping closer as I bent and placed the SED on the ground. I backed away, and they writhed toward the device, seeming to stare down at it.

Their cries were like wind over canyons: hollow, melancholy, eerie. Heat rolled off them in waves, reeking of ash and death. Any sane creature made of flesh and bone knew to stay away from sylph.

That was my plan as well. Soon my friends would be on the path to the city, and then Sam and I would follow. I'd have to leave the SED to keep the sylph distracted, but surely the Council would replace it. But how would I explain this? Call it an accident? Stef and everyone else had seen me pull out my SED with a purpose.

While my friends escaped, sylph swirled around the device as though dancing. Their moans carried across the graying beach, and then one of their cries hit a high note at the same time as the nocturne. The cacophony snapped, a sensation like walking into a crowded room—and suddenly understanding individual voices and words. One mournful wail became the melody, while another sang countermelody. They all chose parts, like they were members of one of Sam's orchestras.

Near the path, Stef—the last to escape—turned around, her mouth hanging open. I motioned for her to hurry, and she turned back to the path.

The nocturne swirled around the beach, above the swish of waves and alongside the rustling of pine boughs. It was beautiful, all of them singing. Part of me wanted to lose myself in the haunting sound, but I knew better.

The nocturne ended.

Sylph fluttered around the SED, waiting. A tendril of shadow hovered over the small device, but nothing happened.

I glanced over my shoulder. Stef and the others were still visible between trees, and if anyone from the guard station was coming, I couldn't hear them.

Sam and I weren't nearly close enough to the path off the beach. Not that reaching the path would magically make us safe. Sylph could fly between trees and catch us in no time.

I shot Sam a pleading look, silently urging him to stay put while I started toward the sylph and my SED again. He nodded once, watching me with an intense protectiveness. But he'd let me do what I needed to do. He always did. And all I had to do was program the SED to play enough music to give us time to get back to Heart.

Sylph whistled and moaned, watching my approach like I might attack them. My heartbeat thundered in my ears as the sun dipped behind mountain peaks. Golden shafts of light spilled across the beach and the dusk-gray water, and the sylph grew darker. Taller. They hummed at the crunch of my boots on sand.

"Back away," I whispered, and put my hands palm-out as though I could push them. "Back away."

A line of inky shadows shuddered away from the SED, keeping an even distance from me. Sam gasped.

Shivering in spite of the heat billowing off the creatures, I bent and retrieved the SED. "Stay back," I murmured, tapping the SED's face and selecting all of Sam's music. Typically, selling recorded music was part of how he earned enough credit to feed himself, but as his student—and other things—I was able to access all his music. I'd been grateful before. Now his music would save lives.

The opening chords of Sam's Phoenix Symphony flowed from the speakers. I put the device back on the sand. The sylph stuttered forward in unison, and stopped when I held up my hands.

A weak, panicked laugh escaped me. I was holding up my *hands*? The same hands a sylph had burned less than a year ago? Sometimes my idiocy astounded even me.

As before, the sylph began to dance, writhing like dark flames. They flowed in and out of one another, moving closer to the SED as I took measured steps away.

Soon, one picked up the melody, sang the notes *just* behind the piano, violins, and flutes. Close. So close.

Sam reached for me when I glanced backward. I moved as quickly as I dared. My heart raced and my hands shook, but I didn't want to give the sylph any more indication of my fear.

I was halfway back to Sam when one of the sylph trilled and turned its eyeless gaze on me. The weight of its attention made me stagger as dusk deepened across the beach.

"What?" My words came as a whisper.

The sylph trilled again, twisting closer to me as it took up its part in the music once more.

It wanted me to sing? I stayed where I was, boots planted in the sand, conscious of Sam behind me. But when the sylph trilled again, I hummed the next few measures of the melody.

As though electricity surged through the sylph, they all shivered straighter, taller, and closer to me. They seemed eager and—welcoming?

That sounded ridiculous, even in my head, but the last thing I wanted to do was anger them. I held up my hands as though pushing, stepped forward, and kept humming.

They breezed backward, eerily intent while they sang.

I could feel Sam's attention on my back, and hear the edges of hushed orders in the forest. A rescue, I hoped, because it was obvious the sylph wouldn't let me go. At least one had recognized my plan to escape. If I tried again, they might attack.

The sylph eased back as I moved forward. Music played between us, warm and joyful, with a flute duet and bass thudding like a heartbeat. We all—the sylph and me—stepped on the beats.

"What in the name of Janan?" A boy's voice carried across the twilight beach, stunning the sylph, stunning me.

Someone swore. "What is she doing?"

"She controls the sylph."

I spun around, too shocked to respond, and suddenly the sylph fanned around me like an escort or army or dark wings, all heat and ashy reek. They keened, voices so high my ears ached, and two of them shot forward to attack the intruders.

"Stop!"

At my cry, the sylph halted and their wailing silenced. Breath rasped across the gloom, the only sound in a pause between movements of the Phoenix Symphony.

"How did she do that?" The growling voice was familiar. Merton? That guy was everywhere.

"Janan has indeed forsaken us," someone else muttered. "Nosouls will be our ruin."

"Shut *up*," I hissed. "I don't control sylph any more than

you control the weather or your own reincarnation. They like music. That's all." Was it?

Councilor Deborl stepped forward, holding a brass egg the size of two fists. "We'll take care of them now, Ana." Physically, he was younger than me, but he held himself with all the importance of his rank. Even his tone was a reminder of his true age.

Darkness shuddered on either side of me: sylph. Heat bloomed against my bare face and hands; I could even feel it through my coat. But the sylph never moved too close—close enough to boil me alive, anyway. Any sylph was always too close.

And yet, they'd responded to music. Now, with the second movement beginning on the SED behind us, one sylph hummed quietly along with the bass line.

I glanced at Sam; the way he stared at the sylph told me he heard it, too.

"Do the eggs hurt the sylph?" I bit my lip, regretting the question immediately. Now Deborl and the guards would think I sympathized with sylph.

"Does it matter?" Deborl moved forward, and a dozen others followed. They all carried eggs. "Sylph will burn you alive. They almost did before, remember? And they were just about to attack Lidea and the other newsoul. I thought you cared about them."

"I do!" Too shrill, too desperate, but the sylph waited

beside me as Deborl, Merton, and the others approached. "I do care, but look, they're not hurting anyone. What if they just left on their own?"

Sam shook his head, a warning.

"Ana," Deborl said as he neared the first pair of quivering shadows. The sylph didn't move. Why didn't they flee? They would be trapped. "Ana, clearly the sylph listen to you. You're a special soul."

Hah.

But I couldn't forget that night at Purple Rose Cottage, or the way they'd stood guard outside Menehem's lab. Why were they following me everywhere?

He continued. "Word of this will spread. If you use your gift to help us, perhaps the popular view of newsouls will change."

Oh. He wanted me to tell the sylph to get inside the eggs, though why would they do that just because I said? Anyway, they weren't supposed to be able to understand words.

They weren't supposed to be able to come inside Range, either. These had been very clever, and very determined to get here. Why? To sing at me again? To attack Anid?

They *hadn't* attacked him, though. They'd moved toward him, yes, but a group of adults posed no barrier if the sylph had wanted to kill him. They could have killed all of us.

But they hadn't.

They'd chosen not to kill Menehem during his experiments.

"Ana?" Sam moved closer, though sylph stood between us and he looked torn. Risk the sylph to stand by me, or stay put.

Near the first two sylph, Deborl and Merton twisted the eggs to activate them, and within seconds both shadows would be sucked in—

"Run!" I shouted. "Fly away. Go!"

Obsidian-black shadows shrieked and surged into the woods, moving *around* people and the eggs meant to trap them.

People yelled, Sam rushed to my side, and soon Deborl and his guards surrounded me. Blue targeting lights flashed against my coat: the guards aimed lasers at my chest.

"What are you doing?" Sam stepped in front of me, reaching behind himself to touch me, make sure I wasn't dead. "You can't *shoot* her."

Deborl motioned, and everyone lowered their weapons. Targeting lights flickered off. "No one is shooting anyone."

Yet.

"Ana," the Councilor said, "why did you tell the sylph to flee?" There was no fear in his voice, only calculating curiosity.

I stepped out from behind Sam. I didn't need a human shield. What would I have done if he'd gotten shot? "It was the right thing to do." My voice shook. I swallowed and tried again. "They hadn't hurt anyone, and they were listening to me. I don't know why."

"So you took their side?" Deborl cocked his head.

"I didn't take their side. I accomplished the same thing you were trying to do, but without trapping them inside eggs, and without anyone accidentally getting burned. They'll go away now." I hoped.

"Hmm. Perhaps." Deborl reminded me of Meuric, the Council's former Speaker, and the boy I'd killed inside the temple. They were both short and skinny, physically younger than me, and devoted to Janan—though Deborl's devotion seemed to depend on the season, the phase of the moon, and whoever happened to be standing within earshot.

I hadn't trusted Meuric; I didn't trust Deborl, either.

I stood as tall as I could make myself, trying not to shiver in the evening breeze, and with the adrenaline fading from my system. "We're going to leave now." My voice trembled.

"Very well." Deborl twisted his sylph egg to deactivate it, then pressed the cold object into my hands. "Try not to get into trouble between here and the Southern Arch. And"—his gaze flickered to Sam—"I expect to see both of you in the Council chamber in the morning. Tenth hour."

"But we have—" Music practice, but Sam touched my hand and shook his head. "Fine." I turned away to reclaim my SED, still determinedly playing the second movement of the Phoenix Symphony. Sand swished as Deborl, Merton, and the guards headed up the path.

"Are you all right?" Sam touched my shoulder, my cheek. "I can't believe they threatened to shoot you."

He wanted to know if I was all right because of Deborl and the guards. Not because of the sylph. The sylph, as crazy as it seemed, had been ready to protect me. From people.

Oh, how our lives had changed. "I'm all right." I hugged Sam close, my cheek pressed against his chest so I could hear his racing heartbeat. "We're both all right." Because they'd pointed lasers at him, too.

Then, in silence, we packed what was left of our afternoon with friends and trudged toward Heart.

The huge outer wall blocked the sky as we drew near. Solar panels and antennae glimmered like needles in the moonlight. From the center of the city, the temple rose into the clouds, a shining beacon.

I kept my eyes on the Southern Arch, nearly big enough for a dragon to fly through, but the temple seemed to watch my approach no matter how I avoided looking at it.

Janan's presence hung over the city as thick as ash. I imagined I could feel the heat of molten rock and boiling mud churning just beneath my feet. If Janan cared about his people at all, why had he built Heart over the most powerful volcano on the planet? Surely not even the temple would survive if Range erupted.

"What will we tell the Council?" Sam pressed his palm to the soul-scanner, and the gate swung open.

"I'm not sure." I bit my lip, confused and frustrated and ready to collapse into bed. "They'll think I like sylph now. Or that I'm like Menehem."

One thing was for sure: I'd just made life for newsouls a lot worse.

10
QUESTIONS

IN THE MORNING, Sam and I headed to the Councilhouse, a firm plan in mind: deny. They would get nothing about the research Menehem had left to me, and even less about the lab east of Range.

I fidgeted with my notebook as we headed up South Avenue, wondering if I'd done a good enough job hiding the folders and diaries Menehem had left, and the books I'd stolen from the temple. I still hadn't figured out how to read the temple books, though not for lack of trying.

"Let's walk around the right side," Sam said as we approached the market field.

I craned my neck to see why we were heading for a different doorway into the Councilhouse, but all I could see ahead were people walking, talking, sipping from cups of Armande's coffee. "What's going on?" I was too short to see over the crowd.

"Nothing," Sam said too quickly, and winced when I eyed him askance. "One of Merton's public rants. He's on the steps getting people worked up."

"Ugh." Fortunately, there were more doors into the Councilhouse. After what happened yesterday, I really didn't want to go anywhere near Merton.

"Just last night, the newsoul set sylph free by Midrange Lake," Merton cried. "She controlled them. They did as she said. I was there. Janan forbid, but what if all newsouls have this power?"

Shouts rose up, sounding afraid, defiant, angry.

Merton roared louder. "Newsouls will rip Heart asunder! We've spent five thousand years perfecting our lifestyle and honing our talents, and now *this*."

I sighed and stared at the cobblestones. "I'm sorry, Sam."

"Why?" He walked between Merton and me, guiding me through a thin spot in the crowd.

A few people sneered at me. One shouted, "Sylph-lover!" but most just frowned and turned away. Maybe they didn't completely believe what Merton was saying. It *did* seem too fantastic.

"For dragging you even deeper into this mess." I ducked through the door when Sam hauled it open for me. "After our trip"—I didn't specify where, in case anyone overheard us—"and what we learned there, you must be pretty nervous."

Darkness flashed in his eyes, something he wasn't telling me, but it vanished quickly. "I want you to feel safe. I'd never regret your feeling safe." He followed me inside. "If I can't give you that, I at least want you to have answers. I'll help you find them however I can."

"I know people have started calling your SED to yell, now that Stef blocked them on mine." I hated that they were trying to make him miserable, too.

He shrugged. "It's okay. I can deal with them."

Why? Why would he endure all this for me? Was this what it meant to be loved? If you loved someone, could love make you strong like that?

I hoped I could become that strong.

Sam rested his palm on the small of my back as we walked through the ornate halls of the Councilhouse. Paintings lined the walls, most depicting faraway places with cliffs or endless stretches of sand. Closer to the library, there was a painting of tropical fish in a coral reef; that was one of my favorites, though I'd never been to such a place. One day, I would. I hoped.

When we reached the Council chamber, we were told to wait. I filled the time by writing in my notebook. Sam spent the time frowning at a wall. "The piano needs a little work, don't you think?"

I glanced up. "Maybe?"

"It sounds off. I'm going to look at it when we get home."

The piano sounded spectacular to me, but I didn't have his ear, so I just smiled and leaned on his shoulder.

When we were called, I followed him into the Council chamber and dropped my notebook onto the table, which ran the length of the room. It was an ancient piece made from a dozen species of wood, inlaid with beautiful swirls of metal. Once a month, the Council called me in for a progress report; while they droned on about the importance of mathematics, which I already knew, I had ample time to search for patterns across the smooth face.

Ten Councilors sat across from Sam and me, some familiar faces, some new since Templedark. Four Councilors had been confirmed dead that night, and the fifth, Meuric . . . they'd never find him. The replacements were mostly young, one barely past his first quindec, the age when people were allowed to start working again.

"Hello, Dossam. Hello, Ana." Councilor Sine brushed aside a wisp of gray hair that had escaped her bun. "This session is closed for now, but later the recording will be archived and available, all right?"

It wasn't really a question, so I didn't respond.

She went on. "The Council has been informed of yesterday's incident. Please, tell us about it."

"Okay." My heartbeat fumbled as I sat and tried not to pay

attention to everyone looking at me. "A bunch of us went to the beach yesterday. Sylph came. I brought out my SED to message you."

"I remember," said Sine. "Go on."

"Then I turned on the music."

"Why?" asked Deborl.

I was a terrible liar. "Um." A really terrible liar. "I think Menehem mentioned something to me during Templedark. He said music calmed sylph."

"And you never told us that before?" Councilor Frase lifted an eyebrow. "That would have been very useful information to have."

"I forgot. I only remembered at the lake." How much deeper could I dig this lie? It made me feel dirty, even though they'd throw me out of Heart if they knew the truth.

"Then the sylph followed your orders," Councilor Antha said. "Yesterday, at the lake. Reports say you shouted at them to flee, and they did."

"Do you have any idea why they did that?" Sine laced her fingers, not at all the friendly Councilor she'd been when we first met. Now she was the Speaker, always looking to see where people had cracks in their armor, and whether they might be lying. Her attention made me want to shatter.

"I—" The lines I'd prepared seemed like someone else's words now. Everyone would know I was lying, and I couldn't look to Sam for help, because these questions weren't for him.

"I don't think sylph are stupid," I blurted.

"Oh?" Sine waited.

"Well, people saw it yesterday: sylph sang along with music. They knew enough to recognize it as music and sing along with it without ever—I assume—having heard it before."

"That's fascinating," Councilor Finn said, and his tone turned mocking. "But did you tell them to run away by singing it?"

I cringed. "No. What I'm saying is that if they're smart enough to recognize music, maybe they recognize the similarities between humans. They fled Menehem during Templedark. Isn't it possible they realized I look like him? Or perhaps they saw me with him that night and remembered?"

The Councilors exchanged glances, frowns.

"We don't know what Menehem did to the sylph." My lie grew a little more confident. "And we won't until he's reborn."

They muttered at one another, and Sam gave me an encouraging look. This was his part. "Tell them the other thing you remembered about Templedark," he said.

I bit my lip—real nervousness, not feigned—and the room quieted again. "I forgot about this too. I'm sorry, the night was just so—"

"It's all right." Sine almost looked like her old self again, like she cared about me. "People do tend to forget traumatic things. It's your mind's way of protecting itself."

It seemed unlikely I could feel worse about all these lies, but if I didn't tell them *something*, they'd keep pressing me. As long as I didn't tell them *how* I knew things, I could give them some peace, and a reason to stop being so suspicious of me.

"The other thing Menehem told me was that whatever he did to Janan, it wouldn't work again. No one would be able to make another Templedark."

Several people exhaled and sat back in their chairs. No more newsouls. No more oldsouls would be lost. I hated not knowing how I felt about that, like I should be relieved too, but pieces of me felt disappointed and guilty. Why did I get to live? Why not all the others, too?

Would there only be seventy-three of us, and then we'd die, forgotten after our generation?

"So that's your theory?" Deborl asked. "Menehem experimented on the sylph for eighteen years and they decided you were in on it too. That's why they listened to you out there?"

It sounded stupid when he said it. And it *was* stupid. But it was better than claiming I had no clue—or admitting I'd been to Menehem's lab and knew all about his research.

"Let it go, Deborl." Sine didn't look at him. Wrinkles spiderwebbed across her face. They were deeper than when I'd first met her. Visible stress of being the Speaker. "Ana's brought us valuable information, and whether or not she should have told the sylph to go into the eggs doesn't matter anymore. They might not have done it, anyway."

"The problem," Deborl said, "is that Ana made a choice. She chose *them*."

Sine eyed me, disappointment flashing through her expression. "That is true."

"Can you blame her?" Sam asked. "If she did choose sylph, can you blame her at all, considering how people have treated her? Deborl, surely you recall that your friend Merton suggested newsouls should be killed like centaurs."

Deborl and the other Councilors had the decency to look ashamed.

"Let's not forget that ever since Anid's birth, people have been throwing rocks at Ana, and the Council's response has been to tell her not to fight back. Not to defend herself." Sam stood hunched over the table, leaning on his fists. "Even if you don't think she's worthy of being treated like a human, what happened to the law *you* passed about not letting people attempt to kill her? It's very poor leaders who won't enforce their own laws."

Frase and Deborl lurched to their feet. "I think that's enough," said the latter. "Dossam, we understand you're frustrated—"

"*Frustrated?*" Sam pulled himself straight. "We went to Purple Rose just to get away from people looking at Ana like Templedark was her fault. Lidea won't even take Anid through the city without several friends along. She doesn't trust people not to try to kill him."

"We can't control everyone's actions—" started Finn.

Sam raised his voice. "You say Ana made a choice. So has the Council. I'd have chosen the sylph, too."

"All right." Sine rose, balancing herself with long, wrinkled fingers on the table. "That *is* enough."

I edged closer to Sam, humiliated he'd had to stand up for me, but grateful he was brave enough to do it.

"The Council has been busy with city repairs and seismic studies. I'm afraid that we've been unable to focus on as many things as we'd like." Sine glanced at everyone in turn. "However, we should make this issue higher priority. The arrival of more newsouls is no longer a possibility; it is a promise."

Sam, still with an edge, said, "So you'll discuss it now? Ana and I can wait while you all decide to uphold the laws you put in place. It shouldn't take long."

"No, not right now." She slumped into her chair. "Now, Ana, I'm sorry, but I must ask you to leave the room." Exhaustion filled Sine's voice. "We need to discuss some things that wouldn't be appropriate for you."

Because it was so much worse than what I'd already been through? I scowled. "I can handle it."

She sighed and glanced at Deborl and the other Councilors. "It's not that we don't think you can. It's— Do you remember the law that was passed a few years ago?"

Ugh. The law that didn't allow anyone to be a citizen unless they'd owned a home in Heart for a hundred years. They wouldn't even have let me into the city if it hadn't been for Sam offering to become my guardian and ensure that I was properly educated. Sam and I had done everything the Council asked, including lessons with every type of work someone would teach me, monthly progress reports, and a curfew.

"The next part of our meeting is for citizens only," Finn said.

Sam's knuckles were white as he gripped the edge of the table. "So you care about *this* law, but not—"

I touched his elbow. "It's not worth it." If we provoked them too much, they might threaten to revoke his guardianship.

Anger-clouded eyes met mine, and he'd drawn his mouth into a thin line. I pressed my hand against his elbow until his expression grew easier. "As you wish."

"I'll meet you outside." I gathered my coat from the back of my chair and my notebook from the table, and left without acknowledging anyone else.

11

BLUE

WHEN I CAME out the side door, the market field was still busy with people walking around, chatting, and listening to music on their SEDs, but not as crowded as before. Merton's group was gone, though the effects of his speech lingered. People eyed me with distaste, and some had gathered into small circles of gossip.

I slumped on a bench and fumbled for my mitts.

"Hey, Ana." Armande sat next to me and offered a paper cup of coffee.

"Thanks." I balanced it on my knee and watched a group of children chase one another through the market field. They weren't really children, though. They were five-thousand-year-old children, burning off the excess energy of their age. Would I know what that felt like, being a kid again but remembering everything I did now? I wanted the chance—ached for it—and acceptance.

"Don't worry, Ana." Armande gave me an awkward sideways hug, somehow knowing what I was thinking about. If I was that easy to read, surely my lies in the Council chamber had been, too.

"Did Lidea and Anid get home safely yesterday?" I asked.

He nodded. "Thanks to you. Wend is with her, of course, and Stef waited a few hours to make sure everything was all right. I think she's rather taken with Anid." Armande grinned. He was Sam's father in this life, so the physical similarities between them were striking: dark hair they both wore perfectly shaggy, wide-set eyes, and strong builds. But that was where their likeness ended. Sam was quiet and graceful; Armande was outgoing and . . . less graceful.

I liked trying to figure out which traits were inherited each generation, and which traits had become habits.

"How'd it go in there?" He jerked his chin toward the Councilhouse.

I sipped my coffee, letting the heat flood through me. "The Council is angry with me."

"The Council is always angry."

"Deborl thinks I can control sylph."

Armande snorted. "That's like saying you control dragons. Ridiculous."

I tried to smile, but I couldn't forget the way the sylph had responded to my voice, to physical gestures, and my words when I shouted for them to flee. Maybe they'd have fled simply because I was shouting.

"It's curious how there were so many, though. Aside from Templedark, we haven't had an attack that size in centuries."

It hadn't even been an attack. Maybe. No one had been hurt—besides my reputation—so did it still count? In hindsight, it seemed like the sylph had just wanted to look at us.

We sat in silence while I waited on Sam, and Armande . . . made sure no one threw rocks. His stall was close enough to keep an eye on it while he kept an eye on me, too. I hated that, but I really didn't want the girl across the way to yell at me, or the guy on the Councilhouse steps to call me names, so I said nothing.

"I'm worried about Anid." I placed my coffee on the bench beside me. "About how he and other newsouls will grow up. The Council isn't going to do anything."

I couldn't help but remember my first conversation with Councilors. Sam and I had just reached Heart, and I wasn't allowed into the city. They'd insisted the no-Ana law was because they hadn't been sure the city could support newsouls. Who would feed us and teach us? But there'd only been me.

Now there were two.

Soon there could be more.

"I expect there will be fierce debates from both sides, not

just from those afraid of change. Lots of people like you and are looking forward to meeting more newsouls." Armande patted my shoulder fondly. "If nothing else, the next few months will give you an idea of whom to avoid."

I hated knowing this was something I had to do, not only for myself but for other newsouls. "At least when policies are finally made, we'll know what kind of things to watch out for. Like if they say it's legal to throw rocks at us. I think I still have a bruise from the last one."

Armande didn't laugh.

"Ana!" Cris towered above the crowd, features sharp in the near-winter sunlight as he moved toward us.

I waved.

"I didn't realize you knew Cris," Armande said, voice low and tinged with something I couldn't identify. Memories? The past? Definitely something he didn't want to tell me.

"We met him at Purple Rose Cottage when he was on his way back here." I took another sip of my coffee as Cris approached and sat on the other side of me, placing a rose across my knees. Velvety indigo petals shivered in the breeze, and settled as I brushed my fingers up to the tips. It was the same kind of rose I'd tended in Purple Rose Cottage, though the thorns had been clipped off this one. "Where did you get this?"

He cocked his head, shadowing his expression. "I didn't abandon them all."

Oh, right. Like I'd accused him of doing. "I'm glad to hear that. I didn't realize you'd kept growing them."

"It's not something someone stops doing just because other people don't agree about color."

"Technology didn't agree either," said Armande. "They tested whether the color registered more red—like purple—or blue."

Cris smiled. "What do you think, Ana? Blue or purple?"

I held up my hands, torn between being stunned and pleased someone had asked my opinion. "I'm not getting into this." My chuckle came out high and shaky. "This is clearly an inflammatory topic, and I think it's safer not to have an opinion."

Cris laughed. "Very well. I was more curious whether you'd like to continue gardening. You've been taking lessons from everyone, right? Are you still interested in roses?"

I nodded toward the southwestern residential quarter. "I've been tending the roses at Sam's house. It's not nearly as involved as what you're used to, I'm sure, but I enjoy it."

"That's good to hear." He motioned toward the rose still on my lap. "Were you interested in learning more about the genetics and how to begin projects like these roses? We've actually learned a lot about human genetics by breeding plants to see what traits pass on."

That was something I didn't want to hear about—how carefully the Council and geneticists decided who could and couldn't have children. Maybe I was only sensitive to it because I was new, or maybe they'd become *de*sensitized after living with the awkwardness for millennia.

But since I was interested in the first part—making new kinds of roses and things that required more gardening knowledge—I said, "Sure. I need to check my schedule to see what days are free. Last week I had to learn about automated sewer maintenance. Soon I'll be accompanying Stef and a few others into a mine to rescue a broken drone. I'm supposed to help fix it." I made a face. More than likely, I'd be holding a flashlight.

"Gardening won't be quite as physically exhausting as that."

"You can't trick me. I've fought weeds before." I fondled the rose petals, soft against my fingertips peeking out from my mitts. It was just like the roses from the cottage, even the sweet scent. "We usually go to lessons in the afternoon, unless another time is better for you."

"We? Sam goes too?" He raised an eyebrow.

I frowned. "Is that not okay? The Council makes him report everything." Plus, it was nice having him around in case we ran across someone like Merton—not that I would admit that out loud.

"It's fine." His expression had darkened, though. "I just didn't realize Sam accompanied you. But please call when you're ready to schedule."

"Thanks. I look forward to it." I offered back the indigo rose, but he shook his head.

"That's for you." With a quick smile, he headed off, almost lost in the crowd again, except he was so much taller than everyone. Did he have to duck to get through doorways? How did someone even get that tall? I stared enviously as he vanished behind a crumbling statue of someone riding a horse.

Armande shifted his weight and hmmed. "That was kind of odd."

"I agree. Why would he just give me a rose when people are supposed to pay for them?" Maybe he'd request payment during the lesson, or hint at Sam later since I, of course, had no credit.

A dark figure appeared around the Councilhouse, hair tousled as he scanned the thinning crowd for me.

I placed the rose and my coffee on the bench and met Sam halfway. He hugged me so tightly my feet lifted off the ground, and then he pressed his mouth against my neck.

"Everything okay?" His coat collar muffled my voice.

"Better now that I have you again." But he didn't sound happy, and across the market field, someone made rude comments to their companion. Something about how boring it must be, being with a newsoul. Sam cringed and dug his fingers into my coat. "Don't listen to them. There's nothing boring about you."

Face red, I stood on my toes to kiss his cheek. "Thank you for standing up for me in the Council chamber."

"I don't know if it will make any difference, but it's better than silence." His voice sobered further. "Stay away from Merton if you can."

That guy again. Had he gone into the Council chamber after I left? Perhaps that was why Sine wanted me to leave. Perhaps she yelled at him for the way he'd behaved in the hospital, and the way he kept holding public rants. "I hadn't planned on asking him to be my new best friend."

Sam didn't smile. "I think he's the person who attacked us after the masquerade. With Li." He held me tighter when I winced. "I don't have proof, but I asked Sine if someone would keep watch on him. For now, the best we can do is avoid him."

"I understand." I glanced at the temple, so high it made me dizzy to watch the clouds drift around it. "Can we go home now?" When I was aware of it, the building seemed more solid, taller and wider and hungrier. It seemed like it *hated* me, and if a building could hate, it would be the one Janan inhabited.

Sam kissed my forehead. "Home sounds good." He slipped his hand around mine as we headed over to wish Armande a good day.

"Hi, Sam." Armande stood, and his gaze flickered toward the bench where I'd been sitting.

Sam's followed. "Someone gave you a rose?"

It took me a second to realize that was a question for me, not Armande. "Cris did. I'd accused him of abandoning the ones at Purple Rose Cottage. I guess he wanted to prove he hadn't." I plucked it off the bench. "He offered gardening lessons. I said we'd call him."

"Okay." Sam and Armande exchanged more silent communication—most of which came from Armande—but it was the kind that came from knowing each other forever. I couldn't read it.

When we left Armande with his pastry stall, I tossed my coffee cup in a recycle bin and asked, "What was that look about?"

Sam didn't answer.

Okay. Question for later, then. "What happened in the Council chamber after I left?"

He just shook his head and didn't speak until we turned onto his street, like he'd been putting the words together the entire walk home. "They wanted me to remember the truth about newsouls."

12
SPIRALING

"THE TRUTH ABOUT newsouls?" I couldn't breathe.

"No one's sure how to respond to Templedark," he admitted at last. "At first, the community was in shock. We reacted how we always react to battles: tend to the wounded; rebuild the city. We could do that in our sleep. But eventually, we woke up and realized." Sam's voice broke, and he stopped walking. "So many souls are gone forever. We'll never see them again. No one knows what happens after you die like that."

Almost a year ago, he'd said the scariest thing he could think of was no longer existing. True death.

Living in Heart and witnessing Templedark gave me new appreciation for how frightening that thought was. I still didn't know what would happen to me when I died.

I didn't want to stop existing either.

"People are born in patterns. For me, it's just usually being male and being born in the Year of Songs. Nothing special. But others have the same mother or father so often it's eerie. Most keep their close friends through generations."

I knew all that. Sam and Stef had been friends since the beginning—five thousand years—and Whit and Orrin had practically built the library together in the first Year of Binding.

Sam went on. Fire-colored leaves floated to the ground behind him. "Some of those best friends and perpetual parents are gone. I keep thinking, what if Stef had been one of them? Or Sarit or Armande or Sine? They've been my friends for thousands of years."

I couldn't imagine. Didn't *want* to imagine. I just wanted him to stop hurting.

He began walking again, fast, clipped steps like he could outrun the pain. "People want revenge." His words almost didn't carry over the breeze, the rustle of conifers, and the tapping of naked deciduous branches. "But Menehem is gone, at least for now. There's no one to punish."

Waiting for his return had to be unsatisfying. I was the next logical choice.

"The Council wants to search your room for anything Menehem might have left you."

"Why?" I hugged my notebook to my chest as we turned

onto his walkway. A chill breeze tugged at the rose in my fist, and leaves skittered across the cobblestones.

"They're afraid Menehem might have left clues for you, and they're afraid of what would happen if you knew how to put Janan to sleep."

"*Oh.* Even though I just told them it isn't possible?" Maybe they'd seen through my lie after all. The thought made me sick and dizzy. "Anyway, how could they think I'd risk sacrificing my friends? Or you?"

For a moment, I hoped he might joke about being upset that he wasn't my friend, but he just turned his face to the sky and sighed.

"You know I'd never risk you." The wind nearly stole my words away. I stepped closer, heart aching. "You know I'm not like Menehem. I don't want anyone to get hurt. I'd never do what he did. You know that, right?"

"I know." He stared far away, cracks showing in his normally calm demeanor. They'd planted something nasty inside of him, and it was growing, bursting out. "I think they're imagining what it might mean, you not being the only newsoul anymore. Having more has never been a possibility before, but if you knew how to do it—"

"I'd *never* risk you. You know how I feel." Didn't he? Maybe he didn't, if I couldn't say it. "And it seems like everyone else knows how I feel, too." Given how often they gossiped about our relationship.

I shifted my belongings to one hand and touched his shoulder. We stood there in the middle of the walkway, underneath one of the skeletal fruit trees and a sky full of clouds. Chickens and cavies rustled in their pens, softly clucking and wheeking as they waited to be fed.

The world moved around us while I waited for him to look at me. While I waited for him to believe me.

"You know how I feel," I repeated, heart twisting into knots. "But maybe the newsouls being born, like Lidea's baby, won't have the same problems I did." I stopped myself before adding, "Still do," but only just. He knew.

"Are you"—his words came like dread—"happy that newsouls are being born? That you're not the only one?" His face revealed no hints of his true question.

"Yes? No?" I dropped my hands to my sides, notebook and rose still clutched in my fist. "It's not safe for newsouls, and I'm terrified we'll never be accepted. So no, I'm not *happy* they're being born into this life. And I'm not *happy* that darksouls are gone. Friends, families. I did everything I could to avoid losing anyone."

"I remember." The words became white mist, and he didn't look at me.

"Some souls aren't coming back. There's nothing we can do for them now. So in that, I *am* happy newsouls are being born. It's better than no one being born." Gooseflesh prickled over my skin as I stared at the sky, searching for answers in cloud formations. "Ever since Anid was born—since I realized I hadn't just gotten stuck or left behind five thousand years ago—I've been thinking there must be a place full of souls waiting for a turn at life. Waiting and waiting, never having a chance because Janan makes someone else reincarnate instead."

His voice turned low and careful. "And now almost eighty will have a chance. Do you think that's a fair trade?"

"Nothing is fair. Not even souls being reincarnated for a hundred lives while newsouls never get one."

"Well, now they'll live, and Devon won't. Neither will Larkin or Minn. Neither will Enna, my current mother, or four Councilors." His voice shook with barely restrained grief. "They were here five thousand years. They were part of our lives. Julid, one of the greatest inventors, is lost forever. Rahel kept watch on Range, making sure we never overhunted, making sure the caldera wasn't going to erupt. People who were necessary to our lives are gone. Thanks to Menehem's meddling, the entire world has changed. You've tried to understand that, I know, but you can't. Not this life. Maybe not your next, either."

My heartbeat raced in my ears. My notebook and rose dropped, purple-blue petals vibrant against the gray stone, like paint on canvas. Shouts itched to get out, and I almost succumbed. I didn't. He was already hurting enough.

Instead, I turned up my chin, keeping my gaze and voice

steady. "If not for Menehem's meddling, I wouldn't be here."

His mouth dropped and his eyes went wide. "Ana . . ."

I scooped up my belongings, swallowing anger. We were both right, and he knew it. There was no *good* answer. There was no fair answer. "Let's just go in." My voice rasped with tears.

Sam watched me a moment longer, then nodded and went for the door. I trailed after him, and when he sat at the piano—to work on it or practice, I wasn't sure—I headed up the spiral staircase, through the hallway, and to my bedroom. Not even watching Sam play the piano could lift my mood right now.

Like every room upstairs, mine had interior walls made of sheets of silk, and pinned together by delicately carved wooden shelves. So when Sam started playing downstairs, I could hear every note perfectly. He began with scales and warm-ups, playing with such force that his discontentment and confusion cascaded through the house.

Jaw clenched to cage frustration, I gathered up the books I'd stolen from the temple. To keep anyone from noticing them, I'd hidden them separately, in drawers or behind other books. With the Council's promise to search my room, I would need to come up with better spots.

But for now, I sat at my desk and placed one of the books in front of me.

More than ever, I needed to understand Janan, and what

was happening with the newsouls. I hadn't magically been able to decipher the symbols in the books yet, but I'd definitely never be able to read them if I didn't try.

The binding creaked when I opened the first book. Dashes of ink stood dark on pale paper, grainy and thick, as if it had been made hundreds of years ago. I let my thoughts drift as I searched the page for anything familiar, and Sam's practicing seeped into my consciousness like water. His practice sounded better than my playing, even when he stopped to work through a section. His music was beautiful even when he was angry and exasperated, emotions spiraling out of control.

Spiraling.

Spirals.

Snail shells. Rose petals. Hurricane clouds. Faraway galaxies.

The nonsense markings jerked into place.

When I blinked, they were random again. Nevertheless, I'd found the pattern, like when I'd first taught myself to read, or when Sam had played music and I'd been able to follow the dots and bars—but never for more than a few seconds. At first.

I pushed the book aside and opened another and another, making a rainbow of ancient texts across my desk.

I couldn't read anything, and it took practice to see it again, but every page in every book had the same structure: a spiral.

Seeing the spiral was difficult at first. After straining my eyes for an hour, I realized my problem: I'd assumed the lines, for lack of a better term, were all the same size, like bars of music were all the same height.

But like looking into a pit with stairs spiraling down, they appeared smaller toward the center. A two-dimensional representation of something three-dimensional. I'd seen it in my mathematics studies, but it wasn't part of my curriculum, so I hadn't had time to pursue it.

Once I realized that, I could see the spiral as clearly as any other line of text, though the characters themselves still made no sense. Not to mention why they'd go in a spiral, forcing the reader to turn the book around and around.

I copied symbols into a notebook to view them flat, but they still looked like random scratches.

Downstairs, Sam's playing stopped, and he played the same note several times, as though testing it; he'd said earlier he wanted to work on the piano.

I put in my SED earpieces and tapped the screen for a random recording of his music. There was so much, I hadn't managed even a quarter of it in my months here, and I still had my favorites and pieces I had to study for lessons. A random piece would be good for me.

A flute sang, low and breathy, reminding me of earth. I'd listened to Sam's playing enough to recognize his vibrato, and the power that lurked behind the gentle sound. A lute joined in a moment later with a light, delicate voice, and soon both played together in an unfamiliar minor key.

The rhythm unfurled oddly, unpredictable almost, though there *was* a pattern I could almost hear—

Then I lost it.

The peculiar beauty swept me along in the sweetness and warmth, and just as it ended, I glanced at the title on the screen. Blue Rose Serenade.

Shivers marched up my spine.

The second player . . .

I pressed my hands over my mouth as though I could smother the stab of hurt. Why couldn't Sam really be a boy my age, with no more experience than I had? No past lives, past loves.

Why couldn't he be only for me?

I hated feeling jealous. It was petty, and I knew he loved me. He'd *told* me. And still my inability to believe he'd choose me over anyone—it squirmed in my gut and made me sick.

I turned the music down as the next piece came on, letting nocturnes and minuets seep into my thoughts while I focused on the temple books.

"This looks like a crescendo symbol."

I jumped as Sam's forefinger touched the paper. I hadn't heard him come into my room, but there he was, leaning on the corner of my desk.

Blushing, I removed the SED earpieces and shrugged. "Maybe. Or grow, expand, increase, swell. Or none of those things. Chances are just as high it means something else." Still, I wrote "Crescendo?" next to the lines.

"How are you getting these markings?" He didn't sound skeptical that I saw them, just curious.

"Here." I slid one of the books toward him and grabbed a pencil. "Watch." Lightly, so I could erase later, I traced a spiral under the text, starting from the center.

"*Oh.*" Sam glanced at the other books and flipped a few pages, just as I had done. "That's incredible. I don't suppose you've translated everything *but* the crescendo symbol, hmm?"

"No, unfortunately." I leaned back in my chair, stretching cramped muscles. "But I've looked at these things how many times? I'm glad for any progress."

"I've no doubt." He picked up the rose, which I'd left on the edge of my desk. It was tiny in his hands, delicate, and the way he gazed at it was more mysterious than the books. "What else are you looking at here? I see the size changes from the center to the outside."

"It does, and I couldn't tell you if you read it outside to inside, or inside to outside. Or why anyone would write in a spiral, making you have to turn the book around."

"It does seem like a lot of trouble."

"I've tried to write down when I see symbols in patterns,

but it's hard to tell when I'm not even sure of the direction of the text." I spun my notebook to face him. "Does anything else look familiar?" Maybe if more were music symbols, that would offer a place to start. But he shook his head.

"Not yet."

I let my thoughts wander through all the information I'd learned about Heart, its history, and where people had come from. He'd told me about tribes, people discovering Heart already built.

"Once, you told me you'd found bones in the agricultural quarter?" I watched him from the corner of my eye. "They might have been from a civilization before you."

He wore caution like a mask. "That was a long time ago."

I refused to be discouraged. "If people lived in Heart before you, perhaps these were their books."

"Perhaps."

How unhelpful. I tried again. "Do you remember anything? Any writing on rocks or trees? Anything like this?" Knowing who wrote it might give clues to what it said.

"Ana, that was a *long* time ago." His gaze dropped toward the rose bloom, cupped in his hand like a puddle of twilight. "And it wasn't my specialty. I avoided the agricultural quarter whenever I could. The only thing I wanted to do then was carve whistles that sounded like my favorite birds."

"Whose specialty was it? We can look at their early diaries. Or just ask." People expected me to be interested in strange things, and as long as I wasn't rescuing sylph, I doubted any-one would mind.

Of course, after the sylph incident, they probably minded when I breathed.

Sam avoided my eyes. "We'd have to talk to Cris."

"I thought he grew roses." I nodded toward the one Sam held.

"He does. They've always been his love, like music is for me, but his talent was more practical in the earlier genera-tions."

I supposed no one cared which animal hide made a better drum skin if they really wanted to use it as clothes. I man-aged a smile and nod, because I knew how it felt to be useless.

Sam gazed through me, though. He had that familiar somewhen-else expression. "Cris had a way of making things grow, and finding the right spot to plant crops, which can be difficult over the caldera. The ground isn't always thick enough to support anything with roots deeper than grass."

That fit with what I knew of all attempts to dig beneath Heart. The sewer had been especially tricky.

"Cris was the first to find skeletons in the ground. It's possible he saw something else while clearing farmland. An object with one of these symbols on it." Sam came back to himself, back to the present. "Something you could use for reference."

Something *I* could use for reference?

I didn't want to be the one who figured things out. Everyone else was so old and experienced. Why couldn't they do it? Why couldn't I just focus on music and making the city safe for newsouls?

"Ana?" His voice was soft.

Without even realizing, I had hunched over the notebook, buried my face in my arms.

He touched the base of my neck, caressed all the way down my spine. He was solid and warm, and I wished things were the same as before we'd come back to Heart. Life hadn't been perfect then, but I hadn't felt this rift.

Chasm. Fissure. Canyon. Even with his palm on the small of my back, I felt like the entire Range caldera stretched between us.

I pulled away. "Let's call him for a gardening lesson. Tomorrow afternoon, if he can fit us in." I copied several symbols onto a fresh sheet of paper. "I'll ask if he's seen any of these and say"—I bit my lip—"I caught you doodling, but you couldn't remember where you'd seen them before."

"Okay." His features twisted into a mask of uncertainty.

I started closing the books, but paused when I remembered the look between Armande and Sam when he'd discovered the rose. And the awkwardness between Sam and Cris in Purple Rose Cottage. I hadn't thought much about it then, but . . . then there was the Blue Rose Serenade. "Did *you* want to ask?"

He cocked his head and searched me, as though I wore

the correct answer on my face. "I'd rather not," he said after a moment.

Because he thought that was what I wanted to hear?

No. As I studied him, his expression shifted like shadows on darkness. Memory. "What happened? Did he do something to you?"

"No." Sam laid the rose back on the desk, voice deepening. "He's never done anything awful to me, or to anyone else. He's one of the best souls in Heart."

"So what is it?" Maybe I didn't want to know, but the question was out.

Sam strode toward the window, where he did not answer me, just gazed outside like he'd rather be anywhere else.

Tough. Surely I deserved *some* answers. I followed him, but paused when I noticed him leaning his forehead on the exterior wall. Paintings and furniture covered most of it, but here by the window was a clear spot. And he'd touched it. For comfort? Revulsion shuddered through me, and his worn expression made me bite back my questions about his relationship with Cris. For now.

"If Cris can't help me with some of these symbols," I said, "I have to go back into the temple and look for clues. Maybe Janan will answer me."

"No." Sam gripped my arm.

I looked up so sharply my neck stung.

"Ana." His jaw clenched and his voice pulled taut. "Don't

you understand that I *love* you?"

I recoiled. Why would he ask that? "Apparently I'm too stupid to understand."

"You've told me how terrible it was in there and—" He paused, looking frantic while he searched for memories. He had enough difficulty remembering I'd been in there; anything more was almost impossible. "You can't even bear this wall, let alone standing next to the temple. How would you manage *inside*?"

Confusion flashed in his eyes—perhaps the question of how I would get in, because he couldn't remember the key I carried—and his grip tightened painfully around my arm. I wrenched myself away.

He must have realized he'd hurt me, because he held his hands before him in surrender. "Sorry. I'm sorry." He said it as a lament, breathing hard and staring at his hands like he didn't know whose they were. "If you want to go, I can't stop you. I won't try. But I *will* go with you."

"Thank you," I whispered. I had never imagined anyone could feel that strongly about me. "Because I'd rather not go alone."

He lifted one hand, hesitated, and caught my chin to tilt up my face.

Our eyes met, and everything inside of me twisted.

His thumb slid along my jaw while his forefinger held me up. If I spoke, I'd nudge his hand off me. I closed my eyes and let my head drop back as he slid his palms across my cheeks and into my hair.

His mouth was warm and soft. We kissed like a bow and violin strings. I wasn't sure who was which, but we made a melody that lasted only a breath.

He pulled away a fraction. "I didn't mean to start fights."

"I know." I kissed him again, my fingertips grazing the smooth skin of his jaw. His cheeks, his throat, his ears. Barely-there touches that made him shiver and sigh.

"I lived ten lifetimes in that kiss, and it still wasn't enough." He tucked a strand of my hair behind my ear. "I was weak in the Council chamber, after you left. They knew just how to exploit all my insecurities."

"Is that an excuse?"

"No." He retreated to sit on the corner of my bed. "Yes, it is an excuse, but it shouldn't be. I'm sorry, Ana."

Sorry because something terrible happened? Sorry because the Council had pressured and he'd slipped, telling them about Menehem's lab? Something worse? I could imagine a thousand horrible things he might apologize for.

"Why?" I couldn't stop the shaking in my voice.

"For letting their talk get to me and"—he slumped, elbows braced on his knees—"I don't know. I'm angry about Templedark. It hurts thinking about the darksouls." He buried his face in his hands. "When I see Menehem again, I can't say what I'll do."

He wasn't the only one to feel like that, either, but at least he didn't want to punish me for what Menehem had done.

Sam met my eyes, apology in his expression. "But I wouldn't want to undo anything that allowed you to be with us. Lidea feels the same about Anid." He looked so torn. "No matter how horrible Templedark was, it allowed for newsouls and you're right. That's better than no one being born at all."

I flashed a tight smile. He'd been right, too: I couldn't feel the same pain he did. That didn't make my caring any less, though.

"Sometimes good things come from unexpected places. Life out of death. No scars after a sylph burn." I showed him my pale, pencil-smudged hands. "And roses that taught me how to care for things, even though no one else thought the roses' color was good enough."

Sam glanced past me, toward the bloom on the desk. "How did you get so wise, Ana?"

"Someone strong and patient showed me." I sat next to him, looping my arm with his. "Will you say it again? The thing you said that night at Menehem's lab." It probably wasn't fair to ask him to say it when I couldn't say it back, but that didn't stop me from wanting to hear it more.

He must have caught the tension in my voice, because he twisted to face me, expression anxious. "You don't think I'd stop loving you, do you? Or change my mind?"

"No." Maybe a little.

"We might fight or disagree sometimes, but that doesn't change that I love you."

What a *powerful* feeling, love, able to withstand time and distance and disagreements. No wonder I wanted it so badly. "I haven't forgotten what Li told you," he said, "that nosouls can't love." He lifted our hands to his chest, fingers knotted with mine. "I haven't forgotten the way you tried to run away when you accidentally said the word 'love' that day in the cabin."

I couldn't forget it either, when he'd asked what made me happy and I'd answered, *Music.* I'd slipped, used a word I knew I shouldn't.

Love. I'd said I loved Dossam, his music.

I hadn't known Sam was Dossam then.

He kissed my fingers. "You may think you aren't capable of love, but I feel you are. I *know* you are." His breath came warm against my skin. "But don't feel rushed or pressured. I can wait if you need time."

How could he be so confident when I could hardly accept his emotions toward me? "It helps. Knowing someone can"— I gathered my courage—"love me, it helps."

His smile grew relieved. "I'll tell you as many times as you need to hear it, so you'll never doubt." He touched my cheek. "A hundred times? A thousand?"

"Start now and I'll tell you when." Part of me wanted to cry again, not from fear or disbelief, but from joy. As incredible as it was, Sam—Dossam—*loved* me, and he wanted me to understand. To believe.

I was Ana who Had Love.

Sam swept his fingers through my hair, down my arm. "All right." His voice was light and deep and open. "I love you because you're clever. I love you because you're talented." He touched my chin. "I love you because you have a perfect smile. I love you because you bite your lip when you're nervous and I think it's adorable."

I ducked my face. "Go on."

"I love you because you're good and honest. I love you because you're brave." His tone shifted, filled with melody that made me shiver inside. "I love you because you're strong. I love you because you don't let anything get in the way of doing what's right."

He went on, touching my hands and hair as he spoke. His words kindled a fire inside of me. I grew familiar with each sound, each letter. I memorized the softness in his voice, and the way he made "love" sound different and the same every time.

Maybe he was right: I didn't have to decide whether I could love. Not right now. All I had to do was accept and enjoy the idea that someone else could love me.

13
JUNGLE

CRIS SAID HE'D be happy to fit us in, so the next afternoon, Sam and I headed through the city, toward the northeast quarter.

The walk through the market field involved no fewer than three rude gestures, two rocks—one that Sam caught before it hit me—and at least a dozen not-quite-hushed conversations discussing my relationship with Sam or sylph.

I kept my head down while he navigated the crowd, not relaxing until we reached North Avenue. "How does someone make a living gardening?" I asked, because I didn't want to talk about what people were saying about me.

Sam eyed me askance, but let me avoid the subject. "Same as with music. He grows things people want. His passion is roses, but he also works in the agricultural quarter. He's the most knowledgeable person when it comes to growing seasons, which crops to plant where, and when to send the harvesting drones out."

"Sounds like the city would starve without him."

"Probably." A note of pride and respect filled his voice. "But he gives lessons as well, or assists when someone does something seemingly irreparable to their private gardens."

And hadn't Cris said he helped geneticists' research by breeding different plants to see what traits were passed on? "I don't understand how anyone can get so much done and still have time for hobbies and friends."

Sam's grip slackened. "It's best to keep busy. A lot of tasks no one wants to do are automated now, like mining or recycling waste, but other things"—his gaze shifted into the distance—"it's better to do ourselves, even when we could have machinery do it for us. Five thousand years is a long time, and there can be joy in mundane tasks."

"That's why you always write music by hand, even though Stef could create a program to make it easier?"

He nodded. "I enjoy the process, even when I make mistakes and have to go back a hundred measures."

"You haven't had much time for that lately." Aside from the music he'd written for darksouls and the memorial, anyway. He was too busy walking around Range with me, escorting me to lessons, doing all the things the Council required of him if he wanted me to stay in Heart. He'd put so many things aside for me.

Sam shook his head. "I've had a lot of time to do a lot of things, and I'll always find time for what I enjoy. Don't forget, I do enjoy you."

His words warmed me as we continued to Cris's house.

I didn't have to ask to know when we arrived: the entire yard was a garden. Vines climbed over an iron archway wrought into silhouettes of hawks and storks and grouse. Hedges lined the path toward the house, hidden behind immense trees.

From the main walkway, more paths broke off like cracks in glass. One grew into a tiny wooden bridge—posts capped with flowerpots—that went over a stream so small it wouldn't get your ankle wet to step in it. Benches, birdbaths, and huge stone flowerpots with leaves spilling over the sides stood in a tiny clearing. Statues of the Range megafauna lurked in corners or at a fountain, as though lapping water.

Leaves hissed in the wind, and ancient maple trees rattled. Mourning doves cooed, jays and wrens and shrikes sang, and a woodpecker tapped rhythm. The scents of green and water and flowers replaced the fumarole stench, and I drew a long breath, smiling.

"What is it?" Sam touched my elbow.

I looked up at him, a dark figure against the bright sky and foliage. "I can hear music."

"Don't let it go. Keep it in your head until we get home and you can write it down." His voice lowered as he leaned toward me. "I want to find out if it's the same music I hear."

His was probably better than mine, but I smiled. "This way?" I motioned in the direction we'd been going.

To either side of the white stone house, which was covered with climbing roses, a pair of long glass buildings reached just as tall. Their windows were fogged, but it was impossible to ignore the *green* inside, and my heart jumped when I caught sight of familiar indigo roses near the door of one.

I squeezed Sam's hand. "Where do you think he is?"

His tone was easy. Happy, almost. "Somewhere in the garden, I assume."

Really helpful. The entire place was a maze, shades of green plants, gray cobbles and stonework, and the occasional squirrel or chipmunk peering from hidden houses someone had built as nests. That seemed like something Cris would do, sheltering animals others treated like pests.

He emerged from a greenhouse and waved us closer. "I was just cleaning up for your visit," he said as we approached. "Come inside. I think you'll enjoy this."

Though I smiled and thanked him, I felt clumsy trying to watch my step, to make sure I trampled nothing. Sam, of course, glided through easily, and the plants barely seemed affected by his passage. I watched enviously, trying to find the same footing through a patch of tall—I didn't even know what they were without blooms—plants, but my foot slipped on a rock, and I had to grab his shoulder for balance.

"Step this way," Cris said, offering a hand. "I just watered that area, so it's still damp. Sorry."

I nodded, keeping one hand on Sam, and used the other to take Cris's. We made it safely over a cluster of slick stones without incident, then onto a path that led to the greenhouse door.

The air glowed verdant with the many-tiered shelves running the length of the building. It was hot and humid, a weird shift from the coolness outside. No breeze, either.

But the colors were amazing. Shades of green certainly dominated, leaves and stems and buds, but splashes of orange and yellow and pink made dizzying patterns on shadows and glass.

I slipped away from Sam and Cris, letting my bag drop as I tried to slow my frantic heartbeat. There were so many roses, all shapes and colors, and the sweet scent was overwhelming. I felt like I could open my mouth and breathe it all in, capture the perfume in my chest, next to my heart.

He didn't have just white roses, but ivory and cream and old lace; and not just red roses, but ruby and scarlet and burgundy. I leaned to smell individual flowers, fiery petals tickling my nose and chin.

My face must have burned as bright as the roses when I glanced up to find both boys watching me. Sam had picked up my bag and hung back while Cris approached.

"These are Phoenix roses," he said, indicating the ones I'd just been sniffing. "Do you like them?"

I gazed at the perfect red, the spiral of petals, and the spicy scent so thick I could almost taste it. "Very much."

Cris chuckled. "That's not a surprise. They're Sam's favorite, too."

My face grew hotter as I stared at the rose.

"It still surprises me to see roses in colors other than blue," I said, before the awkward silence could fester. "I only saw the ones at Purple Rose Cottage for eighteen years." Because Li had never bothered to teach me colors, it had taken me years to figure out the difference between purple and blue, what with the name of the cottage. I'd thought they were two names for the same color.

"Blue, huh?" Cris raised an eyebrow. "I thought you weren't getting into that debate."

"I've had some time to think about it."

Cris grinned like I was his new favorite person.

For the next hour, we followed him around the greenhouse, Sam with his hands shoved in his pockets, and me with a notebook, scribbling to keep up with his lecture. Later, I'd copy everything again into more readable handwriting.

"The pruning shears are here," Cris said, motioning to a shelf with empty pots and jugs of liquid. "Especially in the greenhouse, you'll want to be careful to disinfect the shears between every plant. Otherwise you can spread a disease."

My pencil stopped over the paper. "Disease? I didn't know plants could—" No, that was wrong. I'd seen trees in the forest with strange fungus growing on them. "Never mind. But in the greenhouse? In the wild makes sense, but everything is safe here, isn't it?"

"Humidity." Like that explained everything. "I want to go over the main ways of reproducing roses and the results you can expect from them. Growing seasons, when to put fertilizer on them, when to prune. That kind of thing."

"It sounds like a lot for one afternoon." Not to mention the symbols I wanted to ask him about, if only I could find an opening.

"We can schedule lessons. Every week or every month." His gaze flickered toward Sam so, for a moment, I wasn't sure who the next words were for. "Whatever works for you."

I answered before Sam had a chance to look around awkwardly. "Every week would be great."

Cris beamed and drew me toward the workbench, explaining the difference between cuttings and budding.

We spent the next three hours in the greenhouse, me filling up pages of my notebook, before Cris declared that was all for the first lesson. We headed outside. Wind snaked between trees and bushes, stealing perspiration off my forehead and the back of my neck.

"So you'll call when you figure out a time to come every

week?" Cris asked as Sam wandered off to look at something growing in a stone basket held by a stone rabbit.

I nodded. "Before we go, I was curious about something. Sam said you were the best person to ask."

Cris glanced at Sam, expression blank, and returned his attention to me. "Okay."

I pulled the folded paper from my pocket. "I caught Sam doodling and asked what they were. He said maybe something he saw a long time ago, but he couldn't remember exactly."

Cris raised his eyebrows. "And he thought I might know?"

I gave a one-shouldered shrug. "They look old, and I heard there were remnants of things before everyone came to Heart. And that you discovered most of those things because you put the agricultural quarter together."

"Hmm." Cris studied the paper, turning it on its side and upside down. "Some of these look familiar, but even if I'd seen them before, I couldn't tell you if they meant anything."

"I was hoping you might remember something like a label." I shifted my weight to one hip. "I know it's unlikely."

"Sorry. It was a *long* time ago"—he sounded just like Sam when he said that—"and we didn't keep records like we do now."

"Oh." I couldn't stop the disappointment in my tone as I reached for the page. It wasn't like I'd thought he'd have all the answers, but even a hint would have been useful.

"If you don't mind, I'll hold on to this. Maybe I'll think of something later and need to double-check." He glanced again at the paper as I nodded. "If you're looking for evidence of a civilization here before us, don't forget there were centaurs and trolls all through Range before we settled. They're not all bright, but they're not without their own means of written communication."

"Like scratchy drawings?"

"Sure. Or any other number of things. But I'm not the one to ask about that. There are books in the library you could start with. If you still have questions, I can give you a few names of people who—"

"Who don't mind newsouls?" I hazarded.

"Yeah." He smiled, looking relieved. "It's awkward to say that without *saying* that."

"You'll have to get used to it. With me, just be blunt. It's not like I don't already know what half the people think. The newsouls coming now will learn soon, too."

"Thank you for the advice." His gaze slipped to the paper again, and his smile faltered.

"What is it?" It was the same dazed look Sam wore when he suddenly remembered something he shouldn't.

"Several lifetimes ago I traveled to the jungles along the equator." His tone drifted, almost singsong. "The air was as thick and hot as a greenhouse, and the plants were incredible. They were immense, and everywhere, taking up every bit of earth. The air buzzed with the noise of bugs and animals calling territory."

I could feel it. Hear it. What an alien cacophony it must have been.

"You couldn't even drink the water. It wasn't safe." He traced one of the symbols on the page, paper fluttering in the fading autumn breeze. "And then it seemed like out of nowhere I came across these piles of enormous stone, so old and weathered some of them were breaking apart, but I could see where they'd once made a wall."

"What kind of wall?" I whispered.

The remembrance began to fade. "I'm not sure. . . ."

"Was it white?"

"What?" He blinked, and the memories vanished. "I'm sorry. I must have been thinking about something else."

"You were telling me about stones you found in the jungle. You said they'd once been a wall. Was it white?"

Cris shook his head. "I . . . don't remember that. Sorry." He slipped the paper into his pocket. "But thank you for coming this afternoon. It was nice seeing you again."

When we finished polite small talk and farewells, Sam and I headed from the garden maze. His voice came low and soft. "Nothing?"

If Cris couldn't remember the conversation about the wall in the jungle, neither would Sam if I told him. And the fact that Cris had difficulty remembering it made me think Janan was involved somehow. Ugh. If only he'd said a little more. Described a heartbeat in the stone, maybe. Except the wall had crumbled, which meant what?

Sam had found a wall in the north, in dragon territory. Cris had found one in the jungle. Neither could recall the encounters clearly.

"Ana?" Sam touched my shoulder, looking worried. "Are you all right?"

"Yeah, sorry." I shook away my thoughts of other cities for another time. "Cris said he'll look at the symbols more."

"Then he will." He said it with utter certainty.

It killed me not knowing what had happened between them. They thought so highly of each other, and yet.

"So what now?" he asked.

I pressed my palm over the pocket where the temple key rested. "What I said I was doing before: going into the temple to look for more clues." I sounded as enthusiastic as I would have at the idea of cutting off my hand with a rusty knife, but I was still glad he'd demanded to go with me.

"Oh, right." He didn't sound upset or disappointed. More as though I'd just reminded him of something. "You can get in."

"Yes. I have a key, remember? It makes doors."

"I remember. It's silver."

I stared at him. He'd never remembered before. Cracks were loosening the magic that kept his memories locked.

It had never been challenged, and if everyone had the same selective amnesia, then it didn't have to be *good* magic. But he'd spent so much time with me, with my questions—

I shivered with hope. Maybe I could break the magic.

14
CREVICE

THROUGH THE WINDOW glass, the sky turned velvet indigo as the sun hovered below the city wall and horizon.

My backpack grew heavy as I filled it with dried fruits and crackers, bottles of water, and painkillers. When I'd met Meuric in the temple before, and he'd tried to trap me, he said I'd never get hungry or thirsty. Maybe that was true, but I didn't want to take chances.

"Got enough stuff?" Sam said as he came into my bedroom and watched me shove a small blanket into the bag. "Sure you don't want to add the piano? I bet you can make it fit."

I made a show of looking back and forth between him and the bag. "I'm not convinced you can carry all that."

He pressed his hand over his heart in mock indignation.

"I could. And I'd carry all your books. Your flute. Your rose, too."

"Oh! My rose!" I grabbed it off my desk and threaded the stem through my braid. "Even if I can't take the piano, I should be able to take something good. Besides you, I mean. I'm glad you're coming." The rose was starting to dry, though. Petals rasped under my fingertips. "How's that?"

"Beautiful." Sam snapped my backpack closed and pressed his mouth into a line.

"What? You don't like my hair like this?" Too bad for him; I did. I'd get a hundred roses and put them in my hair.

"Oh, I do." He put on his coat, then pulled the backpack on over it. "It just startled me for a moment. Cris used to wear roses in her hair, too."

Her hair.

Blue Rose Serenade.

"Ah. Clearly it's the best way to show off flowers." I tugged my coat sleeves over my arms, then checked my pockets for the important things. SED, knife, water bottle, temple key, and notebook. Not that I would have time to write in my notebook in the temple—or I'd have too much time—but I didn't like going out without it.

The awkward moment passed, and Sam kissed my cheek before we headed downstairs and out the door.

My SED chirped with a message from Sarit, and I stifled a laugh as we took to the dark streets of Heart. "Sarit just said to have fun and to make sure you massage my shoulders. I wish we really were just sneaking out for a few days of romance. It sounds like a lot more fun."

"I think so, too." Sam walked close to me, cutting his steps short so I didn't have to run to keep up.

With a sigh, I put the SED back in my pocket and took my flashlight out instead. The moon shone brightly, but it wasn't quite enough for someone who hadn't been walking around Heart for five thousand years.

As we came to the road, I caught sight of the temple rising above the city, and the white glow of shifting patterns. It was almost hypnotic.

"What's it like in there?" Sam asked. I'd warned him several times already, about the everywhere-light and the unsound, but that was knowledge he kept losing. The forgetting magic had cracked, not shattered.

I told him again as we walked to the market field, and his face grew pale and drawn, lined with fear. "You don't have to go." I spoke gently, and he really didn't need to go, but I wanted him to. I didn't want to go by myself. The time I'd been in there had been terrifying. Having Sam with me would make it easier.

"I'm going," he said, and in the temple light, I caught his determination, and that strength he got from loving me. It made him brave.

Answers beckoned from across the market field. I

couldn't help but imagine everyone all across Range looking up one night to see a strange, beautiful light, five thousand years ago. Of course they'd been drawn to the city. Sam had said they'd lived in tribes for a while, fighting over Heart before they realized it could easily house everyone. Maybe they'd been fighting over the light, too, if it brought them comfort.

My stomach turned. I couldn't believe I was going in again. Willingly.

For the newsouls, for answers, I would do anything.

I stashed my flashlight away and took a quick drink of water before heading across the market field. There was no one out this late, so the way was clear as we approached.

There was a crevicelike place where the Councilhouse and temple huddled together; Sam had told me earlier that in a few of the back rooms, there were spots on the walls that glowed at night, though none of them were big enough to use the key to create a door. It would have to be done outside.

"Ready?" I pulled out the key and squeezed into the hidden place. It was just big enough for elbow room—for me. Sam stood a little outside.

"Yeah." He took a deep breath, as though preparing himself, but tensed instead and looked over his shoulder. He swore quietly. "It's Stef."

"Sam!" Stef's voice carried across the market field. "What are you doing?"

Sam swore again. "What will happen if we just go in with her looking? Will she forget?"

"I don't know." I really didn't, but being pinned between these two buildings made me itch. "Go see what she wants."

He nodded. "I'll hurry." Then he trotted toward Stef, who was halfway to the temple, and halfway to spotting me clutching the key and ready to make a door.

I held still while they greeted each other.

"Going somewhere?" Stef motioned to the backpack.

"Ana and I are taking a short trip out of Heart. Didn't you get my message?"

"Yes, but you're here in the middle of Heart. In the middle of the night." She put her hands on her hips.

"So are you."

I swallowed a groan. This wasn't going to end well.

"I," Stef said, "am going home after working on Orrin's data console, since he insists he needs one at his house, too. *I* have been working on it for the last seven hours, because he decided he wants to track seismic activity in Range." Her pause was sharp, daring. "Where's Ana?"

"She's waiting on me. So we can go." Sam shifted his weight and didn't glance back at me, but his shoulders twisted like he wanted to.

"At your house? At a guard station? We can walk together." She hooked her arm with his. "Come on."

"No, it's fine." Sam pulled away, and it seemed unlikely anyone had ever looked more suspicious.

The buildings pulsed around me, making my skin prickle. Being this close to the temple made the faint taste of acid crawl up the back of my throat.

Stef's false cheer faded. Her posture straightened and her voice deepened, showing real hurt. "What's going on, Dossam? You're always off with Ana, caught up in your own private quests no one understands. You left Heart because you said Ana wanted time away, and that's great, Sam. She's cute, and I'm glad you're having a nice time with her. You both deserve happiness.

"But ever since you came back to Heart, you just look more and more stressed. Whatever you did in Purple Rose must not have been very relaxing or fun. We've been friends for thousands of years. You don't have to tell me everything that happened, but don't pretend I don't know you've been hiding something."

I wanted to shrink until I vanished between the cobblestones. She meant Menehem's lab. It weighed on him, what we'd learned, but it seemed like there was something more. Something he hadn't told me, either.

"Stef—"

She cut him off. "Your friends are worried. The Council— well, you know the Council. They're looking for a reason to toss Ana—and the other newsoul—out of Heart."

"They wouldn't." Sam shook his head. "They wouldn't, because we've done everything they've demanded."

"They're waiting for you to make a mistake." Her voice lost some of its bite. "I just wish you'd let me help. How can we be best friends when you don't let me into your life?"

Sam bowed his head. "We *are* best friends. But we've had five thousand years."

"And she's still working on her nineteenth. I know. So you'll spend the next seventy years shutting me out. And if she's reborn, what then? Do I cease to matter?"

"You know that isn't true—"

"What about the rest of your friends? You hardly visit like you used to."

"What are you talking about?" Sam raised his voice. "I see people as often as I always have. More, perhaps. But I've always needed time alone. You know that."

"You're never alone anymore. She's always with you. And when you go out to see people, it's for her. Introductions, lessons. Everything you do is about her." Her anger made the last words fall like punches.

There wasn't much Sam could say to that, and he seemed to know it. He *had* devoted a lot of his time to me. The moments he took to think about his response gave Stef another opening.

"You know what they're saying," she said, "about Ana and

the sylph. About *newsouls* and the sylph."

"It's not true." He didn't sound even slightly convincing.

"I was there, Sam. I saw Ana go right for her SED. I saw her when she immediately knew how to distract the sylph long enough for the others to get away. And I saw what happened with the sylph when Deborl and everyone came with the eggs."

"Surely you don't believe—"

"What am I supposed to believe? You don't talk to me about things anymore. People keep asking me questions, because they think I must know what's going on, but the only things I ever hear are rumors." Her voice cracked. "I miss you. I miss how things used to be."

Sam's shoulders slumped.

This fight would last forever, and I couldn't stay hidden in the crevice any longer. Every moment made me feel worse, and listening to them . . .

I couldn't go out there. Stef had shown all her anguish, and she would be furious if she knew I'd overheard. She'd never *hurt* me, not like Li would have if I'd witnessed that kind of vulnerability, but I didn't want her to be angry with me, nonetheless.

Sam couldn't end this—Stef wouldn't let him—and I couldn't stay trapped here between walls that made me itch. Sam would know where I went.

Silver shone in temple light as I lifted the key and pressed the shapes engraved into the metal and squeezed. A gray door swirled into existence.

With one last look at Sam and Stef arguing in the market field, I stepped into the temple.

15
WEEPER

NO SOUND EXISTED inside the temple, not even ringing in my ears, like silence after a loud noise. Temple silence was thicker than regular silence, like stone was thicker than air.

I clutched the door device to my chest, waiting for my eyes to adjust to the everywhere-light that left no shadows. The glow that emanated from the white walls wasn't actually bright, but the reflections and lack of darkness made my eyes water.

Mysteries surrounded the temple like a cocoon. Everyone knew it was empty, and yet no door existed—not without the key I held. As far as I knew, the only other person who'd been inside the temple was Meuric.

The air pulsed with the temple's heartbeat, making my

skin prickle. Janan was here. "Hello?"

No answer. Just the flattening of my voice in dead air.

Wishing I had the backpack, I tucked the door device into my pocket and tried to decide which way to go. The room was immense, though I didn't think it was the chamber from the last time I'd found myself in the temple. Neither was it the hall with books, or the room with an upside-down pit where I'd killed Meuric.

Carefully, I strode across the chamber toward an archway, nearly invisible in the strange light. My footfalls made no sound, and not because I was trying for stealth. Sound simply did not carry.

Moans rippled through the walls.

I halted and waited, but they didn't return, so I continued along my original path. I couldn't let Janan intimidate me just because he was a powerful, incorporeal being older than everyone in Range. Just because—by all accounts—he held dominion over life and death and reincarnation.

Right. None of that was intimidating.

There were no stairs at the archway like last time. It just opened into another room, and when I crossed the threshold, the archway vanished, cutting me off from the original chamber.

The new room was smaller, with archways scattered across the walls that made gentle ripples like curtains. They did nothing to create shadows, but successfully conjured a headache behind my eyes. I pulled out my flashlight, gave it a few twists, and shone it across the room.

It wasn't perfect, but at least I could tell how far away things were, judging by the size of the beam.

I couldn't trust my perception completely. The last time I'd been here, I'd found stairs that looked as though they went down, but actually went up. Nothing in this place was what it seemed.

The key's weight in my pocket suggested I could make things easier for myself while in the temple, but I had no idea how to do that. Too bad Meuric hadn't left instructions.

Determined to stop wishing for things I didn't have, I slipped through another archway and lurched into a sideways room.

I yelped and dropped my flashlight. It flew left and shattered against the wall—or another floor.

My feet stayed planted on the floor where I walked, but my weight pulled to my left, as though I stood on a wall. The other floor was shiny and lumpy, bubbling around the shards of my flashlight like an unfortunate batch of cheese soup I'd once made. All the cheese had coagulated and the milk scorched; the house had smelled terrible for hours.

In the temple, there were no scents, save for what outsiders brought in.

Awkwardly, I sidled through the nearest archway and staggered as gravity righted itself underneath me. My stomach flipped, and I swallowed repeatedly until I was sure I wouldn't throw up.

The room was small, only the size of my washroom. An empty white box with no archways, not even the one I'd come through. Only the occasional groan and gurgle shivered through the tiny room.

Suddenly, the air grew sharp and crushing. The heartbeat pulsed louder until it rattled in my ears, and my chest ached with the fight to breathe. It seemed all the air was being sucked away.

"Now what, Janan?" I could barely speak.

No answer.

I withdrew the door device and jabbed at random symbols. The silver box swirled in my fading sight until I wasn't sure I was actually pressing buttons, just hitting and jamming my fingers. I felt right side up and upside down, and on both of my sides. All at once. Acid crept into my throat.

My body ached as though I were being ripped apart, and my lungs burned with all the air pushing and sucking and swirling around. Vision grayed, and the only thing I could hear was the incessant weeping and moaning.

Janan's hollow whisper silenced everything. "That is not for you." It came from everywhere and nowhere. A place on the nearest wall rippled as though something moved beneath the stone, or inside it. I tried not to look because it made my vision worse, but it was impossible to ignore.

"Let me go." I gasped at the thinning air. "I'll keep pushing buttons."

Pressure gathered around the lump inside the wall. For a moment, it looked human-shaped, though its proportions were wrong. Limbs too long, waist too narrow, head too wide.

Then the shape scattered in all directions, ripples smoothing into the glowing stone. A black archway shimmered where the shape had been, and noise returned in waves.

Whispering.

Moaning.

Weeping.

The air remained stifling, but I could breathe. My vision returned to normal as I replaced the key in my pocket and staggered toward the opening. Losing the key would surely end with my being trapped forever.

I'd gone through a black archway before. It had been as quick as stepping into another room, like any other archway, though they looked frightening.

This time, I stepped into ink and starless night. The blackness coated my skin like oil and made breath . . . what I imagined it would be like to breathe liquid and not die. It sloshed through my nose and windpipe, and I felt ever nearer to drowning.

Three more steps and I still wasn't through. I stretched out my arms to feel the walls, but there weren't any. The archway either led into an empty black room, or I hadn't made it through before the portal vanished.

That meant I was trapped in the walls. With Janan.

Groans and whines pursued me like sylph. There was no telltale heat or strange singing, only the heartbeat and pressure, and what might have been my hair—or someone's fingernails—brushing my arms.

I ran.

The wailing grew all around, tangible, and Janan whispered right by my ear, "You wanted somewhere to go. Now you have everywhere."

I pushed my legs harder, away from his voice, but the fingernails scraping my skin never ceased. If I stopped, he'd hurt me worse. He didn't have to say it.

When I slowed enough to wrestle out my SED, hoping for some kind of illumination, the onyx air only swallowed the light. If anything, the darkness closed in further, though I couldn't fathom how complete blackness could become even more perfect.

Hours passed. Or longer. It was impossible to measure time, if time even mattered in here, but my hips and legs ached and I had the vague sensation that I should be hungry or thirsty.

And then I was, because I knew I should be. I slowed to grip my stomach. I was *starving*, though Meuric had said before that I wouldn't need to eat or drink in here.

"I am hungry, too," Janan murmured, "and I am sure you are delicious."

My hiccups fell flat on the liquid air. I wished Sam were here. I wished we didn't know about Janan. I wished we were sitting at the piano playing a duet, our legs pressed together because neither of us were thinking about music, not really. I wished it all so hard that for a moment I thought I was there, but then a scream cut through the blackness, and I remembered the temple and running and Janan.

"No tears." Not Janan. Not a real voice, either, but a thought that wasn't mine. "The Devourer is incorporeal. He has never been able to touch the other one."

My feet caught on themselves and I stumbled, dropped, and hit the floor. Stabbing pains raced up my palms and knees as I searched the darkness for the non-voice. If it wasn't me and it wasn't Janan, perhaps it was one of the weepers.

I struggled to catch my breath, then fumbled through my coat for the bottle of water and drank half of it. The sensation of claws on skin never faded, but the non-voice was right. The feeling was just in my mind, and stopped when I rubbed my palms over my face and neck and hands.

Janan's words, and the weeper's—they meant something, but my head was too fuzzy to let me think clearly. The darkness remained overpowering.

Maybe I was blind. No matter how I forced my eyes open

wider, I never caught light. I tried my SED again. A white glow pierced the dark, but illuminated only blackness when I held the screen to the floor. And blackness all around.

Trembling, I tried to send a message to Sam, but the SED beeped in error. I put it away and pushed myself to my feet. I couldn't let the screaming get to me, or the crying, or the fingernails raking across my skin. They weren't real.

They weren't.

Determined not to let Janan stop me, I stepped forward, and the whole world changed.

16
TRUTH

I crumpled to the floor, clutching my face and stinging eyes as pressure drained and the weeping no longer followed. Now just the hiss and scrape of cloth, ragged breathing that wasn't mine, and a reek like copper and ammonia so strong it made my head spin.

I wasn't alone.

"What are you doing here?"

The voice was broken, garbled and raspy at the same time, and came from across what appeared to be the bottom of a large hole, though a stairway spiraled up.

I wiped tears from my eyes and focused on the dark lump of bones and rags. Blood stained his face and hands, and a rotted wound hunched like a spider where I'd stabbed his eye out. But the other seemed to work, and it watched me.

"Meuric."

"Nosoul."

He couldn't be alive. It wasn't possible. I'd shoved him under the upside-down pit. The fall must have shattered every bone in his body. It had been months. And still.

I felt only a little better knowing I hadn't actually killed him. And then I felt much worse, imagining the pain he must have been in all this time, trapped at the bottom of a pit with stairs offering a way out—except his bones were splintered and he couldn't move from this spot.

Blood and other fluids seeped around his filthy clothes, but the rest of the floor was clean. No, he definitely hadn't moved.

"You tried to kill me," he gasped.

"After you tried to trap me in here so you could tell everyone I was dead."

Dried blood cracked and flaked when he smiled. Black rot filled the creases between his teeth. "And now I'm trapped. Does that make you feel better?"

"No." His stench made my head spin. I squatted on the floor and leaned against the wall for balance. It didn't help the dizziness, but my back and hips creaked with relief.

The pit was ten paces across. A fair size. When I looked up, the opening was invisible with the everywhere-light. It must have been deep enough to shatter all his bones, and shallow enough so he wouldn't die. How cruel of Janan to arrange that.

"Why aren't you dead?"

He laughed, like bubbles rising from the mud pits around Heart. Then wheezing and coughing, then groaning and silence.

I almost wanted to help him, but couldn't bring myself to go near him while he remained slumped, breath whistling as though there were holes in his lungs or throat. I couldn't get over the creeping feeling that, if I did go over, his body would miraculously mend and he'd grab me.

That thought coiling in my gut, I pressed my spine to the wall and sat properly, waiting for him to regain the strength to speak. How long had it been for him? As long as it had been on the outside?

"Janan won't let me die." His good eye was trained on me. "Do you have the key?"

I pressed my hands to my knees. I didn't want to slip and reveal the key's location.

"I need it," he whispered, managing to lift one arm toward me. "I need it to live after Soul Night. You have to give it back."

"What happens on Soul Night?" I'd come here for answers, after all, though I hadn't expected Meuric to provide them.

He wheezed laughter. "You won't stop it."

I stood, trying to make myself formidable. "What happens?"

"Give me the key." His glare followed me as I marched toward him. "Give, and I'll tell you."

Not a chance. He'd said he needed it to live after Soul Night, so what happened to everyone without a key?

I hovered just out of arm's reach, ready to run for the stairs if he so much as shifted his weight. "You've been down here for months," I muttered. "You must be very hungry. And thirsty. When was the last time you had anything to drink?"

His eye widened, and he groaned.

I felt sick taunting him like this, but I knelt so I was level with him. "Tell me what you know, and I'll give you the rest of my water."

His thirst must be horrible, even if he hadn't been thinking about it before. Janan couldn't fix everything . . . as evidenced by Meuric's broken body.

"So thirsty." The eye closed. The other remained a rotted hole, impossible not to look at; its reek rode the steady heartbeat of the temple. There were no screams currently, just muffled whimpering, as though they were waiting to find out what I'd do.

I checked to make sure the stairs were still an option. "If you tell me what's going to happen, I'll give you water."

"Soul Night."

The spring equinox of the Year of Souls. "Yes, I know that's when it happens."

He nodded. It was frightening how ancient he looked now, though this body was only fifteen years old. Months of dehydration and starvation, incredible physical damage . . . If he'd succeeded in trapping me in here before Templedark, this could have been me.

"I didn't think it would work." His once-high voice sounded like gravel now. "His plan seemed too fantastic, but if anyone could succeed, it would be Janan, so I convinced everyone to let him try. And then he did it. He really did it."

"What did he do?" I wanted to shake him and force him to speak clearly. Instead, I stayed on one knee, ready to bolt.

"He made himself greater. He made people like phoenixes." Meuric held out his hand again. "Water."

"That's not an answer." Phoenixes were another dominant species, like centaurs or trolls, but they appeared to reincarnate as people did.

They were rare—reports said there were perhaps a dozen in the entire world—but once someone had observed a phoenix in the jungles on a southern continent. It built a nest of dry brush, then settled down as though to lay an egg. Instead, it exploded into a rain of sparks and died.

The explorer had stayed at the pyre for hours, trying to figure out why the creature had done that. And then sunlight broke through the jungle canopy and shone on the ashes, dazzling him. When his vision cleared, a tiny phoenix chirped. It looked at him with the same ancient expression the other had worn, and then it flew off, trailing sparks and ash.

"It *is* an answer." Meuric's garbled voice grew panicked. "Water."

"No. What is Janan trying to do?"

"What has he already *done*, you mean." His good eye squeezed shut. "You're so *stupid*. It's already done. Soul Night is inevitable now. He will rise."

"Like a phoenix?"

"No. No, nothing like that. Come Soul Night, you won't care about phoenixes. No one will. Birth is so painful."

Okay. Something terrible would happen. We'd gone over that. Maybe he didn't know exactly what would happen. Or maybe he was too crazy to express how awful it would be.

I forced myself to meet his good eye, though he seemed to have trouble focusing. "When I came here before, I found books. But I don't know who wrote them, and I can't read the symbols."

"No one wrote them. They were simply written." He groaned and dropped his hand. "Give me water. You promised."

"Tell me how to read the books."

"Same way you'd read anything. Learn the language." Oil-dark fluid seeped from his ruined eye, down the crevices of

190

his face, and into cracked lips. He swallowed it.

"What's the connection between sylph and Janan?"

"Janan is nothing like sylph!"

"Don't lie to me. I know there's a connection." The poison wouldn't have worked on both of them otherwise.

"He is greater than them. He has always been greater, and they deserve to be cursed."

Cursed? "What are sylph?"

"They are betrayers!"

"Did they betray Janan? Did he curse them?" Maybe all their attacks on Heart were about revenge. But why did they seem to like me?

"Oh, they betrayed Janan," Meuric said. "But he didn't have to curse them. I don't know who did, but if I had to guess, I'd guess a phoenix did it."

A phoenix. No, that seemed too incredible.

"Give me water!" Meuric's body tipped toward me.

I stood and stepped backward in one motion. "You're not getting anything until you give me answers. Real answers."

"There are no real answers."

"Look, Meuric." Ugh, wrong thing to say, because he grinned widely.

I fought hard not to gag. Meuric's odor of ammonia and bile made my headache increase. Soon my body would stop breathing out of self-defense.

I tried again. "Here." I pulled the bottle of water from my

coat. "Half-full." I sloshed it. "I'll give you this water, but you have to answer questions for me."

"What questions?"

I put the water away and found my notebook, wishing I had the list I'd given to Cris. Still, I remembered lots of the symbols, and I flipped to a blank page and began drawing. "See this mark? What does it mean?" I showed him the symbol that looked like a crescendo.

"Less."

"What?"

"It means less than. Math. Or it could mean 'speak louder.' I don't know. Context. You must tell me more for me to tell you anything. Honestly, I can't believe how stupid you are. Do you think I'm a data console, able to call up information when you press the correct buttons? Or a vision pool? Oh, I remember those. We used to think the hot springs would give us visions if we stood there and inhaled the fumes long enough. And they did give us visions! But not of the future or past or anything useful. Headaches. Like you're giving me now."

I blinked and glanced at the page, desperately hoping it wasn't a math symbol and that all the books weren't written entirely in mathematical equations.

"Okay, let's try another. Maybe it will be less ambiguous." I offered a symbol that looked like an up arrow, but with four points along the shaft rather than one at the top.

"Hmm. Another."

The next was a circle with a dot in its center.

"Still wanting answers from those books." Meuric shook his head, as though disappointed but not surprised.

"Do you know what these mean?"

"Of course."

"You must tell me everything. No leaving out details. If I think you're lying, I won't give you this water."

"Very well." Meuric coughed, flecks of blood and mucus spattering across the floor. "The second symbol means rising or higher. Ascending. You may sometimes read it as Janan, though it isn't his name, simply a reference to him. The third symbol means city, or Heart—but only Heart in the way the other means Janan."

"How do you tell which it means?"

For someone in his condition, he did an admirable job of looking at me like I was an idiot. "Context. Of course."

"Oh, of course," I muttered, scribbling notes to myself. "What about the first symbol? The 'less than' mark."

"It is but a modifier, changing the meanings of the words around it." He gave examples of how the symbol might affect others.

I showed him several more symbols and he answered readily, the whole time grinning as if he believed I would regret all this questioning. But I continued on, and he told me how and why different meanings might be assigned to different marks. Then, too soon, I couldn't remember any others well enough to ask about them. If only I'd found the stack of books again when I came in.

"Okay, you can have the water now." I put my notebook away and retrieved the bottle.

"Yes! Give it." Meuric lifted his arm, which drooped in unnatural places. When I handed him the bottle, it fell from his grasp and rolled across the floor. As it bounced against the far wall and settled, he just stared, desolate and unable to go after it.

Pity gnawed at me, and I fetched it for him. "Do anything I even *think* might be an attack, and I'll shove this in your other eye. Got it?"

Meuric nodded, as I removed the top and held the bottle in front of him. All he had to do was lean forward, but I didn't think he could. He should have been dead. Bone shards should have pierced all his organs and he shouldn't be breathing, let alone talking.

Whatever Janan had done to Meuric, it wasn't a favor.

I tilted the bottle over him until water trickled into his mouth. He drank, sputtered, coughed, and I backed far away. I didn't trust all those sudden movements.

"Answer a few more questions and I'll give you the rest." Unless he started coughing on me again. Maybe I could leave the bottle next to him and call it the end of our agreement. But he couldn't drink it on his own. I hated that I felt obligated to make sure he got what he'd bargained for.

"You want to know how to stop Janan. There is no way to stop him, least of all for you. You are nothing to Janan. Insignificant." He kept staring at the bottle, even as water dribbled down his chin.

"I'm not insignificant to you. I have the water." I shook the bottle again. All this protest. All this insistence on my insignificance. Meuric was afraid of me, of what I might do, because I was the only one against Janan who could remember everything others were supposed to forget. Because I was new. Different. Asunder.

Maybe special.

I steeled my voice. "Now tell me how to stop him."

"Nothing can stop him. Already the world quivers with anticipation." He glared up with his good eye, and the bad one gaped wider. "Why are you even here? You should have been like these screams, these crying souls never born."

Terror flurried inside of me, and I whispered, "What do you mean?"

"You weren't supposed to be born. You keep interfering and because of you, more oldsouls have been taken from Janan forever. More newsouls escape." Meuric cackled, rough and bubbling. "But it doesn't matter. You came too late to have any effect on him. He won't notice the loss of your tiny spark."

"But the others?" My tongue might have been paper as I

asked, "Will he notice the darksouls, and the newsouls born in their place?"

Meuric settled into the position I'd first seen him in, obscured by ratty cloth and blood. "He may notice, but it's too late to stop him. Your trials are for naught. You've secured a few short years for yourself, and a few short breaths for others. But the death you'll soon experience will surely be a hundred times worse than your original fate."

My boots hissed on stone as I backed toward the stairs. "And what was my original fate?" I asked, thinking of the weeper and what it had called Janan. The Devourer.

When he grinned, a cracked and bloodied tooth dropped from its socket. "The same fate of all newsouls, caught to allow an oldsoul to be reborn. The same fate of all the new-souls you hear right now with their little screams and lives never lived.

"They're being eaten."

17

KEY

THE WATER BOTTLE dropped to the floor, spilling open, and Meuric howled with laughter.

I threw myself up the spiral stairs, around in circles higher and higher. My thighs burned and my head throbbed, but I ignored my own pain. It was nothing. Janan was replacing souls, letting the old live and keeping the new for himself. The weeper, the non-voice that had comforted me in the blackness, was being consumed.

As I climbed, the sobbing and wailing grew louder, and I imagined the souls were calling me back, though whether to save them or die with them, I wasn't sure.

Up the stairs, I emerged into a spherical room. I didn't stop running, and the entire chamber rolled under my feet as though I were trapped inside a giant ball.

Remembering how the upside-down pit had sucked Meuric upward, I stopped while the hole was still on the side of the room, then fumbled for the door device with my pulse thundering in my ears. I pressed the combination that had opened a path to freedom before. Gray misted on the white stone, and I ran into scorching daylight.

Even as the door vanished, Meuric's words pursued me: *they're being eaten.*

All the weeping, all the whispered cries for help. Newsouls.

Light rained around me and the temple pressed against my back, echoing my pounding heartbeat. All I could see were the cobblestones under my boots and my shaking hands as I thrust the key into my pocket. I blinked to clear my vision, but it didn't help.

I gasped at air, gulping the scent of sweat and burned coffee and sulfur from an erupting geyser beyond the wall. Steam wafted across the agricultural quarter, through the orchards and fields. Two more geysers erupted in the north and east, their loud gush and whoosh audible even over the market field din. Water sprayed high, reaching over the immense city wall.

Hands closed over my shoulders and yanked me close, and I screamed.

A man I'd never seen before shoved me and slammed me against the temple. Lightning snapped through my vision and thoughts, and I cried out as the stranger pinned me to the wall. I couldn't get away. The temple thrummed against my spine, and the back of my head ached where it had hit. The stranger dug into my pocket and seized the temple key.

"This," he growled, "doesn't belong to you." He grabbed the front of my coat, jerked me around so I hit the wall again, and then he was gone.

My head pounded as I struggled to find my feet, to go after him, but I staggered a few steps and hit the ground. Stone scraped my palms and fingertips, all gritty and cold. I stared up at the real world, such a shock after an eternity of solitude.

At least two dozen people milled around the market field. Some gaped at me. I hadn't seen them before, hadn't thought to be mindful when I emerged from the temple. There wasn't supposed to be a door. Had they seen the man attack me? Had they noticed my appearance?

Had anyone heard the souls crying? The temple loomed behind me, immense and infinitely horrible. Maybe it wasn't a heart, but a stomach.

I tried to track the man who'd attacked me, but my eyes were bleary with pain and grief. His large form stopped by a smaller one—Deborl?—and moved on. I lost him.

I'd lost the key. I'd lost my biggest advantage.

I collapsed over my knees and sobbed.

"Ana!" Sam fell beside me, wrapped his arms around me.

"Where have you been? What happened?"

"Someone took the key."

"Your key? Who?"

"I don't know." I buried my face in Sam's shirt and let tears fall. My eyes were heavy with the weight of them, like I could cry seas.

"Ana," he murmured. "Oh, Ana. You're safe now."

I didn't have the breath to tell him I wasn't worried about myself. It was the others. It should have been me, too, except Menehem's experiment had gone wrong. His meddling.

Trying to swallow my sobs so we wouldn't draw a crowd, I burrowed deeper into Sam's embrace. I inhaled the scent of sunshine on his skin, shampoo in his hair, and coffee on his breath as he squeezed me tighter.

"I was so afraid for you, but you're here now. You're safe. You're safe." He whispered comforting nonsense while he peeled my hair off my wet cheeks and neck. I smelled salty, sweaty, and perhaps I'd carried Meuric's odors of blood and pee, because Sam dragged his hands over me as though searching for injuries.

My worst injuries were on the inside.

A narrow shadow dropped over us. Sam's weight shifted when he looked up, and his voice rumbled in his chest against my ear. "What?"

"Just checking to make sure everything was okay." Councilor Deborl's voice was strained, as though he were trying to make it deeper than it really was.

"Thanks, but we're fine." Sam stood, drawing me with him. I had just enough time to dry my cheeks, not that it mattered. Dark stains on Sam's shirt revealed the oceans of my crying.

"When people scream, it's rude to leave them in the middle of the market field." Deborl leveled his glare on me. "Especially when her guardian is the one to frighten her so badly."

I edged closer to Sam. "There was someone else. He pushed me and took—"

Deborl cocked his head. "And took what?"

Took the key, but I wasn't supposed to know about the key. No one was supposed to be able to remember it, and what if the stranger hadn't just paused by Deborl, but given him the key, too? If I accused Deborl of having the key, there'd be questions of how I came to possess it. Questions like what happened to Meuric, and why had I been hiding such an important object?

I slumped against Sam. "The man shoved me. He was big. . . ." Everyone was big compared to me. "He had brown hair. He walked right by you."

"I'll look for him," Deborl said, but he didn't leave.

"Everything is okay, Deborl." Sam kept his voice even, and only the way his arm tightened around me belied his tone. "Thank you for checking."

Deborl glanced between us, scratching his chin where red lines marked cuts from shaving. "I hope you haven't been letting her get hurt a lot. After all, the Council trusts you to care for her." His eyes narrowed when he smiled. "You know, half the population thinks she's responsible for Templedark, and the other half isn't convinced that she's *not*. And now they're talking about the incident with the sylph."

Sam's hands curled into fists, and his shoulders pulled back as though he was ready to hit Deborl. "Ana did more to mitigate a slaughter during Templedark than anyone. And where were *you* that night? Did you turn over and go back to sleep?"

Their argument had begun drawing curious looks. Cris strode toward us as though on a mission. Most others just stared.

"Stop," I said. "Both of you." I couldn't imagine how my voice didn't shake. I locked my knees to stay upright, but it just made me light-headed.

Deborl smirked.

"Hello, Cris," I said as he approached behind Deborl. I was so sore and tired. Maybe someone *else* could keep Sam and Deborl from coming to blows. Then I could curl up on a nice rock and go to sleep for a year.

He nodded in greeting, exchanging a questioning look with Sam. Something heavy passed between them, though I couldn't decipher the flickers of expression.

"Is this your plan, Sam? Get people to feel sorry for new-souls by parading around a tearful Ana? It won't work. It's pathetic." Deborl sneered. "People will never accept newsouls. Everyone knows you're blinded by"—he eyed me—"whatever you two do together. Disgusting."

Sam's arm tightened around me. "Don't you have some-thing important to do?" He glared at Deborl. "Maybe you could find whoever assaulted Ana?"

The Councilor showed teeth when he smiled. "Little Ana missed her progress report the other day, and you haven't rescheduled. Some Councilors are wondering if she doesn't really want to be a member of the community."

The other day?

"I told you, she was sick—"

Sam had needed to make an excuse for me?

"You have until the end of this week to report to the Council." Deborl's glare didn't shift away from me. "That's in two days. Be there no later than tenth hour, or your status as Dossam's ward will be revoked and you will be exiled from Range." With that, he marched into the dispersing crowd. A couple people patted him on the back, pleased with the idea that I might be kicked out.

Armande strode up, coffee in hand. He offered the paper cup to me, and I clutched it to my chest, trying to absorb its warmth.

"So." Cris turned to Sam. "I see you found her."

"You were looking for me?" He'd known exactly where I was. He'd been ready to go, too. How did I go from being sick to missing? What happened to the original plan of letting everyone assume we were off kissing somewhere?

"You were missing." Sam's fingers curled over the small of my back, as though to draw me close again. "We all went out to look for you that night, and the next. Cris and Armande stayed out late with me every night, but we couldn't find you."

That night? The next night? *Every* night? How many had there been? I reached back and touched the rose I'd braided into my hair, but it felt the same as it had when I'd put it there: a little brittle, but certainly not *that* old.

"We were all worried," Cris said. "Sarit is a wreck. Someone should call her."

My head throbbed so hard I could barely think. I just wanted to sleep, but the temple loomed at my back, a thousand times more frightening than it had ever been. Meuric's words still haunted me. The souls still haunted me.

I licked my lips. "How long was I"—not in *there*, not with Armande and Cris present—"missing?"

"A week." Sam's expression was sober, lines around his mouth and between his eyes. His skin was pallid, his eyes bloodshot and circled with hollowed darkness. "You've been missing for a week."

My cup slipped from my hands and slammed onto the cobblestones. The lid popped off and coffee splashed over shoes and pant hems, but I couldn't muster the energy to apologize, let alone back away from the liquid flying everywhere.

Coffee seeped through the cracks in stones, like rot dribbling from Meuric's eye—

Sam caught me when my knees buckled. "It's all right now. I'll take you home."

18
CRASH

I MADE IT as far as South Avenue before my legs refused to work anymore, so Sam carried me. Safe in his arms, I closed my eyes and listened to the melody of voices.

"Where was she?" Cris asked. "I'd thought you must have found her this morning and you both came to the market field. . . ."

"I don't know," Sam said. I couldn't tell whether he remembered where I'd been. "I wish Deborl had minded his own business."

Armande snorted. "You know he can't. Just as I bake, you play music, and Cris gardens, Deborl must interfere in others' business. It's the only thing he's got going for him."

With my face pressed into Sam's coat, I managed a smile.

Sam tightened his hold on me. "Someone told Lidea that Ana was missing. She's been calling every hour, worried Ana had been kidnapped, and they might come after Anid next. She refuses to leave her house, and she had Stef set up all manner of monitoring systems in the baby's room. Not that it matters, because Lidea sleeps next to his crib to guard him."

Guilt burrowed in my stomach. A week. It hadn't felt like a week. My rose . . .

I drifted in and out, and it seemed like forever before they carried me up the front steps and through the parlor.

A cup was pressed against my mouth, and water trickled in. I swallowed hesitantly at first, but as my throat grew used to the motion, I gulped the water down until my stomach hurt.

Bundled in blankets on the sofa, surely I was safe.

Sam showed the other two to the door, thanking them. It might have been my state or blurry vision, but while Sam seemed easy with Armande, his posture changed when he faced Cris. Slumped shoulders, weight shifted toward the other boy. Cris stood like his mirror.

"You didn't have to do so much," Sam said. "But I'm grateful. Thank you."

"She seems nice." Cris hesitated. "Well, a bit testy, but I suspect she's nice underneath all those thorns."

"When we first met, she had scars all over her hands. It took me a while to figure out how she'd gotten them." Sam hooked his thumbs in his pockets. "Or why they looked familiar."

Cris held up his hands; I couldn't see clearly from my place on the sofa, or with the current foggy state of my vision, but I imagined they were both looking at the scars he wore, too. You'd think someone who had been tending roses for hundreds of years might figure out about gloves.

"I saw the roses at the cottage." Cris lowered his hands. "She did a good job with them. Maybe I'll bring a few more by to cheer her up."

"She'd like that." They spoke a moment more, offers of further assistance, and Cris turned to leave. "Hey." Sam shifted his weight and his tone lightened. "I always thought your roses were blue."

Cool fingers touched my cheek. "Ana?"

"Mmm?" I tilted my head toward the window, where light could burn beyond my eyelids; I didn't want to wake up in the dark.

"Where did you go?" He sounded broken. Shattered. He sat on the edge of the sofa. "I looked everywhere for you."

My arms were too heavy to lift all the way to his face, so I settled for his elbows and dragged him downward. "You really don't remember?"

"You didn't tell me. I thought we were going somewhere together, but I can't remember. I had a backpack. I tried to call you."

The memory magic had closed over the cracks in my absence. I groaned.

"It's okay," Sam murmured. "We can talk about it later, if you want. I've called Lidea and Sarit. They want to come see you."

Opening my eyes was painful. No way could I smile for guests. "Not now."

"Not now," he agreed. "Can I get anything for you?"

I spoke without thinking. There was one thing I always needed. "Music. Play for me."

Sam kissed my forehead and retreated to the piano in the center of the parlor. Long, low notes filled the room, bouncing off the polished wood and stone figurines. This room was meant for music, and I sank into the sound as though it were a pile of feathers.

I dreamt of black rooms and black tears, and my fate narrowly avoided.

I awoke trapped in the tangled embrace of blankets. I thrashed and tumbled off the sofa, ran for the nearest washroom, and lost everything in my stomach.

Outside the washroom, I heard Sam growling into his SED. "Tell them to postpone the deadline. She's in no condition to leave right now. . . .

"She's very ill. . . .

"No, she *was* getting better, and then someone attacked her in the market field. Deborl cornered her right after. . . .

"You're the Speaker, Sine. Overrule them. . . .

"Stand up for her. Stand up for all the newsouls and do something to *help.*"

More than he knew, someone had to stand up for them. Someone had to stop Janan from hurting newsouls. Someone had to.

I had to.

I sobbed until I crashed into dreams again.

When I finally opened my eyes without panicking, Sam brought tea and a plate of buttered toast. The lines and dark smudges were gone from his face, so I must have slept for quite a while.

I'd lost a week in the temple, lost more time sleeping after my escape. If I kept this up, I wouldn't have any memories at all. I might as well be one of the newsouls trapped in the everywhere-light and darkness.

I lowered my teacup mid-sip, and Sam brushed a tear off my cheek. That was all I had left: a few tears. No energy left for a big cry.

"I wish I hadn't gone in." I gulped my tea and set the cup aside, scrubbed my palms against my face. I really wanted a shower. A week of real sleep. No nightmares. "Where are my things? My notebook?" I needed to work on translating the temple books.

"In your room. Do you want to go up?"

"After I finish this."

Sam frowned, but waited while I ate my toast and found my feet. I felt like a memory of myself, after no food, after crying. It made me heavy and light at the same time, and I swayed on aching legs. Were they thinner than before? If I took off my clothes and looked in the mirror, could I count my ribs? I felt so hollow.

I managed to get upstairs without crumbling, without forgetting I wasn't still climbing out of Meuric's pit. Sam followed me into my room, staying close while I found clean clothes. He didn't speak when I went to shower.

Hot water burned off layers of memory. The reek of sideways and spherical rooms, the rancid odor of Meuric and his eye, and the stench of my own sweat. I watched it spiral into the drain.

Dressed again, I sat next to Sam on my bed. "Did you sleep in the parlor today? Last night?" My window showed a deep purple sky, a pale dusting of stars. Evening.

"I'm afraid of what will happen if I look away from you."

"If you were afraid I'd been kidnapped, why did you tell everyone I was sick?"

A line of thought formed between his eyes. "We checked

everyone who's ever publicly acted against you, like Merton, but I was afraid that—no matter what actually had happened—people would find a way to twist the truth. You were kidnapped because everyone hates you, or you ran away to live with the sylph. I don't know. Scared people are creative people. They would have come up with something, so if I only said you were sick and no one knew the truth—that you were missing—I could control what people said."

"Sam." I tried not to imagine how frightened I'd have been if our positions were reversed. I couldn't blame him for the way he watched me now. "Sam," I whispered again, because the only thing I could say was his name.

He pressed his hand over mine, resting on my lap. "I don't think I've ever been as afraid as when I couldn't find you that night." His breath was long and shaky. "I've been inside every darksoul home, every warehouse and building in both the agricultural and industrial quarters, and every closet in the Councilhouse. I don't think I slept for more than five minutes at a time.

"When we first met, you asked about the scariest thing I could think of."

The day had been clear and cold, filled with questions. I hadn't even known who he was then, just that he pulled strangers from frozen lakes. I wished he could pull me from the frozen shock now. "I remember," I whispered. "You said not knowing what would happen if you died and didn't come back. Where would you go? What would you do?" My gut twisted.

"When I couldn't find you that night, I realized that wasn't my answer anymore." He pulled my hand up, placed it over his heart. The beat raced under my fingertips. "If you asked me now, I'd say the scariest thing I can imagine is losing you."

I didn't know how to respond.

"I wish I could tell you all the things you make me feel. I tried putting them into music, but even that wasn't strong enough."

I wanted to ask how he knew, how he could tell the difference between love and infatuation. But I couldn't force my mouth to form the words, because then he kissed my fingers one at a time and my focus sharpened, narrowed to all the places we touched. Our knees, his hands over my wrist, his lips on my knuckles.

When each finger had a kiss, he turned my hand palm up and cupped it over his cheek. "You're part of me, part of my existence." Muscles in his jaw shifted under my fingers. "Everything was dimmer without you."

If he'd been the one missing, I'd have crawled onto him to keep him from leaving ever again. Even in my imagination, I could feel him beneath me, bones and muscles and the solid presence of *him*. In my imagination, he lay there beneath me and never left.

I was both relieved and disappointed that he didn't have the same impulse. Or he had better restraint.

Sighing, he released my hand. "I'm still not sure you won't vanish if I'm not holding you." He glanced at my fingers, now curled on my knee. He started to reach again, but hesitated. Maybe he did want to crawl on top of me after all. "But you just got back, and there are so many things we need to do, which means anything I want will wait. And whatever happened to you, it must have been terrible."

The odor of Meuric's nest, the blackness with weepers, and Janan's voice by my ear. My breath came like a stutter.

Sam tucked my damp hair behind my ear. "Can you tell me?"

"You don't want to know," I whispered, hating myself for all the terrible things I was about to make him feel. "But it's important that you do, anyway."

He waited.

"First, you have to know that for a little while, you knew exactly where I was. You were going to go inside the temple with me."

"That's not possible."

"It is. I had a key." But it was gone now. Had the stranger given it to Deborl? What would they do with it? "We were going to go in together. You insisted, and I didn't want to go by myself. But Stef spotted you and I had to go in alone, before I lost the chance. It's just, Janan plays with your memories. You aren't allowed to know certain things, so you forget them, and you don't question inconsistencies because none of you notice them."

"That sounds crazy," he whispered. "We remember everything, from the very first lifetime."

"You don't." I touched his hand. "You don't remember everything. And that's not the only thing." I told him what Janan did to souls like mine.

19
TRANSFORM

AFTER TELLING SAM everything that happened in the temple, I didn't have the energy to attempt translating the books, though I'd hoped to try.

Instead, I started crying again, and Sam grew somber and distant as he led me downstairs. Dusk had fallen long ago, leaving only lamps and reflections off polished wood to illuminate the parlor. I wrapped myself in blankets on the sofa, listening to his footfalls in the kitchen. Cabinet doors opened and closed, boiling water hissed, and a spoon clanked on ceramic as he stirred honey into my tea.

He left the mug on an end table for me, then went to work on the piano, adjusting strings beneath the gleaming maple lid, then testing pitches. Every so often, he'd stop working to play, always making sure to ask if I had any requests, but most of the time I was content to watch and listen.

Nocturnes and preludes lulled me into dozing, and I awakened to find morning had arrived, covered in a film of snow. Sam and I dressed warmly and headed to the Councilhouse for my very late monthly progress report.

Predictably, the Council quizzed me mercilessly on my supposed sickness and symptoms, expressing false sympathy. Well, Sine's concern might have been real. She worked hard to steer the conversation back to my progress report, but the general suspicion was clear: the Council thought I was up to something.

And wasn't I? I'd discovered Menehem's poison-making machine, Janan's terrible hunger, and their fellow Councilor alive inside the temple. I possessed the only unaltered memory, books from the temple, and—until recently—the key to the temple. Sylph sang for me.

It wouldn't matter that Janan had even more sinister plans for Soul Night. The Council couldn't trust someone like me.

Fortunately, Sam had foreseen the Council's questions about my illness and prepared me, so I described sleeping through a fever that involved lots of snot and throwing up.

"I died from that once," Sam added as we descended the Councilhouse stairs. An icy breeze scoured the market field, though it didn't deter devoted gossips and workers.

"Um." I hunched beneath my coat hood, conscious of glares

in my direction. Merton was out again, reminding people about the sylph incident at the lake, and how disgusting it was that Sam was in a romantic relationship with me. The Council's advice on this was the same as it had been: ignore it. "If you died from the illness," I asked, "is it a miracle I'm alive?"

He slipped his hand around mine and squeezed. "Well, yes. But that was several lifetimes ago. Medicine has come a long way since then. Don't worry. The medic who supposedly treated you is a good friend. She won't say anything if they ask."

"Oh, good."

We stopped at Armande's pastry stall, sipping coffee and eating muffins until he was satisfied I wasn't starving to death. Sam kept checking his SED, but otherwise held a long conversation with Armande about what they each planned to have for lunch. It seemed suspicious to me, but we sat a good distance away from the temple and Merton's gathering, and Armande continued giving me snacks. I didn't complain, but I couldn't ignore the voices from the Councilhouse steps.

"Newsouls are a plague," a woman shouted. "Punishment for our lack of devotion to Janan."

Her theory and the truth were as far apart as the sea and the stars, but it was a popular sentiment.

"They have no skills," said a man. "Why should we feel obligated to care for anyone who can't offer anything to the community? We don't have resources to shelter and feed them. What happens if there are more and more? There are—*were*—a million of us. And only a million. We used to think we were the only souls in existence, but that's been"— the man's voice thinned, like he didn't believe what he was about to say—"proven false. Now whatever limit was set has been broken. What happens when they outnumber us?"

I glanced at Sam and Armande just in time to see them cringe.

It was a good question. I didn't know, either. Of course, this man was leaping to conclusions. For all anyone knew, newsouls might be limited, too. Eventually, by counting how many newsouls were born, they'd be able to tell how many oldsouls had truly been lost during Templedark. At least seventy-two. Probably more. But it seemed to me, once we reached that number, that would be it.

Then we'd either be reincarnated or we wouldn't.

At noon, Sam wished Armande a good day, and we headed back to the southwestern residential quarter. Snow flurries pushed through the streets, and the day was just cold enough to allow a layer of white on the ground.

When we got home, tracks in the snow led to the front door and away, scuffed enough that I couldn't tell anything about them except the intruder had been through a lot. Light seeped from the parlor windows. Perhaps the Council had finally made good on their threat to have my room searched.

If they took my books and research, and Deborl had the key—

Fear splintered through me. "Sam?"

"It's all right." He took my hand and drew me to the door, where I caught a sweet scent. And when I stepped inside, roses transformed the parlor into another world entirely.

Shades of red and blue clustered in vases on tables and shelves. They rested alone on the piano's music stand and on the edge of each step of the staircase. They peeked from stands, from instrument cases, from behind the decorations that served beauty and acoustics.

The perfume was intoxicating, so rich I could taste it. A subtler, spicy aroma filled me up, warming me as the front door shut and Sam stopped beside me, wearing a smile. "I like it."

"Did Cris run out of room in his greenhouse?"

Sam chuckled. "Not as far as I know."

I drifted through the room, touching petals. "I like the way they're all mixed together, the red and blue. Are these"— I bent to sniff one—"Phoenix roses?" They had more petals than the blue roses I was used to, like ruffles of wisp-thin paper.

"They are. As many blue and Phoenix roses as he could stand to lose." Sam tugged off his boots and leaned against the piano, tracking my progress through the room. "I haven't seen you look this happy in a long time."

"It's like a greenhouse exploded in our parlor and left—"

I swept my hands around. They were everywhere, changing the way light and color caught my attention, drawing my eyes to places I hadn't looked since I'd first come to Heart. They were by the cello, resting on the harpsichord, and threaded through my music stand.

And by my new flute, resting on its stand and polished to a shine, lay the most perfect blue rose I'd ever seen, with smooth petals so flawless they didn't look real. The bloom bent under my fingertips, as soft as air.

I turned. "Why would you do this?"

He smiled as I stepped into his embrace, and his arms wrapped strong and solid around my waist. "Why not?" He pulled me tight, and when I lifted my eyes to his, he kissed me.

I lost myself in the brush of his lips, the thrill of his fingers against my cheek and neck and shoulder, and thump of his heartbeat under my palm. So engaged in the way his mouth fit with mine, I almost missed the purr of my coat being unzipped. When he paused his kissing, I stepped back, and he slipped my coat off my shoulders; I dropped my arms and the cloth fell with a soft *whump*.

"I love you. Have I told you that since you got back?" He curled his hands over my hips and didn't wait for me to answer. "I want to tell you every hour. Every minute. Ever since you returned, all I can think about is how close I came to not having you at all. And how close you came to being—"

He looked away, expression grim.

"You remember that?" I would be so grateful if I didn't have to keep explaining it, or reminding him that I hadn't actually been missing. "You remember everything I told you about being inside the temple?"

He nodded, looking wrecked. "I keep remembering it."

"And the white wall in the north? Right before the dragons?" I bit my lip.

Recognition flickered through him, but he shook his head. "No. A little, but no." He grew quiet, seeming distracted by my hair. It tugged and tingled across my scalp where he pulled his fingers through the waves. "There are things I should remember, but I don't."

"Yeah." My heart thudded.

"You remember them."

I offered a pale smile, relief that my newness was good for something. "I wasn't reborn."

"And there are things I'm remembering because of you."

"Yes." At least, it seemed to be my doing. It was unlikely that after five thousand years, the magic would suddenly begin breaking down in the middle of this lifetime. I was the only thing that had *changed*.

A tiny sense of importance surged through me.

"I'm glad you're here," he said.

I looped my arms around his shoulders and pulled close. "Because I make you remember things?" I didn't want to think about Janan right now. I wanted Sam to kiss me.

"Because of a lot of reasons." He read my mind, or read the way our bodies pressed together, only bunched clothes between us.

Our kiss stopped time, stopped thoughts. All I knew was the feel of his mouth, the gasp and shuddered breath, and the calluses of his hands on my back. Cool air fluttered where he'd lifted my shirt, sharp contrast to the way he made me burn with desire. I didn't have words for what I wanted with him, but if I could push closer and closer—

"No one would believe Ana was terribly ill for a week if they saw this." Amusement filled Sarit's voice, and I spun to find her—and Cris and Stef—crowding the kitchen doorway. "Oh, I'm sorry." Sarit grinned, not sounding sorry at all. "I didn't mean to interrupt, but I thought you should know we brought lunch."

My face ached with embarrassment, but I didn't miss the way Cris looked sort of blank and Stef looked . . . upset? Angry? I couldn't tell.

"Lunch?" My voice sounded pinched, and I wasn't sure if I could actually eat after Armande fed me half his pastry stall, but to make the awkward moment go away, I'd eat anything.

The five of us spent the next hour over plates filled with roast cavy and vegetables, catching up, and admiring the roses.

"I recruited Stef and Sarit's help. I didn't think you'd mind them wandering around the parlor." Cris's plate was empty, but he eyed mine, which was still half-full. He couldn't still be growing, as tall as he was. Surely he couldn't. But when I surrendered my leftovers, he seized them as though he hadn't eaten in days.

"I don't mind at all." Sam grinned and found my hand under the table. "Stef lives here part-time anyway, and lately we have Sarit more often than not, too."

"To be completely honest," Sarit said, "I must admit that my increased presence since another musician moved in is not a coincidence." She winked at me. "In fact, didn't you miss your practice this morning? You should probably play for us now. Call it payment for all the work we did arranging these roses."

Before I could come up with a response, her SED chirped and she excused herself, vanishing around the corner to the other end of the parlor. Cheerfulness drained from her tone as she spoke, and when she returned, she almost looked her age.

"That was Lidea. Someone smashed a window in Anid's room. Lots of his things were taken. He wasn't there, but the threat was clear. Lidea is a wreck, and Wend doesn't know what to do." She pressed her mouth in a line. "I'm not sure Wend is handling the stress well. Everyone he lost during Templedark, and now this? It isn't the first time they've received threats, but it's certainly the worst."

I couldn't think around the rushing in my head. Someone had tried to hurt Anid.

As much as I wanted to be shocked that anyone would do this . . . I knew how I'd grown up, how Li had always treated me, and how people still leered at me. They would keep trying to hurt Anid.

"This will only escalate," I whispered, and everyone faced me.

"Ana, dear." Stef's tone turned comforting. "Lidea is strong. She'll make sure Anid is safe. You shouldn't worry about it."

"No." My voice broke as I lurched to my feet. "I *must* worry about it. Newsouls will keep coming, and they'll all face this kind of hatred. If I don't stand up for them, who will?"

"We all will," Cris said. "We're your friends. We want to help."

Sam gazed at me, waiting. He looked proud, which made my heart flutter.

"I know what to do," I said after a moment, and counted days in my head. Less than a week, but maybe . . . "I have an idea, but I need to speak to people. Tonight."

Part of me was ready for them to try talking me out of it. A smaller part expected laughter and placation. But Stef's expression grew serious, focused, and she pulled out her SED. "All right. Who do you want?"

Relief poured through me. "Trustworthy people. You guys. Lidea and Wend. Orrin and Whit. Armande."

"What about Sine?" Cris asked.

I shook my head. "I think this would conflict with her office too much." She'd been different toward me lately, anyway. Probably because she was the Speaker now and the Council pressured her more than ever, but her being the Council Speaker made the decision easier.

I listed off a few more people, and everyone was on their SEDs, sending messages. Warmth replaced the horror of Sarit's announcement. I could do something. I might not be able to do anything for the souls inside the temple, but I *would* convince the Council that newsouls deserved to be treated like real people.

Even though I'd invited them, everyone's arrival still surprised me.

Some, like Moriah and Lorin, were Sam's friends who'd given me lessons in various subjects. But Whit and Orrin were my friends, and liked to tease me about how much time I spent in the library. More than a few times, they'd tried to convince me to become an archivist with them.

Lidea, Wend, and Anid arrived last, the baby bundled in a hundred blankets. Wend hauled a small nursery in a bag, shooting me a strange look as he followed Lidea inside.

Armande appropriated the kitchen to make coffee and tea, and after everyone had a turn cooing at Anid and admiring the roses, they settled on chairs, music benches, and the sofa, waiting to find out why I'd asked them here.

Well, there was no way I could see everyone from the floor, and Sam wouldn't appreciate it if I stood on top of the piano. I climbed up the first few stairs, leaning my elbows on the rail so I could look at everyone.

From his place beside Stef, Sam gave me an encouraging smile. He made me feel strong.

I gathered my thoughts and cleared my throat, and everyone looked up. "I want to start by reminding you what happened the night Anid was born.

"It was, from what I understand, a normal rebirthing. Lots of people were present, hoping a friend would be reincarnated. But when the Soul Tellers announced Anid was new, everything changed. Some of you were there. You remember how people yelled, threatened him, even though he hadn't done anything except be born."

People nodded, and Lidea held Anid to her chest as though she relived those minutes, not knowing whether the crowd would hurt her child. Her eyes shone with tears, and Wend sat stiffly next to her, his expression hard.

"The fact is, more newsouls are going to be born, and there shouldn't be a need to guard the birthing room. I know people are afraid of what this means, or angry that some souls aren't coming back. Those both are perfectly reasonable reactions, but—"

I stopped myself before getting into the same discussion

Sam and I had after the Council pulled him aside. I thought it was better that newsouls were being born—rather than no one being born—but for others, newsouls would be a constant reminder of Templedark and the souls who'd been lost.

"My point is—" I smoothed the shaking from my voice, needing to sound stronger. "Unless we do something, people will continue acting out against newsouls. I'm sure you've all heard Merton and his friends in the market field, yelling about me."

"Anid, too," Lorin added.

At least Merton had a reason to yell about me. The way sylph behaved around me *was* suspicious. But Anid hadn't done anything.

"I want to tell you what it was like growing up. Not just because of Li"—people hissed at her name—"but being different, and understanding how different and hated I was before I could even speak. You need to understand what it means to be a newsoul: knowing everyone wishes you were the darksoul you replaced."

Haltingly, I spoke about the previous Soul Night, now nearly a quindec ago. I tried not to pay attention to the winces and mutters as I recounted how the revelers had stared at me from across the campfire. I told them how I'd needed to teach myself to read and do chores. How I'd always known nothing I did was new or innovative; someone else had already accomplished it, or figured out a better way.

"It's humiliating to be new. To be the only one." My voice dipped low as I found Anid cradled in Lidea's arms. "And now there are all these new people coming. They could be anything. Scientists, explorers, musicians, warriors. But they're going to feel out of place and confused, always knowing what happened to allow them to have a life. They might feel guilty for something they had no control over. They might feel like a mistake."

Sam tensed, his unease a silent reminder of all the times he urged me to know I wasn't responsible for Ciana's absence. But knowing didn't mean it was easy to believe; the people who threw rocks at me knew I hadn't done anything to Ciana. So did Merton, but he still ranted about me at every opportunity.

"I want to talk to people who are pregnant," I said. "Any of them could give birth to a newsoul, and don't you think most of them will want basic rights and protection for their children?" Surely they weren't all like Li. Lidea wasn't; she gave me hope. "I wasn't even allowed into the city without a lot of bargaining with the Council and many of you agreeing to help. I don't want anyone else to have to go through that kind of fight, just to be allowed to live with the rest of civilization.

"We need to make people understand that the newsoul they give birth to will—" My voice caught like I didn't know how to say the word. Maybe I hadn't until now. "Their child will love them no matter what. And they'll need to be loved, too."

Sam sat up straighter, this time at the word. It felt strange in my mouth.

He probably wondered if I'd loved Li in spite of every-thing. Her death *had* upset me, but I'd never loved her.

"If more people knew, it might help." My voice faltered. I tried to look anywhere but others' eyes. The harp or honey-comb shelf. Maybe they'd all think I was making eye contact with everyone, just hadn't reached them yet. "What I mean to say is, it's worth discussing newsoul rights. The break-in at Lidea's is inexcusable. What were they going to do to him? Kill him?"

Across the room, Lidea shuddered and held Anid close. Next to her, Wend shifted and stared at me, as though sur-prised I could consider such awful things happening.

"Anid—and the others who will be here soon—are worthy of a champion. They'll bring new ideas and insights into the world, but right now there are no laws to protect them. How can they ever feel like part of the community if no one will stand up for them?"

"I agree." Cris flashed a wide smile from the back of the crowd. "We've been so consumed with the loss after Templedark, we haven't thought of what we're about to gain. Nearly a hundred *new* people."

"They've talked about it in Council meetings," Stef said,

"but of course they don't come up with solutions or anything concrete. They keep circling the issue like there's all the time in the world."

I nodded. "I guess it's easy to forget that time is different for us. You do have time. Newsouls . . . we don't know yet." And probably wouldn't until I died.

"And like Ana said," Armande added, "the newsouls will have their own talents and ideas. We should be ready to embrace that, to encourage it."

Lidea glanced at her baby. "We weren't ready for Ana, and in spite of knowing he was a possibility, we weren't ready for Anid. But they won't be the last."

"There's still time for him," I said. "To him, every second will count. Days will seem like years, and years will seem like centuries."

And for everyone else, those days and years went by as fast as heartbeats.

Sam dropped his gaze, and Stef watched him from the corner of her eye. For a moment, she looked softer.

"I'll talk to anyone who wants to know what it's like to be a newsoul. I'll tell you anything you want to know." My mouth had a mind of its own. I hadn't meant to make such a huge offer—tell *strangers* about Li laughing the first time I menstruated?—but as soon as the words came out, I decided to stick with them. This was for Anid, and those not yet born. For those who would never be born.

"That's very generous of you," said Lidea. "I actually had a few questions, but I was hesitant to ask."

"I'll help however I can." I forced myself to move on to the next step, the reason I'd actually brought them all here. "The first thing I want you to do is meet up with friends and figure out whether they would be open to supporting newsouls. I expect most won't be, but we have to try."

Orrin lifted his eyebrows. "I don't think you'll have as much trouble as you're imagining."

"And that's where the rest of us become necessary?" Moriah guessed.

"Exactly." I relaxed as everyone said they'd help. My idea wasn't stupid after all. Orrin thought people would be receptive. "I made a list of pregnant women I know"—minus a couple I knew about through Sarit's gossip but wasn't supposed to—"and thought we could start with them."

"Seems reasonable." Sarit's smile was all innocence, as if she hadn't given me most of my information. "We can all speak to a couple of people, give them the basic proposal, and if necessary we can set up a meeting with you."

"It sounds so much easier when you say it." I grinned. "But we'll have to do this quickly, because the next part comes on market day, when everyone is in the market field."

Cris took a sip of coffee. "That's less than a week away."

"Yes, which means we have a lot of work to do, if everyone is willing to help."

"It will be easier with everyone helping," Sarit said, and all my friends nodded.

I couldn't believe it. I'd asked them here because I *hoped* they would help, but the confirmation made my heart swell with gratitude. "First," I said, "we need to call Sine and make sure we can use the Councilhouse stairs. Sam is going to play his piano."

Sam looked surprised but delighted, and a few people cheered.

"While we have everyone's attention, I will speak up for newsouls. I want the Council to hear people supporting newsoul rights, for them to know that people are discussing the arrival of newsouls, too. Not just people who hate us." I urged strength into my voice. "And if anyone else wants to say something so I'm not alone up there, I'd really appreciate it." Sam, Sarit, and Orrin raised their hands to volunteer. Others weren't far behind.

I stepped down from the stairs, meeting Sam's eyes, and smiled when he mouthed, "I'm proud of you."

Warmth filled me as I took a seat on the sofa arm, my list in hand so we could decide who would do what. This might actually work.

20
EXPLODE

AFTER EVERYONE FINISHED deciding who would do what for our market day demonstration, we broke into smaller groups. I talked with Lidea, giving her more details about what I wished I'd been taught growing up. Cris, Moriah, and Orrin discussed the possibility of lessons for parents of new-souls, and newsouls themselves.

The melody of voices livened the parlor, bright as noon, and the scent of roses warmed everyone. The baby cried, and Lidea carried him to the other side of the room for a change. When she came back, she offered to let me hold him.

He wasn't heavy, but he startled in my arms. Then he went still. "He's beautiful." Much more than the first time I'd seen him, all wet and red. Lidea and Wend probably didn't want to hear that, though.

"I know." She bounced on her toes. "He's the most amazing thing. I love him more than anyone. I mean"—she eyed Wend, who fake-pouted—"he's tied with someone else for my greatest love."

They flirted back and forth until Cris and Sarit walked over. "I just had the best idea," Sarit announced.

"We." Cris rolled his eyes. "We had an idea."

"Sure. *Cris and I* had an idea." Sarit leaned against the back of the sofa. "It had to do with roses. *We* think they should go all over the Councilhouse stairs when we speak, like you have here tonight. Not only would it be pretty, but Cris was telling me how special the blue ones are to you."

"We have things in common." I smiled, imagining the Councilhouse columns wreathed in red and blue. Phoenix roses for oldsouls. Blue roses for newsouls. "Are there enough roses?"

"We might have to steal some of these," Cris said, "but I think we'll make it. Sarit volunteered to do all the arranging, and I can run to the cottage and get a few more blue ones if necessary."

"Thank you." I hugged both Cris and Sarit, gratitude filling me up. Maybe—hopefully—others would notice the significance of the roses, too, and see how beautiful they all looked together. Heart could be like that.

"The stage will be gorgeous! Don't you think so?"

Lidea nudged Wend, who nodded.

"Now it's my turn to hold Anid." Sarit held out her hands. "Give him, or no flowers for you, ladybug."

I laughed and handed him over, and when Sarit, Lidea, and Wend moved toward the piano, Cris sat on the arm of the sofa and lowered his voice. "I've been thinking about those symbols of yours. I meant to bring the list."

"Oh." I shuddered, too easily remembering Meuric trapped in the tower, the grating of his voice, the fluid seeping from his eye. His delight when he told me Janan was consuming newsouls. I clutched my stomach and tried to swallow the acid taste in the back of my throat.

"Are you all right?" Cris touched my shoulder. "What's wrong?"

"I think I need some water."

Cris slipped off the sofa and led me to the stairs. "Sit here out of the way. I'll get you a glass."

When I was settled on one of the upper steps, looking down at all my guests chatting and admiring the roses, I tried to relax. I was out of the temple. Safe. I would help the newsouls coming to Heart. I would learn to read the books from the temple. I would discover the connection between Janan and the sylph. I would . . . what?

I still had no idea what Janan had planned for Soul Night.

"Focus," I whispered to myself, wrapping my fingers around the stem of a blue rose. First the newsouls.

236

Stef's voice came from just below my stair. "Did you see her holding Anid earlier? Babies holding babies."

I clenched my jaw.

"Ana is an adult," Sam said. "Almost four years past her first quindec. If newsouls had full rights, she could have had a job years ago."

I appreciated him standing up for me, but it wasn't like I'd always known what I was going to do. I *liked* learning about everything.

"Physically," Stef said, "nearly four years past first quindec describes you too. But that's physical. She's cute, and anyone can see why you like her, but stop pretending that five thousand years don't matter."

"She's accomplished more in these last months than many of us did in entire lifetimes. Even before we met her, she'd taught herself how to do things it took us ages to learn. She hasn't been a *child* in a very long time."

I certainly didn't feel like a child.

Sam spoke so quietly I almost didn't hear. "There are a million things she can teach us, simply by virtue of being new and seeing things differently."

"Like Templedark?"

His voice was a razor. "Ana rescued both of us that night. And hundreds more. Everything else was Menehem. You know that. Ana is no more responsible for his actions than you."

"You're really hopeless about this, aren't you?" Stef gave

a long sigh, and her tone turned to steel. "Listen, Dossam. People are talking about your relationship with her. Whatever you've done with her? Inappropriate. Whatever you *want* to do with her? Inappropriate. She's five thousand years younger than you, and even if she doesn't know better, you should."

I squeezed my eyes shut, glad I was on the stairs where no one noticed me. More than anything I wanted to march over and tell her to mind her own business, but there were still so many people around, all chatting and having a nice time.

"People don't know anything about it. One day," he growled, "you're going to have to accept it. I don't care if she's eighteen or eighteen hundred. I love her more than—"

"What?" Stef's voice was low and dangerous. "More than music? More than me? More than everyone you've known for the last five millennia?" She paused, and the silence was heavy like the moments between a lightning strike and a roll of thunder. "More than all the darksouls?"

I gripped the rose stem so tightly it cracked. Did Sam love me like that? Was that kind of love even possible?

"Yes." His word was barely a breath. "More than all that."

Relief and horror poured through me. Stef had listed herself in there.

"It's unfair to ask me to rank feelings," Sam muttered.

Then Cris was back with a glass of water, still much taller even when he sat a step lower. "Were you just listening to them down there?" He kept his voice soft, and when I shrugged, he leaned on his elbow toward me. "Don't let it get to you. She's probably hearing a lot of cruel gossip—probably more than you or Sam, since she's been his friend so long and people know . . ."

"She loves him," I whispered into my water.

Cris lowered his eyes and nodded. "It makes people do strange things sometimes."

"It's fine." I put down the rose I'd been holding and took a long drink of water, trying to think of a way out of this. Cris was nice, and I'd have to remember to talk to him about the symbols from the books, but right now, I just wanted to make it through the night. "Thanks for the water. I'm going to see if anyone wants to play some music."

Cris unfolded himself to rise, then offered a hand to help me up. I headed downstairs with him and took my flute off its stand.

That was enough to draw looks. Sam and Stef first, both dark-faced from their fight. Then the hum of conversations drained, and others began to claim instruments or find stands. Most, as far as I knew, played at least a few instruments. They were *Sam's* friends, after all.

When everyone had chosen, Whit and Armande ran upstairs to the music library and returned with appropriate music for each instrument. Sam adjusted the lights so everyone could read.

We started with scales to warm up, then moved on to a

few pieces we all knew. At first I thought they'd chosen simple songs because I was new, but after a few squeaks from
Lorin on the oboe, I realized they weren't going easy on me.

As unlikely as it was, I was a better player than a few of
these people; I practiced several hours a day, while they practiced when they felt like it and when Sam scheduled a group
performance.

Of course, as soon as Moriah, Orrin, and Whit played a
dizzying reel on a cello, violin, and clarinet, my pride vanished. *They* practiced every day. Someday, I would be as good
as them. Better.

Sarit sang a ballad to Stef's piano. Others moved in with
duets, trios, their favorite pieces. They made lots of trips to
the music library upstairs, and I had a brief surge of worry
that they'd stumble into my room and find the temple books
hidden all over, but no one was gone long enough for that.
Anyway, Sam would have heard someone walking into the
wrong room.

My heart swelled as we played more group pieces, broke
off into more small ensembles. How did I get this lucky?
Friends—surely they all counted as friends now—who were
willing to help with the newsouls, *and* play music with me?
It was too incredible. Too wonderful.

Music swirled around the parlor, bringing the room to
life. I struggled not to grin around my embouchure as we
came to the coda of a waltz.

"What about"—Stef hmmed—"Blue Rose Serenade? Did anyone see the lute?"

"Um." Sam glanced at Cris as awkward silence fluttered through the room. People glanced at me, at Sam, at Cris, at the roses all around. "One of the strings snapped. I haven't replaced it yet."

"Maybe whatever you and Ana are working on?" Cris lowered the clarinet he'd been playing.

"Oh, I don't know," I said. We'd been practicing flute duets, and Sarit and Stef had listened a few times, but more people?

"Come on." Sarit batted her eyes. "Let everyone hear."

Sam gave me a look like it was up to me, so I nodded, mostly to stop the awkwardness. He had never mentioned Blue Rose Serenade before. He'd probably forgotten about it when he'd given me the code to add all his music to my SED.

Later, I vowed, I'd ask what had happened between them.

Sam warmed up on the other flute while I found our music, and my heart thudded at the weight of everyone watching. Listening.

But as soon as he met my eyes and silently counted off, my fear evaporated. I stood up straighter, rolled the flute in where my high notes tended to go sharp, and played like I never had before. Every time I glanced at Sam for a fermata or tempo change, he looked as though he wanted to smile.

Before I was ready, we came to the last note and held it until Sam nodded, and our duet ended.

When everyone left, I shut the door and locked it, and Sam and I cleaned up, talking about who needed to practice their favorite instruments more. I wanted to ask him about his fight with Stef, but how did one even open a conversation like that?

"What's this?" Sam bent to retrieve something from the floor. He pinched a tiny wire between his fingers. "From a flute?"

"Ugh." I checked mine. Sure enough, the wire was a spring that had popped out. A set of keys flopped pitifully. "Lorin was messing with it earlier. Guess she got a little enthusiastic when she was pretending she knew how to play."

Sam smirked and handed me the spring. "She's banned from holding flutes from now on. Will you take this upstairs? I'll show you how to fix it tomorrow."

I nodded and carried the flute and spring to the workroom, which held a dozen instruments in various stages of repair, as well as tools to fix them. Building and repairing instruments wasn't Sam's job, but he insisted it was important for every musician to know the basics. All this looked like more than basics to me, though.

I left my flute on the workbench and headed back downstairs. Just as I reached the last step, thunder tore in the north, and the ground rippled. "Was that an earthquake?" Range was constantly shifting, but most earthquakes were too tiny to feel.

"No." Sam was pale, staring northward with wide eyes. "I think it was an explosion."

I raced for my coat and then into the cold. Nearby, an orange glow raged against the dark sky.

Sam followed me out, a water bottle in his pocket and his SED pressed to his ear. "Alert all the guards and medics. Hurry."

We ran down the walkway as secondary explosions shattered the night. Crashes and bangs, pops and screeching. I ran as fast as my legs would carry me. Sam raced across the street ahead, not waiting.

From the fiery glow beyond a line of trees, smoke poured into the black sky, obscuring the moon and stars. The acrid reek burned through my nose and throat, caught in my lungs. The sting made my eyes water, and we hadn't yet come in sight of the fire, except where its light shot between trees.

The roar of flame covered the sound of my footfalls beating the ground—I could only feel the heavy *thud, thud* travel up my legs—and the shaking in my breath from icy air.

Hot brilliance blinded me as we broke through the trees, reaching the house. Dark and light. I couldn't see because my eyes didn't know how to adjust.

I crashed into Sam. He held his sleeve over his face, using his free hand to press a wet cloth into my hands. I wondered where he'd gotten the water, but then remembered the bottle stuffed into his pocket.

"Put this over your nose and mouth." The fire tried to consume his words. The rush and groan were louder now that we stood in the yard. Heat billowed toward us, bringing smoke and sparks. In spite of the inferno, I was glad for my coat to protect my skin. I'd already experienced enough burns to last several lifetimes.

"We have to help whoever's inside the house." I squinted at the trees silhouetted between bands of firelight. "Who lives here?"

"You're not going anywhere until you put that over your face." He pressed the handkerchief over my nose. Breathing turned wet and heavy, more difficult than inhaling smoke. He wasn't wearing a wet handkerchief.

"But you—" I bit off my words when I saw his expression, like pieces of him were being ripped out and hurled into the flames.

"I can't stop you from going in," he said, probably at a normal volume, but the fire made his words soft. "I can only try to help you make it out alive."

I pinned the handkerchief against my face and gave a curt nod. We dashed toward the house.

Outbuildings had collapsed in the initial wave, but the white stone remained solid. Janan's doing. At least the entire structure wouldn't fall in on us, though there was still furniture to dodge inside.

And the fire.

We went in. All the doors and windows had blown out—glass crunched under my boots—and tables and chairs were nigh unrecognizable. Everything was black and red, blazing hot. I didn't even have time to sweat beneath my wool coat; the dry air sucked the moisture out of me, and out of my handkerchief as I searched through the terrible heat and burning remains of someone's home.

The fire roared and rushed. It seemed impossible I'd be able to hear anything else, but I caught the ragged sound of coughing. Metals clattered against stone.

Smoke and fire. Debris piled up. I couldn't find the source of the noise.

There, between a fallen bookcase and the remains of a large stringed instrument, lay a woman on her side, facing away from me.

At my approach, she rolled over. Her stomach bulged like Lidea's had while she'd been pregnant. Geral. I'd taken lessons from her, about building roads and constructing outbuildings.

I rushed for her, screaming her name, and as I jumped over the wreckage I lost track of Sam.

"Geral!" Smoke suffocated my voice as I reached her, but her face twisted with confusion. "I'm here to help."

Her eyes focused as I pressed the mostly dry handkerchief over her nose and mouth. It took some maneuvering and shifting her weight, but finally I got her arm around my shoulders and used every muscle in my legs and back to haul her up. By my ear, her breath came shallow and weak from inhaling smoke.

We turned toward the direction I thought I'd come, but the room had changed. Beams had fallen, burning brightly. Blackening rubble blocked our path. And where was Sam?

I coughed at the smoke singeing my lungs, and shielded my face with my free arm like Sam had. It didn't help.

"This way." Maybe it wasn't a good idea to talk, but it helped me focus through the dizzying heat, and she relaxed—only slightly.

Windows and doors were in the same place on every house, and there was some kind of opening on every wall. Any direction was better than standing still. I guided Geral, both of us coughing. Only the fact that the upper level had collapsed on the other side of the house saved us from suffering worse; the smoke had somewhere to go.

I hoped Sam wasn't over there.

Our journey to the wall was unbearably hot. My eyes watered, and Geral was too heavy for me to carry, but that wouldn't stop me. We stumbled again and again.

I reminded myself—maybe out loud—that I'd endured worse, with my hands inside a sylph. But this was everywhere, and I wasn't alone. Geral counted on me to get her to safety.

The world swam with blackness. I staggered, Geral heavy

on my shoulders, but as my knees hit the ground, a cool mist bathed my face.

Someone lifted Geral away from me.

I tried to watch where they took her, but I was blind now that I'd left the too-bright house. No matter how much I blinked, my vision wouldn't work right after peering through smoke and heat. Maybe my eyes had boiled out.

Cold pressed against my face, then air. Fresh air. I inhaled as deeply as my lungs would allow, like I'd never get another clean breath again.

Strong arms encircled me, picked me up, and I was carried away from the heat and roaring fire. My skin cooled when I sat on the ground, and at last my vision fizzled toward normal. A youthful face floated before me.

"Sam?" Was that my voice sounding so wispy? I sucked on air from the mask again. Coughed. Breathed.

Sandy hair and sharp features. Cris shook his head and smiled. "Wrong admirer. Sam is over there with Stef. He got Orrin out."

Orrin had been here? My head pounded, and I tried to focus. Sam was okay. Cris had given me air. I was sitting on the hard, cold ground.

"I thought you'd be across the city by now." My voice sounded like a toad. That wasn't much of an improvement.

"I stayed to visit with Orrin and Geral. A little after I left, I heard the explosion." He gazed around the ruins. "Good thing you and Sam got here so quickly."

"Will she be okay?" I couldn't find her in the mass of people around the house. They aimed hoses at the building, spraying the same mist I'd stumbled into.

His tone was gentle, and so was the way he wiped a cloth over my face; it came away soot-black. "I don't know."

I appreciated his honesty.

The fire died, leaving only electric emergency lamps to light the ruins. Smoke still rose like giant sylph as people shouted orders, darted around. Their silhouettes were strange and long in the illumination, but I saw Councilors Deborl and Sine speaking. Arguing? I couldn't tell from where I stood.

When I lowered the mask—I'd forgotten I still held it to my face—I caught a familiar shape across the yard, sitting near a tangle of fallen and blackened pine trees. Sam.

Stef crouched over him, hands on his shoulders. I couldn't hear their conversation, but Stef glanced my way, darkness obscuring her expression.

She was in love with him. Cris probably was too. I could only think of maybe six people who wouldn't be.

Gravity dragged at me, but Cris caught my elbows and kept me from slumping over. The mask wasn't so lucky. It bounced when it hit the dirt.

The reek of smoke permeated the air, but everything seemed so quiet now that the fire was out. The roaring, blaring, consuming fire. All around, people were still gathered in groups, talking and pointing at various places on the house.

Strange that the white stone remained as if nothing had happened. I hadn't expected anything less from Janan, though. I'd seen the temple mend itself after Templedark, and other structures of white stone withstand onslaughts they shouldn't. It was wrong. Creepy.

"Can you stand up?" Cris held my shoulders.

"I don't know." But I gave it a try, climbing to my feet, using Cris's shoulder for balance. Across the yard, Sam got up, too, and started toward me, leaving Stef to trail after him. "Thank you for helping me." I was always too slow with politeness, but at least I'd remembered this time.

"Of course." Cris smiled. "We've got a lot of work to do, you especially. I can't let you go around with smoky lungs when market day is so close."

Lights shone in a mobile medical vehicle. Geral was probably in there. "I hope she and the baby are okay."

"They have a chance because of you."

I wasn't sure how that was supposed to make me feel. Good? Proud? Mostly I felt overwhelmed and exhausted.

"Ana." Sam's deep voice filled me, sweeter than smoke, sweeter than the burst of fresh air from the mask. Soot and ash stained his face and clothes.

I stepped forward into his arms, relieved just to touch him.

Warm. Solid. Real. Neither of us had gotten burned up.

He swayed, but stayed upright as my weight settled against him. "I'm so glad you're okay," he murmured into my hair. "I lost track of you in the smoke. I was worried." Hands pressed hard on the small of my back.

"Any idea what caused the explosion?" Cris asked behind me. I'd forgotten he was here.

Sam shook his head. "Let's not bother Geral about it, but Orrin is over there. We can ask if they were doing anything unusual."

"Should I walk Ana back to your house, Sam?" That was Stef. I'd forgotten she was here, too. "No need to burden her with this, and she looks like she could use some rest."

I peeled myself off Sam. "I'm fine. Besides, Stef, I'm sure your scientific mind will be more useful here than taking me home."

She looked ready to argue—probably that I was so young and shouldn't be exposed to such horrors—but just then light bloomed on the far side of the city. The ground trembled.

"Was that—" she started, but seemed incapable of completing the thought. Like it was too terrible to comprehend.

The words were ash in my mouth. "Another one."

This was not an accident.

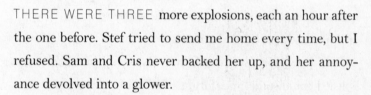

21
SMOKE

THERE WERE THREE more explosions, each an hour after the one before. Stef tried to send me home every time, but I refused. Sam and Cris never backed her up, and her annoyance devolved into a glower.

"She shouldn't be here," she told Whit. "She's too young. This will traumatize her."

I turned to watch flames die under the fire-suppressant mist. Floodlights burned across the city, and smoke billowed into the sky, so completely veiling the stars they might not exist anymore except in memory. I'd grown used to geyser steam rising at all hours, but this was nothing like that. Smoke plumed dark and angry, evidence of destruction and hatred.

We waited for the sixth explosion. Everyone wore tight faces and worry, but we stood there by the smoldering ruins of the fifth house and nothing happened.

I stared at the white shell of the house—now streaked with cinders and dust, but whole—and hated Janan. I hated him for what he did to newsouls, how he'd deceived everyone for so long, and that he'd never let anything happen to his precious white city as long as he was awake.

My hand found my knife inside my coat pocket, the cool rosewood handle smooth under my soot-darkened fingers. As I had in Menehem's laboratory, I wished for a weapon against Janan. Something that would *hurt* him.

But even if it were possible, Janan reincarnated souls who meant everything to me; I wouldn't be able to do it.

That made me hate him more.

Sam drew me homeward, into his own white shell of a house. I could sometimes forget about the exterior walls with all the parlor instruments, the honeycomb shelves, and the perfume of roses.

At some point I must have showered, because when I realized I was sitting on the sofa, tense and waiting for another explosion, my clothes were clean and my hair wet. I no longer stank of smoke and ash. A glass of juice sat on a table beside me, half drunk.

Unnerving.

Sam came downstairs, wearing nightclothes the colors of

winter forests. Hollows darkened under his eyes, and he carried weariness like chains. "It will be dawn in a couple hours."

Would the sun even shine through all that smoke? "I can't sleep. Maybe ever again."

Birdsong skittered outside, hesitant. Sam sat at the piano like he'd play accompaniment, but his hands rested on his knees, unmoving. "I know. I keep thinking what if our house is next?"

Our house. I liked that he said that, though I wished our house were his cabin in the woods, or Purple Rose Cottage. "It won't be."

He raised an eyebrow.

"I'm not pregnant."

"*Oh.*" His posture evaporated as he realized what I had: every one of the attacked homes had belonged to someone carrying.

Some had been no more than a month or two, so it wasn't obvious like with Geral. Two women had died in the explosions, and a third had miscarried. The three babies might have been newsouls. If they were oldsouls, they'd be reborn none the wiser. But newsouls . . .

Escaped Janan's hunger only to die before they were born.

Sam swore so softly I almost couldn't hear the words, but they hissed through me and left smears of despair in their wake. "Someone did this on purpose."

Of course someone had.

"No one has resorted to this kind of terror in three thousand years." He faced the nearest window, looking somewhen-else, like he always did when talking about the distant past. "Violence like this only infuriates people. They'll be reborn and take revenge again and again until they feel they've had justice."

And every death and rebirth meant another newsoul went to Janan.

"Honestly," he muttered, "it's easier to live with one another and stop fighting, no matter how much you hate someone. They're not going away. Ever." He glanced at me, eyes shadowed. "Until recently."

"I'm afraid that was the point." I crossed the floor to the piano bench. He stayed on the edge, facing away from me now, so I put my legs on either side of the bench and pressed myself behind him, my cheek on his shoulder blade, my thighs against his. "Someone wanted to send us a message."

One of his hands fell to my knee. "They attacked Geral's house first because she lives close to us. We wouldn't be able to miss it."

"I didn't even know Orrin and Geral were together."

Sam gave more of a breath than a chuckle. "He keeps quiet about his relationships. Don't feel bad that you didn't notice."

I squeezed my arms around his ribs. Comforting my stupid worries even when . . . this . . . was happening.

"Can I tell you something?" He sounded like I felt. Kind of desperate. Depressed.

"You can tell me anything." Because I wanted to know everything about him.

He threaded his fingers with mine, our hands wrapped together in delicate knots. "I used to worship Janan. We all did, long ago. And now I find out that he'd have consumed your soul if not for an experiment gone wrong."

Didn't he know I thought about that every day? Every hour since my return from the temple?

"I keep wondering how this happened. Why we get to live and newsouls get . . ." His whole body trembled against mine. I could imagine the dark, angry look in his eyes. "When we first arrived in Heart, you asked if I felt betrayed that Janan never aided us in a crisis, never protected us."

"I remember. You said you did, a little, and that you wanted to believe you were here for a purpose."

"That's right." His voice grew quiet. Distant. "And now I discover that all along our purpose has been to replace new-souls. Our purpose has been to help feed a monster."

The words made me shudder.

"I do feel betrayed," he said. The rest seemed to tumble out. "We worshipped him, and he used us. I resent the time I spent caring, even though it was forever ago, and I resent everyone who tried to shame me when I stopped. It *hurts*, this betrayal."

His confession and anguish filled me, made me want to shatter. I wanted to draw it out of him, encourage and comfort him like he always did for me. "Why did you worship him?"

"For most of us, it was Meuric's suggestion. We listened to what he said. The rest was us simply not wanting to feel alone." He sounded melancholy. "The inscription on the temple said he created us, gave us souls. It said he was responsible for our reincarnation. It said he would protect us."

"We know the reincarnation part is true," I whispered. "But it's not as if no one's ever changed written history to suit their own purposes. You told me Deborl changed and omitted things from the history books I read in Purple Rose."

Sam nodded.

"So let's go by what we know. In five thousand years, Janan never protected you?"

"He kept the walls impenetrable, but since he *is* the temple and his heartbeat runs throughout the walls, that might be him protecting himself more than anything."

I squeezed his hands. "Did he help you when you needed him?"

Sam shook his head.

"Does he love you?" I asked.

Silence.

Roses filled the parlor, evidence of love: Sam's love for me, Cris's love for his garden, and my friends' love for one another. I'd seen over and over how they demonstrated their love, and it made them giving, compassionate, and kind. Sam's love made him brave, selfless, and willing to protect me when I needed it.

Maybe Sam was thinking about the same things, because he said, "It seems love is the most important thing. Someone who doesn't love us and uses us to hurt others was never worth our devotion." He let out a long sigh, deflating. "I know now he's real, but before Templedark, I hadn't believed in Janan for thousands of years. But then, when I did, it was comforting thinking there might be some kind of power protecting us."

"There might be. It's just not Janan."

"I love your hope. You make me want to have hope, too." Sam kissed my knuckles, and exhaustion filled his tone. "Are you really all right after earlier?"

"I am. Really." Though I would never forget the heat and horror. "What will happen now? Will there be an investigation into the explosions? Will the survivors be cared for?"

Sam nodded. His damp hair brushed my skin when I lifted my face. He smelled like soap and shampoo, no traces of tonight's events.

"There will be an investigation, but it will take a long time to question so many people. It was already night when this happened, and most live alone. There will be few alibis, few reasons to believe anyone. People who've actively spoken out against newsouls will be the first suspects."

"That's a good start." It wasn't enough, though. "I doubt everyone who hates newsouls is stupid enough to blab about it before planting explosives."

Sam snorted. Had that been a dumb thing to say? I started to lean back, but he tightened his fingers around mine, keeping me pressed against his spine.

"You're right," he said. "There are people who hate newsouls but will have kept quiet until they were ready to act."

I shuddered, wondering who those people might be. "It's easier when you know who your enemies are."

"Really is."

I bit my lip, like that would keep in what I didn't want to say. Maybe I held my breath, too, and my heart slowed down, or maybe I tensed. At any rate, Sam knew I was trying not to just blurt out my every thought.

"What is it?" he asked, and I could almost hear the resigned smile.

I pressed my face against his back, though his shirt was tight against his skin so there wasn't anywhere to bury myself. "Promise you won't be upset."

He just kissed my forefinger. Not a promise.

"It"—at least I didn't have to explain what *it* was— "happened so soon after the meeting, whoever did it must have known our plan."

He was very still. A statue of a musician.

"Maybe I'm wrong. Maybe it's just a coincidence that it happened so soon after I asked for help. People have been throwing rocks and breaking into nurseries. Maybe this was their next step and it had nothing to do with tonight." I peeled off Sam, off the piano bench. He hadn't moved, but I couldn't stay still. In spite of the wretched day that wouldn't end, everything in me itched to run. To go somewhere. The grief inside me needed to escape.

I stalked around the parlor as though my anxiety might leak out from the force of my feet hitting the floor. I made the perimeter twice before Sam came to life again and began tracking my progress.

"I hope you're right," he said at last. "I hope it is just a coincidence, because the idea of one of our friends being responsible is too horrible."

My insides twisted into knots as I stopped before him. We were both exhausted and heartsore. Maybe right now wasn't the best time for this talk.

When the light shifted in the window behind him, casting him as a silhouette, he looked my age. I trailed my fingertips over the soft curves of his cheekbones, down his freshly shaven jaw, and across the thick lines of his eyebrows. At my touch, he swallowed hard, and little by little the tension drained from his shoulders and neck. He dropped back his head. His lips parted and his breath shallowed.

"I miss being outside of Heart," I said. "I want those days

in Purple Rose before the sylph came." I caressed the frown line between his eyes, how I always knew he was thinking too hard about something. Then I found the line by his mouth, a long curve from his smile.

"Me too." His hands breezed over my hips. I didn't fight the urge to lean toward him, press my body against his.

Just us, the parlor instruments, and the early morning quiet, it was easy to imagine we were the only people. No explosions, no sylph, no Janan.

My fingers came to the end of their wanderings on his forehead. I smoothed back his hair and kissed him. "Sam." A shiver ran through his body when I said his name. "Will you sleep in my room with me?"

A wicked smile flashed, and his hands dipped from my hips to my bottom to my thighs. "I'd like that."

My skin burned with his touch, even through my clothes, and I ached to discover what he might feel like without the layers of cloth between us.

Before I could suggest it, he drew away. His hands fell to his knees and the longing faded from his eyes, shifting to regret. "But I should sleep in my own bed." He spoke softly, but that didn't dampen the pain of his words.

I stood there like a moron, feeling trapped in another rejection, trapped in the memory of when I'd first arrived in Heart. We'd faced each other in the kitchen so close, so tense I'd thought he might kiss me. But he hadn't.

He stared at his hands, as though remembering the same event. "Ana." Just a breath. "I do want to, but maybe we shouldn't."

"Why?" I knew why. I'd heard why earlier.

"I . . ." Resolve steeled his voice. "It wouldn't be proper."

Proper.

"I heard your fight with Stef." My voice trembled with effort to speak softly. "The night of the masquerade, after you were arrested, Li kept saying things like that. She insisted the way we danced was inappropriate. Then Deborl said it that day outside the temple. People have said it in the market field. Have you been hearing it from friends, too?"

"Everyone has opinions."

"And why should we mind? Have I given you a reason to believe I care if other people think our relationship is inap-propriate?"

"I'm glad you're not worried what they think." He closed his eyes, expression drawn as though he'd rather be having any conversation but this one. "But have you considered that despite how you feel, this might truly be inappropriate?"

My mouth fell open.

"Stef had a point. I'm *old*, Ana." He shoved himself to his feet, all fire and passion. "It doesn't matter what I look like. The truth is that I have done so many things in other lifetimes. I don't mean composing symphonies or exploring the world beyond Range. I mean intimate two-people-alone things."

Pieces of me were unraveling. Was he *trying* to hurt me?

"I hate that." My heart thundered. I'd just wanted to be near him while we slept, and suddenly everything spun out of control, all my unspoken fears and insecurities so bright and blinding. "Every time you remind me how much older and more experienced you are—I hate that. You think I don't know?"

"I think you don't care."

"Well, I don't." I was a liar. I did care, but not nearly as much as I did other times. "I want things—whatever kind of things—to go normally. Whenever they're supposed to happen, that's when I want them to happen."

His face was stone. "That's the problem. Normally both parties know all the details. They have the experience, even if it's not with each other. This relationship is different. There's nothing normal about it. How am I supposed to know how far to go with you? How am I supposed to know when you're ready, and for what? I want to be honorable and do the right thing, but I don't know what that is."

"You could let me decide." I crossed my arms. "Aren't both people supposed to have a vote in a relationship?"

He shifted his weight, myriad expressions crossing his face before he settled back to the same stone as before. "Do you know what you'd be deciding?"

Caught. My face ached with scowling. "I'm an adult, Sam.

Nearly four years past my first quindec. You said that just last night."

He towered over me, body tense and voice sharp. "Really, Ana."

I resisted the urge to back away. "Like many things I had to figure out on my own, the books I had access to didn't specify how to do certain activities."

"So you don't know. You can't make an informed decision like that."

"You could tell me."

He massaged his forehead. "I can't even imagine how strange it would be for you to hear about it. Even thinking about how I'd explain it makes the whole thing seem a lot less fun. It might even sound scary."

"No, that isn't what I meant." I shook my head. "I meant showing me with—with *you*. Like you promised the night of the masquerade." He'd said he had a thousand things to show me, places he'd kiss me or touch me. My whole body ached with anticipation under his hands, and I'd thought he felt the same way. I said more softly, "Don't you want to?"

"*Yes.*" He sounded raw. "Yes, but I don't want to take advantage of you."

"Your stupid honor is going to make me crazy. As far as I can tell, Sam, we're going to spend the rest of our potentially short lives not doing anything more than kissing."

He looked uncertain. A crack in the stone. "You could ask Sarit?"

How could he be so clueless? "You're missing the point."

He waited.

"I should be able to count on you, but you're telling me I can't."

"Ana—"

"No. I understand this whole thing is weird. You don't know how to reconcile what has always been acceptable and what you feel is honorable in this case. I've always admired your need to do the right thing, so I appreciate it. Really."

He didn't look convinced, and it was hard to believe that less than a day ago, we'd been standing here by the piano, surrounded by roses, kissing, his hands up the back of my shirt. . . .

"We may not be able to decide whether our relationship is or isn't appropriate. We have emotions invested." I struggled to steady my voice. "But we can decide if we care about appropriateness. If you don't care, then we'll decide together what we do."

His voice was rough. "And if I do care?"

"Then I suppose nothing will ever change." Or everything would. "I don't want to be sixty and still unenlightened about these matters."

"I'm sure by then—"

"It will be appropriate?" My head buzzed with exhaustion

and sadness. "When does that happen? When do I magically become old enough for you? There will always be five thousand years between us."

"I don't know." He dropped his gaze. "I just don't. I'm sorry."

Ugh. I saw his dilemma, but that didn't change the fact that we weren't going anywhere until he made a choice. It was *our* relationship, so what other people thought shouldn't matter. "I'm going to bed."

He nodded.

Why couldn't he just be whatever I wanted, whenever I wanted? Why did things Stef said have to matter so much? Why couldn't Sam truly be eighteen—almost nineteen— like me so we didn't have to deal with any of his issues from being so *old* and my being so new? I didn't care. Usually. He shouldn't care either.

I almost asked him to reconsider my offer. Instead, I just said, "Good night," and turned away. My courage was as thin as silk, but I held it around me like armor and urged myself up the stairs, dragging the remains of my dignity.

22
ABSENCE

WHEN I GOT up a few hours later, I started coffee and took care of all the chores. I hadn't slept well—or at all—and even during a crisis, chickens and cavies needed to be fed.

Then, at the kitchen table with a cup of coffee, I closed my eyes and inhaled steam, absorbing the silence of no explosions and no fighting with Sam.

The scrape of ceramic on stone yanked me out of my peace. Sam poured coffee at the counter, his face lined with exhaustion. Just seeing him from the corner of my eye, he might have been a stranger. Even his clothes were rumpled.

I settled into a comfortable glower when he faced me.

"Do you want to see if we can talk to the survivors in the

hospital?" His voice was hoarse with no sleep. "See if they saw anyone?"

"I was already going to do that." I gulped down the rest of my coffee and stood. "Are you ready to go?"

"I guess." He combed his fingers through his hair—it didn't make much of a difference—and finished his coffee.

When we were dressed for the chilly weather, we headed toward the Councilhouse. He didn't try to make excuses for earlier this morning, which was good. He didn't even talk to me. Just as well. It left me time to focus on not paying attention to the ashy reek, or the rubble strewn around Geral's property.

Charred bits of *something* littered the road. Sam picked them up. To carry to a recycling bin, I supposed. I couldn't let him feel morally superior, so I grabbed some, too.

We dropped everything in the appropriate bins when we reached South Avenue, then turned north, and I couldn't help but see the temple. White on gray sky, though it wasn't just smoke up there now. Clouds thickened, threatening snow or sleet.

I shivered and eased my strides closer to Sam. He was nice enough to pretend not to notice.

"Tonight," I said, so he'd think my walking closer to him was about secrecy rather than comfort, "I'm going to work on translating the books. Cris said he meant to bring over the paper I gave him before, so I want to get that, too." I had the notes I'd gotten from Meuric safe in my pocket.

"Okay." Sam kept walking.

We wandered through the hospital wing of the Councilhouse until one of the medics told us where Geral and the other two survivors were being treated. I wrinkled my nose at the scent of rubbing alcohol and burned flesh—a reek too familiar to me. My hands were folded up and tucked beneath my chin before I realized.

Sam touched my back. "This way."

I flinched, but followed through double doors that led into a reception area the size of Sam's parlor, with walls of white synthetic silk sheets, pinned in place by steel shelves; the walls seemed to glow in all the light. People at the desk glanced up at our entrance, then back to their work.

"Sam. Ana." Sine approached, her gray hair pulled into a tight bun. She wore a medic's smock and gloves, and a deep frown. "Is something wrong?"

"We came to see Geral and the others," Sam said. "Do you know anything about who caused the explosions?"

"I think you mean *what* caused them." She glanced around the room; a lanky teenage girl watched us, while another man—Merton?—muttered into his SED as he vanished behind a partition. Sine spoke at a normal volume. "It was only gas leaks and corroded wires. Walk with me over here."

Sam's face was stone as he nodded, and we headed into

a hallway off the main chamber. Several curtained rooms waited on one side. Recovery rooms.

We went all the way to the end of the hall and took the last room. It was unoccupied, as were the five before it. Sine must have wanted a lot of privacy.

She motioned at the chairs around the bed. "Sit close so I don't have to yell."

Sam and I scooted our chairs toward hers.

"For now, the Council is giving the gas story." Her voice was so quiet I strained to hear. "But I assume you two have already figured out what really happened."

"Someone hates newsouls." I wanted to be sick.

"Yes." She leveled her gaze on me. "I *can* stop you from investigating this, but I won't. I know this is something you're passionate about, Ana. I want to caution you, though, before you do anything reckless."

Because someone had told her about the meeting last night? Or she just knew?

She went on. "Whoever planted those explosives is already willing to risk Council repercussions, not to mention several lifetimes of people exacting revenge. Hurting—or killing— either of you isn't going to be a problem."

"But the law about killing me—"

She shook her head. "They don't care, Ana. Any of those unborn could have been newsouls. The law protects them, too, but . . ."

"There should be better laws." I crossed my arms, and neither Sam nor Sine disagreed. "What about Lidea and Anid?"

"Wend took everything they needed to my house. Whoever is doing this won't suspect Lidea and Anid are with me, at least for a few more days. Hopefully we'll have answers by then."

"I suppose you've already questioned the survivors?" Sam asked.

She nodded. "As much as we could. Some were badly burned, and their medication is making them, ah, interesting to talk to. But Geral was asking about you, Ana. And you'll be relieved to know that, while the shock did send her into labor, she gave birth this morning. They're both fine."

"She did? They are?" I twisted in my chair like I'd be able to see through the layers of silk walls. "When can I see her?"

"Now, if you'd like. She's in the first room in this hall."

I was up and at the curtain before I realized they weren't with me. "You aren't coming?"

"We have a couple of things left to discuss," said Sam. "I'll join you shortly." He sat straight with his hands on his knees. How had they both known to stay? How had one communicated to the other there was something they wanted to talk about without me? There must have been some signal I'd missed.

I hated being new. I hated being excluded. "Okay." I shoved the curtain closed behind me, though it wasn't terribly accommodating with slamming. It swished and floated back into creepy templelike perfection.

I found Geral's room. There was nowhere to knock, so I swished the curtain around until she laughed and told me to come in.

She reclined on the bed, a swaddled baby in her arms. The medics and birthing assistants had cleaned her up, but there was a bandage on her forearm and stitches along a cut on her jaw. I should have found her sooner, before she'd gotten injured.

"Would you like to come the rest of the way in? If someone else stops by, they're going to run over you." Her smile would have been serene if not for the flinch at her cut. "I was hoping you'd visit," she said as I crossed the room.

"Oh." I tucked my hands into pockets. "I actually came to ask if you saw who blew up your house, but—"

"It was a gas leak and corroded wires."

I tipped my face downward and raised my eyebrows. Stef had used that look on Sam several times, and it always made him tell the truth.

She gave a breathy laugh and hugged the baby tighter. It was sleeping, and I couldn't tell if it was a boy or girl. "Well, no, I didn't see anyone. Neither did Orrin. Cris was there a while, but he wouldn't have hurt us."

"No, of course he wouldn't have." I stared at the wall, wishing I knew why the arsonist had chosen last night. Coincidence? My meeting?

"Would you like to see my baby?" Geral whispered, tired and hopeful and sad, and I managed to feel even worse than I already did. She'd just wanted to share her newborn, and I'd been caught up in other problems.

"Sure." I stood. "I'm sorry. Everything is just overwhelming. Who did you have?"

"Ariana." She tugged the baby's knit hat downward, though it had been just fine a second ago. "I hope you don't mind."

"Why would I?" And then: "Oh." There'd never been an Ariana. It was a new name for a newsoul. *"Oh."* The last came out perhaps more startled than I'd intended.

"I'm going to be a good mother." Defensiveness edged Geral's tone. "And you of all people should be accepting—"

"I am!" I pressed my hand to my mouth. "Sorry. I keep getting surprised. I'm as used to people being reborn as everyone else. I may not have had five thousand years for it, but it's still been my entire life." And that felt like a long time.

Her gaze flickered toward the curtain as someone entered. "It's all right. After last night, I'm nervous about how people will react to her. I already love her so much."

Why couldn't she have been my mother? Or Lidea? Aside from the fact that they were currently too young.

"I understand." I gazed at Ariana, her dark skin and silky hair. I wanted to tell her how she'd escaped Janan, how others hadn't been so lucky. Even this life where people threw rocks at newsouls—it was better than never having the chance.

And I wanted to tell her I'd do anything to protect her, because we newsouls had to stick together.

I didn't say any of that, though. Not in front of Geral and whoever else had come into the room. Sam. I recognized the sound of clothes rustling as he shifted his weight. "I was just alarmed by her name," I said at last. "But I'm honored."

"You saved her life." Geral blinked away tears.

My face burned. "Next time a newsoul is in danger, I'll send Sam. So far I've got two named after me, and he doesn't have any."

"I am a little jealous," he said from the foot of the bed. "She's beautiful, Geral. Congratulations."

We chatted a little more, and then it was time to go. "Keep her safe," I whispered as I hugged Geral. "Don't trust anyone."

Sam and I finished speaking with the other two survivors, but they knew even less than Geral. We left the Councilhouse and sat on a market field bench as the sun dipped toward the west. Not that it made much of a difference. The clouds from this morning had thickened, and delicate snowflakes spiraled toward the ground. I caught one on my mitten, but it melted.

"How do you feel about it?"

I couldn't tell if Sam was asking about the snowflake or the direction the planet rotated, so I just raised my eyebrows and waited for him to figure out why I wasn't responding.

"Ariana. Anid. People naming newsouls after you."

The temple loomed behind me, already lit with shifting patterns: signs of the evil entity inside. He'd wanted to consume us, the newsouls. So we had that in common already. Now our names. "It doesn't matter how I feel about it."

"Of course it does."

If how I felt about anything mattered, why didn't he tell me what he and Sine had been so secretive about? He could have asked how I felt about not understanding the sylph, or not having had a chance to study the temple books.

Instead, he wanted to know how I felt about newsouls being named after me?

"I think a lot of people whose names sound like Ana are going to consider changing them."

"So as not to be associated with newsouls?" He sipped from a bottle of water like he didn't really care about my answer. I wanted to rip it from him and hurl it across the market field.

There were people out, though. Councilors loitered on the steps—Deborl kept glancing at me—and a couple holding hands walked by. One muttered, "Sylph lover," and probably wished she had a rock to hurl.

A trio of children caught snowflakes on their tongues; I'd done the same thing when I was that age, but it was surprising to see anyone else do it. These children were five thousand years old. A characteristic of their physical age, perhaps, like people currently teenagers were attracted to other teenagers.

I didn't look at Sam as I spoke. "We should speak to everyone who was at the meeting last night. Everyone who knew our plans. Not to accuse them of anything. Just— Just to see if they have any ideas."

Sam capped his water and checked the time on his SED. "Where first?"

I hadn't expected it to be that easy. Maybe he knew better than to argue with me. "Let's start on the far side of the city and work our way home."

"That could take a while." Ah, there was the disapproval I'd been waiting for.

"Did you have plans this evening?" I wanted to work on the temple books, but I could do that after he went to bed.

He glanced at the sky, snow dropping harder now, and shrugged. "Best start with Cris. He'll be out covering the plants, if he hasn't done it already."

Sam set a brisk pace, leaving no breath for talk. No problem. I lengthened my strides, but still had to take two for his every one. Also no problem. It helped stave off the cold.

Darkness loomed by the time we reached Cris's house, though in the temple light, and light from our SEDs, it was easy to see nothing had been covered or moved into greenhouses like Sam had predicted. Nor could we hear Cris's movements.

Most flowering plants had closed themselves for winter, but they were still vulnerable to the cold; I'd lost several roses at Purple Rose Cottage before I realized they needed protection, just like people.

"Where is he?" Sam marched down the path and headed toward one of the greenhouses. "Check the other one. If he's not there, we'll look inside."

I almost snapped at him for telling me what to do, but the last thing we needed was another argument. Fuming silently, I did as ordered.

Inside the greenhouse, warmth and humidity washed over me, a sudden and unpleasant shift from the crispness outside. "Cris?"

There was no response as I walked between the rows of orchids and other flowers I didn't recognize. This was the second greenhouse, the one I hadn't been inside yet; I wished Cris were here to tell me what all these flowers were.

I turned off the light and shut the door behind me, and met Sam on the front steps, picking the lock. Why did anyone bother to lock things?

He ushered me in first, out of the falling snow. "I called his SED. He didn't answer."

"He might have gone back to Purple Rose Cottage to get those roses. He said he might." I stepped farther into the cluttered house. "Cris?" I yelled again. Only the eerie quiet answered, thickened by the sheet of white forming outside. If he'd gone to Purple Rose, surely he would have covered his garden here first.

Plants and journals filled the parlor and all connecting rooms I could see. Shelves held pots and trays of seeds. Heat lamps stood in two corners, though I couldn't tell what they warmed. It was practically another greenhouse, though some of these plants looked edible. The whole place smelled green and loamy and floral.

I followed Sam into the kitchen. "What's that?"

He was in the process of lifting a tray of seedlings and picking out a folded sheet of paper from beneath it. "This is yours."

How could he tell? "Yeah, he said he had a few thoughts."

The paper was damp and smudged with soil, but Sam carefully unfolded it on the tabletop to reveal the list I'd given Cris after our gardening lesson. "Look." He brushed away dirt.

I pressed my shoulder against his and peered at the new lines on the page. "'Gate or portal? Arch?'" The symbol next to Cris's guesses did look like an archway, but only if I tilted my head.

"That seems reasonable enough."

Hmming, I swept more dirt aside. Damp grains stuck to my fingers. "I remember this one." I tapped a symbol that was a pair of vertical wavy lines, thick slashes between them like shading. "'Shadow. Darkness. Nighttime.' I was looking at it the wrong way."

"How do you mean?"

Thoughts snapped, clicked together like the first time I'd understood a waltz had three beats, not four. Suddenly it made *sense*.

I bounced on my toes. "I get it!"

Sam put on his most expectant look. "The writing?"

"No, why paper cuts hurt worse than knife wounds." I rolled my eyes. "Of course I meant the writing."

"All right. I don't get it."

I made my fingers like a spider on the paper and turned it around and around. "This is what I was doing when I was trying to read the spiral. Turning the book upside down when I reached the top of the spiral. That's also how I copied the symbols, like this one." I pointed at the one Cris had marked "gate."

"But?"

"Why would anyone write like that in something as unwieldy as a book? They'd spend all their reading time turning the book around and getting dizzy. This symbol"— again I pointed at the gate symbol—"was on the side of the spiral when I copied it. That's why it's sideways now."

Understanding bloomed on Sam's face. "So you read in a

spiral, but all the symbols are oriented the same, no matter their location."

"Exactly." I bounced again, and Sam twitched a smile. "I get it! I love that feeling. I want to go read all the books right now."

He stared at me like I'd grown a second set of eyes. "You said lo—" His mouth made a line as he looked away. "Well, Cris isn't here. Shall we try the next person?"

As soon as he spoke, I halted mid-bounce. I'd said *love*. Out loud. Did I mean it? Did he expect me to say it to him now? There was a huge difference between loving a feeling or event—and loving a person.

I felt like a whirlwind, with all my thoughts and emotions. Or maybe they were whirlwinds, and I was just a butterfly or blue rose.

"Sure." Trying—and failing—to pretend like nothing happened, I shook the rest of the soil off the paper and put it in my pocket. Cris had left only a few guesses, and they might be wrong, but they'd be good places to start.

"Whit is next." He led me through the maze of potted plants and out the door. Snow fell thicker, a solid white coat. "I don't think the weather will let up any time soon. We may have to quit early, before it gets too difficult to walk. Home is on the other side of the city."

As we emerged onto the road again, I looked southwest

toward our house, but there was only dark and snow. And the temple light making a million flakes shimmer as they fell.

The dark streets remained empty, our passage the only sound. I wished we were at home having music lessons, because playing in a group last night had given me ideas. And music was far less hurtful than thinking about the explosions, or our argument.

Cold swirled and made me shiver as we passed by a white shell, which had once been someone's house. Now the occupant was gone, lost to Templedark. Someone had cleared away the debris from outbuildings. I wondered if there was anything left inside, or if the darksoul's belongings would stay there until they rotted—a memory of someone loved and lost.

We kept walking. The silence and weight of history drowned me.

"What happened between you and Cris?" My words turned into mist, barely visible in the temple light.

"It's nothing." Roughness edged Sam's voice.

I knew better than to push, but— "I don't think it was nothing to him. I see the way you are together, and the way he looks at you."

I didn't think he was going to say anything at first, but then: "It was two lifetimes ago." He had that somewhen-else tone again. Good memories or bad? Suddenly I wished I hadn't asked. "Cris was working on the roses, and I was composing a nocturne about them, so I asked to stay with her a while and study how they grew, how she cared for them."

Sam had lived in Purple Rose Cottage? With Cris? I tried to imagine I'd always felt his presence there, even before I became aware of music and what it meant to me. "What happened?"

"It was fine. I went between there and my cabin, learned more about roses than I thought possible, and after a while, we grew to appreciate each other's company—more than I want to talk to you about."

"More than I want to hear about, I'm sure." I wanted to pretend he was really only eighteen and everything he was telling me had actually happened to someone else. I wanted to pretend he'd only ever loved me. "The song you composed—"

"Songs have words. You can't use 'song' for everything."

I smiled. "Your *song* ended up being a serenade? For Cris?"

He nodded, his movement barely discernible in the darkness. "We played it as a duet. I'd mostly forgotten about it."

Would he forget about the waltz he'd written for me? Most nights, I fell asleep listening to it on my SED. It wasn't as good as hearing Sam play it on the piano for the first time, but it always made me happy, made me remember the evening I'd discovered he wasn't just Sam, he was *Dossam*, the musician.

Oblivious to the way my heart tied itself into knots, he continued. "After that, it was my fault. We wanted different things, we argued, and she told me not to come back to the cottage until I was less selfish. So I left. I could have stayed and tried to work things out, or find a compromise, but I didn't. By the time I was reincarnated, I realized I regretted my decision."

"What did you fight over?"

He glanced at me and shook his head. "I don't— I don't want to talk about that."

It must have been huge. Dedication-of-souls huge? What else could drive them apart if they still looked at each other awkwardly, hopefully? I couldn't forget my first morning in Sam's house, when Stef had whispered, *Don't let him break your heart, sweetie. He never settles.*

Now I knew part of that was because she loved him. Cris loved him. He hadn't stayed with either of them.

And did I love him? The word still made me choke. Even more frightening was the sudden understanding that my feelings for him—whatever they were—might be bigger than his feelings for me. I didn't want to end up like Stef and Cris, pining lifetimes later.

Cold sapped moisture from my skin. I licked my lips and ducked into my scarf. "So after a while," I said, "you regretted the decision not to find a way to work it out?"

He nodded and guided me around a corner. Snow built

up in yards and on trees, reflecting temple light enough to illuminate our path. "I've lived long enough to know there are things worth regretting, but there's nothing you can do to change the past. And yet, sometimes it works out anyway, in ways you don't expect."

Did he mean me? I couldn't bring myself to ask. The things I wanted to say and do but didn't know how—they felt like a wall between us. "Do you still regret it? Whatever it was you couldn't agree on?"

"I regret that I hurt her so badly. And that we didn't speak for a hundred years because of it. By the time he presented the roses and no one thought they were blue—that was both of our last generations—I felt like saying anything would just make it worse for both of us."

My face did something between a smile and a grimace. "I hate admitting when I'm wrong, too."

Sam pulled out his SED. The glow shone on his frown, and the line between his eyes. After a moment's hesitation, he tapped the screen a few times and pressed the device to his ear.

I blinked away light and let my eyes adjust to the darkness once more. "I'm worried we haven't heard from him. Even more worried he didn't care for his garden."

"Me too." Sam replaced the SED in his pocket. "After the blue rose challenge was first issued, Cris packed up everything and built his cottage so he could work without everyone watching and criticizing his progress.

"One spring, he came back to Heart for supplies. It had been an especially unfriendly winter, but it was warm when he set out. Of course, as soon as he got home, a blizzard came through. He'd left his plants ready for spring, so they were still delicate. As soon as he realized how bad the weather was going to get, he turned his horse around. He made the entire trip in a day and a half and saved all his roses at the last minute. Didn't lose even a leaf."

That sounded like the Cris I sort of knew, and solidified my worry. Had something happened to him?

"There." Sam pointed to a glow ahead. "Whit's home, at least."

It was almost a relief to go back to thinking about explosions. Thinking about Sam's long history of one-sided relationships— My heart couldn't take it.

23
FREEZE

INSIDE WHIT'S HOUSE, warmth prickled across my face as I unwrapped my scarf and pulled off my coat. I'd just have to put them on again, but I didn't want to risk sweating inside and then freezing outside later.

"We were curious if you'd heard anything about the explosions last night." Sam pocketed his mittens. His cheeks were flushed dark with chill.

"Just what everyone was told. I saw Jac's house go up last night." He glanced at me, his expression somber. "She was on our list of people to speak with. So were most of the other victims."

"All of them were," I said, "but I didn't bring up a couple last night because only a few people were supposed to know."

Sarit had told me privately she'd talk to them.

"How did you know, then?" He cocked his head.

I shrugged and fiddled with my mittens. "Sometimes people just tell me things. I don't know why." Mostly a lie. People told Sarit, and Sarit told me because she didn't think it was fair if I didn't know just as much gossip as everyone else.

"I see." Whit sat on the arm of his sofa, a monstrosity of faded gray and orange fabric that dominated the room. The rest was all bookcases and what looked like old board games on a long table. "I wish I had answers for you, but I came right here after the meeting. I walked part of the way with Lorin and Armande, but eventually we did have to go our separate paths. Orrin stayed behind to visit Geral. Cris, too."

I nodded. "Have you seen Cris today?"

Whit stared through a bookcase. "No, but that doesn't mean anything. People often go days or weeks without seeing even close friends."

That sounded crazy and lonely to me. I wanted to see my friends all the time. But maybe friendship was different when you'd been at it five thousand years.

"He isn't home, and all his plants are uncovered." Sam looked worried again. "We were just there."

"Well, that's a bad sign." Whit scowled.

"To put it mildly." Sam didn't smile. "I was just telling Ana about the time he raced back to Purple Rose Cottage to beat the frost."

"Cris would do anything for those plants." Whit shook his head, a fond smile tugging at his mouth. Then it dropped, like he remembered Cris was missing. "I'll call a few of his friends. Maybe they know something."

"It's strange," I said, "that the explosions would happen just after the meeting. It could be coincidence, but . . ."

Whit shook his head. "I can't imagine anyone in that crowd doing something like that. They're all good people. You chose well."

The compliment drifted by. I'd chosen well, but somehow, people had still been hurt. I should have done something different. Something *better.* "The Council is telling everyone it was gas leaks and corroded wires. They should be putting all the pregnant women somewhere safe."

"Keeping them together makes them an easy target," Whit said.

"Then not together. There are lots of places in Heart that aren't being used right now."

"Don't take this the wrong way, Ana, but it's unlikely anyone on the Council would tell you what they have planned. They might very well be doing exactly what you've suggested, but the fewer people who know the details, the safer everyone will be." Whit leaned on a table, near a board game with tricolored tiles and pieces shaped like horses in various stages of rearing or running. "I wish I could give you answers."

"What about Deborl?" I asked.

Whit lowered his voice. "He's a Councilor."

"Who hates newsouls." Maybe I didn't know Deborl well, but I knew enough about him and his choice of friends. Merton had attacked me, spoken out against me, said those horrible things after Anid was born. And Deborl hadn't seemed to care when someone attacked me in the market field. "Do you think anyone might have let it slip to Deborl—"

"That fast?" Whit shook his head. "Everyone was at Sam's for a long time after the discussion. No one left early, right? No one had time to speak to anyone, accidentally reveal our plans, and then the second person go out and set explosives. There just wasn't time."

How long did it take to set up an explosive and get away? Or not get away, if it was Deborl? He'd been at Geral's. "SED messages."

Neither Sam nor Whit argued with that possibility.

"What are you trying to prove?" Red veined Whit's eyes; I was upsetting him. "Do you want someone to have betrayed us? Why are you pushing so hard?"

"Someone has to." My throat tightened, making my voice pinched and desperate. "I hate the idea of someone betraying us, but I swore I'd protect newsouls to the best of my ability. I have to."

Both men stayed silent, just watching me like I might burst.

At last, Whit spoke softly. "Would it be easier if one of our friends were somehow responsible for this?"

"Easier than watching more newsouls die." I swallowed hard. "Easier than not being able to do anything at all."

Whit glanced at Sam, something passing between them, and then Sam touched my elbow. "We'd better go."

I wanted to apologize to Whit, but I wasn't sure what it'd be an apology for. Instead, I thanked him for his time as I pulled on all my warm clothes again. Sam and I headed out.

"I can't protect newsouls from Janan." My eyes stung with tears and cold. "I can't pull them out of the temple and bring them to life, no matter how much I wish I could. But I *should* at least be able to protect the ones who escaped. I *should* be able to protect them from *people.*"

Who was I kidding? I could barely protect myself.

My hand fell on my tiny knife, and I squeezed it until my knuckles burned. Not much protection.

"Let's go." Sam sounded like he didn't know how to respond to my confession. I didn't blame him. I wouldn't have known, either.

Before, snow had left a white sheet on the ground; now it coated cobblestones like a blanket.

"I think we should go home," Sam said, linking his arm with mine. I wasn't ready for this kind of closeness, but he knew his way around the city in the dark. I tightened my arm with his.

"But we need to speak to everyone."

"Not tonight."

"And if there are more explosions? I won't be able to live with myself if another newsoul dies because we stopped just short of catching this person." There was no wind and the snow fell in silence, but my voice still rose as if we stood in the middle of a blizzard. Icy air snaked inside my clothes, making me tremble.

"Ana, you're shivering already, and we haven't been out but two minutes. How many times do you expect me to keep you from frostbite or hypothermia?" He brought his face so close to mine I could feel the heat of his words. His skin. "You enjoy making me worry, don't you?"

"No, I hate it." There wasn't much vehemence, though. "I want to do the right thing."

"Sometimes"—he tugged me closer to him—"that means not freezing your fingers off. We still have tomorrow. Anything that happens between now and then is not your fault. Let's go home."

"Fine." I hated when he was right. Snow was piling up; if we waited too long, getting home would be more of a challenge than either of us could handle, especially on empty stomachs. "But first thing tomorrow, we're either going to see people, or be making a lot of calls."

He glanced toward the sky, though it was just dark with

swirls of snow. "Calls, unless this lets up. Which I doubt."

I almost asked how he knew, but right. He was five thousand years old. He could probably tell by the smell or the size of snowflakes.

Our trek back to the southwestern residential quarter was long and cold and slow. We passed the temple—Sam had somehow maneuvered so he walked between the tower and me—and still had a long way to go when the wind kicked up. What had been a beautiful, if annoyingly timed, snowfall became rough and stinging.

Snow flew horizontally down South Avenue. It howled like a sylph as it cut through narrow places in the industrial quarter. Trees whipped in a frenzy. Sharp wind scoured the cobblestones clear, and if not for Sam, it might have carried me off, too. I was a rose petal in a snowstorm.

Drifts stood knee-high against buildings, though Sam managed to find walkable paths. I held tight to him, wishing we were already home. My legs ached with cold and fighting the wind. My muscles burned with exertion, and it felt like I should be sweating, but frigid air stole the ability. It was hard to breathe.

Once we reached our street, thick conifers buffered us from the wind. The night was black and snow. My eyes burned. Every bit of me was freezing, even inside my wool coat and mittens.

"Just a little farther." Sam drew me to our walkway, where more evergreens sheltered us from the screaming wind. He breathed hard, too.

Finally, we reached the house, and Sam's mitten slipped on the doorknob as he spoke. "I wanted to ask you something. You've been talking about making your own decisions, wanting to do things for yourself." He tried the knob again, but snow and wool slid across each other.

"And?" I scrubbed my mittens on my coat and grasped the knob, a dim shape in the glow from the window. It turned.

"Do you want your own house? Li's or Ciana's?" His words tumbled over one another as the door swung open. "I'm sure Sine could convince the Council if you did."

I felt like I had a mouthful of snow as I stared up at him. Both houses were across the city, in the northeastern residential quarter. Had he changed his mind? Decided he loved Stef or Cris more?

Maybe remembering why he and Cris had separated made him realize the same thing would happen with me.

Or— I'd probably gone too far, ruining things for him all the time. The Council, the talk with Whit, the way I'd dragged him into my research of sylph and Menehem's machine. Nothing had gone right for him since he'd found me in Rangedge Lake.

How was I supposed to respond? Say yes, I wanted to leave? I didn't. I wanted to stay, because even when I was mad at him, I still liked being with him. But if I said I didn't want to leave, he'd say okay whether or not he really meant it. And I'd keep ruining things for him. There was no right answer.

Sam wasn't even looking at me as I stood there in the doorway like an idiot. He'd dropped my arm and taken one step into the parlor, and he didn't move.

I shuffled the rest of the way in and edged around him. If I was going to cry, I'd at least do it where my tears wouldn't freeze on my eyes. The door slammed behind me, leaving us in silence. "I don't understand," I whispered at last.

"Me neither," he murmured. He wore a stricken expression. But *he'd* been the one to suggest it.

No, that wasn't why he was upset. I blinked through the tears blurring my vision. The parlor was different.

Destroyed.

Every instrument had been completely demolished.

24
FADE

"NO." SAM DROPPED to the floor with a thump, staring confusedly at the wreckage. He gathered up bits of something now unidentifiable and turned it over in his hands, looking lost. His agony might kill me.

Low light illuminated the parlor, golden on the hardwood floor, braided rugs, honeycomb shelves between here and the kitchen.

Every time I thought I was free from the horror, though, my eyes were drawn back to the splintered maple wood and shattered ivory keys strewn about the parlor. Ebony keys dashed into slivers. Snapped wires curled on themselves as though trying to hide. Hammers and levers and tuning pins, often overlooked pieces that made the music happen. He'd wanted me to understand them while learning to play the piano, understand their true importance.

Here they were. On the floor.

Then, my eyes acknowledged a twisted length of silver that wasn't part of the piano. Sam's flute, its keys stripped off, leaving gaping black holes across its body.

Cracked pronghorn bones, shredded osprey feathers. Heavy curves of carved wood lay scattered across the floor with harp strings hanging on like cut ligaments. The corpse of a violin rested at my feet, bow broken in half.

I stepped over it, careful not to damage it further. As if that mattered. Glass crunched under my shoes, and I winced, but Sam didn't notice. He stayed by the door, staring as though dead.

Centuries' worth of instruments lay destroyed on the floor.

Blue rose petals were scattered like drops of paint. Their stems and stamens dripped from vases and off shelves. Only the Phoenix roses had been left unharmed.

I scanned the parlor like there might be something left, but even the careful stacks of cases had been demolished, and the walls raided. Some of the carved shelves hung at awkward angles.

Dreading what I'd find, I crossed the battlefield and checked the kitchen, but everything was eerily normal. I could almost hear echoes of mocking laughter.

Sam didn't look at me as I stepped around a crushed sheet

of maple, remnants of the piano lid. I tried not to look at him, either, but it was hard to ignore the way he shook his head, muttering to himself. Then, a wild darkness in his eyes, he hurled a length of metal at the wall. It clattered against the wooden shelves, bringing a cascade of rose petals.

Heart breaking for him, I climbed the stairs to check for more damage or anything missing, but it was hard to see what was missing when it wasn't there.

The rooms between our bedrooms held the oldest surviving instruments, sealed in airtight containers to slow decay. They appeared untouched, and so did the workroom and library of sheet music, recordings, and notes on how all his instruments had been constructed.

The harp in his bedroom stood whole. It wasn't much, but it might help, if only I could get him up here to see it. My bedroom looked the same as it had earlier, but I checked all my hiding places anyway.

The books I'd stolen from the temple were missing. So was Menehem's sylph research.

First the temple key. Now the books and research. They had everything.

Almost. They didn't have the translations I'd gotten from Meuric and Cris; those were still in my coat.

My fingers felt like ice as I dialed Sine and told her about the break-in. My voice was too calm, as though my body did all these things on its own now.

"I'm sorry, Ana," Sine said. "Do you want me to send someone over to help clean?"

Outside, the wind howled. Snow pattered on the window. "No." I stared at the empty hiding places and touched the pocket where I used to keep the key. "You aren't going to like this, but can you have someone watch Deborl and Merton?" I wished I knew the name of the guy who'd stolen the key, but I couldn't even remember what he looked like, besides big and scary.

"Deborl and Merton? You don't think they'd—"

"I think they both hate me. I can't prove they've done any-thing, but—" My voice broke. "Please, Sine."

"All right." Resigned, she hung up.

I put my SED back in my pocket, feeling defeated. They'd taken everything.

Downstairs, the front door stood ajar, and snow dusted the floor. Sam was nowhere in sight.

I leapt off the last few steps and hurtled outside. Snow and darkness veiled the night, but a black shape marched down the walkway.

"Sam!"

He didn't stop.

I raced after him, steps heavy with cold and snow, and caught him just as he turned onto the road. "Sam!" Without thinking, I grabbed his arm.

He spun, and his palm landed on my chest—

There was no force behind the almost-blow. His muscles

tensed under my hands as he must have realized who'd run after him. "Ana." Wind captured my name and carried it far away.

"Where are you going?" Only faint light came from the house; I couldn't see his face, and the cold made me shiver so hard I might fall apart.

"I'm going to find who did this. I'm going to hurt them." That wasn't his voice at all. In all the time I'd known him, he'd never sounded so *broken*. "They— My instruments. Everything I've worked for."

"I know." Even in the dark, my hands could find his face, just as they could find piano keys without looking. "Do you know who did this?"

He shook his head; his skin was icy under my palms, and all the rage was burning out. "I have to go. I'll find someone."

"Come inside."

"I have to find—"

"No, Sam. Not right now." We'd both freeze if we didn't get in soon; already, shivers racked through me, and I could barely speak through the cold. "Let's go inside."

Head dropped, he gathered me into a tight, uncomfortable hug. He shivered, too. Or wept. I couldn't tell, except he spoke the same muffled words over and over. "They're gone. I can't believe they're gone."

I had no words of comfort. There was no way to fix this, so I held still and let his grief wash over me in torrents.

298

Not soon enough, we went back inside and shut the door.

"Let's get your coat off." My words hissed harsh and loud in the too-silent room. I peeled off his gloves and hat and dropped them into a basket, then helped with the buttons and zippers on his coat. Our snow-crusted shoelaces were almost impossible with the burn of ice, but we managed.

His focus drifted to the piano as we reached the stairs, and he was silent as I guided him to his bedroom. There, he collapsed by his pillows, face streaked with sorrow.

I sat beside him and held his hands, warming them, wishing for anything but this. His instruments hadn't been just one lifetime's work, but many. I wondered if that made him feel like none of those lives had happened now.

After a minute, he leaned his head on mine. "Who would do this?" His tone was hollow, hopeless.

I didn't voice my suspicions. It wouldn't help. "What do you need right now?" I grimaced. He probably needed his instruments, and for me not to ask stupid questions.

He sighed and looked at the ceiling, misery making lines around his eyes and mouth. Cold still stained his skin red, and we both needed hot showers to warm our insides, but I couldn't see Sam caring right now.

"I don't know." He closed his eyes when I stroked his face. His skin was cold, but he didn't respond to my touch. "I don't think there's anything."

"Okay." I'd find warmer blankets, at least. I wanted to hold him, share heat, but I couldn't forget what he'd asked me on the doorstep. Did I want to leave? "Everything in the library and workroom is fine, including construction notes. I'll start cleaning, but is there anything you need me to save to help you rebuild?"

"Build new instruments?" He made it sound like the most horrible thing.

"I assumed you'd want to."

"Yeah. I guess. I hadn't thought that far ahead." His breath came raspy, and I couldn't imagine rebuilding lifetimes of instruments, either. But I didn't want to just leave everything where it was, in case he came downstairs. "The ivory," he said at last. "It's from far away, and it's hard to get more. But only if the pieces look like they're worth gluing together."

He told me a few more things, then let me help him lie down. I stacked blankets on top of him, wool and silk and bison fur, and went downstairs to heat soup and tea. When I brought them up on a tray, I forced several good sips into him before leaving the room. If I had just lost a thousand years of work, I would want to be alone, not awkwardly trying to accept someone's comfort when there was no way they could understand the chasm inside.

In the parlor, I picked up a few pieces of ivory, but most looked useless. Little was salvageable. Either the intruder knew exactly what to destroy, or had just decided to smash anything that looked important. Even the steel frame had been heated and melted so it would never be useful again.

Sam's flute was a wreck of silver. I hugged the remains to my chest, and blue petals floated out of the tube. Whoever had destroyed it had thought it was my new one. They couldn't tell the difference.

It was likely the instruments had been distractions, which was even more upsetting. But the books and diaries were gone. How long until they discovered Menehem's lab? How long until they discovered I'd been there?

The Council had suspected I'd been given Menehem's research, but no one should have known about the temple books.

No one *should* have known, but someone did.

I worked until my muscles clenched and sleep threatened every time I blinked. Since I couldn't move things outside right now, I set them by the door, a blanket beneath to keep from further damaging the floor.

Too worn to go upstairs, I dropped myself onto the sofa and woke when dawn speared my eyes from a crack in the shutters.

Outside, the snow was piled as high as my knees, and though the sun shone, more clouds huddled over the horizon, barely visible around trees and the immense city wall.

My lungs ached as I lugged broken instruments outside; when the snow thawed, maybe Armande or Orrin would help me separate materials for recycling. But now, I just needed them out of the house. If the sight of them hurt my heart, Sam's must be shattered.

To keep him busy for a while, I brought up more tea and soup. The other mug and bowl were only half-empty, but that was better than nothing.

"You should shower." I sat next to him on the bed. "You stink." As if I didn't smell like sweat, too.

"Doesn't matter." That wasn't Sam's voice. At least not the Sam I knew. Too rough, shredded into black ribbons. "It's all gone."

I wanted to touch him, hug him close, but my muscles wouldn't budge when I tried. "Finish your food and shower. I'll come back up in a little while."

Though Stef's house was usually only a five-minute walk, it took longer in the snow, and I was shivering when I arrived. Her place had the same outbuildings and snow-frosted fruit trees as Sam's, but was sparser, as she didn't garden or keep animals herself but helped tend Sam's in exchange for a share.

I took the steps two at a time and banged on the door.

Wind rattled evergreens, making a loose board on a shed bang in a staccato tempo. Otherwise, the place was silent, waiting for more snow.

Either she wasn't home, or she was avoiding me after the fight she'd had with Sam. I bit my lip and tried the doorknob. It turned.

I'd only been in her house a few times. When it was her turn for giving me lessons, she hadn't wanted to lug over the equipment for teaching basic machine repair; we'd started with water pumps and ended with solar panels. Mostly she went to Sam's if they wanted to visit.

Before I lost my nerve, I pulled open the door and stepped inside and stomped snow from my boots. Sunlight streamed through the parlor windows, glowing across the hardwood floor, landing on the small piano pressed against one wall. While Sam's walls were delicate shelves, most of Stef's were made of bookcases stuffed with notes and diagrams on fascinating subjects like automatic recycling machines.

"Stef?" I slipped around the chairs and sofa, with faded, patched upholstery and blankets thrown across the backs. She had more rooms on the first floor than Sam, most of them filled with inventions in various stages of completion. The stairs were hidden away in a corner, leading to the equally packed second story.

Floorboards creaked under my weight. I listened for any noises other than my own—nothing—and crept around the house, finding a library, a washroom, and a bedroom. Like Sam, she was usually male, but she didn't keep separate bedrooms for male and female incarnations. She just tossed her extra things in trunks for a lifetime, so now her bedroom was filled with dresses.

I started to leave, but a familiar photograph caught my

attention. Hating myself for the intrusion, I looked closer. The photo I'd recognized was of two men, their arms slung around each other's shoulders, both smiling. That was Sam and Stef in their previous lifetimes. Other photos on the shelf were new to me, but I recognized some of Sam's previous incarnations. Sometimes he was alone, but most of the time he was with another person. Stef, I assumed.

Next to the photos rested a stack of papers: letters in Sam's handwriting, written while he was on trips and saved up until he returned to Heart to deliver them. I skimmed only a couple of them, loathing myself as I did because they were private, but they only talked about places he was going and things he saw that she might like.

There were a lot of them.

The last photograph was of the Sam I knew, sly smile and dark, messy hair. I recognized the shirt, too; I'd helped him choose it during a summer market day. For a moment, I thought she must have taken it while I was trapped inside the temple. Surprising that he let her, because he hated being photographed. But his head was turned and one arm was outstretched. He held a smaller hand in his. Mine. My hand was the only part of me in the picture.

I stepped away.

Half of me expected Stef to appear in the hallway and demand to know what I was doing, but the house remained quiet. Feeling confused and betrayed and jealous, I left the room.

I'd known they had history. I'd even seen photos from previous lifetimes where he was kissing someone. It bothered me, but sometimes I could imagine those Sams weren't *my* Sam. Those had been older, occasionally female, sometimes overweight or too skinny. I could find pieces of my Sam in all of them, but I could trick myself when it hurt.

She loved him. I couldn't imagine why anyone wouldn't. It was the intensity of her feelings I hadn't anticipated.

"How hurt does someone need to be to do something desperate?" I whispered, then felt sick. Stef would never hurt Sam like that. She might antagonize him, try to convince him that our relationship was improper. But she would never destroy what Sam loved most. Never.

"I'm sorry," I said, even though she wasn't here to hear it. It had been a petty, jealous thought, and I scrubbed my hands over my face as though I could wipe it away.

Time to go home. I went outside, finding sunlight had dimmed as gray clouds covered the sky, ready to drop more snow.

I shivered with winter chill by the time I opened the door to Sam's house again. The parlor was still a wreck, and the upstairs was quiet. Hopefully he was sleeping.

Fending off tears, I found a large bin and continued

throwing away unsalvageable pieces of Sam's instruments. Any time the bin got heavy, I carried it outside and dumped it out with the rest.

When I couldn't stand any more, I climbed upstairs to shower and change into something not covered in sweat and dirt and splintered memories of a hundred broken instruments. Outside, snow fell heavy and white and wet.

It was almost night by the time I called Stef's SED. No answer. Nothing from Cris, either. Where could they be? Worry gnawed deeper; I tried Sarit.

"Hey, Ana."

"Thank goodness." I slumped to the sofa, relief like a waterfall through me. "You're there."

"Yeah, freezing my tail off. Cris didn't answer his door yesterday morning, and there weren't enough blue roses in the greenhouse. I'm on my way to Purple Rose to see if I can salvage any from there. You owe me. A hundred concerts, at least. Write a song for me while you're at it, cricket."

I shook my head, even though she couldn't see me. "With this snow, they're probably already gone. Just come home." She might have been my best friend, but she was also crazy.

"No way. I'm getting those roses for you. I'll keep them alive with my sunny personality."

"You're insane." I stared around the wreck of a parlor and tried to breathe right. "I'm glad I can get hold of you, though. Stef and Cris aren't answering. They're not at home."

"Cris still isn't there?" Worry crept into her words.

"His garden is collecting snow. And when Sam and I came back—" My voice caught. I tried again. "Sarit, someone destroyed the instruments. All of them."

"Oh." Her voice softened, deepened. "Oh, Ana. Your flute too?"

"No." I took a shaky breath. "It was in the workroom. Lorin accidentally popped a wire out, and Sam was going to show me how to fix it."

"But everything in the parlor . . ."

I gazed at a length of steel I hadn't been able to pick up. "Even the piano. Especially the piano." The words choked me, and my throat tightened with tears.

She didn't speak.

"And you know about the explosions, right?" When I closed my eyes, I could still see the fire, the smoke. I could still feel Geral's weight in my arms. "They're telling me to stop."

"How do they know what you're doing?" she asked.

"I don't know." I squeezed the SED, wishing I could tell her about the books, the key, the research—everything. I could tell her about the fight Sam and I had, and that he'd asked if I wanted to leave, but not right now. Not when she was so far away. "I wish you were here," I whispered into the SED.

"Me too." She hesitated. "You aren't going to give up, are you?"

"No." I clenched my jaw. "No, they can tell me to stop, but I won't. I'm not giving up."

"Good." She sighed, and a minute shivered past. "I've been riding hard to Purple Rose. The road has been snowy, but fine. A drone will come through if it gets bad."

"So you'll be home soon?"

"Yeah, a few more days. This horse is going to hate me, though." Something clanked in the background. "I've been calling my people. I checked in with Lidea and Moriah, and they've been in touch with their groups. Everyone is doing their part. You just get ready for yours and don't worry about the rest of us."

"That's hard to do with Cris and Stef missing." With explosions, people destroying parlors, and nursery break-ins, anything could have happened.

"I'll call their lists. It's fine, Ana. I'm sure they'll turn up soon." She didn't sound convinced, though. "I bet Sam could use your company right now. Go be with him, and I'll talk to you soon. Love you."

The SED clicked, and she was gone. Just in case, I tried Stef and Cris again. They didn't answer, so I left messages. Then I readied another tray of food for Sam, hoping he'd finished the last, hoping he'd gotten up to bathe.

He hadn't. He didn't break his intense study of the floor. His scowl never eased as I replaced his food tray.

Heavy with dread and worry, I did the only thing I could

think of that might rouse him from his misery. I sat at the tall harp and positioned my hands like he'd shown me a few months ago—right hand close, left hand far—and plucked at the first string my fingers found, then the next.

On the bed, facing the other wall, Sam sat taller. He tilted his head.

I played another string, and another. Long, low ringing filled the bedroom like gentle snow. It was slightly out of tune, but I didn't know how to fix that. I'd only played the harp a few times before, though the strings on my fingertips, the curve of wood against my shoulder—they felt natural.

My fingers wandered into familiar patterns from Sam's brief lessons. I played a simple tune, belatedly recalling how to work the pedals to change key. My playing wasn't what anyone would call *good*, but as I continued, I heard silverware clank on ceramic, a mug thunk on the nightstand. A few minutes later, the shower started.

He came back into the room—water still running in the background—while I fumbled across a series of notes I couldn't remember; I was used to having music in front of me.

"Here." He took my hand and placed it on the correct string. "The arpeggio begins here." His fingers fell off mine, skin grazing skin.

I nodded, continued playing, and watched while he took clothes from his wardrobe and drawers, then went into the washroom. Steam wafted from the door he'd left ajar.

My music soared through the house, even when my fingertips started to hurt and I lost track of which strings were which. I needed the music, too.

Shower water silenced, and a few minutes later Sam appeared in clean clothes, his hair chafed damp against a towel. He sat on the bed near me while I kept playing the harp.

"I remember building it," he murmured, almost a countermelody against the delicate harp. "The piano. I remember covering it with coats of clear finish to let the natural wood shine through, fitting the cloth into corners and creases to ward away bubbles and drips. It felt like it warmed under my hands, like it was alive. I could already hear all the music I'd make. Preludes and nocturnes, sonatas and waltzes."

My fingers found a darker melody to match his mood.

"I never imagined choosing a favorite instrument, but even before I played the first note, I thought the piano could be it.

"Each piece of ivory and ebony came from faraway lands. I carved and polished every one myself. I cut the maple from forests near Range, and mined the ore—to be smelted and purified for wires and such—with my own hands."

Which hands were those? Ten generations ago?

"It took half a lifetime to plan and gather the materials, learn the necessary skills for constructing what I envisioned. I couldn't do it all by myself—some things just need more hands—but I worked so hard on it. When it was complete, I was an old man and my fingers ached from all that I'd done to create this thing, but when I touched the keys and played the first notes, it was so beautiful. So wonderful. Even now, I can almost hear the echoes of music from centuries ago."

I leaned my cheek against the smooth wood of the harp and let my hands rest on my knees. The music faded.

He watched me with dark, haunted eyes, his damp hair pressed against his skin. Anguish shone raw on his face: the strained set of his mouth, the way he made breathing look like the hardest thing in the world.

"I didn't make other people's pianos. I gave the construction plans to people who could do a better job. I'm a musician, nothing else. But I was proud of that piano."

"Nothing I say will help." I lowered my eyes. "I'm sorry."

"Your music helped." He reached as though to touch my arm, but I couldn't stop remembering what he'd suggested before we came in and found the parlor. He wanted me to leave. He wouldn't have suggested it unless he meant it.

I pulled away from him; I had to protect what was left of my heart, too. "The temple books are gone," I said, standing up. "And Menehem's research."

Sam said nothing.

"Stef isn't answering her SED. I went over there to see her, but she's gone."

He dropped his gaze. "She probably decided to wait out the snowstorm with another friend. I doubt she felt welcome here."

"Because you two were fighting." About me. Did that make it my fault? "She should have answered her SED, anyway. I called a million times and left a million messages."

He clenched his jaw. "She's angry with me. Maybe she's ignoring you by association."

I doubted that was it, but I wished he were right. Stef avoiding me was better than Stef being missing.

"We've been at such odds lately." He dragged in a deep breath. "I thought she would be happy I was happy. I don't understand why she's been acting like this."

Really? He didn't understand? How could someone with so much history and experience be so oblivious?

I'd reached the end of what I could take. Every piece of me felt like it was vibrating so fast it might fall off. A piano wire. A harp string. I'd spent the last day dragging off pieces of instruments I loved, too, to be sorted into scraps later. I'd frozen, seen friends killed, and Sam had asked if I wanted to leave. So what did it matter if I told him?

"She's in love with you, Sam. Really, really in love." My throat ached, and my heart felt dashed into a thousand pieces. "She's jealous that you've spent so much time with me. She just wants you back."

He was shaking his head. "No. We've had relationships in the past, but nothing like you mean. She can't."

"Because you said?" I raised an eyebrow. "You don't get to say how other people feel or don't feel. You can choose to be blind, but that doesn't change what everyone else sees. She *loves* you."

He seemed lost, like he didn't know where we were or who I was, let alone the language I spoke.

But I'd told him. Now he had to choose what to do with the information; I'd already decided what I'd do with everything he *hadn't* said. "I've been thinking about what you asked. I'll go." Speaking the words aloud made them true.

"Why? Where?"

"Li's or Ciana's, like you said. Maybe Sarit's until I get my own things." I bit my lip, wondering at what point my heart would crumble under the weight of my decision. Any second now. "I hope you don't mind if I stay here until the snowstorm is over."

His mouth dropped open, and he just stared for what seemed like hours. Like after the instruments, this was going to break him. I couldn't feel bad, though. Wouldn't. He'd suggested it. I'd have stayed forever if I thought he wanted me.

But in the hours that were really minutes, he didn't beg me not to leave. He didn't say he hadn't meant it. When I stood, his gaze just followed me up. Then I was a shattered blown-glass blue rose, and every step away from him made my shards clatter and chime.

25
SNOWFALL

AS I LEFT his room, I wanted him to stop me. I wanted it so badly I could almost hear the perfect words he'd say to convince me to stay, but when I breathed, those words were lost. They'd never existed. I braced myself on the nearest shelf as my vision tunneled and faded, and up and down became the same direction. Another step. If I could just make it to my bedroom—

Arms wrapped around me and my knees buckled. "No." Sam's cheek grazed mine, fresh-shaved stubble. "Don't go. I need you."

I jerked out of his arms. "You asked if I wanted to move out. You can't take back a question like that. Words don't just go away."

His voice came from behind me, soft and stricken. "I didn't say you had to go." But his tone sounded like he was figuring it out, how there had been no right answer to his question. Did I want to leave? Live somewhere else?

No, I wanted to be here. I wanted him, the music. "I don't want you to worry about what's appropriate or not, or feel like you need to make those decisions without me." The words barely fit in my mouth. "I know I must seem very young to you, and why would anyone trust me to make choices about anything important? But I've been deciding things on my own my whole life, because no one else ever cared enough to help. Not until you."

Behind me, there was only silence.

How could my heart hurt this much? It shouldn't be possible that it ached more than my sylph-burned hands. "I don't feel young," I whispered, "and I don't feel like anything we had was inappropriate. I still don't care what others think. I still don't think it's inappropriate for us to touch or kiss. Maybe strange, but strange and inappropriate are different things."

And maybe I was talking to empty air. Should I turn around?

"I am an idiot." He said it like tumbling, like if he didn't get it out quickly enough, we'd both fall apart. But weren't we doing that already? "I asked if you wanted to leave because I wanted you to know you could. I don't want you to feel trapped here."

I stared at my socked feet and focused on breathing, suddenly aware of the entire house around us. Rooms filled with books and instruments, bedrooms with personal things, the parlor that used to be a haven, and the white shell around everything. Snow and wind beating on that shell.

He held his hand near mine, not touching. "I hate what people say about you. Everyone knows we live together, and everyone knows how I feel." His words rustled hair across the back of my neck, making me shiver. "The assumptions about us aren't kind."

I knew.

"I don't need that kind of protection, Sam. I've lived with gossip my entire life. I can deal with what other people think or assume. Whatever is appropriate for them—*they* made those rules for *them*. Not for me.

"While I am"—I snorted—"*lucky* to have the benefit of everyone's experience and wisdom, the truth is it's been so long since any of you were truly my age that you can't fathom what it's like. Even if you do remember, the world is different now. *You've* made the world different. That leaves me with the responsibility of deciding what is or isn't appropriate. If they want, other newsouls might be able to use my experience to decide when they're ready, but who knows how the world will have changed by then?" According to Meuric, nothing would matter after Soul Night, anyway.

"So does that mean you're staying with me?"

"Is that what you want?" Hope blossomed in my heart, but what happened the next time someone suggested a five-thousand-year-old teenager and a real teenager shouldn't be together?

"More than anything, I want you."

What happened the next time he saw Stef?

But he'd followed *me* out here to apologize. He'd danced with *me* at the masquerade, maybe even attended because of me. He'd been ready to go into the temple so I wouldn't have to be alone.

I slid my heel back and let my weight follow until I pressed against his chest. His arms closed around me. Warmth filled me everywhere he touched.

"Ana," he whispered. "I only wanted to do right by you, but I should have talked to you about it, too. Better than I did the other morning."

"You and your stupid sense of honor." My words held no bite. I was too drained, and he'd already apologized. Asking him to do it again would diminish the words.

"I agree." He kissed the tip of my ear, sending prickles of heat all down my right side. His arms stayed around me, and when I tilted my head and he kissed my neck, it was as though we'd never left the masquerade. Only the music of our heartbeats and wind outside, surrounded only by silk and wood and cool air.

"Try not to be so dumb again." I faced him, took his hand,

and tried not to think about what I was admitting. "I'm not that strong, Sam. I can't forget the past as easily as you. For me, it's all right here, smushed together. Not stretched over thousands of years."

He cupped my cheek and nodded, his jaw clenched tight.

"I've never been able to trust anyone before." And the things I didn't say out loud, but hoped he understood: *please don't hurt me again; be the person I need you to be; show me what it means to be in love so I can decide whether that's what I feel.*

Fingertips traced lines over my cheek, down my jaw. "I'll do my best to deserve your trust."

I lifted my face and kissed him, tasting the salt of my own tears, inhaling the scent of his soap.

He lifted me off the floor, held me tight against him. My skin slipped against my sweater until my toes touched hardwood and air touched my bare spine. He gave a breathy, nervous laugh as he hitched me up again and this time supported me with a hand on the back of my thigh. "Is this okay?" he whispered.

I had lost all power to breathe, but managed to hook my legs around his waist. It was strange, like we were too close and not close enough. His hips moved when he walked, and he kept one hand on my back, and one under my leg so I wouldn't fall.

He placed me at the foot of his bed, and I recaptured my breath as he knelt before me. "You are beautiful." His hands rested on my knees. "And wiser than anyone has given you credit for. The world does need you, Ana. You challenge us, make people think and open their eyes to the truths that we've been ignoring for too long. Sometimes I'm so aware of how close the world came to not having you at all, and it terrifies me. Our immortality is not without a price."

"Neither is my life. There was Ciana, and other darksouls."

He shook his head, black hair falling across his eyebrows. "I'm sorry that I disappoint you sometimes, Ana. I know I'm not perfect. No one is."

I tried not to think about how many times I would inevitably disappoint him. I'd want his forgiveness when I did. I could forgive him now.

"There is something I *am* good at." He ducked his head as though to hide a blush, and his hands on my legs forced my insides into taut coils of yearning. "At least I hope. I imagine you would tell me if I've been doing it wrong this whole time."

"Music?" I bit my lip. I'd never heard him so much as play an out-of-tune note.

He raised himself, leaned so close his words touched my mouth. "Kissing you."

I couldn't move. "Prove it."

His sly smile flashed as he tilted his head and tipped his chin toward mine. Our lips brushed, but instead of kissing me, he rested his teeth against my skin and gave a gentle squeeze. His voice was so low it rumbled in my stomach, too. "I just wanted to find out if it tasted as good as I imagined."

"And?" He hadn't hurt me, but I could still feel the slight pressure where his teeth had been.

Maybe he'd do it again.

He leaned close and whispered by my ear. "Better."

Wind and snow pattered on the shuttered window while we kissed. He touched my face, throat, collarbone, making me feel like a piano must under strong, skilled fingers. But his movements dragged, and even the cadence of his breath sounded off, as though he was trying not to yawn.

"When was the last time you slept?" I cupped my hand over his cheek, feeling the way his jaw moved when he answered.

"I don't remember."

Not since we'd found the parlor, I was certain. Even before that had merely been a couple of hours in the early morning. He must be exhausted.

"Lie down. I'll turn off the light."

He kissed me again, as if to prove he wasn't *that* tired, and then stretched across the bed. "Stay with me," he said, as I made the room fall into twilight.

I paused, wanting him to mean it.

"Please," he whispered.

"Okay." I emptied my pockets and laid my belongings on his nightstand. Then I crawled into the bed, facing him.

Everything was so dark, I could barely see the shape of his body, and for a moment, my frantic heartbeat seemed the loudest thing.

"Blanket?" He reached around behind him to find the end.

"I am cold," I whispered. And if he heard the shaking in my voice, maybe he'd think it was from chill.

He swept the sheet and down-filled comforter over us. "Closer?"

Yes. Definitely. I reached for him, relieved to find him reaching for me, too. His hands found my waist and pulled me tight against him. "Sam, I don't know—"

His tone sounded like a half smile. "It's okay. We'll figure it out another time. I just want to hold you right now."

That was good. I wanted—*something*. But I didn't want to do it wrong and embarrass myself. I probably would, anyway, if we ever got that far. But for now, I turned over—awkward in my day clothes—and pressed my back to his chest. Our legs intertwined, and I knotted my hands with his at my chest.

I slept.

And later woke to perfect snow silence outside, no wind or rattle of trees or clucking of chickens. Light seeped in around the shutters. I found which legs were mine and reclaimed them, then turned in Sam's grasp. His hands were slack and heavy with the carelessness of sleep.

He rolled onto his back as I finished turning, and blankets

pulled away. The susurrus of silk and our breathing were the only sounds.

Pale light shone around him, making highlights and deep shadows around the ridges of his face and neck, down his torso and arms. Hesitating—what if he woke up?—I combed dark strands of hair off his face, then traced the lines of his cheekbones and smile.

He didn't react; he must have been exhausted.

Brave when he wasn't watching, I pushed onto my elbow to get a better angle, then kissed the same path my fingers had taken. He smelled like laundered sheets and hints of sweat.

My fingers had wandered down his chest while I wasn't paying attention. Through the thin shirt, I explored hills and valleys of muscle, relaxed while he slept. I discovered the plains of his stomach and lifted his shirt to the bottom of his ribs, finding smooth skin, warm with sleep. He moaned.

I froze. "Are you awake?" Barely worthy of being called a whisper.

Muscles tensed beneath my questing fingers. "I am now."

My face might have been on fire as I withdrew, but it was dim enough—I hoped—that he couldn't tell. "Sorry."

He dragged in a shuddering breath and gazed at me for a long moment. "I wasn't expecting that kind of wake-up."

"You didn't think I'd still be here?" I could have gone back to my room, but he'd been so warm and—

"No, I'm glad you were here." He pushed himself up, covers

swishing around his legs. His shirt slipped back down, settling askew on his shoulders, and his smile was warm and shy. Boyish. "I like seeing you first thing."

"Oh, good." I doubted it was possible for my face to burn any hotter.

"Just the way you—" He dragged his fingertips from my shoulder to my wrist, making me shiver. "I didn't realize we were doing that now."

What? Touching? We touched all the time. Or maybe I'd ventured into one of those places I didn't know about, just wanted to. Well, this time had been different: he'd been sleeping, which might have been a little creepy of me, but I doubted that was it. My hands on his stomach, though . . .

My own stomach muscles tightened when I remembered the way he'd caressed me during the masquerade. Tickling. Tingling. Deeper. "Oh." The word came as a breath. "I think we should. Be doing that now, I mean." Maybe right now.

His smile grew slowly, as if he knew my thoughts. I sort of hoped he did. "Did you sleep well?" he asked instead.

"Yes." I scooted to the edge and let my legs dangle off. My toes brushed the floor as I gazed around at the bookshelves and old instruments crowding his bedroom. As long as I kept my back to the exterior wall, it was a safe room, all dimness and comforting things. Music. Sam. "Your bed is softer than mine."

Sam chuckled and sat beside me. "They're exactly the same."

"They are not. Yours is better." I didn't *really* want to argue, but little bickering neither of us would take seriously—I knew how to deal with that. It was easier than asking him to show me what else we were doing now. I could barely think those words, let alone say them.

"Very well. It *is* better." His mouth grazed my cheek. "When you're with me."

Eventually, my skin would stain red. Permanently. "Do you think it's still snowing?"

"Sounds like it. Can't you hear?"

I held still, listening as hard as my ears could manage. "It sounds like settling. Breaths drifting and sighing. The quiet groan of trees and roofs as they bear more weight."

"Yes." Covers hissed as he scooted closer and wrapped his arm around my waist. "I love that you hear it, too. That it sounds the same to both of us."

I did, too. "I want to learn everything, Sam. All about music, every instrument. I want to compose things I hear in my head at night—things that aren't yours or anyone else's—and I want to find a way to mimic the sound of snowfall."

His fingers twisted in my sweater, drawing my gaze to meet his wide, dark eyes.

"Maybe you want to do it alone," I whispered, "and I understand if you do. But if you'll accept, I want to help you rebuild everything that was in the parlor."

He kissed me, warm and hard enough to make me dizzy,

but his arm around my waist stayed; he didn't let me spin away. "I love you." It was his voice, but his lips rested against mine so my mouth made the shape of the words.

"I wish I could tell you that, too." My heart thudded too quickly. "Whenever you say it, I feel so good and happy. But guilty for keeping the goodness to myself."

"That's not how it works." He kissed me again, as if the act would force me to accept his way of thinking. "Besides, I can wait."

Another benefit of being ancient: immeasurable patience.

My feelings were deep and overwhelming and confusing, but at the same time the emotion filled me with a sense of belonging. This boy. This soul. We were tied together with something stronger than anything physical. With him, I was not a soul asunder.

A quiet rumble came from the front of the house, drawing me to my feet. "What's that?" I grabbed my things from the nightstand and wandered into the hall, to a front-facing window.

"A plow." Sam followed. "It's like the drones we saw on the way back to Heart. There it is." He held a curtain aside, revealing a vehicle with a large scoop on the front. It heaved up to the steps—shoving a pile of snow to block the door— and turned to clear the other half of the walkway.

"Okay, so it works here, but what about people like Cris who have about three places you're allowed to step?"

"The price of filling your walkway is the plows don't clear it for you. And they're not very good about the doors. It's going to be tough to escape. I might need your help."

Because I was so strong. Right. But I caught the way he tried to stop his smile, and I rolled my eyes. "I'm worried about him and Stef." I could see slivers of her house from this window. Or maybe that was just more snow.

Sam released the curtain and leaned on the wall, something I still couldn't make myself do. "Me too."

I checked my SED, but she hadn't replied to my messages. I sent another, and one to Cris, asking again if they were okay. I hated that neither were home during a storm. "Where could they be?"

"Wish I knew." The thinking line deepened between his eyes. "After the explosions and what happened downstairs, their absence is especially worrisome."

"I think it was Deborl. Merton. Their other friends."

Sam frowned. "He's a Councilor."

"So was Meuric, and he tried to lock me in the temple. He got Li and Merton to attack us after the masquerade. Being a Councilor didn't stop him, and it wouldn't stop Deborl."

Sam gazed at nothing down the hallway. "You think he'd set explosives to kill people who *might* be pregnant with newsouls? Or break into our house and destroy"—his voice hitched—"my instruments?"

"I have no doubt."

Sam reached for my hand, squeezed my fingers. "All right, so what do we do? If he's attacking newsouls, we need proof."

"Sine is having someone watch them."

Sam nodded. "That's a start. Who knows? Maybe he'll get himself caught."

I rather doubted that, but since I'd definitely get caught and thrown in prison—or worse—if I tried to sneak into Deborl's house and see if he had my things, Sine's people would have to do. "You know what still bothers me?"

"I can't even count that high."

I stood on my toes and messed up his hair, then started down the hall. Just being close to the exterior wall made me squirmy. "If the explosions were coincidence—not a response to the meeting—all right. But how did they know about the books and Menehem's research?"

Sam shook his head. "Did you talk to anyone else about it?"

"No." I leaned on the balcony rail. "Well, Cris told me he had some ideas about my symbols, but no one else was with us. Sarit, Lidea, and Wend had just walked away."

"Cris wouldn't have done any of these things."

No, he wouldn't have. "So now they have the key, the books, and the research. They have everything and we don't have anything." I slouched, despair building inside me. How could I protect newsouls if I couldn't even protect a few inanimate objects?

Sam put his arm around my shoulders. "They don't have everything."

I shivered deeper into his embrace. I wanted to say something nice to him, anything to let him know how much I appreciated him and how glad I was we weren't fighting anymore. But I didn't want to sound stupid. There was one way to show him.

I pressed my palms on the balcony railing, overlooking the ruined parlor. "I'm ready to share something with you."

He waited.

I refused to hesitate. "My notebook isn't a diary." I pulled it out and flipped it open to the first page to reveal hand-drawn bars of music, scribbled words in the margins, and doodles everywhere. "Maybe it sort of is, I guess. Just not like the ones everyone else keeps." I gave Sam the notebook. "I don't think I'm very good at being like everyone else."

"I wouldn't want you to be." He sat on the top stair and turned pages, reading the words and music; they were both his language.

I sat next to him, elbows braced on my knees while I fidgeted and felt naked. Paper fluttered as he turned another page, and another. When he hummed a couple of measures, I cringed, but he kept reading without comment. Then he closed the notebook.

"It's not finished," he said, giving it back.

"Not yet." Maybe not ever, but I hadn't been writing it to finish something. I'd been writing emotions, because I didn't always have words for what I wanted. But there was always music, and sometimes it seemed like the most powerful thing in the world.

"Have you played any of it?"

I held the notebook to my chest, pressing the music against my heart so hard it might leave permanent impressions. "I've been too afraid of what it might actually sound like outside my head."

Sam stood and offered his hand. "It may be time to find out."

Maybe he was right.

26
DEMONSTRATION

DAYS LATER, WE walked to the street and South Avenue, past walls of snow rising as high as my shoulders. Sunlight glittered across the ripples and made the whole city bright. So much light hurt my eyes, but not in the way the temple did. There were still drifts and shadows, dark evergreens against the brilliant snow. White veins shimmered between the cobblestones, and the sky was pale blue, a color almost too impossible to be real.

It was the perfect day for the monthly market, and everything I had planned.

The entire market field had been plowed, along with the wide half-moon stairs leading up to the Councilhouse. It was early, so a few sellers were still assembling their tents and tables, spreading their wares for viewing.

In spite of my coat and mitts and scarf, I shivered as we approached the field, the Councilhouse, the temple pushing into the sky. Cris and Stef were still missing—no one had heard from them—but everyone else had contacted their lists and were prepared to make their speeches this morning. Anticipation and defiance surged through me. Today, my friends and I would show everyone that newsouls were worthwhile. We'd show the Council that some people welcomed newsouls and wanted them to be safe.

I touched my flute case, a velvet-lined tube with a strap that went across my chest; it was easier to carry than the wooden box the flute had come in.

"You'll do fine," Sam said. The market's joyful din clattered across the field as we came in sight of the Councilhouse stairs and wide landing that would double as the stage. Sarit, Lorin, and Moriah were already there, winding evergreen boughs around the columns. "I have to help move the piano from the warehouse. Will you be okay up there?"

"Yep." I stood on my toes to kiss him, then trotted up the stairs, holding my flute case to my chest to keep it from bouncing.

Sarit, Lorin, and Moriah all hugged me, and I began adding the blue roses to the evergreens.

"Sam's getting the piano?" Sarit asked.

I nodded and slipped a rose into the strap on my flute case;

I wanted one for my hair later. "The piano they keep over there." I waved my hands toward the industrial quarter with its warehouses and mills. "He already went twice to tune it, but he said he wanted to do one more pass because it's been so long since anyone has played it. And he's, you know, Sam. It has to be perfect or it's not worth playing."

"How's he doing with"—Lorin gave an awkward shrug— "the parlor?"

I bit my lip and glanced at the market, which grew more crowded by the minute. The only space not filled with colorful tents and stalls was an aisle to the steps, where there was a ramp for the piano. Several people watched our work, and rumors about an impromptu concert trickled through the tents. I tried to find anyone looking especially surprised or upset that I hadn't given up on my plan, but most people seemed to be looking forward to hearing Sam play. They didn't know what had happened in his parlor.

"Sam's angry, of course," I said. "Someone destroyed his work. But he could be worse."

"But they didn't get your flute," Lorin said.

"Because *someone* popped out a spring when she was playing with it, and I had to take it upstairs for repair. It wasn't in the parlor, or they would have." I tried not to imagine my flute twisted up, keys ripped off and holes gaping like empty eye sockets.

Lorin gave me a sideways hug. "Sorry about the spring."

"Thanks for breaking it." I turned to Sarit. "And thank *you* for getting the roses. I don't know what we would have done without you."

"You would not have roses." Sarit's tone was light, but she glanced northeast, toward Cris's house, and her expression tensed. "I hope he and Stef are okay. I wish they'd call or send a message."

If Stef had been the only one missing, I could have blamed it on her being angry with Sam. Cris, though, wasn't angry with anyone. As far as I knew.

Just as we finished decorating the stage and setting up microphones, Sam and some of his friends appeared with the piano. A few people from the market cheered, while others wore expressions somewhere between curiosity and suspicion.

When Sam had the piano where he wanted it and sat to warm up, I went inside the Councilhouse with Sarit.

"Are you ready?" she asked as we moved away from the glass doors.

"No. Yes." I handed her my flute case so I could take off my coat. No one would take me seriously when all my layers made me look like a bundled-up child. I could shiver for a little while if it meant people paid attention.

"Oh, pretty!" Sarit laid my coat on the back of a chair and started braiding my hair. "When did you get this dress?"

I smoothed the gray ripples of wool and synthetic silk that

hung to my ankles—concealing a pair of thick tights so my legs wouldn't freeze. The sleeves hugged my wrists, delicate fingerless mitts covered my hands, and I kept a synthetic silk scarf around my neck. The blue matched the rose Sarit threaded into my braid.

"It's one of Sam's dresses. From before. We had to do a lot of work to make it fit." A few generations ago, he—she?—had been taller and curvier, and wore a lot of dresses. Maybe when you were a boy most lifetimes, you wore dresses when you got the chance. "But I thought it suited today perfectly."

"It looks perfect on you." Sarit stepped back and admired her work with my braid. "Beautiful. Now warm up, or Sam will frown at both of us. I'll get your music."

I pulled my flute from its case and played through warm-up exercises and scales. Outside, Sam played similar exercises on the piano; the powerful sound rattled the series of double doors.

By the time I was warmed up, Sarit had finished organizing my music, which was now written on real music paper and given a temporary ending.

She grabbed the music stand she'd stashed here earlier and nodded toward the doors. "Let's go, dragonfly."

I laughed at the attempted endearment, but just as we reached the door, Councilor Sine burst inside.

"Ana, finally. I've been looking everywhere for you." She took a deep breath, eyeing my dress and flute with uncertainty. "I haven't had any luck locating Cris or Stef. I'm sorry, but I'm sure they're fine."

I scowled, far less sure. "Okay. What about Deborl and Merton? And the guy who shoved me?"

She shifted her weight and shook her head. "I had a few people watch Deborl and Merton, but it sounds like they didn't do anything more suspicious than shovel snow."

I snorted. "I find it suspicious they get up and pee in the morning."

Sine cringed. "I'm sorry I couldn't be of any more help."

Maybe she really was. Mostly, I hoped she was ready to listen to what I had to say, and what my friends had to say.

Sarit went first, taking my stand and music onto the wide landing. She placed it just enough away from the microphone that it wouldn't screech—I hoped.

I clutched my flute and went outside, greeted by cold air, the piano's rich sound, and the fade of conversation around the market as people crowded to look.

"You can do this," Sam murmured from the piano bench. This instrument was dark, as though stained with midnight; it was ink against the white stone and evergreens and blue roses.

My smile felt tight, fake, but as I stood behind the music stand, positioned so I could see both Sam and the crowd gathering below, I reminded myself why I had to do this: for Anid and Ariana, held in their mothers' arms as they paused by a tent with mittens and scarves; for the others who'd be born soon and needed care and protection; for those who would stay trapped in the temple, consumed.

I lifted my flute.

There was a soft *click* as Sarit turned on the microphones.

Sam nodded. I breathed. A long, low chord rang from the piano. The sound vibrated through stone and into my legs, and the world grew silent as we began to play.

My flute whispered at first, evidence of my fear, but I'd played this before, and I could do it again. At home, I'd practiced with Sam, him humming the chords he'd play on the dark piano, because he'd listened to my music and gazed at me with such wonder that I might have flown.

I'd played it a hundred times with Sam correcting my posture and reminding me that cold air would make me sharp. Now on the stage, I pulled myself straight and let my flute sing.

Melancholy melody drifted across the stage, the deep piano chasing after it. I played loneliness and fear, yearning for things unnameable and shining. The sound caught around people, pushed through tents, and heated the air as I gained confidence. My flute stretched, warm and full and silver, and I played as I never had before.

Music grew, shifted into the richer sounds of courage and hope and desire. The piano provided foundation, encouraging my playing, lifting it and somehow revealing new layers of the flute's voice.

I played of sunsets and snow, the way leaves shifted and fell, and the anticipation of a kiss.

Music moved around the market field, raining from speakers to make people look up, look around. Friends and teachers smiled. Councilors tilted their heads, expressions unreadable. Strangers wore a range of emotions, some I didn't want to see, so I turned back to my music, back to Sam, and he smiled.

The music gasped with a kiss, surged with fear, and loomed long and low and lonesome where I'd written my experiences in the temple. Heavy chords were billowing smoke across the stage, and I ended with the four notes that began the waltz Sam had composed for me when we met, a haunting echo of blossoming love.

I lowered my flute, and no one in the market field moved.

They were waiting, which was exactly what I'd hoped, but it was much scarier when it was actually happening, all their eyes trained on me.

I'd played. I could do this, too.

Heart thumping, I stepped around my music stand and up to the microphone. I lifted my chin and found the words I'd practiced; it wasn't much, because others would do most of the talking. I only needed to make an impression.

"I am Ana, a newsoul. The music you just heard is mine,

and this"—I held out my flute, which gleamed in sunlight—"survived in spite of someone's attempt to destroy it and stop me from playing for you today."

A few people in the crowd shifted. Some went back to shopping.

"I've been attacked," I said, lifting my voice. "People have thrown rocks at me. Beaten me. Spread rumors about me. All in response to one transgression: I was born. The same is going to happen to Lidea's baby, and Geral's, and maybe some of yours.

"The reactions to our new knowledge—that more new-souls will be born—have been varied and complicated. Some people have been welcoming. Others have not. I can't ask that everyone accept us. I know that won't happen. But this is my plea to you, the people of Heart, and the Council: protect newsouls. Before dismissing us as inconsequential, give us a chance to prove that we are worthwhile."

I smiled—sort of—and walked toward Sarit, who waited by a column, wearing a wide grin. Sam got up to speak, and I tried to relax. My part was over. Everyone else would do the rest.

"You were great, firefly," Sarit whispered. She took my flute and headed inside to put it away while I listened to Sam.

His words came like a song. "I met Ana when she escaped a swarm of sylph by leaping into Rangedge Lake. That was the first thing I knew about her: she would rather choose her own destiny.

"The next day, we encountered another sylph. In order to rescue me, she burned her hands, even after having been told that any significant sylph burn would grow and kill the victim. A lie, as we all know. But that didn't stop her. That was the second thing I learned about Ana: she is selfless.

"Ana taught herself how to read, memorize music, and survive. Many of you have had the privilege of teaching her and have seen how quickly she acquires new skills. Her very first night in Heart, I left her in my parlor while I cleaned up. When I returned, she was sitting at my piano"—his voice cracked—"and she'd already figured out how to read music. Not long after, she composed her own minuet. The beautiful piece you heard today is only her second composition."

My face ached with heat, from the people staring at me. He wasn't supposed to brag about me, just encourage discussion. This was embarrassing.

"Yet when she arrived in Heart, she was not welcomed. In her absence, a law had been made to keep her from living as an adult, though she was already three years past her first quindec. She wasn't allowed farther than the guard station until she agreed to lessons and curfews and progress reports, as though she were less than human. Less than everyone else simply because she is new."

I wanted to find a cozy rock to hide under. If it were possible for a face to glow with so much blood rushing upward, mine did. People kept looking at me and hmming.

"During Templedark," Sam said, his voice deeper, "when Menehem told her his intentions, Ana did everything in her power to save souls. She warned everyone of the price of dying during those hours. She sought me out when I'd gone to fight—and she rescued me again, this time from a dragon.

"Have any of you ever seen me *not* die when a dragon was trying to kill me?"

A few people chuckled nervously.

"That is what I want you to understand when I tell you we need newsouls. We need them to have privileges and rights, just like the rest of us. We need to encourage their talents and growth. No one will deny education is necessary, but Ana has proven ten times over that she can be trusted, and she will do anything in order to protect our community. It's her community as well."

Just as Sam finished speaking, screams flashed throughout the crowd. A commotion pushed its way between tents, coming toward the stage. Men in black coats dragged something behind them.

I walked back to Sam and the microphone to get a better look. "What's going on?" My voice carried from speakers everywhere as screams grew louder and people hurried to get out of the black-coated men's way.

One was Merton; his huge frame was impossible to mistake as he crashed up the half-moon stairs. Deborl hurried after him, and between them . . .

Meuric.

The reek of his putrid wounds heralded his appearance, all broken and seeping like he'd been before.

I staggered back. Sam caught me, arms tight around my waist.

"Is that *Meuric*?" His tone was incredulous, and the microphone dropped it all across the market field. People rushed like colliding waves, many away from Meuric's decaying body, and even more toward because they couldn't see the horror; they'd only heard Sam's words.

Meuric did not move by his own power. Merton carried him, while Deborl made a show of assistance. Other Councilors rushed in, though I couldn't guess their intentions. They wanted to help him? Keep people away?

"Where's a medic?" Sam leaned toward the microphone. "Rin, we need you on the stairs."

"Don't bother." Deborl shoved his way to the microphone. "Meuric isn't going to live. His bones have been shattered. His eye was carved out. He's been starving for months."

"How is he still alive?" Councilor Frase scrambled up the steps, gaping at the mess on Meuric's clothes and the way his body drooped. "Oh, Janan. Give mercy!" At the top of the steps, Frase bent over and threw up.

I gagged on the miasma of decay and vomit, backing toward the columns and piano like they could save me. Sam turned gray, trying vainly to hide my eyes, as though I hadn't seen this before in the smothering quiet of the temple.

Screams crescendoed as Merton positioned Meuric's fading body where everyone could see it. The crowd pushed around to the front of the steps, leaving tents and stalls untended. Shouts of disgust rang out.

Deborl spoke into the microphone and motioned at Meuric. "This is what the newsoul has done. She obtained a key to the temple, to *our* temple, and took Meuric inside, where she all but killed him. To mock Janan, she left him there, broken. I know such beliefs have fallen out of favor, but Meuric was once called Janan's Hallow. And to leave him there in this state is one of the highest insults."

The screams became cacophony, deafening. Sam grabbed my hand and tried to pull me toward the Councilhouse, but I felt like stone. I couldn't look away from Meuric, and from Deborl, because he was *right*. I had left Meuric there. I'd stabbed him, kicked him into the pit, and then abandoned him. And even when I found him in the temple again, I did nothing.

"Ana!" Sam yanked me, and I stumbled into his chest. "Come on. We have to go."

Go where? But I followed, glancing back to see Meuric crumple to the stage. His head lolled, and as Deborl raged and the crowd surged, I caught one last look at Meuric: the black rot between his teeth when he grinned at me, and the awareness fading from his good eye as he finally died.

I ran with Sam, not sure there was anywhere safe to go, but it was better than watching this.

Sam reached for one of the glass doors, and just as it swung open, I saw the reflection of dozens of people pressing close behind me.

Someone grabbed my shoulders and ripped me away from Sam. I shouted and jerked my elbow behind me. Bone hit soft tissue—a stomach?—and I started back to Sam, but more people appeared.

Hands grabbed from every direction, taking my arms and shoulders and hair. They found Sam, too, and immediately I lost sight of him.

I struggled, but so many bodies created walls around me. I couldn't get away as they push-dragged me somewhere I couldn't see. Above everything, Deborl's voice thundered.

"This is what newsouls do! This is what they will keep doing to us: killing us, destroying us, replacing us."

The bodies blocking me moved aside, revealing me to the mob below. Tents had been thrown on their sides, tables knocked over. People pushed up the stairs, reaching.

I screamed for Sam, for Sarit or any of my friends. Where were Lidea and Geral with their newsouls? What would happen to them?

Someone kicked the backs of my legs and I dropped. Bone slammed on stone, and it felt like my knees shattered, but I could still move my toes. I blinked and breathed through dizziness.

"My friends," Deborl cried, "we cannot accept newsouls. They will rip us apart. For her crimes, the newsoul will be punished."

Cheering rose up. Someone shouted against it, but that voice was quickly silenced.

Fingers gouged into my skin, keeping me on the ground as Deborl approached. He leaned close, whispering into my ear. "You might have thought you could stop Janan. You can't. Nothing can stop him. Meuric failed, but Janan has chosen a new Hallow. I will be the one who welcomes him when he ascends on Soul Night." Deborl gripped my chin and yanked my face around. His eyes narrowed. "And you will be where you belong, trapped where you should have stayed before you were born."

I tried to wrestle away from the people who held me, but they were too strong. Bruises formed under their fingers. I wanted to scream, to make some kind of response, but the noise and heat and rage overwhelmed me.

Deborl shoved me away as he stood. "Take her to the temple wall. I'll put her with the others."

My captors hauled me up, carrying me awkwardly so I couldn't fight or flail. Every time I struggled, their grips got tighter and my existence grew fuzzier.

People banged against me as Deborl's friends carried me through the crowd. No matter how I fought, they kept hold, and nothing I did led to freedom. We left the worst of the crowd soon, and moved between tents. I saw cobblestones, shoes, and trash on the ground. Never my captors' faces.

Until they slammed me against the temple wall, and then I looked up to see Wend. Lidea's partner. Anid's father.

I choked. "You?"

"I do love Lidea," he said, "but the newsoul is not right. He's not natural." Wend backed away, but before I could think about running, I found the blue targeting lights on my chest. The others had laser pistols aimed at me.

"Why not?" I asked. "Other animals live and die and are never reborn."

"We have souls," Wend said.

One of the others chuckled. "Some of us, anyway."

I wanted to be horrified at how Wend felt no attachment to Anid, that he didn't care at all that Anid's existence was partly his doing. But I remembered Li, and how she hated me, how she resented me because I represented everything that terrified her most: the unknown.

"We have Janan." Deborl came around after us, drawing the silver temple key from his pocket. "Janan gives us every life."

"What about phoenixes?" I couldn't stop staring at the

key as he pressed the symbols I'd only guessed at.

"Janan is only for humans. For souls." Deborl sneered and nodded at Wend. "Get her."

Wend grabbed my arm as a door misted into existence on the temple. Did they all know about the temple? Was that how Wend knew what symbols Cris and I had been talking about? And how they knew what to take from Sam's house?

Deborl dragged open the door, and reality hit me. They were going to throw me in.

I struggled, squirming away just long enough for someone to shoot the cobblestone in front of me. Stone sizzled as Wend grabbed me back.

"I'd like to break your bones and gouge your eye before putting you in there." Deborl shoved me into the doorway; I stood half in and half out of the temple. "That way you can feel the pain you put Meuric through. Unfortunately, I only have time for this, but it will do."

He reached back, and Merton slapped a laser pistol into his hand. To shoot me? To burn me just enough so I suffered forever inside the temple? I didn't have a key this time. There'd be no way out.

I searched for a path between the men. Deborl, Wend, Merton, and strangers were too thick. There was nowhere to go.

The targeting light flashed on my shoulder.

Wend lurched forward and shoved me.

346

Just as gray veiled the outside, I saw Deborl turn and shoot Wend. For saving me the pain of being injured inside the temple?

Wend's body crumpled.

I fell backward into the temple.

27
SKELETONS

I TUMBLED INTO the white chamber, all painful glow of everywhere-light and the deafening throb of Janan's heartbeat. I skidded to a stop in the middle of the floor, clutching my head and groaning.

"Ana?" The heavy air smothered the deep voice. The human voice.

I looked up to find Cris and Stef sitting together on the far side of the chamber. Their clothes were ripped, and scrapes crisscrossed their hands and faces.

"Oh. I've been trying to find you two." I struggled to stay upright. "For days."

"Days?" Cris climbed to his feet and started toward me. "What do you mean?"

"You've been missing." I took a deep breath and tried not to think about where I was, but souls began to whisper and cry. The truth was impossible to forget. It was all around me: the incredible nothing that should have swallowed me, too.

"Not days, though. Deborl and some of his friends grabbed me," Stef said, following Cris, "but that was just this morning."

I shook my head, but decided not to burden her with the truth just yet.

"Do you have your SED?" Without my permission, she dug into my pocket.

"It doesn't work here," I warned, and checked to see where we were. Not that it made a difference. Most places in the temple looked alike, all big white chambers and archways. Whispers and murmurs rippled, souls cried. There were no words for how much I didn't want to be here.

"How do you know?" Stef tapped the SED screen like it'd do magic.

Cris offered me a hand up. "I could have sworn they shoved us into the temple, but there's no door."

"This is the temple. Sorry. I've been here before." I bit my lip. "This is my third time."

They both stared at me, confusion bright. "How is that possible?" Cris asked.

The weeping and unsilence surrounded me, heavier and thicker for no reason except that we were trapped without the key. It would be impossible to tell how long we'd been in here, or what was going on outside. The everywhere-light glowed with ever-unwavering determination.

"Meuric had a device. Right before Templedark, he tricked me into coming here, then followed with the intention of leaving me locked in so I wouldn't cause trouble. I took the key from him." And then trapped him in here, caught between life and death. Now he was out, finally dead on the steps of the Councilhouse.

Stef raised her eyebrows. "And you've been coming and going since? *Why?*"

"Not because I like it here. I need to learn what Janan's trying to hide. I came here before because I thought I could find answers." I almost wished for ignorance again; it had hurt less than the truth. "Now I have even more questions."

"Oh." Stef shifted and handed back my SED. "Well, feel free to start explaining things to me any minute. Even the questions."

"Okay." I stuffed my SED into my pocket, wishing I'd brought my knife instead. It was at home, since my dress had only one small pocket, but if I'd known I was going to get shoved into the temple again . . . "Have you been exploring?" As much as I hated moving around the temple without the key, especially when I wasn't sure if they'd throw Sam in after us, it would give me the illusion of doing something.

"A little," Cris said. "But it's empty."

They clearly hadn't reached the spherical room, or the sideways-gravity room. Lucky them. "Stay close, then." We headed toward the nearest archway, and I began telling them the truth about Templedark, my disappearance since then, and the books I was trying to translate.

I told them what Janan was doing to newsouls.

"No," Stef whispered. "Surely no."

Cris's eyes widened with horror. "Why? How? How could that possibly be?"

"Meuric told me," I said. "He might have lied, but I don't think so." Even as I said it, cries grew louder, thicker on the smothering air until they were like black smoke clinging to our clothes and skin. Cris and Stef said nothing, just looked like they wanted to be sick.

It was painful, watching them react to the truth about newsouls. I changed the subject. "I found the guesses you left in your house, Cris. For the symbols."

Cris looked up. "You were in my house?"

"We couldn't find you outside and it was snowing. None of your plants were covered, so we were worried."

"Ah." He glanced nowhere, as though he could see his frost-coated roses. "I was studying the symbols again when someone knocked. I tucked the paper under the tray, and then Deborl, Merton, and a bunch of others took me."

"Why would he take you?" I stepped off a narrow stair-way, onto a floor that looked like white water. It held my weight. For now.

"I don't know." He eyed the floor like it might change its mind about being solid. "Well, Deborl did ask about books and symbols. He said he wanted to know what I knew, which wasn't anything, since you didn't give me details." The last part sounded a little accusing, but I forgave him because it was my fault he'd been kidnapped.

"He asked me the same questions," said Stef. "But I *really* didn't know anything, because you didn't give me even a hint." That definitely sounded accusing, but I forgave her because she was right and it was my fault she'd been kidnapped, too.

Deborl must have assumed Sam and I had told her because they were best friends. If Sarit hadn't left for Purple Rose Cottage, would they have taken her, too? And I couldn't stop wondering what they were doing with Sam right now.

I found an archway out of the water-floor room quickly, before I lost control of my stomach. Stef looked green, too.

The souls around us continued weeping.

"I didn't remember the symbols from anything in Range like you thought I might." Cris's voice was low as we entered a long hall, white everywhere; I dragged my fingers along one wall to make sure I didn't walk into it. "The symbols came from writing I'd seen in the far south, in jungles. I was collecting samples of plants for medicine and experiments, and found giant ruins. A white wall . . ." His voice grew soft and faraway.

I'd been right the day of my gardening lesson: the wall *had* been white, like the wall Sam found in the north.

"I climbed to the top of one of the tallest pieces to get a good view. It was hard to make out with trees and vines and creatures everywhere, but it looked like the wall had once been a ring, like the one around Heart, but there was no evidence of a city inside. Only a razed building in the center, with enough rubble it might have been as big as our temple."

"The ruins looked like a circle with a dot in the middle?"

Cris nodded.

That was the symbol Meuric had said meant Heart or city, but there'd been no city in the jungle. There'd have been *some* kind of evidence otherwise, even if the jungle had mostly overgrown it. "And the symbols?"

"They were etched into the stone, though erosion made them difficult to see. When I left, it was so hard to remember."

Meuric had said no one wrote the books, that they were simply written. But the language seemed to be from the jungle, where phoenixes lived and burned and died and lived again. So what were the books doing here?

Cris focused again, confusion magic evaporating. "Did my guesses help? It was a long time ago."

"Yes, definitely." I wished I'd actually been able to study them, now that I'd acquired a few translations. "You helped a lot. I hadn't realized I'd been looking at some of the symbols sideways."

He offered a warm smile. "I'm glad you trusted me enough to ask."

Stef shot me a dark look, a vivid contrast to the white all around. I wanted to say something comforting to her, but I didn't know what. We were stuck here together, me and two people who loved Sam, and the object of our affections on the outside. Maybe hurt or imprisoned. Who knew what else Deborl had told everyone?

The truth was bad enough.

The hall ended in a black archway. I hesitated, uncertain about this one, though I couldn't tell why. It was the same as all the other black archways, midnight on white.

"That's easier to look at, at least." Cris rubbed his eyes.

"The crying stopped." Stef glanced at me. "Are we going through?"

She was asking me? Perhaps I'd inadvertently given them the idea I knew my way around. "Yeah, I suppose. Keep watch for anything that might help us escape."

There wouldn't be anything. The key was gone. Nothing would help us escape, but they needed the comfort.

We walked through the archway.

The circular chamber beyond was not like the rest of the temple. Here, the walls glowed red, and inky shadows lurked beneath skeletons chained in tarnished silver shackles.

Thousands of skeletons. Maybe a million.

A wide pit waited in the center, large enough for a piano to fall through. Like a spider straddling the hole, a white table stood above it. One body, perfectly preserved, rested on the table with a knife thrust into his chest. His own hands held it in.

Stef's voice dropped low and heavy. "What is this?"

"I've never seen it before." I couldn't move. Everywhere there were skeletons, yellow bones clean of flesh and fabric. They sat on tiers around the room, heads lolled to the sides, bound hands on their laps or the stone beside them.

I'd never seen so much death before, not even in graveyards Sam had shown me. Those had been peaceful, all iron and stonework, flowers and vines. They were bodies kept in mausoleums and caskets where they belonged.

"This one is different," Stef called from across the pit and the man on the stone table.

I stared at the table man as I rounded the pit, not too close. He was short and thick, with bushy brown hair on his head and face. His jaw jutted forward as though he'd died focusing on something important. Mostly, he looked *strong*, like he could wrestle a troll and win.

"Ana." Cris touched my shoulder. Where Stef crouched, another skeleton slumped in its shackles, but away from the rest. It lay prostrate in the middle of the floor, arms outstretched as though bowing to the man on the table.

"That's not the weirdest part." Stef stepped away from the shackled one to reveal a second, which appeared to have been cast aside. Limbs flailed, bones barely held together by worn ligaments. It looked like if anyone touched it, the skeleton would collapse into a pile of dust.

I gazed along the walls, along the ranks of gaping eye sockets and lower jaws hanging precariously. "There." I pointed to an empty spot. Silver shackles sat unlocked on the white stone. "Someone put that one over here."

What Deborl had said about replacing Meuric—

"What's a Hallow?" The question was out before I realized I'd spoken. Deborl actually *had* replaced Meuric. Physically.

"That's a word I haven't heard in a long time." Stef cocked her head. "Meuric claimed the title in the beginning, saying he had a special connection to Janan, but he didn't seem to do anything, really. He eventually stopped talking about it."

I fiddled with my scarf, the cool length of silk only a pale comfort. "Meuric was the first Hallow," I said, gazing at the skeletons on the floor. "Whatever he was supposed to do, he failed when I trapped him in here. Deborl replaced him."

Cris stood next to me, towering. "But why? What does it matter?"

"Meuric and Deborl both said something about Janan rising. Ascending."

"That sounds familiar," Stef muttered. "Ascending."

I waited, but she didn't elaborate. "Meuric was convinced that if he had the key, he would survive Soul Night."

"That's in three months." Cris shook his head. "But we have a Soul Night every fifteen years. We all survive it. What makes this one different?"

Time? Whatever Janan was working toward, was five thousand years long enough? Meuric had been convinced it was happening soon, even before the temple turned him crazy. "If surviving Soul Night requires the key, and the Hallow gets the key, that would certainly be motivation to do whatever Janan wants."

"And what does Janan want?" Cris asked. "Rising? Ascending?"

Not rising like a phoenix, Meuric had said. Something else. Something sinister.

I pointed at the two on the floor. "Those two are Meuric and Deborl." I swept my arms around the room. "And the rest of these are you. All of you. Sam, Sarit, Orrin, Whit, Armande, Sine—everyone."

Cris and Stef gasped.

"What happened here?" It was probably mean of me to ask, since they couldn't remember. Janan didn't *want* them to remember, or know about the other white walls and towers around the world, or consider certain paradoxes enough to know they were ridiculous.

He did something to them every time they were rein-carnated, but maybe now that they were inside the temple, memories would return.

Stef focused inward, a line carved between her eyes. "Janan was our leader. He used to be a man. A human."

I glanced at the body on the table. "Him?"

"Him," she repeated. "He wasn't even anything special. He was our leader, but he was just a human."

How incredible, all this because of one man.

Stef's jaw muscles clenched, and her knuckles turned white with strain. "Every time I think I have it, it slips away."

"It's all right." I laid my hand on her shoulder. "Just tell me whenever you know something. I won't forget."

Sometimes, being new had its advantages.

"You said he was your leader. Just a man." I spoke as much for their benefit as my own. Maybe it would spark more memories. "Had you discovered Heart yet?"

"No." Cris frowned. "And we weren't in tribes across Range like I thought. We were all together. All of us except for Janan. We were going to him."

"The story I was told was this: no one agrees how you got here, but you lived in different tribes. Then you all dis-covered Heart and fought over it until you realized it was big enough for everyone. That was the first time you came together, all million of you."

"Yes, that's right." Cris shook his head. "But that's *not*

right. That's not what happened. Janan was our leader, but he'd been wrongly imprisoned. Everyone came to free him. The city appeared later. After . . . after we did something."

I motioned to the table. "Somehow he ended up there. And somehow you all ended up sitting around the room with chains connecting you. How?"

"I don't remember," Stef whispered. "I know Meuric bound us in the chains, then bound himself beside the altar and told Janan we were ready. I remember white and wind everywhere—and the very next thing is standing just outside the city wall. We all thought we'd just arrived, but no one knew why we'd come." She gestured around the room. "Whatever happened in here, it tied us to him forever. It changed him, made him both less and more at the same time. It made us reincarnate."

Unsilence thickened in the moments between her words, and all of us realized the answer to my biggest question.

I wasn't going to be reincarnated.

Definitely not.

I hadn't been here five thousand years ago. I didn't have a skeleton chained to the walls.

When I died, I'd be gone. Gone, and no one would remember me but through pieces of music and the few notebooks I kept.

I wanted to sit, or speak, or breathe, but it seemed ice radiated from the blue rose in my hair, freezing first my thoughts, then every other piece of me. No matter what I did now—whether or not I escaped here, saved newsouls, and stopped Janan—when I died, that was it. No lifetimes with Sam. No helping to rebuild his instruments, no learning how to play them all, no writing music that sounded like snowfall.

My heart shattered, glass on stone.

Then Janan spoke.

28
TRAPPED

"MISTAKE. IT HAS returned."

Janan's voice hit me from all directions, huge and deep and overwhelming. I blinked away threatening tears and glanced at the man on the table, but he remained dead.

Despair splintered through me. I was a mistake. Asunder. And after this life I *wouldn't* return. I would never be like everyone else.

"You must leave. This place is not for you." Janan's words ripped around the room, and red light gathered on the domed ceiling. It brightened, sucking all the crimson from the walls until they glowed hot white.

The presence faded, leaving the red to bleed back into the walls. Everything became how it had been a few minutes ago.

Except my new knowledge of my . . . temporariness.

"Was that Janan?" Stef's face was pale and drawn as she gazed around. She lowered her voice. "He knows we're here?"

"He does now." I hugged myself. "Usually he doesn't pay attention to me unless I'm fiddling with the key. He can't touch you—he's incorporeal—but he can change the walls. Once he locked me in a small room."

"How did you escape?" Cris asked.

"I threatened to keep pushing buttons on the key." Deep breaths. In and out. I focused on anything but the idea of dying and never coming back. "I don't know how it works, but it must make Janan uncomfortable if he didn't want me poking at it."

Cris nodded. "I suppose if the walls are his body, it'd be like me making your arms move around for you. A trust you'd only give your Hallow."

Janan's voice boomed again, violent as thunder shaking the ground. "You do not belong here!"

I jumped, my bones feeling like they might vibrate out, and tried not to stare at the body on the table. Or the skeletons along the walls. There wasn't really a safe place to look.

"Should we go?" Stef asked, once the rumbling died. Her voice trembled. I hated seeing Stef frightened; she was always so confident.

"No. If we leave this room, he'll trap us somewhere. I don't have the key. There's no way I'd be able to get us out."

"So we stay here?" Cris looked dubious.

"Doesn't that trap us here instead?" Stef eyed the door like she might run for it.

"I've never been here." I didn't want to be here now. "Maybe Deborl made a mistake when he left. Maybe going somewhere in the temple makes it more likely to be available again. All I can tell you is that I've been in the temple twice before, and I've never seen this room."

Stef shook her head. "We're still trapped."

"Important things happened here. This place holds answers. We won't find anything in the rest of the temple."

"I just want to go." Stef edged toward the archway. "There's no way out from here, but the rest—"

"There are no exits." I balled my fists. "I know it's hard to understand, but there is no way out. I don't have the key."

"Sam will free us." Cris looked hopeful.

"No, he won't." The temple had no temperature—not too hot or cold—but chills raced across my body, and I shivered. "He won't save us, because he won't be able to. It was a mob out there. I don't even know if Sam's okay." The last words choked me.

Both of them wore pinched expressions, and Cris touched my elbow. "I'm sure he's fine. He's probably working out a plan to take the key right now."

I shook my head and described what I'd seen. No need to go easy on them. I didn't see how our situation could get any worse.

"Ana!" Stef jabbed a finger toward the archway we'd come from. It was gone. "He locked us in. Now we really can't get out."

"We wouldn't have gotten out anyway!" The constant pulse of the temple made my head throb. "What about that is so confusing? No matter where we are, we're not leaving. Sam can't rescue us. Deborl wouldn't free us if his life depended on it. No one else knows how to use the key. We're stuck."

"All right!" Cris rubbed his forehead as though to press a headache into a smaller, more manageable size. "Both of you, please. We need a plan."

"Like what? Escape?" I scowled and gestured around the room. "The only thing I see is the hole under the altar, and I don't recommend it."

"We're just as bad off as if we'd left," Stef muttered, just loud enough that it was meant to be heard.

I shook my head. "If we'd left, we would be stuck in a tiny box."

"You don't know that. You're guessing on all of this." Stef loomed over me. "You've been leading us nowhere the whole time, with no idea where you were going or what you wanted to accomplish."

"At least I was doing something." My fingernails dug into

my palms, carving crescents into my skin. "You'd have just stayed there all confused. Did you even try to escape Deborl? Or were you too busy being mad because Sam and I didn't tell you what had been going on?"

"Don't pretend like you know anything about me or the way I feel." Her face was pink in the red glow, and I had pushed too hard.

I didn't care. "I know enough." She kept antagonizing Sam about his closeness to me, but *she* was the person keeping a stash of his photos and letters. I wanted to hurt her. "I know how you disguise your feelings for Sam. You fooled him, but he's used to your flirting and never took it seriously. But I know you meant it."

She stared at me like I'd said she had chicken feet or hands growing from her head, but that was Stef. Pretending even now she didn't really care.

I knew I shouldn't, but I said it anyway, my voice low and too calm. "I told him that you love him."

Her face went blank.

A wiser person would have stopped there, but I went on anyway. "If you were as brave as you claim, you'd have told him lifetimes ago."

"And I suppose you have? No, that would ruin your tortured newsoul existence." Her voice grew stronger, angrier. "You can't let yourself be happy, can you? Well maybe this will fix it: you're not coming back. There's no skeleton in here with your name on it, so when you die, that's it. Gone. I'll still love Sam, and thanks for telling him, by the way. Now he'll have time to figure out a response in our next lives when you're not here. Are you happy now? You really are as tragic as you think you are, butterfly."

She might as well have stabbed me; it hurt the same.

There was a whole list of things I shouldn't do, including asking if she could find his skeleton among all these—I could—and telling her about his reaction when he found out how she felt. But I didn't do any of them, because it would be cruel and petty. Not that I'd been much above cruel and petty so far, but I didn't want her to hate me forever. And, romantic feelings aside, she was still Sam's best friend.

"There's no point in arguing about it, Stef." My voice was more level than it had ever been, but surely she could hear the strain. "Because we're trapped. We're never leaving this room."

29
IMMORTALITY

AFTER STARTLING STEF and Cris into silence, I marched over to Meuric's skeleton and kicked the skull.

Whatever magic had been holding it together must have failed when the shackles came off. The skull skittered across the floor and dropped into the pit beneath the table.

I kicked an arm, and several bones cracked against one another, the floor, and a table leg. Pieces of Meuric dropped out of sight, making no sound on their way down. If they ever reached an end, I didn't hear the clatter.

Still angry, I kicked his ribs, hips. Smaller bones turned to powder as my boot hit them. "I hate you," I hissed, as the last of Meuric vanished.

Stepping around the dust, I almost felt bad for kicking Meuric down a pit again.

"Okay," I whispered to myself, and knelt by the skeleton now caught in shackles. Deborl. I hated him, too. More than I hated Meuric. The hate twisted inside me like a snake, uncomfortable, but clean and sharp and determined.

I reached for the tarnished silver cuff to search for a lock. If Janan didn't have a Hallow, maybe he couldn't ascend on Soul Night. It would make being trapped in here worth it, if I could save everyone else from the fate hurtling toward them.

As I touched the shackle, electricity zapped through me. I screamed, and lost feeling in my right side. My arm hung uselessly.

"Ana?" Cris hurried toward me, looking around for whatever had attacked me.

I shook away the buzzing in my head. "Don't touch the chains."

He sat with me until feeling in my fingers returned, and then, more carefully, I climbed onto the table and tried to kick Janan off.

He might have been a human-shaped lump of silver himself. He didn't move. Cris even joined me, but no matter what we tried, we couldn't budge him.

The knife, however, did come away when we worked together. Cris pried Janan's grip off the handle just enough so I could slip it out. The blade was silver at the base, but the end looked as though it had been dipped in liquid gold. Janan's hands returned to their original position, but now they held only a memory of the knife.

I didn't have anything to do with it, though, so I left it on the table.

"You will die!" shouted the walls, incorporeal Janan.

"Why don't you lick my shoe?" I propped my boot on dead-Janan's face. "You won't do anything to us. Not here."

Red light swirled around the chamber, and Janan's screams resounded through the room as he called me names I'd never imagined could be put together like that.

But he was without substance, and we were already trapped.

"You're just a human, like us!" Not quite true—he was powerful, incorporeal, and consumed and reincarnated souls—but he'd started out human. Reminding him of that was satisfying. "Just a short human!"

"Is that your plan?" Stef asked when the screams faded. "Annoy him until he kicks us out?"

"No. I'm working on a better one." I flashed a tight, fake smile. "This is just the beginning." I kicked dead-Janan's head, but numbness rushed through my toes as though I'd kicked a block of ice.

I hopped off the table and marched around the perimeter of the room.

A few minutes or an hour later, Cris fell into step beside

me and I said, "If you're here to chastise me for being mean to Stef, I don't want to hear it." I twisted my scarf in my hands, hating my obvious fidget, but I couldn't stay still.

"No, I thought you'd probably done enough of that yourself."

"Mmm." Noncommittal. I'd picked it up from Sam, and it seemed to work for whatever the other person wanted to hear.

"I've been trying to figure out how to get out of here," I said. The archway was still missing, and there weren't any signs. No words or pictures to indicate what we should do next. "No key means we can't control the walls. We can't make doors or do anything useful. The good news is we won't get hungry or thirsty, as long as we don't think too hard about it."

"Great, thanks. Deborl didn't feed us before he trapped us. Do you have any idea how long it's been?"

"A day? A week? Five minutes?" I shrugged. "Time passes differently here, and not even at a consistent rate."

Moriah had told me time mostly mattered to the person measuring it, which had made me laugh because she built clocks. SEDs and clocks didn't work in here, but now I was extra aware of every second and how they carried me closer to my end.

"So what we need is someone who can make doors."

I raised an eyebrow. "Well, yes. Pretty much."

"Stef?" He waved in her direction. "You don't happen to have anything on you that would make a door in the wall, do you?"

Her glower was dragon acid. "Go roll around in rose-bushes, Cris."

"I don't think she appreciates your humor," I muttered. As if I could blame her. At this rate, we'd be out of Janan's way in a few days because we'd have killed one another. Well, Stef would kill me, then Cris, and then she'd be here all by herself. And I wouldn't feel bad for her.

"Few really do." He kept pace with me easily. "Why are you walking?"

"It feels like if I stop, then I give up. But I don't know what to do." My throat tightened with the confession. He was going to think I was weak, just like Stef did.

"Hey." He tugged my arm. I stumbled and he caught me, one hand on my back. "Sorry. Hey." He faced me, expression serious. "We're going to find a way out, okay? And then you'll rescue Sam from the angry mob, reclaim your books, and find a way to stop Janan from ascending."

"So while I do all these miracles, you'll be where?" My whole body ached, and I really wanted to lose myself in the piano, but it was gone. Smashed. And my flute? Sarit had put it in the Councilhouse, but they might have found it.

Cris said, "I've been remembering, too."

I waited.

"Being here has made me remember a lot of things we're not supposed to know. The memories are so old they feel like dreams or someone else's life, but I know they're real." He looked more serious than I'd ever seen him. No hint of a smile, no friendly stance. He looked sad. "I remember what Janan said he was going to do."

"What is that?" I whispered.

"He wants to be immortal."

"But—"

"*True* immortality. Not like we are, trapped in an endless cycle of birth and death and rebirth. And not like what he is now, trapped in these walls. Before, when he was still human, there was *nothing* in this tower. No rooms or light or shifting walls. It was meant to be a prison."

Even before he started switching old and newsouls, he'd been imprisoned? "Why was he here? Who put him here?" Whatever he'd done, it must have been terrible, and as far as I could see, he was only getting worse.

"Before all this"—Cris gestured around—"Janan took his best warriors on a quest for immortality. People were so afraid of everything, like dragons and centaurs and trolls—"

"And sylph?"

Cris cocked his head. "No, we hadn't seen sylph yet. Only after."

"Okay." That was odd, though. "Go on."

"Well, he said he discovered the secret to immortality, but

that phoenixes were jealous: they didn't want anyone else to know their secret. They made this prison—and prisons all over the world—and locked Janan and his warriors away, one in each tower so they'd never band together again."

"Phoenixes." I'd known they were real, but I'd never heard of them making prisons or really *doing* much besides flying around, burning up, and rising from their own ashes. Well, Meuric had said a phoenix cursed the sylph, but Meuric had been crazy. Maybe. "The other prisons were towers, like this one? With a wall around?"

"I never saw them, but I think so. I think when we came to rescue Janan from his prison, it was just a tower and a wall."

"Like the one you saw in the jungle."

He nodded.

And like the one Sam had seen in the north, I guessed. But none of those towers had anything like Janan. If they did, they wouldn't have been affected by weather and life. So what had happened to those prisons and prisoners?

Cris seemed somewhen else, heavy with his memories. "We all went to rescue Janan, but instead, he said the secret to immortality meant he had to stay in the prison—for a while. He said phoenixes had made this tower, so it was already infused with their magic. And the rest of us were to wait for his success and return." Cris gazed around the red-lit chamber. "Can you imagine five thousand years existing only in stone, just waiting?"

"He's *eating newsouls*." I clenched my jaw. "I'm having trouble sympathizing with him."

"I didn't mean—" Cris lowered his eyes. "Sorry. I didn't mean it like that. It's just, five thousand years. That's a long time."

So long I could hardly imagine it. "I shouldn't have snapped. I'm just exhausted."

"I understand." Cris flashed a pale smile. "Janan shed his mortality, but souls still need something to contain them."

What did that mean for sylph, then? It seemed hard to believe that anything without a soul could love music as much as they seemed to.

"All this time, he's been waiting, growing, gaining power. If he ascends on Soul Night and becomes truly immortal, no need to consume newsouls to survive, then he won't need to reincarnate us."

"What about the Hallow? Meuric said if he had the key, he would live."

Cris smiled grimly, voice low and filled with hurt. "Why should Janan bother? We'll be unnecessary, even Meuric and Deborl. With Janan free of the temple, there will be no need for someone to guard the key."

The key. Another thousand questions revolved around that little box. Where had it come from? "The night of Templedark, Meuric said that birth isn't pretty. It's painful."

"Add the Range caldera to that," Cris said, "and you

have—nothing. When it erupts, there will be nothing left but Janan."

I wanted to be sick. I hadn't even considered the caldera, but the earthquake swarms, the lake level . . .

The caldera beneath Range wasn't just moving through one of its natural cycles. No, it was getting ready to erupt. There *should* have been lots of warning. There *should* have been years of evidence beforehand. But nothing about Janan was natural; the unrest in the caldera *must* have been his doing.

When Range erupted, the devastation would be complete. The ground would be ripped apart. Lava would pour across the forest, killing everything in its path. Ash would fill the air, blocking the sun. The world's temperature would drop dramatically.

Not that anyone would be around to see that happen.

Heart—even Range—would be a hole in the ground.

Cris shoved his hands in his pockets, frowning at nothing. "Soul Night is still months away. There's still time to stop him if you can escape."

"By 'you' I assume you mean 'we.'"

"No, I mean you. And Stef if she'd like to escape as well."

From the other side of the room, Stef called, "What?" and stood. "You thought of a way out?"

Cris nodded as she rounded the stone table. "Ana, I have to confess something first." His tone made me shiver.

"What?"

"Please understand the last thing I want to do is hurt you, but"—he glanced at Stef, who didn't react—"I think you need to know."

I waited.

"Janan is using us, yes, switching oldsouls and newsouls to feed himself. But he didn't deceive us or trap us, in spite of these chains. We were told he'd gain knowledge and power to protect us when he returned, truly immortal. All we had to do was bind ourselves to him and he'd do the rest. We were afraid of the world, and of him, so we said yes." Cris gestured around the room. "We all made the agreement to be bound. We chose to be reincarnated."

It must have seemed like such an easy decision; after all, who wanted to die when you could live forever? "You didn't know about the newsouls?" Surely they hadn't known. Sam had been horrified when he learned the truth, and Stef and Cris were the same. The people I knew would never make that trade.

"Understand that we were young," he whispered, his face ashen. "We were young and in a dangerous land that spat boiling water and mud. There were dragons and centaurs, trolls and rocs, plus the regular animals that live in Range. Half our number had already been killed on the journey here. We were—still are—terrified of death."

Stef dropped her gaze. "It was selfish and desperate,

but those were wilder times."

"No." I spoke as if denying it would change anything.

My heart beat itself into knots. I wanted to say I'd never make that decision, but how I felt now—knowing that no matter what I did, my life would be short—I might accept such a bargain. One more life with Sam, with music, with everything I ever wanted. All it would cost was someone who'd never know what they missed.

This would have been so much easier if I could have hated everyone for what they'd done.

Cris closed his eyes. "I don't want to think about how many souls that is, especially considering how frequently some people die."

"Hundreds of millions of newsouls." Stef's voice turned raspy. "I'm so sorry, Ana."

I was sick and aching. Sam had made the deal, too. Sam who loved me.

It stabbed like betrayal no matter how I reminded myself it was so long ago. My Sam. My friend Sarit. Lidea, who loved Anid so much. Geral, who thought Ariana was the most precious creature. All my friends. Everyone I'd ever trusted.

They'd all made the deal.

The people of Heart were so terrified of newsouls replacing them, but in truth, they'd been replacing newsouls for five thousand years.

A sob choked out, but I wiped my cheeks and tried to put

the grief and anger aside. I was too worn to deal with it now. "Okay. So what's your plan? How does remembering how Janan started all this help?"

Cris was quiet for so long I thought he didn't really have a plan. "Someone needs to be able to open a door. I'll do it."

"Without the key?"

He closed his eyes. *"A* key. Not *the* key."

It took me a minute to follow. "No. You can't."

"I'm the only one who can."

"No." I scrambled to my feet, heart collapsing in on itself. "I won't let you sacrifice yourself."

"I'm sorry, Ana." He stood, too, with ten times more grace. "It has to be me. The world still needs Stef."

"The world still needs *you.*" I was yelling at a rock, because he just shook his head. "Society would have never understood farming without you. Greenhouses. Fields. Orchards. That's because of you."

"That was thousands of years ago." He touched my arm, but I batted him away. "Now I grow roses. A noble endeavor, but not necessary for survival."

"What?" Stef peered between us. "What are you talking about? Why don't you want him to open a door?"

"Because without *the* key, there's only one way to make a door," I said.

She shook her head, looking weary. "Please remember I've been kidnapped and starved."

"Cris"—I pointed and growled his name—"thinks he's going to do whatever Janan did: get rid of his body; become part of the temple."

"*What*?" Stef was on her feet in an instant, shrieking at Cris.

"If you do it, you'll be as bad as him. You'll have to consume souls to survive, and someone will have to be the Hallow, and how will both you and Janan fit in the walls? I'm sure he won't be happy about sharing his space with you."

Stef stood inches from Cris, yelling as loud as she could while he stayed silent, waiting. "Why do you think this is going to work? For all you know, you'll just stick a knife in your chest and die."

"Even if it does work," I said, "in five thousand years everyone will have to stop you and they'll feel bad because you're otherwise nice."

Stef and I both stopped to breathe at the same time, and Cris cut in.

"First of all, I don't have followers like Janan did." He motioned around the room at our skeletal audience. "If I'm not reincarnating anyone, I won't get souls. These skeletons are bound in chains. They're bound to *him*."

"What if it changes?" My throat hurt from yelling, and my head throbbed with anger and betrayal. "What if suddenly you're supposed to switch souls?"

"I wouldn't do it." He sounded so calm and certain, like he

didn't think it would be a temptation. "Ana, I promise. Knowing what I do, knowing you, I understand what we sacrificed so long ago." He touched my hand, softly enough that I could barely feel his fingers tremble. "I'm so sorry, Ana. We don't deserve your forgiveness, but I can try to put things right."

"How is that?" I wanted to hate him and his stupid plan, but now that I wasn't yelling, my body felt limp and heavy.

"I will become part of the walls, like Janan, then open a door."

"No." I crossed my arms. "This is a crazy plan. You don't even know if it will work."

"Wouldn't you need a Hallow?" Stef asked. "I'm not chaining myself up like those two." She pointed at Deborl, and one of Meuric's toe bones I'd missed.

"There's no need for a Hallow." He smiled at her, all grim determination. "Janan needed one to help bind his followers and guard the key, but I won't. No souls. No sacrifices."

"You're talking about sacrificing yourself." My words squeaked out. This wasn't happening. It couldn't be.

"For you." He took my hand, his five thousand years evaporating. He looked young and scared, just like I felt, and his hand sweated over mine. "You haven't had a hundred lifetimes, and even this one has just begun. There's so much you still have to experience. No matter what happens with all this"—he gestured around the temple—"I need to give you a chance."

A million things happened inside me at once, most prominently my heart squeezing up to my throat, and my stomach flip-flopping. Grateful and sick and filled up with misery.

"Cris, no." I didn't want to die, though, or be trapped forever. I wanted to live, to have experiences. I wanted to see the world with my single short life. But Cris . . .

"Think of it as a gift, if it helps. One you can't turn down."

Stef stood nearby, eyes round as if she'd begun to accept what he was going to do.

"Janan is too strong. You can't beat him," I whispered, half saying the words because I knew I should. "He's had five thousand years to gain power. You will be new and weak. He won't let you stay in the walls." He needed to see how futile his plan was.

"I only need a few moments to open a door for you." He cupped my cheek with his free hand.

"What happens if he kills you? Will you be reincarnated?"

"For a newsoul's sake," Cris said, "I hope not."

But I didn't want him to be gone forever. Where would he go? What would he do?

"Ana, you have to live. You have to get out of here, stop Janan from destroying Heart, and live this life. Do everything you can. Don't waste it. Promise me."

"We'll find another way." Why couldn't he see?

"When? How? There's nothing here but skeletons." His

eyes were glassy, and he blinked several times as though trying not to cry.

"Please don't." I looked to Stef for help, but she just watched us with a hard expression, like ice.

Just as I turned to him again, Cris leaned forward and kissed me. Not long, and not desperate. I barely had a chance to register the way his lips tasted like tears before he drew back, looking as surprised as I felt.

"I thought you were in love with Sam." That wasn't what I wanted to say, but it saved me from having to think too hard about the simultaneous thrill and fear and stress of what had just happened. I still didn't understand why *Sam* wanted to kiss me, let alone anyone else.

"I will always be in love with Dossam." He focused inward, somewhen-else. He didn't mean my Sam, but a Sam from lifetimes ago. "And I love you," he whispered, coming back to the present. "Not like Sam does, not nearly. But that's why you have to live. I couldn't bear to let anything happen to you when you've just begun, and I couldn't bear Sam's pain if he lost you."

My breath was too heavy, crushing me from the inside. I couldn't let him do this, but I wanted to escape. I wanted to live and be loved and *not die*. Pieces of me were becoming resigned to it, even welcoming his fate because it meant I might be free.

Stef was still ice. No hope of strength from her.

Cris squeezed my hand. I'd forgotten he hadn't let go. "You're going to live," he said. "You're going to make it out of the temple, and then you're going to use everything you've learned to stop Janan. Save the newsouls."

I hated myself as I nodded, and warmth trickled down my cheeks. He was crying, too, but I didn't know what to say to other people who cried. Instead I just hugged him. His wiry body tensed before his arms went around me, too.

If I spoke, I would be undone. Everything in me would spill out. So I squeezed him until he pried himself loose and said, "I shouldn't have kissed you. I hope you can forgive me."

Because I still couldn't speak, I pressed my fingers to my lips and nodded, and hoped he knew that I understood. He was afraid.

"Be ready to run," he said, "because I have no idea how long it will take, or how long it will last. If I have time, once you're free, I'll try—I don't know. Maybe I can save the souls he's trapped here."

Was that even possible? Maybe it was to the boy who'd ride across Range to save his roses from frost.

"You don't have to," Stef whispered. "I could."

"The world has more need for a scientist and engineer than a gardener, especially right now." He hugged her as well, and kissed her cheeks. "Please don't kill each other after I'm gone."

Gone.

He was going to do it now? Shouldn't he wait?

My legs were numb, my arms useless. My voice had long since abandoned me. I wanted to tell him to stop, to reconsider, but it would only delay the inevitable. He'd already decided, and I selfishly wanted to go home.

Without regard for my silent urging him to wait, Cris climbed onto the table next to Janan, found the knife, and lay down.

I wished I had something strong or brave to say, something that might give him a breath of reassurance. But I had nothing to offer. I was useless.

Stef stood next to me, put her arm around my waist. Crying, I leaned my head on her shoulder and watched Cris settle on the stone and position the knife above his heart. He was really going to do it. There had to be another way, and I was crying instead of figuring it out.

"Please, Cris." The temple smothered my words. *Please don't. Please wait. Please come back.*

He turned his head to look at us, managed a grim smile, and closed his eyes. Silver and gold flashed in red light as the knife pierced.

He died.

30

SACRIFICE

I SCREAMED.

Fingers dug into my arms, through my sleeves, and Stef
yelled my name over and over. I strained against her, reaching for Cris on the table. His eyes were dull and glassy; his
knuckles were white around the knife hilt.

No matter how I struggled, Stef was stronger. I rushed
toward Cris, but Stef yanked me back and shoved me to the
floor, pinning me. "Stop it!" she yelled.

But I wasn't flailing anymore. I was too busy watching a
white light bleed into the table.

The light expanded, flooding around the table legs that
stretched over the pit. It was so bright I had to squint as the
glow encompassed Cris's body.

Tears leaked down my face, from despair and shock and light. All the air swept inward, wind rattling bones and snatching at our clothes; I caught my scarf as it tried to flee my neck. Deborl's skeleton skidded on the floor toward the pit, as though all the air were being sucked down. It strained against the shackles.

The glow flared so bright I had to close my eyes. I wanted to close my ears as the wind howled around table legs.

Beneath me, the floor moved, slick against my clothes.

No, I was moving on the floor, both Stef and me. Shrieking wind pulled us, even as Stef scrambled to help me off my back. Wind-deaf and light-blind, we had to feel our way as the pull grew stronger, like gravity was shifting.

My heart hammered with a surge of adrenaline.

"We have to find something to hold on to!" I couldn't tell if she heard me over the rush and keen, but I reached—her arm reached with mine—and felt along the floor, trying to dig my toes in.

"No!" Janan's voice filled the room, thunder and waterfall-crashing.

I fought the wind's pulling, the way air thinned, and I lost track of Stef. Twice, I felt her bump against me, but I focused on *not sliding* as red light pulsed beyond my eyelids, and white light burned and moved. Even with my eyes closed, I saw silhouettes of my hands splayed on the floor, desperate for traction.

And then Cris's voice: "Ana. Stef. *Go.*"

I couldn't help but sob. He'd done it. Done something. "Cris!" My voice was lost under Janan's rage and the wind still sucking toward the pit. Bones clacked, and silver chains rattled and clanked.

Janan roared words I didn't know, had never heard. His voice was pressure on my skin, hot as a sylph turned solid.

"Ana, now!" Cris again, like sparks catching and burning. "Please."

It was his desperation that made me open my eyes. A gray archway waited ahead of me, just a few paces away, and mostly in the floor so I wouldn't even have to stand. He'd done it. Freedom. His plan had worked.

Jaw clenched, gasping at thin air, I clawed toward the misty portal and hooked my fingers on the bottom lip. I just had to pull myself up and tumble out. Quickly, too, because the outline wavered, shot with streaks of black and white. Changing its destination.

If I didn't hurry, Janan would seize control.

"Go, Ana!" Cris again, choked and smothered. Lights and air pulsed all around the chamber as the two battled within the temple walls.

Stef. I couldn't find her.

Digging my fingers into the stone—what would happen if the archway vanished altogether?—I adjusted myself to get a better look around the room. I shouted her name, but she wouldn't hear me over the stampede of Janan's rage.

The table. If I squinted right, I could make out arms looped around the near table leg, and Stef straining to keep herself from being sucked the rest of the way in.

She had bumped against me before. Nudging me away from the pit?

Her attempt at heroism had almost gotten her killed, too.

I had a scarf, but even if I had been strong enough to hold on to the archway with one hand and pull her up with the other, it wasn't long enough.

There was no asking Cris for help. The shrieking and wind grew worse, and Cris cried out in pain. I had no idea what Janan could do when they were mostly without substance, but the wailing sounded like stars dying.

I pulled myself far enough to the arch and braced my elbow inside it, then lifted my leg as high as I could. My heel caught the edge. Terrified every motion would make me slip, I tied one end of the scarf around my ankle, making sure the knot was secure.

Leg down again, the scarf whipped in the wind, close to Stef but not close enough. I couldn't see her face in the searing light, but her arms didn't move from around the table leg.

Chest muscles aching with the strain of holding on, I switched to my hands again, so now instead of my upper body at the archway, only my head peeked in.

Stef—I hoped Stef—tugged on the scarf, but the weight

wasn't enough to make me believe she'd taken a good hold. It wasn't constant pulling.

Sam would never forgive me if I got this far and didn't save her. I took three breaths as deep as I could, wind stinging my throat and eyes, and lowered myself farther so my arms stretched before me. Only my fingers stayed in the archway as the sucking wind grew stronger.

Red flashed like bloody lightning, and the cacophony grew worse. But then there was steady tugging on the scarf as Stef grabbed hold and began climbing.

"Please let the knot hold," I whispered.

The scarf yanked on my foot, and Stef was more weight for me to keep up. My hands were numb as I struggled to hold on, struggled to keep my foot flexed so the scarf wouldn't slip off. My muscles shook.

A hand closed around my ankle, and another on my calf. My own scream was lost in the din as I begged my arms to pull us up again. If I could just get my elbows over the edge, I would be able to fall through the hole.

Stef used me like a rope, climbing as I worked to bend my arms. The wind pulled and pushed, and lights flared. I focused on breathing, focused on the archway stretched above me. Freedom. If only Stef's arms weren't wrapped around my waist.

She must have been pushing with her feet, because a nudge gave me the weightlessness and strength to move my left shoulder over the lip and hang on with my elbow. Now I pushed instead of pulled, but fire still ripped through my arms and chest as I gained enough strength to move my upper half over the archway.

Stef reached for the edge with one arm. Her other around me slipped.

"Just a little farther," I urged. The wind stole my voice.

Chasms of concentration lined her face. She clenched her jaw tighter, reached again, and caught hold enough to pull herself up next to me.

The archway had been gray when Cris opened it, but now it was midnight dark. Relief for my eyes, but I was pretty sure that meant Cris wasn't in control anymore, and no matter how much I shouted his name, the archway didn't change.

Stef leaned toward me, shouted by my ear. "Why aren't we leaving?"

My tortured voice wasn't even as loud as hers, but I tried. "Gray means outside. Black or white means inside."

She looked ready to cry, but nodded and hauled herself higher on the archway. One foot on the left edge, one on the right. She positioned herself over it like a spider waiting to pounce.

I understood. The second the portal turned to gray, we were going through. I hastened to follow her example, screaming to Cris as loud as I could that we were ready.

But when it did flicker and the black became smooth gray, I wasn't prepared. My foot had slipped and I was trying to push myself up with just one leg. All my muscles felt shredded, though, too worn to move.

Stef grabbed my wrist and dragged me through the gray archway just as it began to change.

Silence.

Real silence, not the temple unsilence where not even my ears would ring.

And air, windy and cold, but it didn't try to pull me places. It was thick enough to breathe.

Frigid skin pressed against mine, and I opened my eyes to see Sine above me. Her mouth moved as though she spoke, but I couldn't hear, so I just blinked and breathed and waited for my muscles to melt. For now, at least, they were too cold to hurt. I reveled in the ability to lie flat on my back and not be *moving*.

"Ana." Sine sounded far away. "You have to get up."

I turned my head to find Stef staring up at Councilor Frase. She looked the way I felt. Dull. Not really here.

The market field cobblestones had never been so beautiful.

"Ana!" Sine's shout brought me back to myself. "Get up before I find someone to carry you."

That didn't sound like a bad idea at the moment, but as I

regained control over my body, I remembered market day, Deborl's speech, Meuric dying in front of everyone, and the resulting mob.

I sat up so quickly Sine almost didn't dodge fast enough. "Where is Sam?" I tried to make my eyes focus on her again, but I'd moved too fast, and dizziness swarmed inside my head.

"Hospital." She stood and offered a hand. I climbed up by myself when I saw Stef finding her way to a more vertical position, too. "With everything that happened the other day, he received a few serious injuries, but he'll live. He just woke up an hour ago."

I wanted to feel numb, not vainly try to patch the cracked dam of emotions. Sam. Cris. Janan. Soon I was going to break.

Just not in front of anyone. Please.

"What day is it?"

"You've been missing for two days."

It felt like a month. Maybe Cris had managed one last favor, letting us out as close to the time we went in as possible.

The dam inside me strained. I should have stopped Cris. I'd as good as killed him.

"Where's Deborl? I'm going to electrocute him and then set him on fire—" Stef gasped as she leaned on Frase's shoulder, hiding her face.

"Deborl and his friends are in prison."

"Prison?" I could hardly imagine good news anymore. "What about Wend? He was there, too." Though Deborl had shot him. . . .

Sine combed her fingers through my tangles. "Wend is dead." Lines creased her face as she frowned, and a tear dropped from crevice to crevice. "None of them will trouble newsouls again, though it's only fair to tell you that they were not ignored."

"I need Sam." I needed to tell him everything that had happened.

"Of course. Corin, please fetch Dossam." She signaled to someone behind me—Corin, presumably—and footsteps retreated. "Where is Cris? They said he was with you."

I gazed at the temple, cold and white and not quite as evil if Cris was still in there. Sam had said Cris had never done anything terrible to anyone. Even after learning they'd all sacrificed newsouls for reincarnation, I still believed that. He'd sacrificed himself for us now.

But I couldn't answer Sine's question.

I was going to break.

I wasn't sure how long I stood there, holding myself together with nothing but threads, but eventually a familiar shadow fell next to mine.

My muscles felt like liquid as I lifted my hand just enough that Sam's closed around it, and then his arm closed around the rest of me.

The dam broke and everything spilled out. Sam hugged me so tightly I couldn't breathe, or maybe the sobs choked me. He touched my hair and face, kissed me. His affection was featherlight, as though he was afraid of crushing me.

I cried into his shirt even though there were other people here. Stef, Sine, Frase. People I didn't know. I wanted to hide, but I was afraid I wouldn't be able to walk. Even now, Sam mostly held me up.

Sam, who, five thousand years ago, had taken immortality knowing the price. How could I ever look at him the same way?

But I couldn't bear to pull away from him. Maybe I wouldn't tell him; it would be hard enough for both of us to deal with the fleetingness of my existence.

I would just die.

Where would I go? What would I do?

So lost in myself, and in Sam's arms, I almost didn't notice the commotion around the curve of the temple.

"What's going on?" I swallowed more tears.

"Sylph. Don't worry. They'll capture it and set it free outside Range." He started to adjust his hold on me, but I straightened and pulled away. "What is it?" Concern lined his face.

"I just had a horrible thought." I wanted to be wrong, but my mind worked no matter how I tried to ignore it. "Help me get there before they put it in an egg."

He looked uncertain, but kept me upright as I limped toward the crowd gathered around a panicked sylph. The tall shadow hummed and sang, caught in the circle of people with brass eggs. It could have burned any of them, but it stayed in the center and shifted as though trying to decide what to do.

Then it saw me.

I gathered my strength and gave Sam's hand a squeeze. "Let me through." My voice cracked, and I had to say it again, but the team with sylph eggs backed off. Maybe they remembered Deborl's claims that I could control sylph.

I stepped through the line of people, Sam close behind, and Stef after him. The column of smoke and shadow grew still and its songs silent. It looked at all of us and slumped, somewhere between relief and exhaustion.

It was too human.

"We shouldn't have let him do it, Stef." I lifted my hand toward the black smoke. People hissed, but when my fingers passed through, there was only uncomfortable warmth. The sylph hummed, calmer.

I raised my other palm toward the midnight curls, but it shivered away from me as heat grew, like it had lost control.

"Oh." Stef sounded like she wanted to be sick. "Cris?"

The sylph twitched—acknowledgment—and a tendril of shadow blossomed like a black rose, then fell to my feet.

I clutched my chest, my heart caged inside. We'd let him sacrifice himself for us, and now he was cursed—

Cursed.

Sylph were cursed.

Cris had said there'd been no sylph in the beginning. I still didn't know how they'd been cursed, but I knew what Cris had done.

"Oh, Cris."

The shadow rose vanished, and the sylph floated between a pair of guards—who stepped aside to let him pass. He flowed like ink down East Avenue, and Sine muttered into her SED. "There's a sylph going through the Eastern Arch. Open the gates wide and let him be."

31
HEARTBEAT

AFTER SPENDING A few days in the hospital, I was taken to the Council chamber. The remaining Councilors were there—nine now, since Deborl was in prison—but none of them looked happy to see me. Most just stared at the items on the table: a stack of leather-bound books, a handful of diaries, and a small silver box.

This wasn't quite everything Deborl had stolen from me, but these things were the most incriminating. The music . . .

I slumped in my chair, grateful when Sam sat next to me; they hadn't let anyone visit while I was in the hospital.

"Today's session is closed." Sine focused on me, her gaze hard and holding back all emotion. "And it will probably stay closed. Typically we are in favor of sharing our decisions with everyone in Heart, but this— Ana." She said my name like heartbreak.

Everyone stared at me, but I didn't look away from Sine. I just waited.

"Deborl's methods were reprehensible, but he did uncover several unfortunate truths.

"First, you were in possession of Menehem's research." She pressed her palm on the diaries, as though she could crush them into dust. "The same research that describes how he created Templedark. You *lied* to us. You hid information regarding our existence and our history. Regardless of whether Menehem left the research in your care, it was never yours to keep."

I clenched my jaw and said nothing, because nothing I might say would help. I had kept the research. I had lied. Those things were true.

"Second, there's Meuric."

The name alone conjured memories of his stench, his grating voice, and his manic laughter when he told me that Janan ate souls. I shuddered and swallowed the taste of acid in my throat. Below the table, Sam took my hand and squeezed.

"Is what Deborl said true, Ana?" Emotion cracked through Sine's voice when she asked, "Did you kill Meuric?"

Had I? I'd thought so before, but then he was alive in the temple. He would have stayed alive, but Deborl brought him out. Both Deborl and I were responsible, but if I hadn't stabbed and kicked Meuric to begin with . . . "It was self-defense. He tricked me into the temple. He was going to trap me there. We fought. I won."

"And you decided not to tell anyone." Sine glanced at Sam, probably knowing I'd told him, but if she was going to punish him for not coming forward, she wasn't going to do it now. "That brings me to the third complaint." She touched the temple key and books, and confusion flickered across her face. The other Councilors, too, seemed unsure what they were looking at.

"Those were Meuric's," I offered. Technically the books weren't, but he could have shared them with the community. He'd decided not to.

"And yet," Sine said, "when you came into possession of them, you hid them."

It wasn't like anyone else would have remembered them. Deborl would have taken everything, and I would have no answers.

Maybe I had too many answers.

"Do you remember what happened to Cris?" My voice caught on his name.

The Councilors glanced at one another, muttering, until Sine shook her head. "He was killed during the mob on market day."

My fists balled up and my jaw ached from clenching it, but there was no point in arguing. They wouldn't remember that

Cris had become a sylph, or what Janan did to newsouls, or that they'd all agreed to bind themselves to him in the first place. The forgetting magic was too strong.

They'd only remember that they didn't trust me. That I'd lied. That I'd kept things from them.

"Ana." Sine leaned on the table. "I know the newsouls are important to you."

She had no idea.

"The Council had several emergency meetings after market day. We did listen to what you had to say, and we've already put laws in place to make sure newsouls are protected. Anid and Ariana are safe. So are any others born."

And me? I'd never feel safe again. Neither would those inside the temple. Still, it was more than I'd expected. "Thank you."

"But," she said, "I'm afraid given what we've discussed today, the Council has decided to revoke your status as a guest in Heart."

Everything inside of me spun, dropped, slammed. She couldn't do that.

"Be reasonable—," Sam started, but Sine held up a hand to stop him.

"This was not an easy decision to come to." Sine lifted her voice, glancing between Sam and me. "We agonized over it, trust me, but the fact of the matter is that Ana has not held up her end. By lying and withholding important information and items, she betrayed our trust."

"No." Sam's voice was low. Dangerous. "You betrayed her trust. She hasn't been safe in Heart since she arrived. And would you have believed her, even if she'd come forward? People have tried to kill her; Deborl—a *Councilor*—and his friends set explosives to try and kill more newsouls. The moment she arrived in Heart, the Council betrayed her by making up laws to prevent her from joining society."

Sine closed her eyes, and her tone was much too calm. "As a result of your actions, Ana, I'm sorry to say you are no longer welcome in the city. Dossam will no longer be your guardian. While we will not force you beyond Range—that would surely be a death sentence—you are hereby exiled from Heart."

"No!" Sam lunged across the table, and within heartbeats, every Councilor was up and shouting.

Exiled.

Screaming and fighting built around me. I stared at my hands on my lap.

Exiled.

Asunder after all.

"I'll go." I stood, and the cacophony stopped; Frase and Finn had Sam pinned against the wall already, fists drawn back as though they were going to punch him. It hadn't been much of a fight, one against many. "I'll go," I said again, "as long as you keep your promise about the other newsouls."

"Of course we will." Sine nodded at the men holding Sam. "Please, all of you. Stop this. Sam, I'm disappointed in you."

Sam muttered a few unfamiliar curses as he jerked away from the Councilors. "You deserve everything coming to you."

I frowned—no one deserved what Janan would do—but I just turned for the Council chamber doors. "I need to pack a few things."

"That's fine." Now that it was over, Sine was gentle. "We can give you two days."

That didn't give me much time to pack and say good-bye to friends, but it was more time than I'd expected.

Afternoon fell in pale splashes across Heart. Sam and I walked home, not talking about the Council's decision. Instead, he called and vented to Stef, who immediately went to demand an appeal. Other friends joined in, once they heard the news, but when they came over later, everyone said the Council had refused to hear them.

When Stef and Sarit left late that night, Sam and I changed into nightclothes and settled in the remains of our parlor.

"I can't believe this is really happening." He sounded far away.

"They'll never accept me." I closed my flute into its travel case, grateful it had survived the mob. "They don't trust me, and they won't believe the truth. But I believe Sine when she says she'll take care of the other newsouls. They have a chance. As far as Janan goes—what can I do against him when the Council has everything?"

"You won't give up against him, though."

"No. But what I want to do, I can't do here."

"What's that?" Hope colored the edges of his voice.

"I'm going to find the sylph." I was closer to finding answers to the questions I'd asked in Menehem's lab, but I needed to know more. And Cris was out there. Somewhere. Maybe— No, he'd already given everything.

Sam smiled grimly. "I'm going with you."

Joy sparked inside of me. "Are you sure? I'd never ask you to leave—"

"I'd go anywhere with you." He touched my cheek. "It doesn't matter where or how far, or even why. I want to be with you no matter what."

"Thank you." Heartbeat thudding in my ears, I met his eyes and let my emotions bubble into words. "I love you, Sam."

It was easy to say. I could love. And I did.

Sam swept me into his arms and hugged me so tight I couldn't breathe, whispering his love again and again. His promises sat warm on my throat, trapped in my hair and shirt collar, and I imagined they wrapped around me like armor.

"I always have," I said into his hair. "I've loved you since I first heard your music, and saw how you wrote about it." I kissed his throat, twisted my fingers in his shirt. "I loved you when you saved me from the lake and put your breath inside me." His face, his hair, his shoulders—everywhere my hands could find, they did. "I loved you that day in the library when you showed me your past lives, and at the masquerade before I was totally sure you were the shrike."

"All those times?" He pressed his cheek against mine.

"And more. When you took care of my hands, when you found me outside the temple. I even loved you when I was angry with you. Maybe especially then." While I spoke, I'd settled myself on his lap, facing him. His heart thudded against mine. "I think no matter what happens, I'll always love you."

Even though five thousand years ago, he'd made the choice to sacrifice newsouls, I still loved him. I couldn't help it.

He'd changed so much since then. The entire world had changed.

We fell asleep on the sofa, tangled in blankets. My cheek rested on his chest, and my arms looped around him. I loved the way he felt underneath me, and the way his hand rested on my ribs. I loved the occasional soft snore.

There were so many times I should have said it since meeting him. I should have told a lot of other people, too.

It was the last night before the new year. The Year of Hunger was passing into memory as I breathed.

I slipped from Sam's arms and let my nightgown fall

straight, then took careful steps around the last of the piano wreckage. Dried and delicate rose petals still speckled the floor, like flecks of cracked blue paint.

"Ana?" Sam watched me from the sofa, my hand extended halfway to the exterior wall. "What are you doing?"

I shook my head, dropped my arm. "Just . . . seeing." I'd feel better about leaving if everyone was safe.

He sat up, blankets tangled around him, his shirt askew and half-unbuttoned. "There's something I need to tell you. Something I did at Menehem's lab."

I picked up a rose petal; it rasped and crunched in my fingers.

"I asked you about the knife. You'd said it made you feel better. You'd said you wanted something like that against Janan."

The petal crumbled and bits fluttered to the floor, and I couldn't forget his guilty expression anytime we'd spoken of Menehem's lab. I'd felt bad about keeping the truth from people, but he'd seemed to take the guilt even harder. "What did you do?"

He met my eyes and drew a shaky breath. "I turned on the machine. It's been making the poison since we left."

"*Oh.*" A hundred emotions flooded through me, shock and dread and gratitude.

"You said it would take an incredible amount to affect Janan even for a moment. I don't understand much about it. I

405

just turned on the machine and input the ratios from the dose that worked on sylph. It may not do anything. It may be for nothing. But I wanted to give you a knife."

"Thank you." I wasn't ready to believe it would work, but my heart swelled with what he'd done for me. Turning on the machine went against his nature, but he loved me and wanted me to feel safe. "So that's where we go first, before the Council looks into it. Unless . . ."

I touched my fingertips to the exterior wall.

The white stone was warm, as usual, but it didn't do anything untoward. I dared a moment of relief.

Shouldn't have.

The heartbeat pulsed faster than ever. I snatched my hand back, echoes of Janan's roaring in my head, visions of Cris a sylph behind my eyes. He'd freed us, but nothing more.

Midnight struck.

The Year of Souls had begun.

ACKNOWLEDGMENTS

ETERNAL THANKS TO:

Lauren MacLeod, my agent, and Sarah Shumway, my editor. Thank you for always challenging me to do better and inspiring me to try harder. I can't imagine this journey without you ladies.

The entire team at Katherine Tegen Books, including Amy Ryan, Brenna Franzitta, Casey McIntyre, Esilda Kerr, Joel Tippie, Katherine Tegen, Laurel Symonds, Lauren Flower, and Megan Sugrue. Hearts and flowers to you *all*.

The amazing people who read early versions (or last-minute changes!) of this book: Adam Heine, Beth Revis, Bria Quinlan, Christine Nguyen, C. J. Redwine, Corinne Duyvis, Gabrielle Harvey, Jamie Harrington, Jaime Lee Moyer, Jillian Boeme, Joy Hensley George, Kathleen Peacock, Lisa Iriarte, Myra McEntire, and Wendy Beer. Your comments, encouragement, and kicks in the butt were invaluable for getting this book from pixels to paper. I'm so grateful that you're all in my life.

Warm thanks and adoration to Jeri Smith-Ready, Rachel Hawkins, and Robin McKinley, who said such nice things about *Incarnate*. Your praise means so much to me, as I'm an incredible fan of your books as well.

Special thanks to the book bloggers, writers, and knit bloggers who helped me launch the *Incarnate* Theater Treasure Hunt the week *Incarnate* was released. Your support, enthusiasm, and hard work amaze me.

Adam Heine, Amanda Miller, Amanda at Loves Books Reviews, Amber Mitchell, Amy Fournier, Angel Cruz, Anna Billings, Asheley Tart, Becky Herrick, Best Tanakasempipat, Bonnie Lynn Wagner, Brenna at Ever After Esther, Charlee Vale, Dot Hutchison, Emily Wright, Enna at Squeaky Books, Gabi Becker, Gabrielle Carolina, Hannah Courtney, Jaime from Two Chicks on Books, James at Book Chic Club, Jessica Reigle, Jodie at Uniquely Moi Books, Julie, Katie, Kaye M., Lauren at 365 Days of Reading, Linda Dao, Mary at the Book Swarm, Mei Jiao Ashley Chen, MG Buehrlen, Michelle and Amethyst at Libri Ago, Michelle Villarmia, Rachel, Sana Reddy, Sarah Nicolas, Shanyn Day, Shellie from Creative Reads, Shelley Watters, Stephanie at Poetry to Prose, Stephanie Huber, Susan Adrian, Tammy Moore, and Traci Inzitari.

Jill Roberts, for being the best, most encouraging mother a girl could ask for. Thank you for always believing in me.

Jeff Meadows, for unending patience and understanding, and willingness to listen to book-crazed ramblings at all hours of the day.

Thanks to God, who I will never be able to thank enough.

And thank you, reader, for picking up this book. I hope you enjoy reading it as much as I enjoyed writing it.

READ ON FOR THE BEGINNING OF
THE YEAR OF SOULS IN

INFINITE

1

ENDINGS

MY DEATH WOULD not be another beginning.

For millennia in Range, death meant another rebirth. Another life. Then someone died the night the temple went dark, and I was born in their place.

A nosoul. A newsoul. A soul asunder.

I was a mystery others sought to control, a frightening creature that made the world reconsider what it knew of life and death and what happened after. But I was only one. I could be desperately ignored as a mystery, a mistake that would never be repeated.

Then my father devised another Templedark, and for dozens of oldsouls, it was their final death. Violent. Terrifying. Inescapable.

Within the year, newsouls were born and the world mourned darksouls even more fiercely, never realizing the sinister truth about reincarnation. They had thought rebirth was natural, but the opposite was true: while oldsouls lived and died and lived again, millions of newsouls were consumed by the very entity that provided reincarnation.

Janan. The Devourer. The once-human who had reached too high and who would soon burn the world.

And then, there would be nothing left but endings.

Midnight struck.

The Year of Souls began with a thunderous crash and rumble from deep within the earth.

"What *is* that?" My voice sounded hollow in the parlor, the floor still littered with the remnants of destroyed instruments and tattered rose petals. Light from the kitchen bathed a square of the dusty hardwood floor, but otherwise, the room was dim with night. We'd awakened only a few minutes ago, having dozed on the sofa after friends left last evening.

Across the parlor, Sam tilted his head and listened. Black hair shadowed his eyes as he searched his memory for the strange crash and rumble.

The floor swayed under our feet. I yelped and braced myself against the wall. Janan's heartbeat thudded under my fingertips.

I dropped to my hands and knees, spreading out my

weight for balance. "What's happening?" Panic pitched my voice high and thin.

Sam staggered toward me, unsteady on the shifting floor. "It's an earthquake. Don't worry. It will pass."

Decorations rattled on the honeycomb shelves that divided the parlor and kitchen. Obsidian figurines danced and dove off the edges of their shelves. Wood and stone and glass thudded to the floor, crashed or rolled or shattered as they struck. Even the shredded rose petals swirled.

The shaking slowed, but it wasn't over. The world jerked again and hurled everything sideways. Furniture crashed upstairs. Trees snapped outside. The whole earth roared. I screamed as the hand-carved shelves cracked and splintered all around the room.

Sam stumbled and dropped, just out of my reach. Surprise and pain flared across his face as he clutched his hand to his chest, keeping his fist closed. His gray nightshirt darkened with seeping blood.

"Sam!" I crawled toward him, fighting the moving floor. "What happened to your hand?" Even as the question left my mouth, I spotted the glass near him, stained with crimson and glistening blood.

"Nothing. It's fine." The world steadied and he sat back on his heels, trapping his injured hand in his good one. "That wasn't so bad."

His idea of bad must have been the whole world rattling

apart. And now the earth's silence stretched through the house, heavy and alive. Waiting.

Not trusting the floor to stay put, I sat up and scooted toward Sam, giving the glass a wide berth.

A couple of weeks ago, Councilor Deborl and his friends had come through and smashed all the instruments in Sam's parlor. The piano, harpsichord, cello, and even the smaller instruments locked inside protective cases. Only the instruments upstairs had been spared, including my flute. It had been in the workroom, waiting on a small repair. Only chance had saved it.

I'd cleaned up most of that destruction right away. What remained on the floor had been pieces that might one day be useful again, as well as dried rose petals left over from a party with our friends.

But now, the parlor was more of a wreck than Deborl ever could have left it.

Shelves hung at odd angles, leaving books and boxes and bits of decorations scattered everywhere. The shelves looked like teeth, ready to bite down.

A lamp had fallen, leaving a glittering river of glass. We were lucky the light hadn't caught fire. Who knew what the kitchen looked like, or the upstairs, or the outbuildings. There'd been so much crashing and thumping; anything could have happened.

"Is your hand okay?" I crouched next to Sam and pried

his fist away from his chest.

"It's fine." A lie. His hand trembled in mine, and his skin was slick with blood. It was hard to see under the red smears, but it looked as if the glass had shredded his palm and fingers.

"We need to get this cleaned up. Hold still."

Sam nodded and braced himself while I picked out bit after bit of glass until my fingertips ached, but I couldn't find anything more. Cleaning the wound would help, but first I needed to stop the bleeding.

"This might hurt."

"It already hurts." Sam's voice was rough.

I wanted to say something reassuring, but I didn't know near enough about what had been damaged to make promises. If it looked bad after we rinsed the blood, I'd call Rin, the medic. For now, I grabbed a big shard of glass and sliced off a length of my nightgown to make a bandage, then wrapped the length of cloth around his hand as many times as it would go. "Hold on to it. Keep pressure."

"My hand will be fine." The words came out hard, like commands. Like he could will the cuts to heal.

"Let's go upstairs and get it properly bandaged. It didn't sound like any of the support beams broke, so the stairs should be safe." Hopefully the water lines were intact, too. The lights and everything else seemed all right. That was something.

I started to stand just as the earth jumped and an explosion sounded in the west. Not another earthquake. Something else.

Sam and I scrambled to our feet, careful of the glass as we hurried to the front door. I slipped into the night, icy air stinging my face. "Can you see anything?" I asked.

Sam shook his head. "No, but it sounded like an eruption."

"Not the caldera." The Range caldera was enormous, stretching in all directions with the city of Heart at its center. If the caldera erupted, there'd be nothing left of Heart.

"Not the caldera," Sam agreed. He put his arm around my shoulders, holding me close against the chill. "A hydrothermal eruption. Like a geyser, but bigger."

"How much bigger?" I peered into the night, but clouds obscured moonlight. Even if there'd been enough light to see by, the city wall blocked the horizon completely. The eruption had been outside the city, but it could have been just beyond the wall. There were geysers everywhere.

"Depends. Sometimes much bigger. They're a response to a pressure change underground."

Pattering sounds filled the trees and yard, tapping on the house in a strange rhythm. A pebble fell from the sky and hit my head.

With his good hand, Sam took my elbow and drew me toward the house. "Hydrothermal eruptions take rocks and trees with them sometimes, but they don't happen very often.

I've seen only two of them, and they were a long time ago."

As he spoke, a second eruption thundered in the north, and a third in the southwest. The world came alive with tapping, hissing, clattering. Animals grunted and darted through the evergreen trees. Birds squawked and took wing, but there was nowhere safe to fly. Earth rained from the sky as though the world had turned upside down.

"Inside." Sam's voice hardened as more bits of stone pattered against the walls of the house. "Inside now."

"How is this possible?" As we turned for the door, a flash of light caught my eye.

In the center of the city, Janan's temple shone incandescent.

2
INTRUSION

THE FRONT DOOR slammed behind me, muting the quiet cacophony of the world falling apart. I hugged myself as Sam moved into the shadows, away from the light of the kitchen. "Did you see the temple?" he asked. "I've never seen it so bright."

"I saw."

"Do you think it's Janan's doing?" He leaned on the wall, head dropped as he clutched his hand to his chest. "The earthquake? The eruptions?"

"It seems likely." I eased into the shadows with him, resting my cheek on his shoulder. His arms circled my waist. My chest and stomach pressed against his, only our nightclothes separating us. "I'm afraid," I whispered. It was easier to be honest when he was holding me, and when we stood in the dark.

He rested his cheek on top of my head. "Me too."

"If the caldera is going to do this a lot from now on, maybe the Council exiling me isn't such a bad thing. It's probably smart to get away from Range. I'm glad you're coming with me."

"I'll always go anywhere with you."

We stood together for a while, listening to each other's heartbeats and the patter of debris on the house. I touched only Sam, avoiding the white exterior wall even more now that Janan's pulse was stronger.

"Let's go upstairs and get this fixed." I straightened and cradled his hurt hand in both of mine. The strip of my nightgown was soaked with blood.

He nodded and allowed me to guide him upstairs. We took the steps slowly, testing the wood before trusting our weight to it. The exterior of the house would be fine after the earthquake—Janan would never allow the white stone to be damaged while he was awake—but the interiors of the houses were all of human construction.

But the stairs were well enough. None of the support beams had snapped.

His bedroom was cool and dark. Shapes hunched within the shadows: a warm bed, a wardrobe, and a large harp. We made our way into the washroom, and I flicked on the light.

Both of us squinted in the white glare. "Sit," I ordered.

He leaned and scooted onto the counter while I closed the door and turned the shower knobs, water as hot and strong as it would go. A sly smile tugged at the corners of Sam's mouth. "Ana, I'm not sure this is the best time, but if you'd like to—"

"Shut up." A relieved grin slipped out. If he could joke, he would be fine. "The steam will help loosen the glass, if there's any left."

"That's less fun." He pretended to pout as he unwrapped his hand and rinsed the blood away in the sink. I found bandages and ointment, and together we picked out the last slivers of glass while steam billowed from the shower. The mirror fogged, and the pounding water on the tub drowned out the sound of the world beyond the room.

"This doesn't look too bad," I said, spreading ointment over his fingers. Most of the cuts were superficial.

"Told you." He held still while I wrapped his hand in clean bandages. "And it's my left hand, which is a relief because I write with my right." The shower made his voice deeper and fuller. "I'll get along fine until my left recovers. And I don't need either hand to kiss you."

With a quiet gasp, I dropped the roll of bandage tape. "We should test that claim. I seem to remember you using your hands quite a bit when you kiss me."

"Hmm." He slid off the counter. "Perhaps this does deserve

some experimenting." He closed the short space between us and smoothed a strand of hair off my face. "Oh," he murmured, "you're right. There's one."

I stood on my toes and wrapped my arms around his shoulders. His lips were warm and soft from the steam filling the room.

"Two," he said, curling one arm around my waist to pull me close. Lips breezed over my cheek and neck. "Three." With his good hand, he nudged my nightgown off my shoulder and kissed bare skin, then trailed his fingertips down my arm. His touch ignited sparks that traveled all the way to my stomach. My breath fluttered. "You're very right." His lips grazed my collarbone. "I use my hands all the time when I kiss you."

I would have melted if he hadn't been holding me up. The steam, his touch, his kiss: they made me light-headed and giddy, in spite of everything that had happened not an hour ago. Safe in his arms, with only the sound of the shower running, I could forget about the outside world and the rest of our problems.

"Do you remember what we talked about last night?" I kissed his ear, his cheek.

Sam gave a low rumble of assent. "You said you love me."

"I did say that, didn't I?" Pleasure poured through me. After years of believing I wasn't deserving of love, Sam had shown me I was. But that was different from accepting I could love others. Wrestling those feelings had been diffi-cult, but last night, I'd said it, and it turned out that I'd loved him all along. "Guess what?"

He pulled away and met my eyes.

"I still love you today."

His smile grew wide and warm.

"I heard a rumor," I went on, "that the first day of the new year is your birthday."

"Did you?" He suddenly looked shy.

"When we first met, you told me we shared a birthday."

"Did I?" Panic flickered across his face, and his cheeks darkened. "I did. Oh."

I kept my face as serious as I could manage, though laugh-ter gathered in my chest and I had to bite my lip to keep from smiling. "So?" I lifted an eyebrow.

His whole face was dark with embarrassment. "Would you believe I forgot when my birthday is?"

I snorted and laughed. That was exactly what I thought he'd say, because when I looked back on that day, I remem-bered the hesitation and momentary confusion before he declared we had the same birthday. He *had* forgotten. "It's all right. I love you on your real birthday *and* on your fake birthday. And all the other days."

He grinned, relaxing. "There's nothing more we can do tonight. Would you—" He seemed to fumble for the right words. "Would you like to sleep here with me? In my room,

I mean. Not the washroom."

The mess would still be downstairs in the morning, and his bedroom had appeared relatively unharmed when we passed through. We could take care of everything else in the morning. Or not. Yesterday, the ruling Council had exiled me from Heart, and Sam was leaving with me. Soon, we'd be on our way east. We didn't *have* to clean the house.

We could put off real life until dawn.

"If you steal all the blankets, you'll be sorry." I reached inside the shower and turned off the spray. After dealing with the Council, visiting friends who'd come to express their outrage, and then the earthquake and eruptions, curling up with Sam was the most appealing thing I could think of.

The shower dripped for a moment longer, and then the house was silent. Maybe the debris had stopped falling outside. The whole world was still, and quiet, and waiting.

I felt behind me for the doorknob and pushed the washroom door open. Soon, everything would be perfect, if only for a few hours.

Sam's smile fell away. A question formed in my mouth, but he grabbed my wrist, yanked, and spun me so I stood behind him. "What are you doing here?" he growled. He reached behind him with his good hand, palm on my hip as though to keep me in place.

My heart raced at his sudden shift. I peeked around him.

A stranger stood in Sam's bedroom, clutching a long knife.

13

He wore a filthy coat that hung to his ankles, but even in the dim light and with the heavy layer of fabric, I couldn't miss the bulge of another weapon on his hip when he faced us.

"Dossam. Nosoul." His voice sounded familiar, but I couldn't place it. "We were hoping you'd been crushed to death."

We?

I twisted my hand in Sam's shirt, desperately wishing I were wearing something more serious than my nightgown as I stepped out from behind him. I didn't need a shield. "You're one of Deborl's friends."

"And you were in prison," Sam said. "With Deborl and Merton."

The stranger showed teeth when he smiled. "Janan used the earthquake to free us." He pulled back his coat, revealing a laser pistol tucked into his waistband. "We have a calling."

"Mat, no." Sam tried to step in front of me again, but I jabbed my elbow into his side. "Why would you do this?"

The stranger—Mat—leveled his gaze on Sam, apparently unworried about our escape. We were trapped in the washroom, after all. "She's an abomination. They all are. The plague of newsouls *must* be stopped."

We were trapped in the washroom.

I stepped back, letting Sam block the doorway. "Newsouls are the natural order of things," he began. "Other animals are born, live, and die forever. Haven't you considered that what we do is unnatural?"

"They're an offense to Janan. He created us. He gave us immortality. And soon he'll return to reward the faithful. He'll ascend. The faithful will ascend with him."

Meuric hadn't thought so. He'd been convinced he needed the temple key to survive Soul Night.

I tuned out Mat's arguments as I considered the items in Sam's washroom. Shampoo, soap, painkillers. I wished for my SED—then I could call for help—but both our SEDs were downstairs.

"Ana's done nothing to you," Sam said. "Nor have the other newsouls."

Gauze. Painkillers. Ointment for cuts and burns. If my nightgown had pockets, I would have grabbed those, because the plan budding in my head involved going outside.

"They were born," Mat said. "They replaced oldsouls. *Real* souls. They take what isn't theirs. Life. Keys."

Mat's identity snapped into place. He was the man who'd attacked me when I'd stumbled out of the temple. He'd stolen the temple key from me and given it to Deborl.

"This must come to an end. I'm sorry, Dossam. I have no quarrel with you, but Ana has to die."

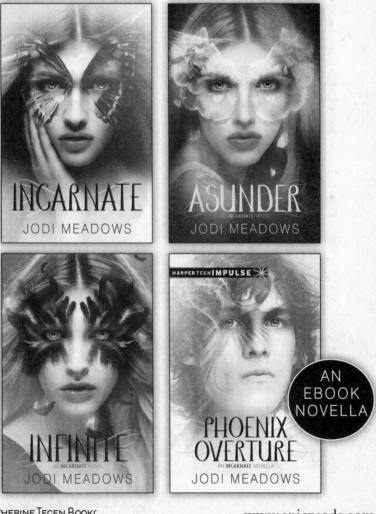